IN THE
Wilderness

BY
ANGELA JOSEPH

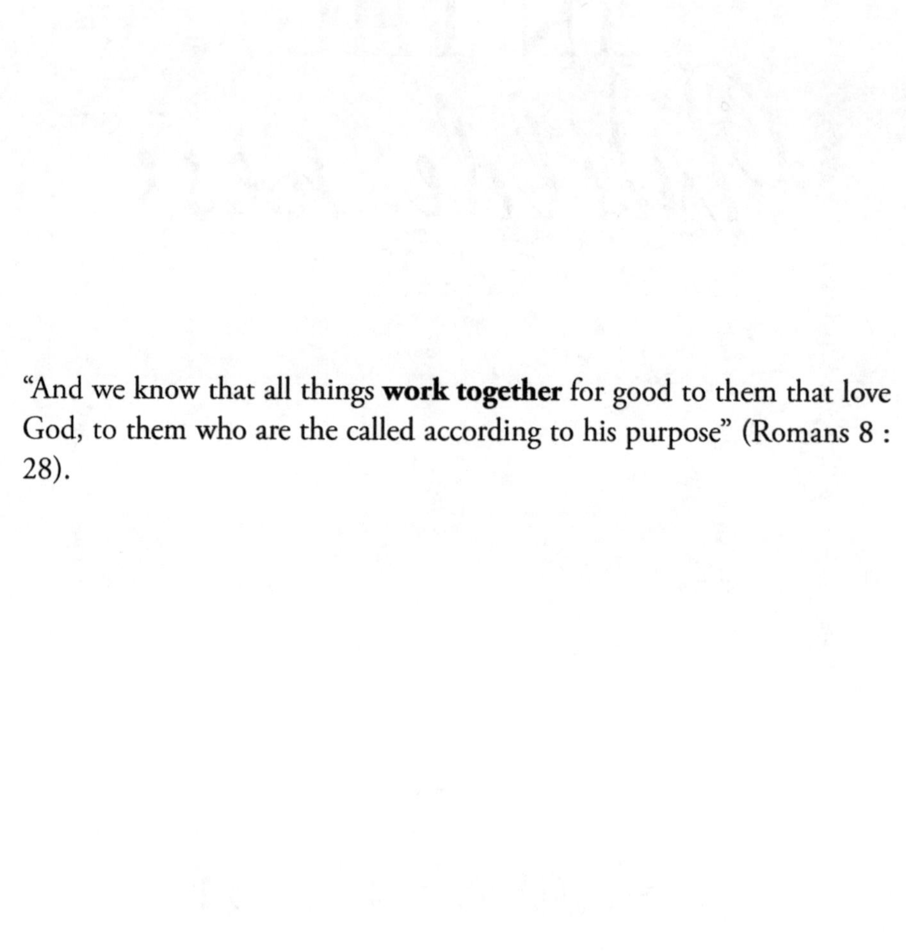

"And we know that all things **work together** for good to them that love God, to them who are the called according to his purpose" (Romans 8 : 28).

ACKNOWLEDGMENTS

To my Sharpies critique group who helped me make this book the best it can be. Great writers, great friends.

For my children and grand-children, the air I breathe.

Copyright © 2017 by Angela Joseph

ASIN B072WB8N25

CONTENTS

CHAPTER ONE

I *killed my father.* The thought exploded in Marva Garcia's mind like a bombshell. She could never say *that* to Miss Stewart. Or anyone else for that matter. Marva jumped up from her chair and hurried out the door.

Down the hallway, second door on the left. The house she was in, Miss Stewart's house, was one Marva knew as well as her own. She and June spent many pleasant times there. No sooner had she entered the small guest bathroom with the lavender walls and purple rugs than someone knocked. She knew June would follow her.

"Just a minute."

She splashed water hurriedly on her face, patted it dry and pasted on a smile. Outside the door, June's beautiful face was etched in worry. "You okay?"

Marva nodded. "I'll be all right."

They walked back into the room where a bevy of activity was taking place. Miss Stewart's wedding was two weeks away, and Marva, who was to be the maid-of-honor, had gathered with the bridesmaids to have their gowns fitted.

If June only knew how difficult it was for her to feign interest in all that was going on around her. Not that she wasn't happy to be part of her teacher's wedding. Miss Stewart had become a mother substitute to her and June over the years, and with the wedding just two weeks away, now was not the time to unburden herself on her. Marva lifted her head and tried to look cool, the way a maid-of-honor should look.

While Marva's gaze roved from one bridesmaid to another, June, who had metamorphosed from a shy, almost mute child – overnight, it seemed

- flitted among the girls, admiring their dresses, helping to fix something, or just being June. Miss Monique, the seamstress, a thin woman with a beehive hairdo, glasses hanging from a chain around her neck, issued instructions to her assistant. Miss Joy, a plump, shorter lady with pins sticking out of her mouth worked as fast as a sewing machine, adjusting hems, necklines, and anything else that needed attention.

Miss Monique stopped in front of Marva. "How's my tall friend?"

A few years ago, the adjective would have irritated her, but now she only smiled.

"You won't be wearing very high heels, will you?"

Marva shook her head.

"Good. Tiptoe for me."

Marva obliged.

The woman got down on the carpeted floor. "Maybe one inch," she said to her assistant.

Marva stood still while Miss Monique swiveled around her, pinning her hem into place. Then she stood and pinched the waistline of the dress. "You have a nice, small waist." She stuck a few pins into the seams and motioned to Miss Joy, who approached with needle and thread. After the lady had moved on to the next girl, June flitted up to her. "This is a beautiful gown, Sister."

Marva fingered the soft petals covering the straps. "It is."

Her gown of lavender chiffon was different from the others. It had a shirred blouse, dropped waistline and full skirt that draped at the back. It fitted her perfectly now that the adjustments had been made. She studied June's short, embroidered dress fitted at the waist with billowing skirt and a long bow at the back. "Yours is lovely too."

June looked down at her dress. "I can hardly wait for the wedding." She leaned over and whispered in Marva's ear. "Try to look a little more lively."

Marva's eyes widened. Had anyone else noticed? Maybe not. June noticed because they were so close and because her hawk's eyes never missed anything.

A door opened and shut and familiar voices floated in. Miss Stewart and Mr. Bowen, her husband-to-be, and the man Marva feared most. She let out a slow breath and tried to relax. Her former teacher knew her well too. She couldn't have her thinking anything was amiss.

Miss Stewart bustled into the room, a petite woman in her late thirties with sparkling brown eyes and an infectious smile. Marva couldn't help smiling. Aside from her sister, there was no one in the world she loved more, and her joy at her teacher's obvious happiness filled her with a pleasant ache.

"How's everybody doing? Hope I didn't keep you all waiting."

Murmurs rose from the group as Miss Stewart circled the room, inspecting each girl's dress. When she came to Marva, she smiled. "Now here's a maid-of-honor any bride would envy."

Marva laughed. "No, Miss. Not if you are the bride."

Miss Stewart embraced her. "You make me proud, my dear." Turning to the seamstress, "You outdid yourself this time, Monique."

"Nothing but the best for you, Cicely."

The first nice dress Marva had ever owned was one Miss Stewart had bought her from Monique's. She was known to be one of the best seamstresses in South Trinidad. Marva could not afford to shop there and she had appreciated her teacher's generosity. Then, two years ago, at Marva's eighteenth birthday, she'd secured another of Monique's creations when June and Miss Stewart pitched in to get her a gorgeous birthday dress. A feeling of pleasure washed over her as she recalled that birthday party when she'd danced with her friend Jason. She would see him again at the wedding.

About an hour later, Marva and June said their goodbyes to Miss Stewart when she dropped them off at their apartment. Inside the house, June babbled on about how much she loved her dress and how excited she was about the wedding. She lifted her long curly mane off her neck and pirouetted in front of the bedroom mirror.

"Miss Monique said I should wear my hair up to show off the V neckline of the dress." She pulled the hair as high as she could, but some still cascaded past her neck. "What you think, Sister?"

Marva summoned some interest. "I think it's a good idea. The hairdresser will know how to fix it."

June turned around. "And a little bit of makeup?"

Marva headed for the kitchen. "Of course. It's a wedding."

The effort to appear excited and happy had left her drained. She wanted to be alone, to talk to God or just mull over what she wanted to say to her teacher. But she didn't have that luxury, not with June as hyped up as a little puppy.

June came into the kitchen and opened the fridge. "What are we going to eat tonight, Sister?"

"We have soup left over from lunch."

June pursed her lips. "I don't feel for that."

Marva had a sudden inspiration. She went into the bedroom and took her purse out of the nightstand drawer. She opened it and counted the bills and change – twenty dollars and sixty cents. Enough for two movie tickets, a box of chicken and chips and taxi fare.

Going back into the kitchen, she found June about to reheat the pot of soup. "Let's go to the movies. We'll get something to eat."

"Yaay!"

"But we'll have to eat that soup tomorrow. We can't afford to waste food."

June's grin faded as she placed the pot back in the fridge.

The movie proved a good idea. It absorbed Marva's attention right from the start and when she and June left the theater, she was much calmer than before. But as they got ready for bed, June surprised her by saying, "I'm glad you're feeling better, Sister."

Marva stared at the young girl getting into her pajamas. "Who told you I wasn't feeling well?"

"Because you had your face like this." June used her fingers to pull her jaw down. "All while we were trying on our dresses."

For her sixteen years, June's perception often amazed Marva. She could see through her with a clarity that was at times almost uncomfortable.

"Well, I hope no one else noticed my face looking like that." She tried to imitate June.

"No one was paying you any attention, but I know when you are worried."

Marva turned away not knowing whether to laugh or cry at June's unflattering response. In the bathroom, she pondered what June had said. Her sister was right, as usual, and she would not let her rest until Marva disclosed what she was worrying about. But Marva didn't want to scare her.

When she returned to the bedroom, June lay with the sheet pulled up to her neck, eyes wide open staring at the ceiling.

"I can't sleep unless you tell me."

Marva flicked off the light and got into the bed. "You're like a cat. As soon as the light is turned off, you fall asleep."

"Not this time."

Marva lay waiting for the sound of June's soft snoring, but it didn't come. Then just as she was about to turn over on to her stomach, "Sister?"

Marva threw off the cover and sat up. "All right, all right. What you want to know?"

"What you're worrying about."

Marva hesitated. "I … I want to confess to Miss Stewart."

The light came on with a snap. June's hazel eyes seemed ablaze. "You want to confess what to Miss Stewart?"

Marva faltered, suddenly feeling like the younger of the two. This was the child she'd looked after and tried to protect during the horrible years of their father's abuse. And this was the child she'd fled Egypt Village with and made a home for in San Fernando so she could get an education and make a new life. Only, she was no longer a child. She was a beautiful young woman with a level of maturity way beyond her years.

Marva's lips trembled. "You know what I'm talking about, Junie. You are smart."

June crossed her legs beneath her. "No, I don't, Sister. We've been living here, quite comfortably I must say, for three years. I'm doing well in school, you have a job you enjoy, and Miss Stewart is about to be married and live a happy life. Why do you want to spoil it, Sister?"

"Because the Bible says if we confess our sins He is faithful and just to forgive us our sins and cleanse us from all unrighteousness."

"Good. Then confess it to God. Not to Miss Stewart, or anyone else. It's not their business."

Marva's fingers twisted the end of the sheet. June's words made sense. Why spoil things for everybody? Because she wanted to be a martyr?

She lay down and pulled up the sheet. "You're right, Junie. Please turn off the light."

June hesitated. "Promise me you'll stop worrying."

Marva smiled. What a sweet child she was. "I promise."

The light went off and June settled quietly next to her. Long after her snores confirmed that she was asleep, Marva lay mulling over what was the best way to make her confession. She could not bear the guilt any longer. She had to tell someone that she was the person who had killed her father.

CHAPTER TWO

It was Friday. Payday. After picking up her pay envelope from the office, Marva left the garage and walked to the street corner where she hailed a taxi to San Fernando. She had saved for the past few months and now at last had enough money to purchase a brand, new Zenith television. She felt the smile spreading over her face as she envisaged June's look of surprise.

Marva would always be grateful for her job at Glen's Automotive, even though it caused her some anxiety in the beginning. Some clients felt a girl should not be allowed to work as a mechanic. They'd advised her to get "a typing job" or "a maid's job." With the support of Raymond - her boss - and other co-workers, she'd learned to ignore them. Once she'd developed her skills, the customers grew to like her and some of them even complimented her on her career choice.

But no one ever looked at her the way they looked at other women. All the mechanics saw her as one of the boys – strong, reliable and capable. Only Carlton, her first supervisor, had overstepped his boundaries. But with the help of a wheel rim, Marva had straightened him out real quick, and he'd steered clear of her after that. No man would ever violate her body again.

Marva wished the wedding was this weekend so she could get her hair and nails done. The hairdresser would fix her hair really nice and she would polish her nails to cover the stains.

With quickened steps, she crossed the street to Stephen's & Johnson's.

Marva's excitement almost equaled June's as the taxi driver brought the huge box into the living-room. Marva ran into the kitchen, grabbed a knife and cut the box top open. Then she and June stared at the shiny, gray object, then at each other. How would they lift it out of the box? How would they set it up?

June came up with the answer. "I'll go and ask Mrs. Maraj if her son can help us."

Their landlady's son was a few years older than Marva and rarely spoke to them, but they knew no one else who could assist them. A moment later, June returned with the short, stocky young man who easily removed the television from the box and set it on the table. The girls looked on anxiously as nothing but snow appeared on the screen after he plugged it in. A few adjustments later, colored lines appeared then a woman's face. June squealed and leaped in the air. Marva felt like leaping herself, not so much for the television, but because June was happy.

After the man left, Marva went into the kitchen, leaving June to flick through the channels. While she stowed bottles of Coca Cola in the fridge, June called from the living-room, "Sister, tonight is *The Love Boat.*"

"Okay, what time?"

"Eight o'clock."

Marva removed a bag of popcorn she'd bought along with the soft drinks for the big event. She and June would change into their night-gowns and curl up on the sofa Miss Stewart had given them and view their first TV show at home. An unusual feeling of satisfaction enveloped her like a warm blanket. As June had wisely said, why spoil it?

They had everything they needed, and soon the sale of their father's estate would be finalized. They would have enough money to pay for June's education and to last them a few years, as long as Marva continued working. Everything would be perfect. If only this feeling of guilt didn't haunt her day and night.

Marva took a taxi to Oropuche, the little seaside village where her aunt lived. She paid the driver and got out at one of the side streets that led to her aunt's house. Yes, there it was. Bitter-sweet memories of the months she and June had spent here resurfaced. The house was a small, concrete structure with galvanized roof and fading beige paint. Rows of potted plants lined the yard and the wooden porch. The anthurium lilies and roses didn't look this healthy four years ago when she and June, desperate to flee the horrors they'd left behind, had landed on their aunt's doorstep. The wooden steps leaned sideways and Marva stepped gingerly on them until she reached the top.

She knocked on the door. While she waited for her aunt, memories tumbled around in Marva's mind. So much had changed since then. Tantie Beulah pushed the door open, jolting Marva back to the present. Her aunt's brown face creased into a smile. "But, child, I so glad to see you. Where the pretty little one?" She didn't wait for a reply. "You have to watch her, you know? She doin' good in school?"

Her aunt allowed her to enter then moved a cushion and some papers off the settee. "Come, sit down, child." She picked up a paper and fanned herself. "Lord, it so hot. You want some juice?"

It really was a hot day and juice sounded refreshing. Marva followed Tantie Beulah into the kitchen where she poured juice from the fridge and added ice.

"You not having some, Tantie?"

"No, child, the doctor say I have to watch my sugar and I had a little bit before you came. So, you getting ready for the wedding? You are the chief bridesmaid? Yes, I wouldn't miss it for the world. Your teacher is such a nice little lady."

Marva smiled. "Yes, she is. I'm looking forward to the wedding too." Then changing the subject, "So how you makin' out here by yourself with Grandma gone?"

"Oh, child." Tantie Beulah pulled a towel from her bosom and dabbed at her eyes. "I miss her so much, but she with the good Lord now and I have to be content. Nex' month will be a year already since she passed away."

Tantie Beulah was her father's half-sister, and her mother was not Marva's grandmother, but she was the only one Marva and June knew.

Their father's parents had died when they were little, and their mother, a Venezuelan by birth, had no relatives in Trinidad. How different their lives might have been if they had close relatives they could talk to.

Marva turned to Tantie Beulah. "Well, I have some news to cheer you up."

"What is that, child?"

"The lawyer said the buyer is getting ready to close any day now."

"Oh, that is good news, child. I really want to fix the roof on the house. It leaking badly."

"Yes, Tantie, and those steps. I don't know how you climb them."

Some time later, Marva said good-bye to her aunt. On the way home, Marva thought of the conversation with Tantie Beulah. They had not discussed how the money from the sale of her father's property would be shared. The lawyer had advised her to give her aunt ten thousand dollars and divide the remainder between her and June. It should be more than enough to make her aunt happy. Her share and June's would be forty thousand each after the legal fees were deducted. Marva had no idea what she would do with all that money, but what mattered most was that June would be able to afford the education she deserved and wanted.

Marva, seated at a table with June and the other bridesmaids, bit into her chicken, her ears hearing the idle chatter of the younger girls, but her mind on her good-looking friend seated a little distance from her with a small group of young men. Jason, one of the groomsmen, cut a striking figure in his dark suit, white bow tie and cummerbund, his wavy hair brushed back from his forehead, his mustache and beard neatly trimmed.

Marva wished he'd been her escort when they left the church, but as maid-of-honor, her escort had been the best man, Arthur Buckie. A nice man, but older and shorter than she. Marva looked across at Miss Stewart - now Mrs. Bowen, but she would always be Miss Stewart to her – seated next to her husband, smiling and chatting while they ate. He leaned closer and whispered something in her ear, and whatever it was,

Miss Stewart blushed, reminding Marva of the kiss in the church. Would Jason ever kiss her like that? She felt her face getting hot, and wiped her mouth on the napkin. She shouldn't be thinking about him that way. He was probably engaged to Joanna by now.

While the servers cleared away the dishes, two photographers circled the room taking pictures, and Marva leaned back in her chair, wondering what next. Mr. Bowen's brother, master of ceremonies, approached the podium. He whisked through the welcome and congratulations to the bride and groom, wished them a long and happy life with lots of kids, to which everyone laughed. Then he called on the groom to say a few words.

Mr. Bowen also welcomed the guests and spoke about his love for his bride. Miss Stewart said almost the same thing when her turn came then the best man followed with a toast to the bride and groom. Marva was glad that all the drinks were non-alcoholic. She had no intention of going back to drinking.

Following the toast, a young lady whom Marva had never seen before sang a song to the couple. More speeches followed from friends and family members. Marva, who had never been to a wedding, found it all fascinating. She wished she could make a speech and tell everyone what her former teacher meant to her. Marva's mind went back to the first time she set eyes on Miss Stewart.

She was nine years old, and it was the first day of the new term at the Egypt Village Government School. A lady, just a little taller than Marva, hurried into the school yard, balancing a bag on her shoulder, a small lunch kit in one hand and books in the other. Marva didn't know what came over her. She ran to the new teacher and offered to carry her books. The lady fixed her with her large brown eyes and smiled. "Thank you, dear. That's sweet of you."

Something melted inside of her as she took the books from the woman's hand and followed her to the principal's office. Marva had been in there a few times before and she hesitated at the door.

The woman turned to her. "What's your name?"

"Marva."

"Thank you, Marva. I'll see you around, okay?"

She sounded different from the other teachers. Years later, Marva learned that the lady had been born in America. Marva nodded and skipped away, hoping she would be in the woman's class, but she wasn't. Still, that didn't stop Marva from hanging around her classroom whenever she could. Sometimes the teacher would acknowledge her presence with a nod or a wave. Marva learned that her name was Miss Stewart and she kept hoping she would one day be in her class.

It didn't happen until three years later. Marva struggled with the math and English, hoping to impress her teacher, but it was difficult. However, Miss Stewart was patient. Sometimes Marva would catch the teacher's worried gaze on her and she would duck her head. Did Miss Stewart have a clue what Marva was going through at home? Did she somehow guess how difficult it was for Marva to concentrate, far less master her lessons? One afternoon as she hung around the classroom, cleaning the blackboard, putting away books, Miss Stewart asked her, "Marva, it's getting late. Don't you think it's time for you to go home?"

Without thinking, Marva had blurted, "Daddy will be coming home drunk."

Miss Stewart didn't say anything, but an unspoken message seemed to pass between them.

The master of ceremonies' words broke into her reverie. "The bride and groom will be coming around to greet their guests personally, then we'll clear the floor for the first dance." Marva rose, anxious to perform her last duty to the bride, but Miss Monique got there before her. She tied the bustle so Miss Stewart could glide around the floor without her train getting in the way.

Marva looked around for June and spotted her in a far corner chatting away with a group of young people. Marva hesitated, wondering what to do with herself.

Someone touched her on her shoulder. "I wondered when I would get a chance to talk to you."

Her heart gave a little flutter. "Jason! How you doing?"

"Waiting for a chance to dance with the prettiest girl in the room."

Marva looked around. Who could he be talking about? June was always the prettiest girl wherever they went, but when Marva turned back to face him, he was gazing at her with an expression she remembered too well. She blushed and studied the tips of her new, white shoes to hide her confusion. Wasn't he supposed to be getting engaged to Joanna Dean? They'd been dating a long time. But she was not with him tonight. The next moment he took her hand. "Let's go join my friends over there."

He led her to a table with two other couples. One of the men was his friend, Steve, easily recognizable by his stingy brim hat. A new one, it seemed. He tipped it to her with an elaborate bow, which made the others laugh.

"Don't mind him," the lady seated next to him said. "He's always so silly."

Steve replaced his hat and kissed the woman on her lips. "That's why you love me."

Jason introduced the woman who had spoken. "Marva, this is Steve's unfortunate wife, Shirley." Turning to the other couple, "and this is Gloria and Earl."

With everyone's eyes on her, Marva forced herself to smile and say, "Hello."

"You did a nice job in the church as maid-of-honor," Gloria said. Before Marva could reply she continued, "I couldn't do that. I woulda forget everything."

Marva opened her mouth to speak, but Gloria went on, "The last wedding I went to, the bride had to keep looking back for her chief to lift her train and help her out. That girl was something else. But Marva, you were like that," she snapped her fingers, "all the time. But that is a gorgeous wedding gown, eh Shirley? That train must have over a thousand rhinestones. And the lace over the top of the bodice. I like that."

While the girl chattered, Marva turned her attention to the bride and groom standing just two tables away, his arm possessively around her waist. They had almost completed their journey around the banquet hall and the servers were clearing the middle of the floor for dancing. Members of the police band began to take their places on the stage at the far right of the room.

Jason leaned closer to Marva and whispered in her ear. "Don't mind her, she doesn't give anyone else a chance to talk. We can talk to each other."

Marva was relieved. She was still shy around strangers, except at work.

Jason ran a finger up her arm. "This is a pretty dress too."

Marva looked down at the lacy, V neck top. "It is, but I don't know when I'll wear it again."

Jason seemed about to say something, but his words were cut off by the appearance of the newlyweds. "There you are. Thank you for helping me so well in church." Miss Stewart bent and kissed Marva's cheek. "You're a treasure."

Marva smiled with pleasure, but before she could reply, Gloria piped up congratulating Miss Stewart on her dress, the food, the decorations, everything.

Before Miss Stewart got away, she bent and whispered in Marva's ear. "Where did she come from?"

This time Marva laughed. Her gaze followed her teacher as she floated away on her husband's arm.

At last the bride and groom got their chance to waltz to the tune of *Endless Love*. Marva could feel the love from the couple flowing out to everyone in the room, even though they seemed to have eyes only for each other. While they danced, a photographer clicked away. Their dance ended, the father of the bride and mother of the groom took their places on the dance floor. Marva was amazed at how well Mr. Stewart danced with his prosthesis. No one would ever guess he had one. But what amazed her more was the connection she sensed between the couple as they smiled and whispered to each other. Mrs. Rose Bowen was a widow and Mr. Stewart was a, what did they call that, a widower?

During the lull that followed, the master of ceremonies announced that the bride and groom would soon make their departure, but before they did, the bride would throw her bouquet. The young lady who caught it may become the next bride. Women jumped up from their seats and congregated in the aisle. Jason nudged Marva, but she laughed and shook her head. "That's not for me." While the band played softly, Cicely turned her back to the audience and threw the bouquet over her shoulder. Gloria screamed as she caught it.

Jason laughed and slapped his friend on the back. "You're in trouble, man."

The poor young man didn't seem to know what to say.

The floor was finally open for all who wanted to dance, and Jason pulled Marva to her feet. She was relaxed and her steps matched his perfectly. Lightly he touched her cheek with his lips. "You're a good dancer."

A wave of pleasure coursed through her veins. "That's because you're so good."

She meant it. If she had to dance with anyone else, she would surely crush their toes. Unlike June who didn't seem to have any difficulty dancing. She was in a different boy's arms every time Marva looked.

Finally, the moment came when the bride and groom once more stopped by Marva's table, this time to say good-bye. Marva understood why people cried at weddings. The couple was spending their wedding night at home before leaving early next morning for their one-week honeymoon in St. Lucia. Short, but to Marva it felt like eternity. June appeared from wherever she'd been and she too looked like she wanted to cry. They embraced their teacher, then withdrew to allow her and her husband to leave in a shower of rice, rose petals and confetti.

CHAPTER THREE

The day after the wedding, Marva and June got ready for church, neither of them speaking. Already it felt like their lives had undergone a big change. They wouldn't see Miss Stewart today. Marva gave herself a mental shake.

She had to learn to detach herself from her teacher and exercise the independence she'd acquired after her mother's death. She'd taken care of the home and June and comforted her during the years of their father's abuse. If she'd done all that when she was younger, she could learn to live without Miss Stewart.

She slipped on her shoes, and June reached for her purse.

"Ready, Junie?"

June nodded, giving herself a last look in the wardrobe mirror. "We're on our own now."

Marva felt she had to break the spell. "That was the most beautiful wedding I ever saw."

June glanced at her. "Sister, it was the only wedding you ever saw."

They chuckled as they went out the door.

Back at home that afternoon the phone rang while Marva was tidying the kitchen. She heard June say, "Yes, she's here. Could you hold?"

June traipsed into the kitchen, a broad smile on her face. "He's on the phone."

"Who?"

June gave her a playful shove. "You know who. Jason."

Marva took her time rinsing the plate before placing it in the dish drainer. She was pleased Jason had called, but she didn't want Little Miss Sharp Ears to hear her conversation. Marva waited until June took her place at the sink before drying her hands on the kitchen towel and going to the phone.

"Hello."

"Hello, Miss Chief. Looks like you were still sleeping."

"Sleeping? I went to church, and was just tidying up after lunch."

"You went to church even after staying up so late?"

Although they had left the hall after midnight, Marva had been up at her usual time.

"I don't like to miss church. I feel empty when I don't go."

There was a pause. "Really? I didn't know you were so religious."

"I don't know if I'm religious. I love God, that's all."

Another pause, then he cleared his throat. "I'll be in San Fernando next Wednesday. I have to do something for my mom. What time you go for lunch?"

"Around 1.00 most days."

"Good. We can go for lunch. Where is your place?"

She gave him the directions and he hung up.

She replaced the receiver slowly to give her heart time to quiet. They'd danced together at the wedding, and she'd enjoyed his company, but this relationship was all wrong. *Any* relationship would be wrong. The one date she'd had with him before had ended in disaster. He'd kissed her when he brought her home, and she'd stood there like a breathing block of ice. After he left, she'd thrown herself on the bed, wishing she could cry, but no tears came. That incident showed her where her heart was. It was with Him. She could never love anyone else.

On Wednesday morning, Marva went through her little hanging wardrobe as if she were searching for something valuable. None of the outfits seemed suitable for a lunch date. She always wore a long skirt and loose blouse to work then changed into coveralls when she got there. To-day, she wanted something different, but not dressy.

June came in, looked at the assortment of clothes on the bed then at Marva. "Sister, are you going somewhere?"

Marva reached for a long brown skirt and cream blouse. "No, just to work."

"Then why …?"

She won't give up if I don't tell her. Marva ran a comb through her hair. "I …er, Jason might be taking me to lunch."

In the mirror, Marva saw June's lips part in a grin. "Oh! And you can't decide what to wear. All right, lemme see."

June got busy, sorting through the outfits on the bed. Eventually, she held up one of Marva's newer skirts – a long, A-line blue and white patterned skirt and blue sleeveless top. "How about this? It's different, but not dressy and the color wouldn't make you stand out too much."

Marva studied them as June held them up against her. June was the fashion expert. She would have to take her advice. "All right." She sighed. "I'll have to walk with some soap, cologne, and a little makeup so I don't look and smell like a grease monkey. This is too much trouble. I should have told him no."

"You can never say no to Jason."

Marva shot her a quick glance. Too perceptive, as always. But June was right. How could she say no to her childhood friend? The one who had helped her fight her battles in Egypt Village, the one she'd danced with on the cocoa leaves near the river and the one – the only one – who had ever touched her lips with his.

Despite her misgivings, Marva enjoyed her lunch date. They ate at Belle Bagai, a small restaurant that Miss Stewart had taken her and June to. The place was very popular and she and Jason had to wait a few minutes for a seat. But Marva wasn't worried. Raymond, her easy-going boss, had winked at her when she was leaving and said, "Make sure you get back before closing time."

She'd blushed and hurried away.

Now with her meal of *coo coo* - a delicious corn dish - *callalloo* – a vegetable soup - and stewed chicken almost over, Marva was glad she'd accepted Jason's invitation.

He covered her hand with his. "Enjoyed the food?"

"It was great. I love this restaurant."

"I'd never eaten here before. I'm glad you suggested it."

"Are you going back to work?"

He shook his head. "No. I took the afternoon off."

She slid her hand gently away.

"What's the matter?"

She looked down at her plate then back at him. "Jay … I have to ask. What about Joanna?"

"What about her?"

"Are you engaged?"

"No. We're just friends, that's all."

Marva paused again. "I heard …"

He chuckled. "Don't believe everything you hear. We're just friends."

She held his gaze. "And we're just friends too."

June and Keith quickened their pace to catch up with Wendy and John.

June flashed them a smile. "You all want to come with us to study for the test tomorrow?"

"Come where?" Wendy asked.

"To my house."

Wendy looked at John. "I'll have to call my mom and let her know where I am."

He shrugged. "I can come. My parents will be home late."

Keith turned to June. "You got any food?"

"That's all you think about. No, we don't have any food."

He patted his flat stomach. "Well, if I have to study I have to fill up first."

The others laughed. Tall and skinny, with a light olive complexion and dark, wavy hair, Keith's sense of humor made him one of the most popular boys in school. June had liked him the first day she set eyes on him, but Marva had been so strict, he could only walk her home after school. He'd never come to the apartment in Marva's absence, but as long as others were present, she shouldn't mind. Besides, chemistry was not one of June's favorite subjects. The only way she could make a good grade was with help from Keith, the class science whizz.

June turned to the others. "There's a *doubles* man at the corner. If we hurry we should catch him."

Doubles, a popular Indian pastry made with ground peas and filled with curried chickpeas, was a cheap and satisfying dish. It would carry them through until dinner.

They counted the money they had between them. Enough for six doubles - the boys would have two each – and a litre of Coke.

Armed with their sustenance, they entered the apartment about a half hour later. June opened up the windows. The boys flipped on the television while June and Wendy went into the kitchen for ice and glasses. Soon they were enjoying their meal. But once it was over, her three friends seemed in no hurry to start studying. Wendy got up and flipped on the radio. A hot calypso was playing and she snapped her fingers to the beat and wiggled her hips. She pulled John up and they began dancing to the music.

Keith looked at June. "A little dance wouldn't hurt."

June shrugged and rose to join him. They were having such a good time she almost forgot why they were there.

The music over, John reached for his knapsack and touched Wendy on her shoulder. "It's getting late. We have to start studying."

June glanced at her watch. Five to four. Marva would be home soon. If she came and found them studying, she wouldn't mind. June began to clear the table, hoping they would take the hint, but another calypso started and Wendy got busy once more. "Oh, all right, just now. I like this song."

June shook her head and took the glasses into the kitchen. Keith followed her with the plates. "That Wendy is crazy. I'll help you tidy up and then we'll go and turn off the music."

June agreed. While she washed the glasses and Keith dried, he said, "It's nice being here with you like this."

"I know. I like that."

"What do you plan to do after CXC?"

"I want to go back and do my A levels and then work in the library."

"You don't need A levels for that."

She handed him a plate. "I know, but I just want to have them, in case I decide to do something else. You still plan on working with Fedchem?"

He shrugged. "My dad's an engineer there. He says it won't be hard for them to hire me."

"You're so lucky."

A sudden silence descended on the living-room. And then came a voice June did not wish to hear at this time. "What on earth is going on here?"

Muffled voices reached her ears.

"Where's June?"

June saw her panic mirrored on Keith's face. He dropped the towel on the counter just as Marva burst into the kitchen. "June? Who are those people? And what are you and Keith doing back here?"

Keith, who had always been afraid of Marva, stuttered, "We … we …"

June took over. "Sister, I'm sorry. We were just going to study."

"To study? With the TV and the radio blasting at the same time? What kind of studying you planned to do? Dance lessons?"

"Sister, it's not what you think. We were going to study chemistry." June made to leave the kitchen. "I'll tell them to go."

Keith trailed after her into the living-room where the other two were putting their knapsacks over their shoulders.

"You all have to leave now," June said.

"Wait!"

Marva stood in the doorway. "You all don't have to leave. If you came to study, sit down and study."

June stared at her sister, then moved toward a chair. "Thanks, Sister. Thank you!" She motioned to her friends. "Get your books out."

But Marva wasn't finished. "Your parents know you all are here?"

The four exchanged glances, then John spoke up. "My mother and sister don't get home until five and my father gets home later, but Keith and Wendy were going to call their parents, if it's okay with you?"

June was impressed. None of her friends ever faced up to her sister like that. Marva seemed to think the same way. She nodded. "Go ahead."

While Keith spoke on the phone to his mother, June cast John a surreptitious glance. He was kind of cute too with his serious expression, dark complexion and a hint of a mustache and beard. He'd started going with Wendy after she'd performed her infamous slip and fall act that day in the auditorium. The senior classes were gathered there for some lecture. Before it began, Wendy had gone running down the aisle, pretended to trip and ended up in John's lap. They'd become a fixture after that.

Keith finished speaking and passed the receiver to Wendy. Her voice cut through June's thoughts. "My mother wants to speak to your sister."

The phone conversations over, Marva turned to the group, "Okay, I'm going to cook. Did you all have anything to eat?"

When they told her they had *doubles*, Marva made a face. "That won't keep you for long. I have chicken already seasoned and a few cans of red beans. Dinner will be ready in no time. One more thing." She paused near the kitchen door. "No one," she fixed her gaze on each of them, her eyes lingering on Keith, "no one is to come here when I'm not here, unless you ask me first. Understood?"

Smiling, June reached for her bag. Her sister was the best. "Yes."

Marva finished fixing dinner and served it to June and her friends who attacked it like it was the only meal they'd had all day. After she'd eaten and done the dishes, she retired to the bedroom with the portable radio. She turned it on low and lay on the bed. An unaccustomed feeling of satisfaction came over her. Despite her warning to June, she was happy to have other people in the apartment.

Marva had just one evening out during the week – Bible Study on Wednesday - while June engaged in a myriad of activities. She would be successful one day, Marva was sure of it, but what about her? As a woman, she could never be a full-fledged mechanic. She had no education. She'd never even passed the Common Entrance Examinations.

At Tantie Beulah's home, and during their early days in San Fernando, Marva didn't feel so lonely. Adjusting to city life, a new job and most of all, trying to avoid detection, had occupied her time and her thoughts. But now that she had settled into her new life, loneliness seared her soul the way Krishna's welding torch seared a vehicle's metal. Even while she was in the company of others, the scorched feeling remained.

Spending time at the Stewarts' home had helped a little. But now with Miss Stewart married and June busy with so many activities, Marva felt the pain of loneliness closing in on her again.

She was only twenty, but she felt like forty. Life was passing her by.

CHAPTER FOUR

By Friday Marva had hit on a partial solution to her self-esteem problems. She lingered near her boss's desk until he looked up at her with raised eyebrow.

"I'm going to start work in a minute, Glen, but I just wanted to ask for something."

Glen waited. He was always a man of few words.

Marva continued, "I want a certificate."

He laid his pen down. "You want a certificate."

"Yes, you know, one like that." She pointed to a framed one hanging among a calendar, other certificates, and paraphernalia on the wall. "That's mine."

She nodded. "Right. I want one with my name on it. I've been working here for three years now. I learned the job and am almost as good as a mechanic. I want something to show for it."

Glen returned to his work, but not before Marva saw the half-smile on his face. She ran down the steps mumbling. Krishna, who worked in the body shop, left his bay and came to meet her. "Marva, what's going on?"

She repeated her request to Glen and what his reaction was.

Krishna smiled. "Why not go to technical school? They'll give you a certificate."

She looked at him in surprise. "I hadn't thought of that. But I can't go there and work at the same time."

"They have evening classes. Check it out."

She turned away. "Okay, I will."

Cicely and David alighted from the taxi, thanked the driver and took their suitcases from his hands.

"Somebody left the gate open," Cicely said as they entered the driveway.

David nodded to the left. "And somebody is here."

Her sister's Hyundai and another car Cicely didn't recognize were parked on the side of the house. She and David climbed the short flight of steps to the verandah. Discarded lumber and building tools and the smell of fresh paint told of the earlier presence of workmen. A sign that said WET PAINT was stuck on the glass front door. Why would someone put a sign there? Cicely removed it and saw writing on the other side. It read "WELCOME BACK!" She laughed and showed it to her husband.

He placed it on a nearby chair. "I wonder who thought of that."

Inside, on the mat was an arrow with the words "Follow Me." They exchanged glances, shrugged and set their bags down in a corner. More paper arrows pointed in the direction of the kitchen. David removed his shoes, and she did the same. They tiptoed into the kitchen and found the table laid and covered dishes set in the middle. There was no one in sight. They peeked under the table, behind cabinets, out on the back porch, but saw no one.

Cicely uncovered a dish of baked chicken. "I guess they wanted us to know we have food."

David took the cover from her hand. "No eating yet. I have to do this first." He scooped her up in his arms, and just then they materialized out of nowhere. "Surprise!"

Sheila, her sister, came first, followed by her daughters, then Cicely's father and David's mother, Rose. Marva and June brought up the rear.

Cicely ducked her head on her husband's chest and he set her down not too gently. "Don't tell me you guys were in the bedroom."

Rose nodded. "That's why we had the arrows leading to the kitchen. You fell for it." She embraced Cicely then David. "You two look wonderful. St. Lucia must agree with you."

Cicely's father gave her a big hug, before turning to David. "Maybe you agree with each other."

David laughed as he pumped his father-in-law's hand.

More hugs and kisses followed, while Marva and June hung back looking on. Cicely went to them with open arms and they fell into them. "I missed you girls. Have you been good?"

They nodded and June said, "We missed you so much."

"You poor baby. I won't be gone for a while. I'm home now."

Marva's face seemed a bit strained, but that was not unusual. Cicely turned back to the table where Sheila was busy setting glasses with juice and ice.

Cicely uncovered another dish while answering questions from everyone. Yes, St. Lucia was beautiful. They stayed in a lovely villa in the mountains. The beaches were gorgeous. They went fishing and snorkeling, played tennis …

Sheila cut in, "Okay, everything's ready. We're out of here."

Cicely's mouth fell open. "Wh … what do you mean?"

Rose touched Cicely's shoulder. "We only came to welcome you guys home. Now it's time to leave you two alone."

More hugs and kisses. Her father said, "I'll call you."

Cicely said to Marva, "I'll call you."

Then they were gone. The house filled with an echoing silence.

David turned to Cicely. "Now, where was I?"

She laughed. "You were about to —"

He cut her off by scooping her up once more and carrying her into the bedroom. He deposited her on the bed. "That's the traditional way."

She sat up and looked around. A vase of flowers stood on the dresser with a card pinned to it. Cicely was about to get up to remove the card when David eased her back down on the bed. "We have to give each other a welcome home."

Sometime later, they went out to the kitchen to have their dinner, now cold, their drinks all turned to water.

Cicely placed the dish of chicken in the oven. "If we keep this up, we'll never eat."

He slid an arm around her waist. "It says somewhere that man shall not live by bread alone."

She swatted him with the dish towel. "Not that kind of bread. In a few days you'll be singing a different tune." She lowered her voice to a growl. "Where's my dinner, woman?"

He laughed. "No way. I married you to be my wife, not my slave."

She touched his cheek. "I love you, David."

He bent and their lips met, then he withdrew and rubbed his stomach. "I agree with you. If we keep this up we'll never eat."

Later that evening, they tackled the pleasant task of opening their presents and signing their thank you cards. Cicely paused with her pen over the card. "You know I just realized something."

He gave her a quizzical look.

"The initials of our first names follow each other; C and D."

"You're right." He took a piece of gift paper. "And if you remove the line from the D and put them together like this, they form a complete whole."

Cicely looked at the circle he'd drawn, then at his face. "We complete each other."

The following Friday when Marva went to receive her paycheck, Glen handed her a larger brown envelope and made a mock bow. She opened the envelope and pulled out the paper with an important-looking border around it. In the middle it read, *Certificate of Completion. Marva Garcia has successfully completed an automotive apprenticeship program at Glen's Automotive.* His signature was scrawled below.

Marva beamed with pleasure. "Thank you, Glen. Thank you. My own certificate."

She ran into the yard holding out the paper for everyone to see. Krishna looked at it and patted her on the back. "So long I working here and Glen never gave me a certificate."

Carlton said, "That don't mean nothing. You can't take that anywhere."

She tossed her head and showed it to Raymond, her new supervisor.

He beamed back at her. "Good going, girl. Frame it and put it on your wall."

She looked down at the paper. That was exactly what she planned to do. With this one and the ones to follow.

When Marva got home that night, she showed June her certificate.

June took it from her hand and examined it then turned to Marva. "I'm so proud of you, Sister. You worked hard for this and you deserve it."

Marva took the paper back from June, stared at it a moment longer, then slowly ripped it once, then twice.

June put her hands to her face. "Sister, why'd you do that? You looked so happy just now."

Marva sank down on a chair, crumpled the pieces of paper into a ball. "I don't know, Junie. What use is this to me?"

"Well, it … is a certificate. It shows you achieved something."

Marva squeezed the paper tighter. "Well, I want to achieve more. Some day. I want to be like you, and Miss Stewart. You understand what I'm saying, Junie?"

June seemed puzzled. "You want to go back to school?"

Marva nodded, but she averted her gaze. It was a stupid idea. She couldn't go back to school at twenty. It would be worse for her than when she was in elementary school. Everyone would laugh at her.

"Sister, that is wonderful. I'll help you study. Ooh, that is great." June clapped her hands and skipped out of the room.

After she left the room, Marva straightened the pieces of paper. What had she done? Still acting without thinking. This might be the only certificate she would ever have. She smoothed out the pieces of paper on the table and went in search of scotch tape.

Seated in their usual spot under the mango tree, June listened with half her mind on the chatter around her while pretending to be studying.

"You should see the nice red dress Mother bought me. It has a scoop neck and a frilly skirt," Wendy said.

"And Mummy got me a pair of black high-heeled shoes. About this high—" Althea measured with her fingers.

That's all they ever talk about. Clothes, shoes and boys. No, that's not fair. I like to talk about those things too, but not today.

June rose from the bench and stuffed her book into her bag.

Althea paused in her conversation. "June, where are you going?"

She turned to walk away. "If you all don't want to study, I'll have to find a quiet spot. Exams are just a month away."

Wendy opened her book. "All right, all right. I hate math, but let's work on these equations."

Keith loved math and was good at it. Maybe June should go look for him instead, but her friends seemed ready to study, so she sat back down. About an hour later, they agreed it was time to break, and June didn't protest. She'd begun to get the hang of quadratic equations. In fact, she was beginning to like algebra and thought she had a good chance of passing it in the CXC.

As she was putting away her books, someone touched her on her shoulder. She looked up and smiled at Keith. "Your timing is good."

John and a Chinese boy named Patrick, who looked too young to be in high school, followed. The six of them sauntered out of the school yard. The boys walked in front while the girls straggled behind.

Suddenly, Wendy stopped and held June's hand. "My mother and father are going to The Great Race in Tobago next weekend."

June had heard about the event where boats from all over the world came to Tobago to compete. Wendy's mother was a nurse, her father a high-powered civil servant, and they were always doing important things.

June looked at her with envy. "Are you going with them?"

Wendy shook her head and smiled, her gaze on the ground. June knew that smile. It was the same one she'd given John when she fell into his lap in the auditorium that day. What was she up to this time?

Althea provided the answer. "She has plans."

Wendy cast a glance at the boys, then back at June. "I'll call you when I get home. Mother will be working late tonight."

They watched as she crossed the street to the bus stop. A year older than June, Wendy was plumper with skin like creamy chocolate. Her permed hair was parted down the middle and held in two ponytails with ring combs. At the end of the ponytail, she always wore two bow clips to keep the hair from coming loose. But that was as far as the little-girl look went. Her ample bosom and flaring hips contrasted sharply with the rest of her to give her a far more mature appearance.

Althea turned off on her street and waved good-bye, then Patrick, then John and finally June and Keith were the only ones left.

"I hardly got a chance to talk to you today," he said.

"I know. It's like the more I study, the more I feel I don't know."

He took hold of her hand. "If your sister wasn't so strict, I could come to your house and study. Or you could come to mine."

She glanced at him quickly. "You heard what she said the last time."

He squeezed her hand. "I want to be alone with you sometimes, June. We never get to be alone. We're always with other people. We're old enough."

June had heard it before. Lately he'd begun dropping hints, and whenever they went to the movies with friends, he would steer her away from them.

In fact, they all broke up once they were in the theater so they could do whatever they wanted. One night he'd taken a small packet from his pocket. "Feel it," he'd said.

She'd gasped. A condom! Where had he got it? Had he gone to the pharmacy and bought it?

"I took it from my brother. He has a lot. He wouldn't miss this."

Memories of her experience with Marcus, an older man, were still too fresh in her mind. She'd promised her sister she would not repeat that behavior and she planned to keep her promise. Besides, she was a Christian now and knew that sex before marriage was wrong. Still, she felt tempted at times.

After Keith dropped her off at her apartment, she thought of Wendy. June hoped she would call before Marva got home. As luck would have it, Marva called to say she was going to be a little late. June took the chicken out of the fridge just as the phone rang a second time. It was Wendy.

June got right into it. "What was that mysterious smile about?"

Wendy pretended she didn't understand. "What are you talking about? I'm just glad Mother and Daddy are getting a chance to go away. They work too hard."

I bet they do. "So, how are you going to spend the weekend?" A sudden thought came to her mind. "I've an idea. Why don't you come and spend it with me? Sister won't mind as long as I ask her first."

Wendy laughed. "To do what? Play doll house, or keep my nose in a book?"

June's face burned. Was she calling her childish or bookish? "That's okay, Wendy. Bye."

"No, wait, June. I didn't mean what I said. It's just that someone else invited me."

"Oh, okay. Have a good time." June hung up the receiver and went into the kitchen. Maybe it was a good thing Wendy didn't want to spend the weekend with her. They would never get a minute of studying done. June wanted so much to pass her exams on her first try. They couldn't afford to pay for her to retake the exams if she failed and still do her A levels after that. Their funds were so meager they had to watch every penny.

Sister was content to wear the same blouse and skirt all the time, but June craved every new style that came in. If she had a job, she could buy her own clothes and help with some of the expenses. She stared at the oil while it heated, then she put in a teaspoon of sugar. As the sugar darkened and bubbled, an idea bubbled up inside her. With a feeling of excitement, she poured the chicken into the pot and stirred.

CHAPTER FIVE

June communicated her idea to Keith the following day.

He spun a soccer ball on his index finger. "My aunt works at KFC. She might be able to help us get a job there."

"Us?"

He held the ball to his side. "I'm not letting you go and work without me. All the guys will be staring at you, wanting to date you —"

June laughed. "You don't own me, you know. I can do whatever I want."

He looked her up and down. "Yeah, I know that. When you want to go down there?"

"I have to talk to my sister first."

Keith frowned. She could tell he thought she was too much under Marva's control, but when he spoke his voice was even. "Let me ask my aunt then. She'll know if they're hiring."

June nodded.

A few days later, Keith informed her they could work at the fast food restaurant one night a week and on weekends. June was ecstatic. She had a job, and she and Keith would be together.

She blurted out the news to Marva when she walked in that night. "I got a job."

Marva stopped in her tracks. "You what?"

"I got a job. At KFC."

Marva continued toward the bedroom. "You can't work. You have to study."

June's jaw dropped. "But, Sister —"

Door closed.

June faced the wall. "You hear that? She says —"

Marva emerged from the bedroom, towel in hand, on her way to the bathroom. "You can't work."

June followed her. "Why not? I need this job."

Bathroom door slammed in her face.

June spun around and headed for the phone. She was about to call Keith and give him the devastating news when a knock sounded on the front door. She rolled her eyes and stomped toward the door. "Who is it?"

"Mrs. Benoit, Wendy's mother."

June glanced around their sparse, but tidy living-room before opening the door. A slim, dark-skinned woman in nurse's uniform stood there.

"Good- evening, Mrs. Benoit." June looked past her to the black Jaguar gleaming under the street light. June remembered her – and the car – vaguely from when she'd dropped Wendy off at Marva's party two years ago.

"Good-evening, June. Is Wendy here?"

June creased her brows. "Wendy? No, she isn't here."

The woman paused. She seemed worried. "Her father and I came back from Tobago sooner than we planned only to find … Wendy gone."

June felt a stab of guilt. Wendy did say she had plans, but she'd not disclosed what those plans were. Did they involve John? She didn't know what to say.

Marva saved her. "June, who is this?"

She turned around with relief. "Sister, this is Wendy's mother. She's looking for Wendy."

Marva stretched out her hand to the lady. "I'm Marva. Would you like to come in?"

The woman hesitated. "Thank you, but no. I … I have to check some other places."

She turned around and left. June and Marva watched her get into her shiny, expensive car and drive off, then they looked at each other, eyes wide.

Marva voiced part of June's thoughts. "That's a nice car. I would love to see inside that engine."

June would love to see inside the car, but right now her mind was on

Wendy. She recalled the girl's secretive smile and what she'd said on the phone about not wanting to play doll house.

Marva closed the door. "Do you know where your friend might be?"

June shook her head. "I've no idea."

Was she with John? He seemed too much of the quiet, studious type for Wendy. Maybe she was at another friend's house. June shook Wendy from her mind and faced Marva. "Sister, I want to talk to you about that job."

On Saturday morning, June and Keith took the bus to High Street for their job interview at KFC. Even though Keith had assured her they would get the job and that the interview was just a formality, June was nervous when they entered the restaurant. Keith's aunt took them into a back room to meet the manager, a short Indian man with spectacles and a protruding belly. Although it wasn't really protruding, just hanging like a big, floppy pillow. Maybe he ate too much fried chicken? She stifled a giggle.

The man waved them to a chair and took some basic information. Where had they worked before? June and Keith glanced at each other and Keith shook his head.

The man peered at them through his glasses. "Never work?"

He wrote something on his paper then looked at Keith. "We have two shifts. Eight to four and four to twelve. Which one you want to start with?"

Keith returned the man's stare. "What's your name?"

The man frowned. "My name? Call me Mr. Rambachan."

"Mr. Rambachan, I can't work so late during the week."

The man laid down his pen. "This is a fast food restaurant. F-A-S-T." He swept one hand across his desk to emphasize the word. "We sell a lot of chicken."

June was beginning to wonder if this was a good idea when the man continued, "We pay you real good."

"How good?" Keith asked.

"Nine dollars an hour."

That was good – if they got the job. She leaned forward. "Do you have special hours for school … I mean, we go to school, and we're studying for exams."

The man studied June's face. "School, eh? You doing your CXC?"

She nodded.

After scratching his head, scribbling and humming, the manager propped his glasses on his forehead and fixed his gaze on Keith. "I can only let you work on a slow night, Wednesday night from four to ten, and Saturday from eight to four. Take it or leave it."

June swallowed. Sister will never go for any of that. She would have to leave it.

Keith spoke up. "I'll take it."

June raised her eyebrows. "You will?"

"Yes." He leaned over and whispered, "Say yes and we'll work out something."

June smiled. "I'll take Saturday eight to four."

The man glanced from one to the other. "All right. But sometimes I might have to cancel you if one of the regular people want your shift, or if we're slow."

"I thought you said you were F-A-S-T." Keith imitated the man's sweeping gesture.

"Don't get fresh with me, young man. You don't have the job yet." He rose and beckoned to them to follow him.

They spent the next half hour meeting the staff and going through the supplies room.

"When you come next week, you will start training and get your uniforms," the man said.

"How long will the training be?" Keith asked.

"One day. If you don't get it by the end of the day, you can't make it."

June left the restaurant wondering if they had wasted their time, but Keith was unfazed. "Don't worry with him. How long could it take to learn to say, "Can I take your order?" or, "That would be eight dollars and twenty-six cents."

June was not reassured. "We still have to learn the cash register."

Marva rung the mop out in the bucket and passed it over the kitchen floor once more. June should be home soon. Marva wasn't sure if she wanted her to get that job. She worried that June didn't get enough rest. No, she corrected herself. June didn't spend enough time with her. Since Marva had loosened the reins, she was always out doing something, while Marva stayed at home. If June got this chicken and chips job, it would be another thing to come between them.

Marva finished mopping the floor, opened the back door and emptied the dirty water. After rinsing the mop and leaning it up to dry, she went back into the house. It was almost two o'clock. Maybe she should call Miss Stewart. It was Saturday. Miss Stewart and her husband might be out, or they might be relaxing at home. She couldn't disturb them. How she missed her teacher. Marva and June could no longer call her on the phone or go to her house whenever they pleased. Not that Miss Stewart would mind, but *he* might.

The phone shrilled, making her jump. She sprinted to pick it up. "Hello."

"Marva?"

Immediately, she felt a wide grin splitting her face. "Miss Stewart!"

"My dear, how are you and June doing?"

"We're doing good, Miss Stewart. I'm sorry - Mrs. Bowen."

The lady laughed. "Don't worry about it, Marva. Just call me Miss, like you always do."

"Junie went to look for a job."

"Really? Where?"

"KFC."

"Oh, that will be good for her. Listen, the lawyer called yesterday. He said that the closing is next Monday."

That was good news. She'd waited so long for the day when the sale of her father's property would be finalized. "Do I have to go and see the attorney?"

"No, I gave him your number. He'll call to tell you where the closing will be."

Marva raised her hand heavenward. "Okay, Miss. Thanks! Does Tantie Beulah have to go?"

"Yes. Take her with you."

"Okay, thanks, Miss."

"All right, dear. See you all in church tomorrow."

Marva replaced the receiver slowly after the click sounded on the other end. She and June would be well off. June would have enough money to go to university, and Marva could go back to school. She lowered herself on to a chair near the phone. What use was it really? When she could end up in jail? June was turning out to be everything Marva prayed she would be – bright, beautiful, ambitious. Why embarrass her?

She pasted a smile on her face as she heard the door lock turning.

On Monday morning, Marva dressed in a light green polka dot suit she sometimes wore to church.

June's eyes shone with excitement. "I wish I was going with you. I like to see how they do all those official things."

Marva smiled as she slipped on her medium-heeled brown shoes. "And I wish you could go instead of me. I'm so nervous."

At the attorney's office, she sat with Tantie Beulah and Mr. Rampersad, the buyer, and signed stacks of papers. She frowned over words like "probate", "clear title" and "intestate". Even though the clerk explained them to her, Marva was painfully aware of her limitations. But with every sheet of paper she signed, her nervousness lessened and by the time she finished, some excitement had seeped into her veins. And when the woman handed her both checks for forty thousand dollars each, she almost wept for joy. She could hardly wait to get home and show them to June and tell her every single detail.

Tantie Beulah was not so reticent. Tears streaming down her face she shook everyone's hand, thanked everyone and told them what a blessed child her niece was.

Guilt prodded her mind.

If she hadn't killed her father, they wouldn't be here today. She glanced down at the envelope in her hand. If it weren't for June, she would tear it up.

Blood money, like she'd seen in a movie.

However, something in her whispered the money was payment for all the years of abuse they'd suffered. Marva raised her head and squared her shoulders. As she did so, Mr. Rampersad stepped forward and shook her hand. "I'm happy to acquire your father's property. He was a good man and his estate is one of the best in Egypt Village." Then he shook his head. "It's a pity they can't find the man who killed poor Garcia."

The words were so unexpected they sliced through Marva's stomach with a clean cut.

The man patted her shoulder. "I can see it's still hurting you, but God will catch up with him. He could hide from the police but he can't hide from God."

Marva nodded and turned away. The germ of an idea implanted itself within her.

June was full of chatter that night. "I can't believe we'll have so much money." She flung her hands in the air. "We're rich."

Marva forced a smile. "Not really. We have to be very careful if you want to go to university."

June's expression didn't change. "I know, but it's still a lot of money."

"Well, maybe you could give up the chicken job."

June shook her head. "Give up seventy-two dollars every week plus tips and all that fried chicken?" She patted her tummy and giggled. "Maybe I'll get a big belly like Mr. Rambachan."

Marva laughed in spite of herself. "You better not."

June suddenly sobered. "Sister!"

"What?"

"You didn't enroll in classes."

Marva groaned. She hadn't forgotten, but the thought of returning to school and being among younger people terrified her. Now she wished she hadn't said anything.

June sat next to her on the bed. "Don't back down now, Sister. Why must I be the only one to get a good education? Why can't you get one too? You want to work on greasy, smelly cars all your life?"

"I love working on cars." She stopped and smiled. The next minute Mr. Rampersad's words resurfaced, and the smile left her face. What was the use of going back to school? What was the use of anything? She rose from the bed and headed for the bathroom.

June's words trailed after her. "We're going down to the center when I get home tomorrow, and you're enrolling if it's the last thing I do."

June was beginning to sound just like her.

True to her word, June was waiting for her when she got home from work the next day. There was no escape. Marva felt like a kindergarten pupil being dragged to school by her mother. After they'd eaten, they took the bus to the center run by the University of the West Indies. It offered courses for the General Certificate of Education as well as vocational classes, such as air conditioning, automotive and bookkeeping. Marva wanted to sign up for the automotive class, but the woman behind the desk raised her penciled eyebrows and said that class was already full.

June beamed at the woman. "My sister would like to enroll in the G.C.E. class."

The woman shifted some papers. "O Level or A Level?"

"O Level, please."

The woman placed some papers on a clipboard and handed them to June. "Have her fill these in and bring them back."

Marva felt invisible as they walked to a bench where a young man sat working on a similar form. June helped her complete the registration, and she took it to the desk. There was no turning back now.

CHAPTER SIX

Marva played the part well. Work Monday to Saturday, classes three afternoons a week, Bible study on Wednesday, and church on Sundays. She tried to appear interested when June questioned her about her lessons, but the germ was growing and taking shape. She couldn't let June suspect she was only biding her time. Exams were two months away. She wanted to be around to celebrate June's success with her. But meanwhile, she had to prepare.

She prayed daily for God to give her the strength to do what she needed to do. No one but she and June must ever know that she was the person responsible for her father's death. Not even Miss Stewart. Especially not Miss Stewart. The light in her teacher's eyes, the glow on her cheeks spoke of a happiness Marva would never experience, and she would not take that away from her.

But the more Marva thought of the lack of her future, the more she was drawn to God. The only time she felt really alive was when she was on her knees, or in church. During those times she experienced a peace, almost a oneness with her Savior. Sometimes, she would whisper, "Lord, I don't want to wait."

He never answered. But daily, two convictions were growing inside of her. Like Rebecca, carrying Jacob and Esau, they warred inside her, torturing her, convincing her that one was the promise, the other the shame. And like Rebecca, she desired the promise.

June slowed to a trot to allow Wendy to catch up with her. They'd done their usual two laps around the playing field and the boys were on their third. School had let out about half an hour earlier, and the grounds were almost empty, except for a few students who lingered, studying or just chatting. A cool, soft breeze fanned her cheeks, drying some of the moisture her running had produced.

Whether it was once or three times a week, June limited herself to just two laps around the field. Their Physical Education teacher, Mrs. Wilkes had advised them to keep up with their exercise.

"A fit body leads to a fit mind," she'd said.

June thought it must be true. Her mind seemed much clearer after she ran.

Wendy came up to her, panting, dabbing at her forehead. "It's so hot. I can't wait to get home and shower."

June placed both hands against a mango tree and extended one leg behind her in a deep stretch, then did the same with the other leg. "And I have to wash my hair."

Wendy eyed June's abundant tresses. "I don't know how you manage it."

"Sister helps me." She picked up her book bag from near the tree trunk.

Wendy picked hers up and slung it over her shoulder. "I have something to tell you." She studied the ground, as if thinking what to say. Keith, John and Patrick's running footsteps pounded toward them, kicking up dust in their wake.

Wendy looked up. "I'll tell you tomorrow."

June shrugged. What could she say that June had not heard before? As they neared a small shop, an advertisement for a Solo soft drink on the front wall of the building caught June's eyes. "I'm so thirsty."

"Me, too," Wendy agreed. "Let's go and get something to drink."

"You buying?" Keith grinned.

"You never have money," Wendy muttered. "Come on."

June dug her hand into the inner pocket of her skirt and pulled out her wallet. She looked at Keith. "You got paid Saturday. Where's your money?"

Keith handed her a few coins as they entered the shop. "I only have a dollar. I'm keeping the rest for the movies this weekend."

June shook her head. "You have more than enough for the movies."

She ordered an Apple J for herself and a Pepsi for Keith. "Next time you have to pay."

As they left the parlor sipping their sodas, June turned to Wendy. "What you wanted to talk about?"

They reached the intersection of Chacon and Rushworth Street. The boys said good-bye and left them.

Wendy slowed her pace. "I'm going away this weekend."

June glanced at her. "Oh, with your parents?"

Wendy sipped her Coke then smiled. "No, I'm coming to your house."

June came to an abrupt halt, spilling Apple J on her white shirt. "Look what you made me do."

"I'm sorry." Wendy held out a handkerchief.

June dabbed at her shirt. "You mustn't play games like that, Wendy."

Wendy laughed. "It's not a game."

June handed the kerchief back to her. "Well, I didn't invite you."

Wendy stopped and unslung her bag from her shoulder. She opened it and took something from the front pocket. June stared with mild curiosity at the photograph of a good-looking Spanish man probably in his late twenties. "Who is that?"

"Daryl."

June gave her a questioning glance.

"I'm going away with him."

June almost dropped her bag. She forced herself to keep her voice low. "What do you mean? Going where?"

Wendy seemed amused. "You remember the last time you invited me to stay with you when my parents went to Tobago? Well, I was with Daryl."

June opened her mouth, but no sound came. Wendy's mother had been very worried, looking all over San Fernando for her, and now she was going to do it again. Only this time she was going to tell her mother she was at June's house?

June grabbed her arm. "No! You're crazy. Don't tell your mother you'll be at my house when …" She clapped her hand over her mouth, suddenly realizing the implications of what Wendy was saying. She was having an affair with this man, and she was using June to cover for her. Of all the lowdown things to do.

"Do you know what you're doing? You could get pregnant!"

Wendy was unfazed. "He uses condoms."

June put her hand to her forehead. "You're crazy, Wendy. You want to ruin your life? Exams are right around the corner. You should be concentrating on that instead of —"

Wendy slipped her soft drink into the side opening of her bag. "I'm not crazy." Then she looked at June. "Everyone knows about the time you ran away to live with that man, so don't preach to me."

June felt the blood drain from her face. That episode with Marcus had occurred over two years ago, and June had put it behind her. An ounce of indiscretion that had caused her a pound of shame and heartache, when, unable to bear her sister's controlling attitude, she had run away from home to meet Marcus. But she'd never lived with him, never had sex with him. Could she tell that to her friend, now staring at her with accusing eyes?

Wendy tossed her head. "I'll tell Mummy I'm with Sharon or Althea. I have other friends."

June stared at the girl's stony face. "Wendy, please don't do this. You're messing up your life."

Wendy quickened her steps and turned into a side street. June watched her for a moment, then on legs that felt like a ton, continued on her way home.

Marva watched June push the rice and peas around on her plate, then get up and dump the food into the garbage can.

"Junie, what's the matter?"

June scraped off the remaining food carefully and placed the plate in the sink before answering, "Nothing."

I know you. Something's wrong. But she also knew that if she probed, June would close up like a *chip chip* shell. June dragged herself out of the kitchen like an old lady, and Marva heard her rustling around in the bedroom before going into the bathroom.

Marva didn't finish her meal either. Something had upset her baby sister, and it upset her too, even though she didn't know what it was. She washed the dishes, tidied the kitchen and mopped the floor, even though it didn't need mopping. By the time she'd done all that, June was seated at the table in the living-room, her books spread around her.

Marva walked past her, pretending not to notice the fingers twirling the pencil in front of her forehead and the eyes staring at nothing. She sat at the edge of her seat, chair tilted forward on two legs in her characteristic studying position. It was a miracle she never fell forward. But today June's frown was not one of concentration, but of worry.

After Marva had taken her shower, she changed into a clean skirt and blouse, placed her math book in her purse and headed for the door.

June's posture had not changed.

"Junie, I'm going down to the center."

She placed the pencil down. "I forgot you have class today. Math?"

Marva nodded. "I'll be back soon."

She reached the door and turned the lock.

"Sister."

"Yes?"

"Never mind. When you come back—"

"You want to talk to me about something?"

She sighed. "It's okay. When you come back."

Marva's hand dropped from the door lock and she went and sat on the couch. "What is it?"

June rose, pushing her chair roughly backward. She rarely wore her hair down during the day anymore, but twisted it into a bun at the nape of her neck. Marva had taken it as a sign of her growing maturity. Her hazel eyes seemed dark this evening. Maybe it was the fading light, or just worry, and she didn't meet Marva's gaze. A wave of fear swirled in her stomach. Was Marcus troubling her again? Or was it Keith? Marva didn't want to fight again.

June's voice cut into her thoughts. "What do you do if a friend is doing something foolish?"

A friend? A friend? Marva wanted to throw her hands in the air in relief, but June's pinched expression told her she was really troubled.

"Who is this friend?"

June's gaze flickered upwards then down again. "I can't tell you … yet, but she's doing something really stupid, and she wants to involve me—"

"Involve you? How?"

A look of panic flashed across June's face. "I … she wants me to lie for her."

Marva frowned. This sounded serious. "Is she a Christian?"

June uncoiled the bun and ran her fingers through her lustrous hair, sending a mass of rivulets tumbling around her shoulders. "She and her parents go to our church."

"Do I know them?"

June hesitated, still looking fearful. "A little bit."

"Do you want me to talk to your friend?"

"No!" June ran her fingers through her hair again. "I shouldn't have said anything. Go on to your class."

Marva rose. She knew when it made sense not to pry. June would tell her about it eventually. "Okay, I'm going. Lock the door."

On the bus to the center, Marva puzzled over what her sister had not said. A secret serious enough to keep June from eating and studying? Nothing ever did that.

Marva bowed her head and prayed, "Lord, there is nothing hidden from you. Whatever is troubling my sister, she won't tell it to me, but I pray she'll tell You and allow You to give her the correct advice, because I may tell her the wrong thing. And, Lord, I pray for her friend, that You will speak to her heart and keep her from getting hurt. Thank you, Lord, for I ask it in Jesus' Name, Amen."

When she opened her eyes, the bus had reached the little incline near the tire shop where she usually got off. She rose and pressed the bell.

When Marva returned home around eight-thirty that night, she found June in much better spirits, chomping on a drumstick and studying with the radio turned down low.

She ran to meet Marva as she came through the door. "Guess what, Sister? My friend called. She said she wouldn't go … wouldn't do what she said she was going to do."

Marva placed her books on the table. "You never told me your friend's name."

June went back to her seat. "Wendy."

"Oh, the one whose mother came looking for her the other night?"

June kept her eyes on her book. "That's Wendy."

"Well, I'm glad she changed her mind."

Nothing more was said on the subject, but as Marva prepared for bed that night, she reflected on the conversation and the prayer she'd offered up on the bus. God had answered. She smiled in the darkness. *I know what I have to do.*

CHAPTER SEVEN

Friday was Cicely's favorite night of the week. It was the beginning of the weekend, and she got to be a real housewife. She let Miss Lucy leave early after preparing whatever Cicely had decided to cook for dinner. Tonight, she was making *pelau*, one of David's favorite dishes.

She removed the chicken, nicely browned, from the pot, poured coconut milk into the skillet with the green pigeon peas, carrots and seasonings. She glanced at the clock. Four forty-five. Ample time to finish cooking, take a bath and get into tonight's get-up, as David liked to call it. She washed the utensils she'd used earlier and placed them in the dish drainer. Everything must be spic and span by the time he got home.

While she wiped the counter, Cicely reflected on how easily she'd slipped into married life. This house, which at one time held bitter-sweet memories for her, had now become her love nest. She didn't need the little plaque Marva had given her as a wedding present that read Home Is Where The Heart Is, to remind her that her heart was planted here with the man she loved.

The sprawling four-bedroom house should have felt empty when she was alone, but it didn't. All she had to do was look at her husband's picture above the television or on her dresser, or their wedding pictures adorning the living-room walls, and she felt warm and comforted. Everything, from the renovated back porch, new windows and furnishings spoke of the new life they'd begun – a life which, a few years ago, she would have never thought possible.

From the corner of her eye, she saw the liquid bubbling up in the pot and hurried to rinse the rice and add it to the contents. She stirred the mixture, then picked up a copy of *Essence* magazine that David had bought her, and reached for a chair. No sooner had she sat, than the phone rang. Was David calling? She hoped he wouldn't be late.

She picked up the phone. "Hello?"

"Hi, Ciss, it's me."

"Daddy? How are you doing?"

"Great. And you?"

"Wonderful. I was just thinking about you."

Her father's voice sounded vibrant. "Something good, I hope."

"Yeah. How is everybody?"

Her father now lived in Port-of-Spain with his sister Elaine and her husband Jonathan.

"They're fine. How's David? Still working hard?"

"Not really. He says it's boring being in the San Fernando Fraud Squad. He says, 'How many checks can they bounce in Trinidad? How many signatures can they forge?'"

Her father laughed. "A man like David has to be in the action."

She nodded, forgetting he couldn't see her gesture. "I'm not complaining, though. He gets to come home early every evening and has every Sunday off and most Saturdays."

"Sounds like a dream job."

During the pause, Cicely wondered if her father had only called to see how they were doing. She glanced at her pot. "Daddy, could you hold one second? I'm cooking."

The rice had swelled and the liquid was almost gone. She added the chicken, stirred the whole thoroughly, covered the pot and lowered the burner. When she picked up the phone again, her father said, "Honey, I've something to tell you."

"Are you okay?" He'd had a heart attack two years ago, but had seemed much better at the wedding.

"Oh, I'm fine, I'm fine." He paused. "Ciss, you've been a good daughter to me all these years, even though I wasn't always a good father —"

She bit her lip. Did he have to bring that up?

" — I've been lonely and, well, what I'm trying to say is … I would like to get married again."

A wave of excitement washed over her. "Daddy, that's wonderful! I'm so happy for you. When do I get to meet my new stepmother?"

"You already know her."

Cicely frowned. It couldn't be Mrs. Alfred from their church, an usher with whom her father had seemed friendly some years ago. Had she moved to Port-of-Spain and their friendship deepened into something more?

Her father's next words almost knocked the wind out of her stomach. "It's your mother-in-law."

The room seemed to spin around her. Her mother-in-law? Mother Rose?

"Hello?"

"I'm here," she replied. Her mind went numb. All she could think was, David would hit the ceiling.

"What do you have to say?"

"I ... er ... congratulations!"

"You don't sound very enthusiastic."

"I ... I'm just a bit surprised, that's all." *Liar.*

Her father chuckled. "I'm still a bit surprised myself. That such a lovely woman would say 'yes' to a man like me. But God works in amazing ways, doesn't he?"

She had to agree. "He sure does."

"Don't say anything to your husband yet. Rose will want to tell him herself."

"Of course." A whiff of an aroma came to her nostrils. "Daddy, I have to get back to my *pelau*. Talk to you later."

Shaking her head, she hung up the receiver and uncovered the pot.

David's contribution to their Friday night party was to bring his new wife a gift, just as he'd done during their courtship days. He stood in the doorway, hand behind his back, a smile on his face. His smile widened into a grin when he saw what she was wearing—one of his old tee shirts that fell just below her knees. He placed the small vase with the single red rose on the table and scooped her up in his arms. "Now I know you really love me."

Laughing, she asked, "What did I do?"

He set her down and eyed her get-up. "If you can wear that old rag, it speaks volumes."

"Well, this is it every Friday night from now on."

He shook his head. "I won't mind a little variety – the strapless dress, the mini skirt, the negligee —"

Cicely swatted him playfully. "I know the last one is your favorite. Go and wash up and come let's eat. I'm starving."

The next morning, she lay languid in bed, listening to the sounds of her husband's ablutions in the bathroom. Minutes later, he stood in the doorway. "Sleepy-head, are we getting up today or no?"

She glanced at the clock. It was six-thirty. They should be leaving the house in the next hour if they were to get in a good game of tennis. But she didn't feel like it.

He came into the room, towel around his middle and sat on the edge of the bed. His arm circled her waist. "I'll make breakfast while you get dressed, okay?"

She scooted up on the bed and kissed him on his cheek. He smelled of aftershave and mouthwash. She loved a man who smelled like that in the morning. She got off the bed and went into the bathroom. By the time she was ready, David had bacon and eggs on the table, a steaming cup of tea for her and a cup of coffee for him.

Cicely looked at the spread. The thought of eating did not appeal to her, but how could she disappoint him when he'd gone to all that trouble? Obviously noting her reluctance, he placed a forkful of egg in her mouth. "You have to get some strength to beat me this morning." She chewed and swallowed. The next moment she was out of her chair and running to the bathroom. He caught up with her just as her stomach heaved, and for the first time since she became an adult, Cicely threw up.

She gave him a sheepish smile. "I wanted to be sure before I told you."

He wrapped her in his arms and rained kisses all over her face. "I love you, love you, love you." He held her away from him just a little. "Today is Saturday, doctor's offices are closed. Do you think your sister or Fred might know someone?"

She leaned against his strong chest. "They might, but I feel better now. What do you say I call my doctor on Monday morning? He'll see me right away. I just want to spend a lazy day with you."

"Whatever you say, sweetheart, but I want you to start taking care of yourself and my son right away."

She raised her head and stared at him. "*Your* son? He's my son too. Or daughter."

He kissed her on her lips. "Whatever it is, I want you to be careful."

"Women have been having babies for centuries without anyone fussing over them."

"You want to call your sister and your father? Then I'll call mom."

Cicely jerked upright. Her father was not the only one with some big news. Thank God, David had something else to cushion the shock of what his mother had to say to him.

"Let's be sure first. What if it's a false alarm?"

He patted her tummy. "It's not. I know it's not."

In the church lobby, Marva sidled near the little table against the wall on which lay some tracts. While June spoke to someone – she was always talking to someone – Marva grabbed a handful of the tracts and dropped them in her purse. With a feeling of satisfaction, she waited on June to end her conversation.

Marva had gotten the idea from the sermon the minister preached that day. Now she could barely wait to put her plan into action.

Next morning, she decided to experiment on her boss, Raymond. After he finished checking the distributor cap she'd just replaced she asked, "So, did you and your daughter enjoy church yesterday?"

"Yes, Debbie say she want to go again." He closed the bonnet. "Go start the engine."

The car hummed smoothly, and they decided to break for lunch. She found a seat in the back of a spacious Kingswood station wagon. She stretched her legs out in front of her, Bible on her lap, while she bit into her ham sandwich. It was a very relaxing position, and she had a whole hour to delve into the book of John. Snippets of the men's conversation, punctuated with their laughter, drifted to her ears. From Carlton she heard the words, "Jehovah Witness" and "hypocrite." Krishna responded in an angry tone, but she couldn't discern what he said. Carlton still hated her because he'd not had his way with her, but at least the others were on her side.

She finished her sandwich and drank the juice from her small thermos bottle then she looked in her bag and found the tracts. Now was as good a time as any. She took six of them, opened the car door and sauntered over to the men. They had finished eating and begun their game of cards.

With her brightest smile, she said, "Excuse me. I have something for you all." She handed two tracts to each of the men. Carlton glared at her, but kept his mouth shut.

Raymond took his, read the heading and smiled. "How to know if you are going to heaven. Thanks, Baby. I want to go to heaven."

Carlton chortled. "I told you she was a Jehovah Witness. Now she bringin' the books."

Krishna retorted, "Fool. This is not a book. This is a …" he raised one eyebrow at Marva.

"It's a tract, to help you learn about God and the Bible."

"Right. I couldn't remember the name," Krishna said.

"What you know about tracts?" Carlton argued. "Indians don't know nothing about God."

Krishna jumped up, hands on his hips. "My uncle is a Pentecostal. I went to church with him a few times, so I know about God. And Marva told me a lot about God, right Marva?"

She nodded. She didn't want to start a fight.

Raymond touched Krishna's arm. "Sit down, sit down. Let us finish the game."

Krishna sat, and Marva turned away. As she walked back to her car, she heard Carlton's irritated muttering. "Woman always causing trouble. I don't know why Glen don't fire her."

Raymond once more tried to appease, "She don't cause no trouble. She's a very good worker."

She bit her lip. Her well-laid plan seemed to have backfired.

Marva had a little success on the bus to her class the next day. A young woman with two small children came and sat on the seat next to her. The younger was just a baby, maybe six months old, the other, a boy with large, dark eyes and a lollipop in his mouth, couldn't be more than three. Marva returned the woman's smile and went back to studying her geography. But not for long. An elbow poked her in the ribs. Seconds later, she felt a kick to her shin. The mother slapped the boy on his leg and pulled him closer to her.

Marva put her book away. "It's okay. Let me help you."

She pulled the child on to her lap. "Do you like cars?"

He nodded, still sucking on his lollipop.

"What colors do you like?"

He thought for a moment. "Red."

"Good. Let's count all the red cars."

The boy pressed his nose against the window, then squealed, "Look!"

Marva smiled. "That's one red car."

By the time the bus neared her stop, she and the little boy had counted seven red cars, and the baby was sleeping peacefully in her mother's arms.

She gave Marva a look of gratitude. "Thank you so much. I'll try that the next time."

The boy touched Marva's cheek with a sticky finger. "You are nice."

She smiled as she rose and pressed the bell. Then she remembered the tracts in her purse. She pulled out one and handed it to the mother who smiled her thanks and began reading.

Encouraged by her success, Marva gave out two more tracts to girls she sometimes spoke with at the center. That night as she pulled the blanket around her, she whispered, "It's all for you, Lord. All for you."

CHAPTER EIGHT

The evening sun filtered through the sheer curtain, casting golden bars on the flowered sofa. From the upstairs apartment came the sound of the television, not loud enough to be distracting.

June watched as Wendy erased the numbers from her paper. "I'll never understand this stupid algebra."

"If you keep saying that, you won't understand it. Look at this. If x squared plus $3x$ minus 1 equals 0, then all we have to do is factor out x."

Wendy propped her cheek on her fist. "Okay, show me."

June sighed. "All right, but you are going to do one by yourself. When we factor it out it will be x plus 4 …"

Knocking on the front door interrupted her. The girls looked at each other then at the door.

"Who could that be?"

June went to the door and opened it. A tall, nice-looking man, neatly dressed in a light gray shirt and pants with matching striped tie stood at the door. He could be some kind of salesman. Why did he seem vaguely familiar? "Good-afternoon."

Chiseled lips parted to reveal even white teeth in a flashing smile. "Good afternoon. You must be June. Wendy told me how pretty you are."

She turned to find Wendy standing behind her, a broad smile on her face. Now she remembered. He was the man in the photograph Wendy had shown her. Hadn't she said she wasn't going with him anymore? Very cunning, but it wouldn't happen again.

"Thank you, but please don't come to my house again to meet Wendy." She turned and stared her friend in the face. "She will not be here."

The man opened his mouth as if to say something then seemed to change his mind. Wendy brushed past her as she went out the door. "I'll see you tomorrow, June."

In stony silence, she watched them climb the steps to the pavement and get into the man's shiny sports car then she slammed the door and stomped over to the table. It took her a few moments before she felt composed enough to resume her studying.

June avoided Wendy at school the next day. If the girl felt any guilt about what she'd done, her actions didn't show it. That evening as June and Keith walked home, he said to her, "What happen to your friend Wendy?"

June kept her tone casual. "What do you mean?"

"She didn't tell you she's getting married as soon as we graduate?"

June halted. Wendy getting married? To that man? "No, she didn't tell me."

"I thought she was your good friend."

June tossed her head and continued walking. She couldn't prevent Wendy from doing what she'd set her mind on, any more than Marva could have prevented her from doing what she did two years ago. She just hoped Wendy wouldn't be hurt.

Keith's next words jolted her once more. "I don't see how she could marry a married man."

"What! He's married?"

Keith smiled. "You look like you saw a ghost."

She couldn't answer. What was Wendy doing? June quickened her pace. "Look, Keith, I … I have to get home."

"I didn't mean to upset you. It's Friday. You don't have to study tonight."

She stopped and turned to him. "You didn't upset me. I … I'm just in shock, that's all. I'll see you at work tomorrow, okay?"

"Okay."

They faced each other on the street with cars and pedestrians going past. June had a sudden desire to be kissed. She wanted Keith to wrap his arms around her right there and make all this mess with Wendy go away.

He seemed to sense it too, for a smile curved his lips and he took a small step toward her. A car honked and the spell was broken.

"See you tomorrow." He turned in the opposite direction and walked away.

June stared after him, knapsack bouncing on his back, the stick he always carried to keep stray dogs away trailing at his side. She sighed and continued on home.

Lady Hailes Avenue was a bustling hive of school children chattering and giggling. Women holding children by one hand, purses and parcels in the other, hurried in the direction of the taxi drivers who called out loudly, "Siparia, Point, Couva." Nearby, the towering San Fernando General Hospital, a city landmark, attracted its own brand of traffic with cars flowing in and out of its gates. Marva's courage wilted as she viewed the scene.

A short distance away, a man removed a cigarette from his mouth, spat on the ground, replaced the cigarette and returned his attention to his newspaper. A young man and woman came out of the little diner near where she stood, holding hands. The girl gave her a curious look. A few people gathered near a stand where a woman sold roasted corn. The aroma made Marva's mouth water. She'd been there almost an hour, but no one had accepted her tracts. They either looked through her or averted their head.

From the corner of her eye, she saw a young man handing out what appeared to be flyers. Like a well-oiled engine, he ran back and forth, holding out his flyers to everyone who passed by him. Most people took one. His smile and his energy made him difficult to resist. He even approached cars that slowed near him. With the agility of a cat, he dodged between them as he ran from one side of the street to the next. His hands seemed to move in all directions at the same time. Up to his forehead to brush away the sweat, then down to stick a flyer in someone's hand.

When the traffic lulled, she walked up to the man "Good afternoon, I have something for you."

Since he was giving things out, she didn't expect him to refuse. He glanced her over and stuck one of his flyers at her. As she expected, it was an advertisement for a fete. Marva took it and handed him one of her tracts. He grinned, showing a mouth full of discolored teeth. "I like that. I give you something, you give me something." He looked at the tract. "This some kind of church thing?"

Marva nodded.

He shoved a bunch of flyers at her. "Here. Gimme some of yours. We'll work together, but don't stay here. Go down the hill near the end of the street."

Marva hesitated with the flyers in her hand. What had she gotten herself into? He waved her away as he pushed a flyer in someone's hand. "The fete is tomorrow night, man."

Marva did as she was told. She took up a position about a hundred yards away where she could still see him at the top of the incline. Smiling, she summoned her courage and managed to distribute a few flyers and tracts.

On the bus that evening, she sent up a prayer for forgiveness. What business did she have giving out flyers for a party when she had set out to do God's work? It must not happen again.

Marva returned to the corner two days later. Though she saw the flyers man, she decided to try and hand out tracts without any help from him. But either she lacked his finesse or people were just not interested. In half an hour, she'd only given out one tract. A little discouraged, she sought him out.

He seemed to recognize her immediately. "Ay, church lady, how you doin'?"

He didn't stop to look at her while he pushed flyers with his enviable speed.

"Can you help me?"

"Sure, I'll help you. As long as you help me." He grinned his colorful grin and flyers and tracts quickly changed hands. Marva read the flyers as she walked downhill. Today they were from a popular fast food restaurant that was giving away a free liter of soda with every meal. This was much better. Maybe she would pick up one on her way home. Her flyers and tracts went quickly after that. Before leaving, she ran up the hill and said good-bye to the man whom she now considered a friend.

"I gave out all your flyers."

"And I gave out all your tracts."

On impulse she asked, "What's your name?"

"Everyone calls me TL."

"All right, TL. See you next time."

"What's your name?"

Marva hesitated. "Call me CL."

He chuckled. "All right, CL. Take care."

Marva smiled. *CL. Church Lady. It suited her well.*

In the following weeks, Marva no longer depended on TL for help. They still exchanged materials, but she'd become so confident, she even spoke to some of the people, telling them about Jesus and inviting them to church. And a few of them came. One rainy afternoon, neither she nor TL did much business. They sought shelter in the diner where Marva had stood that first day. With some guilt, she realized she'd never invited TL to church and she knew nothing about him.

She ordered two sodas for them both and he seemed happy to accept. While she sipped hers, Marva studied his skinny frame, worn shoes, clean shirt, but frayed at the collar. His bronze complexion seemed to have been darkened by the sun and his forehead bore a few frown lines.

"How old are you TL?"

He glanced up with a smile. "Thirty-two next month. You find I look old?"

Marva regretted asking. "No, no. I was just curious."

"And how old are you?"

"Twenty."

"My sister is nineteen."

"What's her name?"

"Carol."

"My sister is sixteen," Marva said. "Her name's June."

TL cackled. "Bet she was born in June."

Marva smiled. "You're smart TL. She was born in June."

He seemed to be taking his time with his soda. Marva ordered two currants rolls and gave them to him.

Surprise showed on his face. "You don't want one?"

She shook her head. "I'm not hungry."

He lowered his gaze and when he spoke, his voice was muffled. "You're very kind, Miss Church Lady."

As if a dam had burst inside him, TL went on to tell her about himself. He lived with his mother, a stroke survivor, and his sister Carol who had Down's Syndrome. He was the only breadwinner, and giving out flyers was his job. He earned ten dollars for every hundred flyers he gave out. If he didn't give out all, he didn't get paid. Sometimes someone might feel sorry for him and give him five dollars.

"I could throw away some and tell them I gave them out, but I prefer to be honest."

Marva studied his bent head as he chewed on his pastry. "I want you to come to church this Sunday. You know the Anglican Church right there on the Promenade?"

His eyes became misty. "I don't have no church clothes, CL. I have this." He touched his shirt. "And three more, one a little better than this, but my pants and them real old."

Tears prickled her eyes. Memories of her life back in Egypt Village as an abused child, wearing shabby clothes and being laughed at by the other children, welled up inside her. She took hold of TL's hand and right there in the small snackette, Marva prayed that God would bless him and his family and bring them to know Him.

The next day, she brought him a new pants and shirt and a dress for Carol. "I hope it fits. I want you to bring her to church too."

The expression on his face when he opened the bag was one Marva would never forget. He took her hand in both of his. "God bless you, CL. You're an angel from above."

"And here's money for your taxi fare."

She wagged a finger at him as he gaped at her, apparently unable to speak. "No excuses."

Marva went to bed that night with a feeling of satisfaction akin to pleasure. She had helped someone just as Miss Stewart had helped her so many years ago in Egypt.

As always, thinking of Miss Stewart seared her with longing. Marva missed her so much. But she'd always known the time would come when she and June would have to go it alone. Just as she knew the time would come when June would be on her own. How could she prepare her? What could she say to her sister who, while self-assured, still counted on Marva looking out for her the rest of her life? Marva rolled on to her side and studied her sister's silhouette dotted with droplets of light from outside. Gently she stroked the silky hair, fanning over the top of the sheet. *God will take care of you. I know He will.*

David opened the car door for Cicely then stood aside. He watched as she turned around, sat on the seat and swung her shapely legs into the car. She was as graceful as the night they first met at James Garcia's wake over three years ago. But that would soon change. She would become heavy and clumsy, and he would be right there for her.

Their visit to the doctor had gone well. Dr. Marcelin, the physician who had taken care of the family ever since they came to Trinidad, had confirmed the pregnancy. David wished he could tell them the sex of the baby. That would have to wait until the baby was born.

David got into the car and gathered his wife into his arms. "I love you. I can't say it enough."

"I love you too."

He released her to buckle his seat belt, while she did the same. As he started the engine, she said, "I'll love you more when our daughter is here."

"I thought you couldn't love me anymore than you do now."

She laughed and touched his face. "It just keeps growing."

He groaned. "You don't know what you do to me."

As he and Cicely entered the house, the aroma of curried chicken floated out to them. There went his plan for a lunch date. He could never resist Miss Lucy's curried chicken. Cicely followed him into the kitchen where the woman was stirring the pot.

"That smells so …" Cicely began, then covered her mouth and fled.

After she'd recovered from her nausea, David sat beside her on the bed "I'm sure Miss Lucy suspects. I guess we have to go out there and confirm it. Should I leave it to you while I call my mom?"

"Yes, but I must call Sheila first."

He handed her the phone. "Of course. Go ahead."

David got up to leave, but Cicely beckoned to him to stay. He listened, smiling as she recounted to her sister everything the doctor had said to them, almost word for word. Women had such amazing memory. Eventually she said, "He's right here," and handed him the receiver.

No sooner had David finished speaking to Sheila than the phone rang again.

He picked it up. "Hello? Oh, hi, Mom. How are you doing?'

Cicely still hadn't decided how she was going to break her big news to Miss Lucy. How many years had it been since she'd become almost like a mother to Cicely? Maybe thirteen. But how do you tell your mother you're pregnant? Even if you are thirty-eight years old and married?

Miss Lucy solved her problem, almost colliding with Cicely as she pushed the swing door. "Oh, Miss Cicely, I was just coming to tell you I'm makin' a l'il beef soup for you."

"Why? I thought the curry was almost finished."

The lady looked her up and down. "Yes, but you can't eat anymore curry now in your condition. It's not good for the baby's skin, or for you."

She wrapped her arms around the woman's soft, pillowy form. "What will I do without you, Miss Lucy?" Her eyes watered as she sent up a silent prayer of thanks for this angel God sent them.

The sound of someone clearing his throat broke them apart.

Cicely stepped into the hallway with David. "Did you tell her?"

He took her hand. "No."

"No?"

He led her to the sofa. "She said she wants to see us to tell us something really important, so I decided it would be better to tell her face-to-face."

Cicely kept her head lowered. She'd all but forgotten her father's startling announcement a few weeks ago. That had to be the reason David's mother wanted to see them.

His words interrupted her thoughts. "She seems to be having a big to-do. She said she's inviting your aunt and uncle and your father, your sister and her family. She even wants us to bring 'those two beautiful girls that Cicely used to teach.'"

Cicely aimed her smile at the chair opposite. "When does she want us to come?"

"This Sunday."

Cicely rose from the chair.

"Where are you going?"

She sat back down. "I was going to call Marva and June, but they won't be home yet." She got up again. "I'd better check and see if I have anything to wear."

He followed her into the bedroom. Cicely had over a dozen outfits that would be suitable, and all still fit. She made a big show of checking her outfits, while trying to give suitable replies to her husband's worrying questions.

"I wonder if she's planning to go on vacation? She hasn't been out of the country since ... since she and your father went to New York."

"Maybe she wants to sell the house. No, she'll never do that. She and Dad were so happy there."

Cicely hated keeping secrets from her husband. After almost losing him because she'd kept her past from him, Cicely had vowed never to hide anything from him again. His brooding over lunch and later when they strolled along the beach did nothing to relieve her guilt.

That night in bed, she ran a fingernail down the middle of his chest. "If you ever leave me I'll die."

He chuckled. "If I ever leave you *I'll* die."

"Even if I kept a secret from you?"

He turned to face her. "No more secrets."

Her finger continued its tracing. "I think I know what your mom wants to tell you."

He jerked upward and stared at her. "You do?"

She nodded, not looking at him. "But I can't tell you. I'll be out of place."

He flopped back down. "You're right."

Before they fell asleep, he said. "I hope she isn't sick. I'm going up there tomorrow. I can't wait until Sunday."

CHAPTER NINE

David turned off the engine of his new Toyota station wagon and got out. He'd bought it after returning to Trinidad just over a year ago, having sold his old Volkswagen when he thought he was leaving the country for good. He liked his new car, but still felt nostalgic for his old tiger that had served him faithfully for more than ten years. But his new wheels were faster and roomier, perfectly suited for Cicely, and for when the baby came …

David cut off his thoughts as he rang his mother's doorbell. His pulse quickened when he heard her footsteps coming to the door, then her clear voice, "Who is it?"

"It's me, Mom."

The door opened and his mother's welcoming smile lit up the morning. At sixty-three, Rose Bowen still had the energy of a woman decades younger and when she smiled, her even white teeth flashed in her cinnamon-colored face. Few women her age equaled her in grace and beauty, David was certain.

He wrapped her in his arms and planted a kiss on her cheek. "Mmm, you smell so good."

She smiled when he released her. "You've been telling me that since you were this high." She lowered her hand to her knee.

He stepped into the cool interior of the spacious living-room. "It's true." He sniffed. "Looks like I'll get some banana bread to take back to Cicely."

She headed for the kitchen. "It's almost done. Did you smell it from San Fernando?"

"Maybe." He opened the fridge. "What? No ginger-beer?"

"No, son, I used the last of it on Sunday, but I'll have some when you come up this weekend." She turned to him. "You are coming, aren't you?"

He removed a can of Apple J from the fridge, pulled up the tab and took a sip. "Yes, but I couldn't wait."

His mother gave her attention to the banana bread.

"Mom?"

She straightened up and looked at him. "What is it, dear?"

"Why the big party on Sunday? What's so important?"

She removed the bread from the oven and turned it out on to a wire rack. "Have a seat. I'll cut you a slice."

He took a chair. "I don't want any bread, Mom. I want to hear your news first."

She sat at the table and fixed him with a mysterious smile. "Okay, want to hear it? I'm getting married."

David almost choked on his soda. "Don't make jokes like that, Mom."

"I'm not joking, son."

He stared at her serious expression then managed one word. "Who?"

"Your father-in-law."

David jumped up out of his chair. His mother's gaze met his, unblinking. She'd always been a strong woman, and David knew his obvious anger would never intimidate her, but still he couldn't control his tone. "Are you out of your mind?"

His mother's voice was even. "Sit down, and don't speak to me like that."

David could not sit. He paced around the kitchen floor, running his hand over his balding head, then clenching and unclenching his fists. Of all the things he expected his mother to say, this was not one of them. Even if she wanted to marry someone, why did it have to be Stewart? The man who had almost destroyed his relationship with Cicely. The man who had abused her as a little girl. The man whom David thought he had forgiven, but now realized he hadn't.

He squeezed the soda can into a small uneven ball. "This is a slap in my face, Mom. How could you do this to me? How could you do this to Dad?"

His mother left her chair and stood before him. "Son, look at me. I'm glad you came this morning so we could have this talk. I had no idea you still felt this way."

He glanced at her, then turned his head. "How do you expect me to feel, Mom? This man did his best to destroy our lives – mine and Cicely's."

She nodded. "You think I don't know it? He has confessed to me in tears the reason he did it. He didn't want to lose his daughter. He felt old and abandoned at the thought of her leaving him with no one to care for him."

"So now you are to be his nursemaid, is that it? The man's a cripple."

"David, stop it! He's not a cripple. I will not have you speaking about him that way."

"Mom, I can't believe you love this man. You and Dad had such a wonderful life. Dad was so strong. Come!"

He took her hand and led her into the little room off the den where the family pictures adorned the walls and a wall unit. He stood in front of a large, framed picture of his father in his full army uniform. David heard the pride in his voice as he said, "Now, there's a real man. General Harold Bowen. They don't come any finer than that."

His mother gave him a sad smile. "General Harold Bowen *was* a fine man. But now he's dead, honey. You have to accept that. Dead. Seven long years. And I'm still alive—and alone."

"What are you saying, Mom?"

She moved to a small armchair and sat. "What I'm saying, David, is that I've been here in this big house by myself with my memories all these years. You kids have your own lives, all happily married, and I thank God for that. I've tried to fill my life with my church and my music, but now I sense God wanting me to do more, to have a fuller life—with Gavin."

David swallowed. She was calling him Gavin. What could he say? His mother had always been stubborn, forthright and—he had to admit—levelheaded. He could never recall her doing anything that wasn't prudent.

He looked down at the distorted can still in his hand. "Have you spoken to Peter and Phyllis?"

"Not yet. I wanted you to know first."

Eyes still lowered, he murmured, "I appreciate it."

"And if Peter can't make it, I want you to give me away."

His head jerked up, then he shifted his gaze. Was God paying him back in his own coins? Sometimes it was best to say nothing.

On the drive back to San Fernando, David tried to reconcile himself to the fact that Gavin Stewart, in addition to being his father-in-law, was now going to be his stepfather. How crazy could the world get? He stamped on his brakes just in time to avoid running in to a car that stopped suddenly in front of him. David realized the reason for the driver's apparent carelessness. A vagrant, clothes tattered and filthy, hair matted, bare feet crusted with months' build-up of dirt, sauntered across the street, heedless of oncoming cars.

"Crazy, crazy, crazy," David fumed.

That was the problem with this world. People sauntered into people's lives and hearts without thinking of the accidents and pain they caused. "Bounce me *nuh*," Trinidadian jay walkers were wont to say, knowing that the hapless motorist would be the one to face the consequences. Well, he wasn't about to bounce Mr. Stewart. He would just be calm and allow this debacle to play itself out. Meanwhile, he would pray for his mother's happiness.

"I need my wife," he muttered as the vagrant, now safe on the sidewalk, allowed the traffic to move on. Only Cicely, with her sweet, quiet wisdom could help him see beyond the tip of his arrogant nose.

He was almost home before he realized he'd not told his mother his big news – that Cicely was expecting. It would just have to wait until Sunday.

That night as he entered the door, she rose from the couch to meet him. Without a word, she tiptoed and kissed him, then folded her arms around him. He rested his chin on her head and for a few moments neither of them spoke.

Eventually she stepped away and studied his face. "I was so worried about you."

He removed his gun holster and rested it on the table. "Never mind. I was a good boy."

"I'm happy to hear that."

He turned to her. "That's not true, honey. I lied. How could she do that to me?"

Cicely put her arms around his waist. "Your mother's a smart woman. I'm sure she didn't make this decision without seeking God's guidance. She'll be all right."

"I know she will. But what about me?"

"You'll be all right too. Am I not enough for you?"

He grinned, his mood suddenly improving. "You are more than enough for me." His lips sought hers. When he released her, he said, "But how do you feel about it?"

"I … actually, I'm okay with it. My father has been alone for a long time. Even with me living with him, it wasn't the same as having someone around his own age to talk to. And I couldn't ask for a better stepmother."

He drew her to him again. "What will I do without you?"

"I shudder to think."

Marva smiled as Mrs. Rose Bowen approached her. The woman moved with a grace that belied the patch of white hair at the front of her short Afro. Her unlined skin and floral gown with matching head-band reminded Marva of pictures she'd seen of the African singer Miriam Makeba. Her smile, easy manner, and gentle voice drew Marva to her in a way that didn't usually happen. If she had a grandmother, she would want her to be like Mrs. Rose.

"What are you doing out here by yourself, my dear? I see you found Chang. Say good-bye to him for a little and come and help us in the kitchen."

Marva patted the golden cat lounging at her feet and uncoiled herself from the comfortable porch chair. Miss Stewart's invitation to spend the day with them at her mother-in-law's house had filled her with dismay, if not a little fear. She was so used to hiding in her wilderness that the thought of being among strangers always made her stomach lurch. But, of course, June had threatened that if Marva didn't go, she wouldn't either. And, not wishing to offend Miss Stewart, she'd reluctantly agreed.

How would she survive almost an entire day in Mr. Bowen's company? She relaxed somewhat when they arrived at his mother's Diego Martin home. This spacious house was sure to provide a few hiding places. Marva didn't mind Miss Sheila and her daughters being there. She was already used to them, but Miss Stewart's aunt and uncle and a couple of Mrs. Rose's neighbors were there as well.

As soon as the introductions were complete, June spotted the piano near the dining-room and asked if she could play, to which Mrs. Rose agreed. Marva retreated to the porch with one of her school books where she met the lovely gold and white cat sunning himself on the mat, and the two soon became great friends.

Marva followed Mrs. Rose into the kitchen. June was still at the piano playing, Miss Sheila's daughters sitting near her. She looked up and smiled as Marva and Mrs. Rose crossed the living-room.

"Your sister plays well. Do you play too?"

A little embarrassed, Marva shook her head. "No."

Piano lessons were part of the myriad of after-school activities June was involved in, but with exams so close, she'd suspended her practice. Laughter and conversation filtered in from the back garden where the men sat at a table under an umbrella playing cards.

The mouth-watering aroma of the dishes on the kitchen counter drew Marva's gaze. Three meat dishes – stewed chicken, beef pot roast and pork chops – two casseroles, a platter of colorful vegetables, a rice dish, banana bread …Marva was suddenly eager to help get this food on the table.

"We'll put the dishes on the buffet in the dining-room so everybody can help themselves," Mrs. Rose said.

Marva reached for a pot holder, and for the next few minutes she forgot her shyness as she and the women laid out food, plates and silverware. The dining-table was not large enough to accommodate everybody, and Marva was happy to take her food out to the porch. This time June and her friends joined her.

Marva discovered another reason to like Mrs. Rose. The woman's cooking was medal worthy. She was also a fine hostess. From where she sat, Marva caught occasional glimpses of her serving her guests. She seemed to be paying special attention to Mr. Stewart, refilling his glass and attending to his needs, even though he was quite capable of doing all these things himself.

As for Miss Stewart and her husband, they sat away from the table in a quiet corner, whispering and giggling together like two teenagers. Marva felt a pang of aloneness – one she should be used to by now, but it always hurt.

After they'd eaten, she assisted in the clean-up, and when the kitchen was restored to order, she strolled through Mrs. Rose's garden, admiring her fruit trees and herbs with Chang at her heels.

June found her stooping, sniffing a mint bush. "Mrs. Rose sent me to call you."

Marva straightened up and beckoned to the cat. "Let's go, boy."

When she got there, Mrs. Rose sat at the piano. Her piercing gaze, so much like her son's, roved the room. "Okay, everybody, I'm going to play "Lean On Me," and I would like you all to join in."

Marva had seen the movie and she knew the song. With everyone singing, it was easy for her to sing along. They all held hands and swayed in time to the music, and Marva forgot her shyness.

The song ended, everyone applauded, then Mrs. Rose held up her hand. "Friends and family, you're probably wondering why I've called you all together. I won't beat about the bush." She placed her hand in Mr. Stewart's. "Gavin and I are engaged to be married."

There was a moment of silence before cheers broke out. The women went to the couple and congratulated them, followed by the men. Mr. Bowen shook Mr. Stewart's hand and whispered something in his ear. Mr. Stewart smiled then slapped him on his back.

When all the commotion had died down, Miss Stewart and Mr. Bowen stepped forward, hand-in-hand. "Well, Mom, we didn't want to upstage your announcement, but we have a big one of our own." He put his arm around his wife's waist. "Cicely and I are expecting."

More applause and cheers broke out, while Marva stood staring. Expecting? Expecting what? She looked for June, but she'd joined the small crowd hugging and kissing Miss Stewart. Marva felt she should do the same. She crept up just in time to hear Mrs. Rose say, "I'm going to be a grandmother," and Miss Stewart's aunt ask, "When's the baby due?"

A baby? Miss Stewart was going to have a baby? Now she could never disclose her ugly secret to her. Face frozen into a smile, Marva bent and kissed her teacher's cheek.

That night Marva listened with half her mind on June's chatter about the day they had spent. Miss Stewart was going to have a baby. But she didn't look any different.

"How was she supposed to look?"

"Well, shouldn't she be walking slow and holding her tummy?"

Marva laughed in spite of herself. "I love the cat."

June frowned and continued as if Marva hadn't spoken. "And fancy Mr. Stewart getting married. Isn't he too old? But Mom Rose is a doll."

"Mom Rose?"

June chuckled. "She told me to call her that. I love the way it sounds. And I love her."

Marva threw her a quick glance. June easily made friends with everyone, but Marva had never heard her say she loved someone so soon. Mrs. Bowen had made quite an impression.

Leaning forward, chin propped on her hand, June said, "I wonder what the baby's going to be." She paused. "I want a girl."

"*You* want a girl?"

"You know what I mean," June said. "I want her to have a girl, so I could dress her up and comb her hair. What do you want, Sister?"

"I want to die." The words were out of her mouth before she even thought about them. June's eyes widened and her face paled. Marva reached out and touched her arm. "I … I mean, I'll miss Miss Stewart, that's all."

June's gaze bore into her. "Why would you miss her? She isn't moving, and with a new baby we'll have to go over there all the time to help her out."

Marva forced a smile. June was so naïve. With a husband and a new baby, Miss Stewart would have little time for them. They were all alone again. She had no one to lean on. No one.

CHAPTER TEN

Marva threw herself into her evangelizing task the next week. June's exams were two weeks away, and Miss Stewart was starting her family. It was time for Marva to put her plans into high gear. But first, she had to get as many souls into the kingdom as she could. Only by doing that could she be forgiven when she stood before God.

She was now confident as she stood on her corner giving out tracts two days a week. People smiled at her, and she smiled back. Whenever someone stopped to talk to her about their problems, she listened, then placed her hand on their shoulder as she'd seen them do in church and prayed with the person.

Her friendship with TL deepened. Most days she invited him to share a soda and a sandwich or some pastry with her. Sometimes he refused, saying he didn't want to take advantage of her kindness, but it never took much to win him over.

On Friday evening, she got on the bus heading home feeling good about herself. But the moment she entered the apartment, she sensed something different in June's manner. Marva's cheery greeting received a cool, "Good-evening, Sister," in return. They were the same words June usually spoke, but today they sounded limp and droopy. As droopy as the macaroni she was now pushing around her plate. Marva was in too much of a good mood to wait for June to tell her who, or what stuck a pin in her balloon.

"What's going on?"

June twisted the long, white strings around her fork and shook her head.

Eating macaroni required a certain amount of skill, one which Marva had never acquired. Sometimes it stuck to her fork just right and at other times, a few tendrils escaped. Today she didn't let it bother her. Putting out her tongue, she lapped the loose ends and slurped them into her mouth.

June gave her a disgusted look.

"If you don't tell me what's wrong, I'll do it again," Marva said, her mouth almost full.

June rested her fork on the edge of her plate. "Were you down by the hospital this afternoon?"

Marva swallowed the rest of her macaroni, then gulped some water behind it. Digging her fork into the sticky mass once again, she nodded.

No more was said until they had finished eating and were doing the dishes.

"Sister, why are you handing out things to people on the street?"

Marva paused in washing a plate. "They are not things; they are tracts. I want people to know about Jesus."

June went on rinsing the dishes in silence as if Marva had not spoken. Finally, she said, "Could you imagine how I felt when my friends told me they saw you giving out tracts on the street corner?"

Water splashed on her arms as Marva dropped the plate. "What is wrong with that?"

June pierced her with her gaze. "It's embarrassing. And I want you to stop."

Marva opened her mouth, closed it and opened it again. "*You* want me to stop? Well, let me tell you something. I'm not ashamed of what I'm doing and I'm not stopping."

June stared at her a moment longer, then threw down the dish cloth and stomped out of the kitchen. Marva's anger cooled as quickly as it had flared. Her sister was at that stage in life when appearances mattered a great deal. And young people loved to make fun of each other. Had June's friends teased her? Marva didn't want to stop giving out tracts just when she'd grown so comfortable doing it. And what about TL? He'd started going to church and had given his life to Christ. He always thanked her for the way she'd helped him. He'd said one day, "You are a real church lady."

If he only knew. She leaned her head against the cabinet door and didn't hear when June entered.

"Sister, I'm sorry."

Marva jerked her head away. "It's okay. I understand how you feel, but I don't want to stop, Junie."

"Why do you have to give out tracts?"

How could she explain to her younger sister? "I … I want God to love me."

June frowned. "He does love you. Isn't that what the minister said? That God loves all of us."

"Yes, but when people do bad things like I did, then He gets angry with us."

"Sister, I don't know. Maybe we should ask Miss Stewart. But I think that even if God gets angry with us, He still loves us." She smiled. "It's like when you get vexed with me, you still love me. Right?"

Marva couldn't help smiling. June was right, but what she didn't know was that Marva was trying to keep God from getting vexed with her. Like the checks she'd deposited in the bank so she could withdraw on them later, she hoped to have enough good deeds to cancel out her bad ones – past and future.

That night as they sat in front of the television, June appeared more relaxed, but she didn't laugh as she usually did when the commercial with the fat lady and the skinny man came on.

Marva turned to her. "Are you still mad at me?"

She seemed to force a smile. "I could never stay mad at you."

Marva went back to chewing her popcorn and focused her eyes on the news once more. Maybe if she shared a little of what she'd seen and done on the streets, June would be more understanding.

"I prayed with a lady the other day. She has a son who's giving her trouble, always in and out of jail."

June turned the force of her hazel eyes on her. "You prayed with her on the street?"

Marva nodded. "And I prayed with the lady who sells *amchar* and red mango too."

"Sister, you're so brave."

Then she told her about TL. "You remember the tall, skinny man and the Down's Syndrome girl I was talking to in church the other day? Well, he taught me how to give out the tracts. He gives out flyers and that's all he does to support himself, his mother and sister."

"You sound like you really like this TL."

"I feel sorry for him. I don't know how he manages to live."

Silence.

"Sister, what about Jason?"

The question caught Marva off guard. She hadn't heard from him since the day he visited her at work. She popped some corn into her mouth. "He's all right, I guess."

More silence.

"How would you feel if I got married after exams?"

Marva jerked forward so suddenly she almost knocked over the bowl of popcorn on the couch. June laughed for the first time that evening. "Gotcha. I've no intention of doing that."

Marva coughed to clear her throat. "I was going to say if it's five or ten years after exams it's okay."

June laughed again, then sobered. "I'm glad you were so strict with me."

That was another surprise. "Really?"

"Yes. If you weren't so strict, I might have ended up like Wendy."

"How is she doing?"

"The last I heard, she's planning to get married right after gradua-tion."

Marva considered for a moment. "That might not be a bad thing. Her parents have money. They might be able to give them a start."

"Yeah, but … the man looks too old for her."

"You know him?"

June nodded, and Marva knew not to expect anything further from her.

~

June's exams began Tuesday of the following week with her least favorite subject, chemistry. It was just as well. She wanted to get past that and accounting, so she could be more relaxed when the time came for her favorites. In the hallway she bumped into Wendy, but her friend's gaze shifted quickly when June's eyes met hers, and her bubbly demeanor seemed to have vanished. June wanted to speak to her, but now was not the time. Later, she left the examination room feeling she'd done her best.

When she and Keith joined some of their classmates under the mango tree to study for the next day's exam, Caribbean history, Wendy was not among them. Later, as they ambled home, Keith suddenly changed the subject. "You heard the news?"

June skirted a water- filled pothole just in time. "What news?"

"Wendy told someone she's pregnant."

June's feet froze to the ground. Her mind went blank and she stared at Keith. "That little fool."

"Why do you say that? The guy's going to marry her. And from what Wendy said, he makes good money as a car salesman."

June stomped along. "She's still a little fool. She had plans of getting a job with the *Express*. She's such a good writer."

"She could still do that." He paused. "So, you wouldn't want to get married?"

June gave him a sidelong glance. "At sixteen? You crazy?"

He linked his arm in hers. "What you say we pack a few clothes in our book bags on the last day of exams and run off together?"

It was the funniest thing she'd ever heard and she told him so. "And what will we live on?"

"Chicken and chips. We still have our jobs, remember?"

June disengaged her arm and gave him a playful shove. "You've been studying too much. Go home and rest."

But Keith was not ready to drop the subject. "And, since Wendy's husband makes good money, they will find a nice apartment and we can rent a room from them."

"Shut up, Keith. Tomorrow is geography. What route you think the Queen will take from London to the Philippines?"

"She's not going. She decided to stay home."

June burst out laughing. Keith could always change her mood.

Marva watched her sister plunge deeper into studying for her exams. June had said, "This is the last hurrah – for now. After next week I'll be like a dried-up orange."

"A dried-up orange?"

"Yeah. These exams are sucking the juice out of me."

Marva laughed in spite of herself, but she worried about her little sister. She would wake up at nights sometimes and find her asleep on the couch, a book on her chest, lights still on. Marva would remove the book, cover her with a blanket and turn off the lights. One night she paused to look at her. Who would look after her when she was gone? She needed to speak to someone.

Since that day two weeks ago when June had told her she didn't want her giving out tracts anymore, Marva had not gone near the hospital. She'd only given a few to some of the students at the center and to people on the bus. But she missed being on the corner, as she liked to call it, and most of all she missed TL. She hadn't seen him and his sister in church last Sunday.

On Wednesday morning, she shoved a few tracts into her bag as she left for work. All day she anticipated seeing TL that afternoon – his springy walk, his colorful smile, his gravelly voice calling, "Flyer for the fete," "Free soda," "Free tire," or whatever he was advertising that day.

She spotted him the minute she got out of the taxi. His movements were as brisk as always, his eyes alert, missing nothing and no one.

He waved a bunch of flyers at her. "Miss CL."

Marva jogged to where he stood. "How you doing, TL?"

"I miss you. You bring any tracts? People asking for you." He shoved a flyer into a lady's hand. "10% off today, ma'am."

Marva was pleased. "Really? Here, take some."

Tracts and flyers exchanged hands, and Marva set off down the hill to her spot.

A man coming toward her said, "You have a pretty smile."

She wasn't aware she was smiling. "Oh, thank you. May I give you something?"

The man stopped, and she handed him a tract and a flyer.

"Thanks." He nodded and went on his way.

Marva was surprised and a little dismayed at the response she received from the passers-by that day. No one refused her offerings, and a few even stopped and chatted with her. The *amchar* vendor she'd prayed with some time before said to her, "People like you. They say you are a nice girl."

Marva smiled. How much longer could she continue to carry her ugly secret? Some days she felt like she had the words "I Killed My Father" engraved on her forehead. Surely everyone must see it. But instead, people liked her? She could never confide in TL. He saw her as a holy person, Miss Church Lady, who had prayed with him and led him to Christ.

Later, when she'd finished giving out all her papers, she joined him at the top of the hill. He had a few left and his eyes and hands were still moving in all directions. "What happen? Somebody say something bad to you?"

"What you mean?"

"Flyers. Flyers." His hands went right and left. "You left smiling and come back moping."

Marva drew her shoulders up. "Come and meet me in the snackette when you're done."

She ordered a Pepsi for him and an Apple J for herself when he joined her about fifteen minutes later.

Looking at her above his straw, he said, "What's up, Miss CL?"

"I'm not coming back over here."

TL removed the straw from his mouth. "Not coming back?"

She lowered her gaze. "I … I have to catch up on my studying. With that and work, it's too much."

"You going to school?"

She sipped her drink. "Evening classes."

"I too old to study anything now." He paused. "I bet your boyfriend don't want you standin' on no street corner."

"I don't have a boyfriend."

He raised his eyebrows. "Well, what in blazes? If I was ten years younger I woulda ask you a question."

Marva laughed. "What kinda question?"

He grinned, showing his discolored teeth. "Never mind."

She placed her empty bottle on the counter. "I love you, TL."

He almost dropped his.

"I mean, I love you as a brother. You're a nice person."

He lowered his gaze and brushed one hand across his eyes. She hadn't expected her words to have that effect on him.

Still not looking at her, he mumbled, "Nobody never tell me that before."

Suddenly it occurred to Marva that if he was a few years younger, had a job, and nicer teeth, she would have wanted him to ask her a question. And maybe if she didn't have this heavy load on her conscience. She studied his bent head covered by a weather-beaten hat. She missed him already. Maybe once June's school closed for the summer, she could resume giving out tracts.

When she got home, the apartment was quiet. June had taken temporary leave from her job because of her exams, but she still went to the library or remained after school to study with friends. This was a good time to write a letter she'd been planning. She tore a page from her notebook and began, "Dear Miss Stewart …

CHAPTER ELEVEN

The next afternoon as Marva entered the apartment, June broke off her phone conversation with "She just came in." She mouthed, "Miss Stewart," and handed Marva the receiver.

Marva smiled, her mood doing a complete one eighty. "Hello."

"Hello, Marva, how are you doing?"

"I'm doing good, Miss. I mean, I'm doing well. How are you?"

Miss Stewart laughed. "Maybe not as well as you. I miss you girls."

Marva gripped the receiver. "I miss you too."

"I was just telling June I'm coming over to see you both this evening. Is that okay?"

"You never have to ask, Miss."

She heard the smile in the lady's voice. "All right. See you around six."

Marva waited until she heard the click on the other end before replacing the receiver. Then she turned to June with a big grin. "I can hardly wait."

June cupped her hands. "Me too."

Marva was surprised at how round her teacher had become in the two months since she'd seen her last. She wore a loose-fitting blouse and skirt, and while her stomach was just barely visible, it was obvious that she'd gained weight. However, her skin and her eyes glowed with happiness, for which Marva was glad.

They hugged each other in a warm embrace. When Miss Stewart released her, Marva stepped back. "You look great, Miss."

Miss Stewart looked her up and down. "And so do you." She turned to June. "And our little scholar here is as pretty as ever."

June smiled and sashayed a little as she'd seen the models do on TV. "Well, what can I say?"

Amidst the laughter, Miss Stewart said, "You'll make a great model, but that's not what we want for you. Right, Marva?"

Marva nodded agreement.

Miss Stewart sat on the couch, opened her purse and took out a small envelope. "I brought you girls an invitation."

Marva took the envelope, addressed to her and June, and removed the pale pink card. It read, "Mr. Gavin Stewart and Mrs. Rose Bowen cordially invite you to their wedding ceremony on August 1st. at the Port-of-Spain Cathedral."

Marva raised her eyebrows. "They're inviting us?"

"Of course, dear."

June whirled around. "Another wedding. Are they going to have bridesmaids and all that?"

"From what I understand, this is going to be a small affair. Just close friends and family. David's older brother is giving away the bride, his sister is going to be the matron-of-honor and that's it."

Marva looked at the card again. "This is so pretty. I never received an invitation before."

June took it from her hand. "August is just six weeks away."

"That's right," Miss Stewart said. "If you want something from Monique's, you should talk to her soon."

June glanced at her sister. "My last exam is on Thursday. Maybe we can go see her this Saturday."

"I can take you if you like. I have to see her too," said Miss Stewart.

After they'd agreed on a time, their visitor crossed her legs, obviously in no hurry to leave. She patted the cushion next to her. "I've missed you girls so much. Come tell me what's going on."

Marva sat next to her on the couch, while June pulled up a chair opposite. June brought her up to date on her exams and her plans to return to school to study for the CAPE, the advanced level courses.

Miss Stewart nodded approval, then turned to Marva. "And you're studying too, I hear?"

Marva suddenly felt shy. She didn't have such glowing reports as June had, but she told her teacher all about the classes she was studying in hopes of taking the CXC exams next year.

"I like everything I'm hearing. Remember, I'm still here for you. Call me anytime you need me before she," patting her tummy, "decides I can't do anymore."

June leaned forward. "Is it a she?"

"We don't know yet. David wants a boy, I want a girl, but we just have to wait and see what God gives us."

A frown appeared on June's brow. "Miss Stewart, I know Sister may not want me telling you this, but I don't want to talk behind her back."

Marva gritted her teeth and made to get up.

June threw her a glance. "No, Sister, I want you to hear what Miss Stewart thinks about evangelizing."

Miss Stewart raised her eyebrow. "Evangelizing? It's what Jesus calls us to do."

Marva leaned back in her seat with an I-told-you-so look.

The woman continued, "What do you want to know?"

June ran her fingers through her hair, a sign that she was nervous, "Well, er, Sister has been giving out tracts on the street, and I … I felt embarrassed."

June kept her eyes lowered, and Marva relaxed even more.

Miss Stewart turned to Marva. "Why were you giving out tracts, honey?"

Marva looked past June's head. "Well, I … Reverend Harris said we must tell others about Jesus Christ, and … and I want to go to heaven when I die."

Miss Stewart nodded. "That's good. We must tell others about Jesus Christ, but we don't have to give out tracts on the street in order to go to heaven."

Marva twisted her fingers in her lap. "Oh, I thought —"

Miss Stewart took her hand. "We don't have to work to go to heaven, my dear. Give out tracts if you want to, but if you didn't, you would still go to heaven." She glanced from her to June. "Girls, I'm glad you brought this up. The Bible says we are saved by grace and not by works lest any man should boast."

Marva raised her eyes to her teacher's face. "What does that mean?"

"It means that God saves us by His grace when we accept His Son Jesus Christ as Our Lord and Savior. That's how we get into heaven. We don't have to work in order to get there."

June frowned. "So then why tell others about Him?"

"Because Jesus says we must."

Marva gave a shaky laugh. "That's confusing."

"Not really. As long as you're telling others about Jesus because you love Him and you want them to go to heaven too, that's okay. But if you're trying to work your way into heaven, that's not what God wants."

Marva understood, and from June's smile, she did too. In reality, Marva was trying to bribe God so that when she stood before Him He would forgive her and allow her to enter heaven because of her good works. Now, what was she to do? Could she still take her own life and expect God to forgive her? She couldn't ask her teacher that.

Marva ran her finger down the page of her concordance until she came to forgiveness. She read each passage of scripture before coming to the book of Mark. There she read, "Assuredly, I say to you, all sins will be forgiven the sons of men, and whatever blasphemies they may utter; but he who blasphemes against the Holy Spirit never has forgiveness, but is subject to eternal condemnation."

She looked up from the page and considered what she'd just read. It didn't say anything about taking one's life, but it did say that all sin would be forgiven, except blasphemy against the Holy Spirit. The seed that had taken root pushed itself deeper into the soil of her mind, branching out and becoming stronger every day. She didn't really want to take her life, but she was trapped between two evils – fear of what would happen if she confessed, and increasing guilt over the crime she'd committed.

But now something else pressed itself upon her already fragile psyche. Remorse. She should have stopped and thought before hitting her father that fatal blow. She'd struck him on the back of his head with the pestle to keep him from hurting June. How could she know he would die? She would pay dearly if she didn't get out of the picture real fast.

If only she had June's boldness, her openness, her motivation to succeed. If she was embarrassed by Marva giving out tracts on the street, how much more would she be when people found out that her sister had murdered her father? No, Marva could not allow her to suffer through that. If she took her own life, no one, except June, would know her awful secret, or why she did it. Yes, she was convinced. Suicide was her only solution.

But how should she do it? She was not a murderer. And she was afraid of pain. She would have to come up with the least painful method. Overdosing on pills and alcohol had not worked the first time. It might not work now. Besides, she didn't drink anymore.

She turned around and ran her hand lovingly over her mother's picture, hanging over their bed. It gave her a feeling of comfort. Her eyes misted. Her mother's beautiful, silky hair was parted in the middle and rolled into a bun. A gentle smile adorned her clear, open features with the plump, rosy cheeks that never needed rouge. How young and pretty she looked. Nothing like the shriveled-up, tight-lipped old lady, Marva remembered, limping around the house, muttering to herself.

June entered, her hair swathed in a towel, body wrapped in another. "You think Mama could see us?"

Marva didn't take her eyes off the picture. "I don't know, Junie. Maybe that's something you should ask Miss Stewart."

June fumbled in the dresser drawer and removed a pair of panties. "Are you still mad at me for talking to her?"

Marva removed her hand from the picture. "No, I'm glad you did. She helped me understand some things."

June dropped the towel and began to dress. "Sister, I don't like you talking about dying. I want you to live forever."

Marva forced a laugh. "Nobody lives forever. Only God."

I'll have to be careful what I say from now on. I don't want to worry her, or make her suspicious.

～

In the weeks that followed, Marva forced herself to appear cheerful. She threw herself into her work and at lunch time found solace in reading her Bible. On Sundays, she went to church and was rewarded by seeing TL and his sister there, as well as a few other people she'd invited. The wedding of Mrs. Bowen and Mr. Stewart drew near, and Marva ordered a simple, but elegant light blue sheath from Monique's. June's dress, a pale pink creation with spaghetti straps and A line skirt flattered her figure and gave a glow to her complexion.

This time Jason would not be there to dance with Marva and make her feel pretty. She hadn't heard from him in a long time. Maybe he was engaged to Joanna by now. She missed him more than she cared to admit.

One day after church, TL told her, "I have something for you. When you could come and get it?"

Curious, she smiled up at him. "Tuesday okay?"

He nodded. "Tuesday."

When she met him, she was amazed at the contents of the large paper bag he held out to her. "Mangoes! Thanks, TL."

Traffic was slow, and for once he was still. "You're welcome. You always giving me things. I wanted to give you something too."

She peered into the bag again. "You have Julie and Calabash, and what's this one?" She pulled out a long, thin mango.

"That's cutlass."

"You have all these trees?"

"No, we have one Calabash in our yard, but it's not bearing yet. My uncle came from Mayaro and bring all these mangoes. When I see how much he had, I tell my mother I have to carry some for my church lady. And she gave me this to give you." He stooped and took out a small, package from his duffle bag.

"More? Sugar-cake."

The pink and white confection was made from grated coconut mixed with sugar and a sprinkle of cinnamon. Marva broke off a piece and popped it into her mouth. "Mmm. Delicious. Tell your mother I said thanks."

Because of the weight of the mangoes, TL walked her to the bus stop and held the bag until the bus came.

"See you in church." She waved to him as she climbed onto the step.

He waved back without answering. As Marva took her seat, she looked back at his lank figure running up the hill.

Cicely paused as she and David neared his station wagon parked outside the doctor's office. She gazed at her husband. "Twins?"

"Twins." His voice was almost reverent. "Are you scared?"

Cicely moved on slowly as if suddenly aware that she had to be extra careful. "I … I don't know. I never anticipated this."

Now she realized why she was always tired and had gained so much weight. David opened the passenger door and waited until she'd got in then closed it and went around to his side. "I'm sure everything will be okay."

She was only four and a half months along, but their Saturday morning tennis games had come to an end a week ago. Getting up early five days a week and carrying out her teaching duties was all she could handle. She knew how important exercise was to her husband, but when she urged him to go down to the club without her, he shook his head. "I prefer to stay home and massage my wife's feet."

But she did force herself to walk around the block with him at least three nights a week, and Dr. Marcelin approved. Her nausea was not as frequent, provided she watched what she ate, and she'd begun to feel movements. The first time she felt it was at night. The sudden flutter in her stomach had jerked her upright, waking David.

She placed his hand on the spot, and nothing happened. Then from the opposite corner came a gentle kick. This time he felt it. She could see him grinning in the dark. Long after he'd fallen back to sleep, Cicely had lain awake thinking about the miracle taking place inside of her.

Now she buckled her seat belt. "Yes, according to Dr. Marcelin, everything will be okay, but he is not the one who will be doing this."

David patted her hand. "You'll be fine. I wish they would allow me into the delivery room though."

She threw him a glance. "I don't know if I want you to see me like that."

"Better me than some strange doctor and nurse."

Cicely knew in America it was the accepted thing to have the father present during the delivery, but in Trinidad it was different. Cicely was having the baby at a private hospital. Maybe the doctor would make an exception.

As they entered Collins Avenue, David said, "I wonder whose side has twins."

"Most likely yours. I never heard my parents mention twins in our family."

Later when David called his mother, she was ecstatic. He reported to Cicely what his mother said. "She wondered when twins would resurface in our family. One of her aunts had twins, but they died in a car accident."

Cicely touched his arm. "How tragic."

CHAPTER TWELVE

June's backpack fell with a happy thud near the others lying on the ground. She whooped as she leaped across the small drain that separated the roadside from the empty parcel of land. This was where she and her classmates had spent many moments – some anxious, some carefree – studying or just lazing, eating *amchar* or red mango and talking about the myriad subjects that saturate teenagers' minds.

Today they'd completed their last exam and wildness was in the air. But this wildness was just a way to mask the feelings of sadness that their time at Polytechnic Institute was almost at an end. Some of them, if they passed the CXC, would be going to other schools where they would spend the next two years studying for the CAPE. Others, like Keith, may be joining the world of work. Those who did not get enough passes could return to repeat their courses. And one or two, like Wendy, would be getting married. But for now, their months of frantic studying needed an outlet, and June could feel herself ready to burst at the seams. A group of kids chanted loudly, *"No more Spanish,*

no more French,

no more sitting on the ole school bench ... "

One boy did a somersault on the grass, and Dale, the class clown, was break dancing to a cheering, admiring audience.

Someone took hold of her elbow. "You going to the Y later?"

June looked over at her friend, Paula. "I wouldn't miss it for the world. A good swim is what I need to cool me down." Then she slapped her forehead. "I'll have to go home and get my swimsuit."

They sauntered over to the break-dancing group where the boys were trying to outshine each other.

After a while, Keith stood and clapped his hands. "Enough! Let's mix up the culture."

He cupped his mouth with his hands, and the sound of a Scottish jig came through his lips as from a mouth organ. June's jaw dropped in amazement. Everyone linked elbows and danced in and out in circles. Minutes passed before they collapsed on the ground in laughter. In the midst of it all, June raised her eyes to the school building in the distance. A lone figure emerged from the direction of one of the bathrooms and made her way slowly toward the gate.

Wendy!

What was she doing there all alone while the rest of her classmates were out here having fun? She had not spoken to Wendy since that last day she was at the apartment. They'd studiously avoided each other, but now that dejected walk tore at June's heartstrings. She jumped up and ran toward the school. Not knowing what kind of reception she would get or what she should say, June called to her while she was still a few yards away. "Wendy, wait!"

Wendy glanced at her, and her steps slowed.

June reached her and matched her steps to Wendy's. "I want to talk to you."

The girl's tear-filled eyes met hers. "About what?"

June's stomach lurched. Wendy was always so proud and carefree. What happened? June suddenly felt at a loss for words. Without thinking, she blurted out, "Want to come to the Y with us?"

The girl stood still. "Are you trying to make fun of me, June? I'm pregnant. Haven't you heard?"

June's gaze flashed to the girl's stomach, which showed a slight bulge. But Wendy had always been a plump girl. "I … I did hear, Wendy, but you seemed to be avoiding me."

Silence. "I had to. You're gorgeous and smart. You tried to warn me, but I wouldn't listen. "

June searched for something positive to say. "But you're getting married; you should be happy."

"Getting married? Ha!" She tossed her head and continued walking.

"That's what Daryl said when we … when we first started going together. Now he says he can't leave his wife."

June remembered what Keith had said. "Oh, my goodness."

A wave of sadness washed over her. They reached the gate, and Wendy paused. June hoped she hadn't come there to wait for Daryl. Before she could ask her next question, Wendy continued, "He wants us to live together. Can you imagine that?"

After all that Wendy had told her, June could imagine it. This Daryl was a selfish, self-centered, egotistical —

"— I'm not that stupid, but June, I love him so much."

Her friend was on the brink of tears, and June could feel her own eyes filling up. "Don't cry, Wendy. Just don't give in to him anymore."

She brushed her hand across her eyes. "Mummy is sending me away."

This was a surprise. "Where is she sending you?"

"To Florida. Her sister lives there. She said I can stay with her until I have the baby."

June threw her arm across her friend's shoulder. "Oh, Wendy, I'll miss you, but I think that's a good thing. And you know what? Maybe you'll be able to stay a little longer and go to school."

Wendy nodded, her face brightening. "I still want to be a journalist."

June smiled. "You can do it, Wendy. Just ask God to help you."

A sleek black car drew up almost without a sound near them. Through the tinted window she saw Wendy's mother.

Wendy turned to June. "Can you come and spend Sunday with me?"

"If it's okay with your mom, I'll ask Sister to let me come after church."

Wendy opened the car door and got in. She said something to her mother, then rolled down the window. "Mummy wants to talk to you."

June stepped forward. "Good afternoon, Mrs. Benoit."

"Good afternoon, June. How are you doing? I would love for you to come and spend Sunday with us."

"Thanks. My sister will call and confirm it."

"Good. See you then."

Wendy and June waved at each other as the car drove off, then she turned and walked slowly back to her friends. What a mess Wendy had got herself into. Her parents' money was not enough to cushion her from the effects of her unwise choices. Maybe being in a new environment and having a baby to look after was what Wendy needed. As she neared the patch of ground where her friends were still acting silly, June broke into a trot.

Marva drew the blow dryer, a Christmas present from Miss Stewart, through June's hair while she listened to June's account of her day. June ended with the sad part about Wendy.

Marva sighed. "I feel sorry for her, but I'll pray that God will help her."

"I know He will. Wendy's a bright girl. Her mother invited me to spend this Sunday with her. I told her I'll have to ask you."

This time she stifled her sigh. June was already gone to her chicken job on Saturday and when she got back around seven, she and Keith might go to a movie. And now she was leaving her all alone on Sunday.

As if reading her mind, June said, "I'm so glad exams are over, I'm not even going anywhere this Saturday."

Marva paused with the hair dryer. "You're not going to work?"

"I'm going to work, but after that I'm coming straight home to crash."

Marva smiled and continued with her task.

Sometime later, as she emerged from the shower, a sharp exclamation from June brought her running to the living-room. June stared transfixed at the television screen, which showed a gray-haired man talking to a reporter. "… even after five years we haven't given up hope of one day finding the murderer. Trinidad is a small country, and this murder took place in a small village. Unless he skipped the country, and we doubt that very much, he should still be in the Point Fortin area."

Marva's heart dropped to the bottom of her foot. The reporter, a young Indian woman, continued, "But do you think the detective on the case did everything he could to find the murderer?"

"Sergeant Bowen is one of the nation's finest. I'm confident he did everything he could, but without witnesses or a murder weapon —"

June pressed the remote and the screen went black. She and Marva faced each other, neither of them daring to say what was uppermost in their minds. Marva struggled to breathe. June's face was pale. Marva uttered a moan, rushed into the bedroom and threw herself on the bed. She stared at her mother's picture for comfort.

"Mama, what to do?"

June bustled into the room. Her face was still pale, but Marva could sense she was trying to be brave for her sake. She buried her head in her hands to avoid the look of fear and worry in her sister's eyes. Memories of that July night rushed back as if it were yesterday.

June touched her shoulder. "Sister, don't worry. They'll never suspect us."

"Mr. Bowen suspected me."

"Only because he was investigating the case, but he doesn't have time for that now."

She sat up and drew her knees up to her chin. "I'm a bad person. I killed my father."

June put her arm around her neck. "I don't want you talking like that. You are the best sister in the whole world. You didn't mean to kill him. It was an accident."

Marva glanced at June. "I ... I don't know what to do. I guess I could go to the police, tell them everything —"

June snatched her arm away. "Never! They'll take you away from me."

The tears rolled down June's cheeks, and Marva couldn't stand it. She lowered her knees and got off the bed. "I can't go on like this, Junie. I can't. Anytime anyone mentions a murder, or if I even think about ... what happened, I go to pieces."

June bit her lip. "I'm so selfish. I'm studying and having fun with my friends when all this time you're suffering so much."

She felt bitter, not at June, but at herself. "I deserve to suffer. I'm a bad —"

June clapped a hand over Marva's mouth. "Stop saying that!"

She went into the living-room and returned with the newspaper. She pointed to a spot. "Look, they're showing *Raiders of The Lost Ark* tonight at the Strand. Let's go. I'll pay."

Marva managed a smile and peered at the place where June's finger was. "*Indiana Jones!* I always wanted to see that. But not tonight. I'm going for a walk."

June folded the paper. "Want me to come with you?"

Marva pulled her sneakers from under the bed. "No, you stay here. I want to think over some things."

She'd not walked far when the black and white dog with the zebra stripes met her. He was such an odd-looking dog. She didn't know who his owner was, but he often followed her on mornings when she walked to the bus stop. He trotted up to her, wagging his bony tail, giving her what she called his doggy smile – mouth open, teeth showing.

Marva patted his head. "Will you miss me?"

He wagged his tail again. She took that to mean yes.

She had no more doubt. Soon the police would be on her trail. She couldn't go through that again. It was time for her to end her life of pain and sorrow, although the thought of actually doing it froze her insides. She couldn't hang herself, drink poison or swallow pills. Anything she did must be away from the house to cause June the least possible distress. It should also look like an accident. Maybe throw herself in front of a car? She shuddered. She would write another letter when she got home.

Despite her efforts to cheer Marva up the night before, June's heart carried a dead weight into the following day at work. While she refilled the mustard, ketchup and pepper bottles, she kept looking out for Keith. He was so funny he always knew how to make her laugh even when she didn't want to. Today she needed to laugh. Seeing her sister's reaction to that interview on the television last night had shaken her. She had no idea Marva was still so balled up with fear.

Becoming a Christian and the passing of time had done nothing to assuage her sister's guilt. It seemed worse now than when the "accident" had just happened. Now, where could they go? Who could they talk to?

June sighed as she replaced the bottles in the exact order the boss wanted them in. She turned around and came face to face with Keith. How long had he been watching her? Mr. R would have his head if he saw him doing nothing.

Keith shook his head. "My, my, my. I didn't think it possible."

"What?"

"That you could be even more beautiful when you are worried."

She was alarmed. "What makes you think I'm worried?'

He looked around before replying. Mr. R was nowhere in sight. "I heard a sigh coming from deep down in my lady's heart, and it made my own heart bleed."

She swatted him playfully with the rag as she moved away. "You're silly – and late. You better hurry up and get your apron on before Mr. R sees you."

"Wait till you hear why I'm late," he said as he rushed toward the door with the employees' sign.

She was mildly curious, but with the usual flow of Saturday morning customers and Mr. Rambachan breathing down their necks, she had to wait until their break to hear the reason for Keith's lateness.

They sat on a bench outside the restaurant. Jameela, another employee, stood a little distance away smoking a cigarette. Keith took his time, sipping his Coke and shaking the ice in the cup, something he knew always rattled her, but today her mind was on other things.

Suddenly, he removed the cup from his mouth. "How much money do you have?"

She rolled her eyes and didn't reply. If he was going to ask her to pay for their movie date again, he would be disappointed.

He leaned forward to look at her face. "I'm serious. Have you saved any money since you started working?"

She hoped her irritation showed in her eyes. "I have, but it's none of your business."

He went back to shaking his cup and sipping on his straw.

June jumped up from the bench. "All right, all right. I don't know how much I have. Why do you want to know?"

"Because we're going to Tobago."

June's jaw dropped. "We —"

Her words were cut off by the appearance of Mr. R looking at his watch and shaking his jowls. "Your break was over five minutes ago. That means you lose fifteen minutes off your pay."

Keith jumped up. "That's not fair, man."

His boss glared at him. "You want me to make it thirty?"

"You do that and I quit."

The man didn't seem to have a reply to that. He opened the door and they followed him inside.

Later, as they walked to the bus stop, Keith said, "I'll be glad when I don't have to see that big-belly man again."

June laughed, feeling a little better than she had earlier. "If you're moving to Tobago you won't have to see him."

"I didn't say moving, I said going. My family and I are going to To-bago for a week, and I told Mom I want you to come with us. It will be a nice present for your birthday."

She took his hand. "Keith, that's so sweet of you."

"I'm sweet, Cat's Eyes. I mean, Catty."

June blushed and looked away. Cat's Eyes was his endearment for her, but when she told him she didn't think her eyes looked like those of a cat, he changed it to Catty. His eyes were a light brown, a shade darker than hers but they didn't turn green in the sunlight the way he said hers did.

"I would love to go, Keith. I love your mom."

"She loves you too. She sees you as a daughter-in-law already."

She gave him a playful push. "Stop it!"

After he got off the bus, June's heart sang. A week in Tobago was the ideal way to help her sister forget her troubles. June had always wanted to see Tobago, Trinidad's smaller sister, with its pristine white beaches and relaxed atmosphere. Even though Marva wasn't invited, a Tobago vacation was just what she needed. But June would have to put things in place before she could approach her.

CHAPTER THIRTEEN

"Bye, Sister. See you later."

As soon as the door closed behind Marva, June rushed to the phone and dialed Miss Stewart's number. After a short conversation, she replaced the receiver and lifted her eyes heavenwards. "Please, let her say yes."

Her birthday was just a few days before she hoped to leave for Tobago. She and her sister would celebrate it quietly. Last year Marva had put on a big bash for her sixteenth birthday, catering the food and inviting all her friends. This year, if everything went according to plans, Tobago would put the icing on the cake. June loosened her ponytail, bent at the waist and shook her hair out. Life was exciting!

Cicely hung up the phone and returned to her perch on David's lap. She ran her hand over his balding head.

He gave a slight groan. "Did I tell you that the three of you are becoming … er rather heavy?"

She jumped off his lap, but he pulled her back. "I said becoming. You aren't heavy yet."

She laughed and nuzzled his neck. "I love you."

For answer his lips found hers. When he released her he asked, "Who was that on the phone?"

"Just June."

"What did she want?"

"She said to tell you hello."

"And?"

Cicely went back to fondling his head. "She wants me to accompany her and her sister to Tobago."

David cocked his head to view her face. "You're kidding, right?"

"No. It seems that June's boyfriend Keith wants her to go with him and his family to Tobago. June wants Marva to go as well, but she thinks the only way Marva would agree is if I go too. As a sort of chaperone, I guess."

"What a clever little planner!"

Cicely smiled. "I agree."

"So what did you say to her?"

"I told her I had to ask my husband first."

He patted her leg. "Good."

No more was said on the subject until they were getting ready for bed that night. As Cicely turned down the bedspread she asked, "What should I tell June?"

David yawned and got into his side of the bed. "Tell her your husband said no."

"David!"

"Honey, there's no way I'm letting my very pregnant wife go to Tobago with a bunch of kids."

She settled in beside him. "Then you come too."

"You know I can't leave now. I'm saving up all my time to be with you when the babies come."

She reached over and kissed him on the lips. "Night, sweetheart. Love you."

He slipped his arm around her bulging middle. "Love you too."

By weekend he'd relented, but only on the condition that her sister accompany her. "At least I'll know you have a nurse with you, but I'll be mad with worry until you return. Those cliffs and hairpin roads over there are something else, and the taxi drivers are crazy. They scared the hell out of me the first time I went there."

~

"Yes!" June shot her fists in the air when Miss Stewart gave her the news. Now her sister would have no choice but to go. A week in Tobago with Keith sounded like heaven. They would go swimming, snorkeling, visit the reef and do all the things she'd heard and only dreamed of. She would even buy a bikini, and Marva wouldn't know until she saw her in it. She only needed to call one more person to make everything complete.

She picked up the phone book and opened it to the Yellow Pages. Under the heading Factories, she ran her finger until she came to Point Fortin Tire Factory. She wrote the numbers on a piece of paper and headed out the door. She would call from the phone booth around the corner so her sister wouldn't see the number when the bill came.

Minutes later, June walked home with a feeling of let down. She'd expected Jason to jump at the chance to be with her sister, if only for the weekend. But instead he seemed hesitant, and when he did agree, he sounded reluctant. Was he seeing someone else? Well, at least Miss Stewart, her sister and her daughters would be there. Marva had no choice.

But as June had expected, Marva showed very little interest. "I have to work."

"Sister, you've never taken any time off since you started working at that place, except for two days when you had the flu. You've been working there over three years now; they owe you two weeks with pay."

Marva smiled, and June knew she would come around. But to strengthen her position she added, "Sister, we both work hard, me studying for my exams and you on your job. We deserve a nice vacation. And besides, Miss Stewart, Miss Sheila and her daughters will all be there."

June was becoming tired of persuading people to do this thing. Why was it so difficult? It didn't cost a lot to go to Tobago, and they had the money. She rose from her chair and shoved it back in place at the table. "If you don't want to go, I'll find other ways to occupy my time."

She regretted it the moment the words came out of her mouth.

Her sister's eyes flashed. "What is that supposed to mean? I didn't say I wouldn't go. I said I have to work. And we don't know how much it's going to cost."

June averted her gaze. "I'm sorry, Sister. I … I just want us to go away and have a good time. Keith said the plane ticket is around one fifty."

"Okay, but we still have to pay for a hotel or something. Krishna went there for Easter and he said it's expensive."

June hung her head. She wanted to go so badly. Some of her classmates had mentioned they were going. It would be nice to meet them over there.

Marva touched her shoulder. "I'll talk to Glen."

Marva would gladly walk on a bed of rusty nails, if that would make June happy. But this Tobago proposition promised to be more painful than nails, rusty or otherwise. June had studied hard for her exams, and Marva expected her to pass all of them, most with distinction. So, yes, she deserved a vacation. But Miss Stewart, Miss Sheila and her daughters were going to be there, so why did June want her tagging along?

She had no idea how much Marva depended on her job. Not for the money, although it was useful. But work was her balm, her pacifier, something to help her get through each day without spending every minute agonizing over her sin. And soon she would be on a permanent vacation, more refreshing than anything Tobago had to offer.

She'd made a lot of progress since she started working at Glen's Automotive. Since hiring a new apprentice six months ago, Glen now had her assisting him with his bookkeeping, organizing his files and answering the phone. She missed being out in the yard, as she liked to call it, but whenever the garage was busy, Glen would allow her to go out and assist. He even let her supervise the apprentice on a few occasions, something that thrilled her no end. And a copy of her certificate hung proudly on the office wall. If she never got a chance to achieve anything else, she'd achieved that, including a ten-dollar-a-week raise in pay.

That night June was already in bed by the time Marva came into the bedroom. She'd fallen asleep with a book on her chest and the light on. Marva gently removed the book, *Doctor Zhivago*, and turned off the light.

Why not make their last days together as happy as possible? No more sighing, no more grumpiness. June wanted them to go to Tobago? Then they would go. It should make for pleasant memories.

June's squeal of pleasure when she told her she'd decided to go was enough to bring a grin to Marva's face. Her sister played her like a fiddle, but she didn't mind. That night as they discussed the clothes they would take on their trip, June leaned forward. "By the way, Sister, you're not going into the sea wearing a dress like you did that time when Miss Stewart took us to the beach, are you?"

Marva laughed. She could still remember the look on the faces of June and Miss Sheila's daughters when they saw what she was wearing. June had not spoken to her all afternoon and when they got home, she'd said, "I was never so embarrassed in all my life. Everybody was staring at you."

Marva could not have cared less. The knee-length, denim dress with short cap sleeves and a scoop neck was the shortest dress she owned. She'd chosen it because it was not clingy and would not reveal her underwear. She would not be caught dead on the beach showing off her body.

She turned to June. "If I do decide to go in the water, that's what I'll be wearing."

"Sister!"

Marva rose. "Otherwise I'm staying right here."

Marva scanned the room. She drew the curtains together, checked the window, shoved June's slippers under the bed and straightened a corner of the sheet. In spite of herself, a feeling of excitement grew inside of her, spreading its warmth until she thought it must show on her face. She'd told her co-workers and a few of the customers that she was going to Tobago. They all wished her well and suggested things for her to do and places to go. Seemed like everyone had been to the sister island except her and June. Even TL, when she saw him in church and told him, had said, "You'll enjoy it, Miss CL. I used to live in Bon Accord with my aunt until I was eleven years, then I came back to Trinidad. Come an' meet me an' I'll give you her number. If you tell her you's my frien' she'll cook the nicest coo coo an' stew fish for you."

Marva had not had the time to go and see him, but she promised herself she would tell him all about her holiday when she got back.

So now she was taking her first, maybe the only, vacation of her life. Going on a plane, also a first, and spending a whole five days with Miss Stewart, Miss Sheila and her daughters and Junie. What could be nicer? She didn't mind that Keith would be there. He was staying with his family, and with the two adults helping to oversee things, Marva didn't have to worry about June getting into any kind of trouble.

Marva picked up their suitcases just as June came rushing back into the room. "I met Mrs. Maraj by the back door. She said she would keep an eye on things for us."

"I know she will."

Mrs. Maraj, their landlady, had eagle eyes and dog's ears. Nothing escaped her. June grabbed the rest of their belongings, and they headed out the door.

As they approached the airport, Marva realized with a shock that she'd never been to this part of Port-of-Spain before. She could feel the excitement bouncing off June's body as she turned her head this way and that, trying to take in as much as she could. A plane roared overhead and dipped lower.

Miss Stewart turned and smiled at them. "That could be our plane."

June stared upwards. "It looks a bit small though."

"They use small planes between here and Tobago," Mr. Bowen replied.

"Why?" Miss Stewart asked. "I thought a lot of people travel to Tobago, especially in the summer."

"That's true, but they have several flights a day and the ferry as well. Some people prefer to take that."

June said, "I have some friends who are using the ferry, but it takes all night, and some people get seasick."

Miss Stewart chuckled. "The first time I went to Tobago was with some teachers during the summer vacation. We took the ferry and it was fun until we got to the middle of the ocean where the waters meet —"

"— the Bocas," June put in.

Miss Stewart nodded. "That's right, the Bocas. My goodness, I'd never been so sick in my life. We were all sick. One girl, Judy, was rolling on the floor, another spent the night in the bathroom. It was awful."

June wrinkled her nose. "I can imagine. I'm glad we're flying. And Keith says it only takes fifteen minutes."

A small welcoming party met them at the airport. Miss Sheila, her daughters and her husband Fred, who had come to drop them off, along with Keith and his family. Finally, they boarded the plane and were greeted by smiling crew members. Marva smiled back, a genuine smile, which faded when she tried to squeeze her legs into the small space in front of her.

June, already seated by the window, laughed at her predicament. "Let's ask them to change seats."

An air hostess directed Marva to a seat with more leg room at the back of the plane. She looked back expecting June to follow her, but Keith had already occupied her vacated place. Marva shook her head and buckled herself in next to an elderly gentleman. She watched as the air hostess pointed out the exit signs and explained the safety precautions. The plane was moving.

No sooner had she begun to admire the floating cotton candy outside her window, than she felt a distinct downward tilt in the plane. The air hostess's voice came over the intercom. "Ladies and gentlemen, we will be landing shortly at Crown Point Airport. Please make sure your seatbelts —" Marva's thoughts of what it would be like to live among the clouds had been rudely interrupted. Still, she was eager to see what awaited them on the ground.

While they waited for their luggage, Keith's father informed them with an air of importance that he'd rented a car. "You all will be taking a taxi?" Without waiting for anyone to answer, he continued, "Taxis here too expensive. It's not like Trinidad. Anytime I come here I rent a car. My company gives me an allowance for that." He turned to Miss Sheila. "If you want I could take you to the car rental place."

Miss Sheila and Miss Stewart considered then decided against it. Miss Stewart said, "We won't be going out much."

June turned to Keith. "Where are you staying?"

"Not as close as you." He looked back at his father. "Dad, how far are we from here?"

Mr. Bishop poured out a mouthful of information. Marva gathered that they would be in Store Bay, which was one of the nicer beaches and boasted the best curry crab and dumplings. Good. Keith and June would not be near each other. Maybe they wouldn't see him, or his talkative father, until they were ready to leave.

From the corner of her eye, she watched Keith pull June's suitcase off the baggage belt. He set it down in front of her and whispered something in her ear. She giggled then caught Marva's gaze and stopped. The two had been inseparable since they got on the plane.

Eventually, Keith and his family had gathered all of their luggage, seemingly enough to last them a month. Marva watched them leave with a sense of relief and a little concern at the way June gazed after Keith as he walked away. He was a handsome young man, she had to admit, with oriental features like his dad and an impish grin. He'd always been polite around her, and Marva could see no reason not to like him. Still, she didn't want June getting too serious about anyone just yet.

Marva and her fellow passengers passed through the terminal with the big sign that read Crown Point Airport, then out of the building. Once on the outside, she paused and drew a deep breath. June tugged at her arm and pointed. "Look, Sister, there's a beach."

In the distance, the shimmering aquamarine water and white sand were like nothing she'd ever seen in Trinidad. Further still, splashes of color, maybe houses, dotted the green, rolling hills.

Miss Stewart caught up with then. "That's Sandy Point, if I remember correctly."

A ten- minute drive in a jitney took them to the guest house, a two-storied, orange building fronted by palm trees, red and purple bougainvillea and crotons. A chain link fence with an open gate wound its way around the sides of the property.

A plump, dark-skinned woman and a short, stocky man came out from a downstairs room to greet them. The woman wore a straw hat and had an apron tied around her waist. She stuck out her hand and they all shook it. "You must be the family from Trinidad," she said in a strange accent. "I am Mrs. Brown and this is my husband, James. Everyone calls me Miss Mabel."

"Nice to meet you, Miss Mabel." Miss Sheila introduced everyone. When she mentioned Miss Stewart's name, the woman smiled. "I had a call from your husband this afternoon. He told me to make sure you are very comfortable."

Miss Stewart blushed. "He's just too much. I can't believe he did that."

Miss Sheila laughed. "I believe it." Turning to the woman she said, "This is a lovely place you have here."

"Thank you."

Mr. Brown reached for the two heavier bags. Marva and June picked up theirs and followed the man into the ground floor which appeared to be the dining area. It was tastefully furnished with tables covered with white tablecloths, table ware and napkins. Padded stools stood around a stained, wooden bar in the far corner. Through the sliding-door, a pool, surrounded by short palms and colorful shrubbery sparkled in the sunlight.

Gemma tugged at her mother's hand. "Look, Mummy, a pool!"

Before her mother could reply, she and her sister darted toward the door, followed by June.

"Wait, girls, wait!" Miss Sheila turned to Miss Mabel whose round face widened with smiles. "Is it okay for them to go out there?"

"Sure, let them go. We'll put your things upstairs. When you're ready, just take the stairs over there."

They all trooped out to the pool where the younger girls ran around it, peered in it, touched the water with their finger, then swirled their hands in it. Marva and the adults walked around, admiring the lush tropical landscape.

June came up behind her and rested a hand on her shoulder. "Sister, there's the beach we saw from the airport."

Miss Stewart drew nearer. "It is. It's one of the most beautiful beaches in Tobago."

They were standing on a cliff above the sea. A low stone wall enclosed the back of the property. Marva left the small group and walked closer to the wall. Behind it, huge rocks and boulders, some polished by the elements and the passing of time, jutted out from among the lush, untamed foliage that covered the steep slope. And down below, powdery, white sand and sparkling blue waters stretched all the way to the horizon.

Marva exhaled. She'd found her Shangri-La. How unexpected! Not here though. Not now. But she'd come to Tobago for a reason. God had given her His answer. What a perfect way to go to Him!

CHAPTER FOURTEEN

That night, over a scrumptious dinner of black-eyed peas and rice, stewed red snapper and salad, Marva had a question for Miss Mabel. "How do we get to the beach?"

From the corner of her eye she noted June's raised brow.

"You have to walk around the other side." The lady pointed in the direction of the kitchen. "My husband will show you when you're ready."

Marva nodded. "Thanks."

While they ate, Miss Mabel suggested a few places in town where they could shop for foodstuff since they planned to do their own cooking.

They occupied four bedrooms: one each for Miss Stewart and Miss Sheila, an adjoining one for her daughters and one for Marva and June. As they prepared for bed, June said, "I can hardly wait to go on the beach tomorrow." She turned to Marva. "Sister, I didn't think you would be that interested."

Marva removed her Bible from her bag. "I've never seen water so blue. I want to get closer to it."

June gave her a curious look as she untied her pony tail.

The jitney that had brought them from the airport arrived next morning after breakfast to take them into Scarborough the capital to do their shopping. Downtown was a place of small shops and narrow streets, bustling with human and vehicular traffic. The driver said, "If you don't mind, I'll come in with you. Once they know you're visitors they like to overcharge you."

Miss Stewart glanced at him. "Thank you so much. We appreciate it. Miss Mabel told us you're a good man."

He accompanied them into the store and helped them select their groceries, then stood at the cash register while the cashier rang up their goods, questioning everything that didn't appear right. Despite this, Marva found that the prices were much higher than in Trinidad. It was true what she'd heard. Tobagonians depended on Trinidad for everything.

Back at the guesthouse, Marva helped prepare a light lunch of ham sandwiches while the girls frolicked in the pool. Afterward, they sat around the pool enjoying their lunch. A blue jay landed on the ground near Gemma's feet. She fed him a piece of bread, which he took and flew off, returning a while later with another bird.

Finished eating, they quickly disposed of their paper plates and cups. Marva kicked off her slippers, stretched her legs out on her lounge chair and closed her eyes. The warm sun felt good on her face, neck and arms. She removed her bandana from her hair and placed it across her face to shield her eyes from the sun. The island's magic had begun to wrap itself around her, imparting a tranquility she'd never experienced before.

When she awoke, the pool area was deserted. She found Miss Sheila and Miss Stewart in the kitchen preparing the evening meal.

"Where are the girls?"

Miss Sheila looked up from the pot of chicken she was stirring. "Keith came and took them down to the beach."

He hadn't wasted any time. Still lulled by her nap, Marva said nothing but engaged herself in the meal preparation.

Miss Sheila covered the pot and turned down the gas burner. "Marva, you and I can go down to the beach once we're done, but my poor sister has to stay here. Orders of her husband." She winked at Marva.

Miss Stewart placed some utensils in the sink. "After looking at those steps that lead to the beach, I have no desire to go down there."

They left her comfortably settled with a book by the pool and headed for the beach. As they picked their way down the narrow, rocky steps, bordered by huge boulders and a few scrubby bushes, Marva said, "I'm really glad Miss Stewart decided not to come."

The breeze grew stronger, whipping the ends of her hair from under her bandana across her cheeks.

Miss Sheila held on to her floppy hat. "Mr. Brown said there's a much easier way around the bend, but it's about a half mile from here."

A few yards from the water, the stairway widened and became more gradual, and they were able to walk side by side. Here, the steps were covered with sand and Miss Sheila remarked that the water probably came in that far at high tide.

They placed their towels on a large, smooth rock and Miss Sheila removed her top, revealing her swimsuit. "Did you bring your swimsuit?"

Marva looked away. "No."

She wore her short, blue denim dress, but with Keith there she didn't want to embarrass June by going into the water like that. "I … I'll wait here."

"You sure?"

She nodded.

After the lady left, Marva got up and strolled along the beach, glancing at the water from time to time. She didn't want to think of her end just then, but it kept wafting into her mind like the salt on the sea spray. What would it be like to eventually find peace? To walk into the arms of Jesus and be rid of all her troubles? To know she was in a place where no one could ever hurt her again?

She removed her rubber slippers and waded into the foaming water's edge, enjoying the gritty massage of the sand under her feet, the warm kiss of the sun on her arms and legs and the comforting roar of the waves. Yes, this was the answer. At another flat rock, she sat and prayed. That God would give her the courage to do what she needed to do. That He would forgive her and welcome her into His kingdom and that He would take care of June. She ended, "And Lord, if Keith is the right person for her, please let her finish her studies first before she decides to settle down with him."

Marva gaped at the black bathing suit that June placed in front of her. She picked it up, turned it over, then threw it back on the bed. "I'm not wearing that."

June gestured with impatience. "Sister, we're going to the Reef. There'll be lots of people. Everybody will be in swimsuits, and you want to wear a dress?"

Marva nodded, almost enjoying the angry expression on her younger sister's face. This time June was not getting her way.

"If I'd known you bought that bikini I would have made you take it back to the store and get something more like that." She nodded toward the swimsuit lying in a forlorn heap on the bed. Then she looked down at the orange bikini. It wasn't really skimpy, but Marva didn't like June showing off her body. She wasn't just arms and legs like Gemma and Glenda, she was a well-proportioned young lady, who would make men stop and stare.

June snatched up the bathing suit and left the room. Marva heard her talking to Miss Stewart next door. She didn't hear the reply, but June returned pouting and threw the garment on the bed. Marva hid her smile and went out the door.

Buccoo Reef and the Nylon Pool proved to be everything Marva heard they were. Two natural wonders that attracted visitors every day with their beautiful coral formation, exotic marine life and calm waters. The Nylon Pool in particular was something Marva felt everyone should see. A large, calm pool in the middle of the ocean, as if God had said to the waves, "Come no further." And the water was so clear you could see a pin if it dropped to the bottom. The boatman said Princess Margaret named it after she visited it and found the water so silky, she said it reminded her of her nylons.

After June's display of disapproval that morning, Marva had thought to stay in the boat, but looking down through the glass bottom made her nauseous, so she got out and joined the others in the water.

Of course, Keith and his family were there along with tourists who had come on other boats. Everyone was so engrossed in what they were seeing that no one paid much attention to what Marva was wearing. With her snorkeling gear on, she got close up to the fishes and the coral, marveling at their radiant colors. The boatman had warned them not to touch the coral as the reef was shrinking because of people breaking off pieces to take with them. She was actually sorry when the boatman said it was time for them to leave.

The boat dropped them off near some thatched-roof huts on the beach where there were changing facilities and bathrooms. After eating their packed lunch under one of the huts, Marva and Miss Sheila sat in companionable silence watching the kids play cricket on the sand, using small coconuts for the balls and the stems of coconut branches for the bats. Later, they joined June and the others for more swimming. By the time they left, Marva felt as relaxed as if she'd been wrapped in a warm blanket and rocked by unseen hands.

At the breakfast table, Miss Stewart buttered her bread. "I can't believe it's Friday already. But I'm glad. I miss my husband." She ended with a chuckle.

Miss Sheila cut into her bacon. "I miss Fred too. They should be here around seven tonight."

Marva stiffened. She didn't know the men were coming. Once Mr. Bowen came, her vacation was over. Not that she disliked him. She thought him a good man, but she felt he saw through her as clearly as she saw the bottom of the Nylon Pool. She finished her breakfast quickly and began clearing the table. She would stay in with Miss Stewart today. Apart from mealtimes, they'd seen little of each other, and once her husband came, they would have no time together.

While the others went down to the beach, Marva tidied the kitchen then found Miss Stewart by the pool reading her book. Marva had also brought one of her text books, *Capitalism and Slavery* by Dr. Eric Williams, the country's first Prime Minister, and now she opened it and leafed through the pages.

Miss Stewart peered at the cover. "Hmm, interesting! I love Dr. Williams's writing. I've read all his books."

Some of the material was above her head, and Marva didn't feel capable of discussing it with her teacher.

"Anything you don't understand, just ask me."

Marva stared at the page. "I never knew slaves had to endure so much … so much cruelty."

"Yes, they did, here in the West Indies and America. They were used as a commodity, a form of goods, in order to increase the riches of the slave owners."

"How did they do that?"

Miss Stewart laid her book on her lap. "The slaves were sold by Africa to work on the sugar-cane plantations in the West Indies and to pick cotton in the southern United States. From sugar, they got rum and molasses, which they exported to other countries for huge profits. Slavery was a commodity that reproduced itself, since children of slaves also became slaves to produce even more slaves and more wealth for their owners."

Marva looked away at the waving palm trees and the clouds floating leisurely in the distance before returning her attention to her teacher's face. Miss Stewart's complexion was a light, golden color, almost like clear honey, her eyes dark brown and her nose short and straight. She could be of mixed ancestry.

As if reading her thoughts, Miss Stewart continued, "My father's grandfather was the son of a female slave. His father was the white plantation owner who, in all fairness to him, helped my great-grandfather gain his freedom. He passed on a lot of stories to my grandfather, who passed them on to my father. He knows a lot about slavery."

Marva studied her toenails that June had polished bright pink. She still didn't understand a lot about slavery, but it reminded her of her abusive childhood. Hadn't she been a slave to her own father? And even now she wasn't completely free. She closed her book and stood.

"Where are you going?"

"To get a glass of water. Would you like one?"

"Yes, please."

She returned with the two glasses of cold water, and minus the book. She didn't want to read anymore about slavery in these lovely surroundings. She and Miss Stewart chatted about the things they'd seen and done in Tobago. The conversation turned to the babies, and Marva's interest peaked. "Are you scared of the … having the babies?"

"You mean, the labor, the childbirth itself?"

Marva nodded, watching her face.

Miss Stewart smiled. "I'm not scared – yet. I don't want to think about it until the time comes. David says he would like to be in the room with me, but I don't think they allow that here."

Her husband in the room while she was giving birth? Marva had never heard of it. How nice to have him there, holding her hand, stroking her hair … Miss Stewart's words reoriented her thoughts. "That hungry pack will be coming soon. We better see about lunch."

They'd just finished preparing hot dogs when the girls came running in, followed by Miss Sheila.

"Sister, you missed a treat this morning. The water was so nice. What's for lunch?" June lifted the towel covering the food.

Marva smiled. "Go and dry off first, or you'll be drinking seawater with your food."

That evening, they were lounging around the pool when Miss Mabel came to announce a call for June. She jumped up with an expectant smile, and Marva knew right away who the caller was. June returned with slowed steps, avoiding Marva's gaze. "Keith asked if he can pick me up tonight to go and see the turtles."

Marva furrowed her brow. "See the turtles? Why? What's so special about them?"

June fixed her gaze on Miss Stewart's face as if she was the one who'd asked the question. "It's the turtle-laying season and they come out at night."

"I think I heard something about that," Miss Stewart said. "What time does he want to pick you up?"

"Around nine. The turtles come out much later."

Marva became impatient. "Much later than nine? That means you'll be out near midnight?"

June turned her hazel gaze on Marva. "It's something a lot of people go to see. His brother and his wife will be taking us."

"If I wasn't pregnant I would go. It's something I would love to see too. Marva, wouldn't you like to go?"

Marva couldn't believe Miss Stewart would ask her something like that, but then teachers had the strangest interests. "To see turtles lay eggs?"

"I know Sister wouldn't like that," June said much too quickly, which almost made Marva want to change her mind. But being on some beach in the middle of the night held no appeal for her. Watching television or curling up in bed with her Bible made a lot more sense.

"Can we go with June, please, Mommy?" Gemma piped up.

Her mother turned to her. "I would take you if your daddy wasn't coming up tonight."

Glenda, always her father's favorite, said, "I want to be here when Daddy comes."

"And I have to be here when my babies' daddy comes." Miss Stewart smiled, patting her belly. "So June, it looks like you're on your own."

June rubbed her hands together, then bent and kissed Miss Stewart's cheek. "Thanks, Miss. Let me go and get out my jeans."

Marva watched her dart away, wanting to say something to stop her. She couldn't believe Miss Stewart had agreed to let her go just like that. Was she the same teacher who had been so strict in Egypt Village?

The woman caught her gaze. "Don't look so worried, Marva. June has a good head on her shoulders, and there'll be lots of people there."

After June left, promising Marva she would be all right and that Keith would bring her back as soon as they'd seen the turtles, Marva tried to settle herself into bed with her Bible. She had reached halfway through the 91ˢᵗ Psalm when someone knocked on her door. Thinking it might be one of Miss Sheila's daughters she called out, "Come in!"

Miss Stewart pushed the door open, smiling. "Marva, someone's out here to see you."

Marva raised her eyebrow. "Me?" She didn't know anyone in Tobago.

Miss Stewart turned away, and Marva slipped on the dress she'd worn earlier, patted her hair and went out into the hallway.

She stopped and gasped. "Wh … what are you doing here?"

Jason stood framed in the hallway light, a smile on his face, a bag slung over his shoulder.

He took a step toward her. "I … came up on the plane with Mr. Bowen and the doctor."

Marva stared at him. He wasn't an apparition. His smile, the clipped mustache and beard, chiseled lips, were all as she remembered them. But how did he know she was here?

The awkward silence hung between them. He answered her unspoken question. "I have a taxi waiting to take me to my aunt's house in Bon Accord. I just came to ask if … if you would like to go for a spin tomorrow."

She found her voice. "You brought Steve's car with you?"

He chuckled. "I'll borrow my cousin's car. I can show you the other side of the island." His gaze never left her face.

Without thinking, she replied, "Okay."

"Mr. Bowen invited me to go fishing with them in the morning. We can leave after that."

"Okay." She could think of nothing else to say.

"I … I'll see you tomorrow."

"Bye."

Marva watched him go down the hall and waited until his footsteps faded before returning to her room. She'd known the men were coming tonight, her main reason for retiring to bed early, but what coincidence had brought Jason here as well? Had he come especially to see her, or did he just find out from Miss Stewart that she was here? Her interest in the Psalm, and June's welfare, disappeared. Smiling, she closed the Bible and turned off the light.

CHAPTER FIFTEEN

David settled himself in bed next to his wife and drew her into his arms. "I've missed you all so much."

Cicely stroked his cheek. "We missed you too. We had no one to kick."

He patted her tummy. It felt hard. "I'm surprised they haven't greeted me yet."

"They haven't been very active lately. Maybe the tranquil atmosphere of Tobago put them to sleep."

"So, what have you been up to?"

She filled him in on the things the others had done so far, ending with, "All I did was eat, sleep and read – as I was ordered to."

He kissed her lips. "My poor darling. You must have been miserable."

"Just a little, except when I was planning what I would do to you when I saw you."

It was wonderful to be with her again. The four days they'd been apart had seemed like four years.

Cicely shifted her position on the bed. "So, what have *you* been up to?"

"Lots of nice things, like painting the nursery and getting in Gerard's way."

Cicely chuckled. Gerard was the cabinet maker they'd hired to build the cabinets in the nursery. He'd worked for them before and was very particular about his work. Gerard never failed to show his disgust with David's attempts at helping him, even though he had his own assistant.

"I can just hear Gerard growling under his breath like an angry dog."

"That's exactly how he sounds, but he did help me paint the ceiling."

"You painted the ceiling?"

He nodded. "Wait till you see it. And Mom is busy sewing curtains." Even though the room was almost dark, David could see the wide smile on his wife's face. He kissed her lips again. "She hopes to have them done by the time we get back."

"She doesn't have to rush. We still have more than two months."

"Yeah, but you know Mom. She doesn't drag her feet with anything."

"I just love her."

"She sent her love, to you and the girls." He paused. "By the way, did you give June permission to go out tonight?"

Cicely twisted again. "Yes, leatherback turtle- nesting."

David hooted with laughter.

"What's so funny?"

"You sent her out at midnight to a beach with a teenage boy to watch turtles?"

"What's wrong with that? His brother and his wife are taking them."

David stroked her hair. "Honey, all the ingredients for the loss of innocence are present – the sea, the dark, a teenage boy with raging hormones, and a beautiful young girl. Worse yet, if there's a moon."

"You sound like you're talking from experience, but June's a trustworthy girl."

He laughed again. "Maybe. But is the boy trustworthy?"

Small pockets of people had already gathered on the beach by the time June and her party got there. She and Keith, holding hands, stayed close to his brother and sister-in-law, making small talk. Keith's brother Roger approached a white couple standing a little apart from everyone. "Who is the person in charge?"

The man pointed to himself and the woman. "We are." He spoke in a hushed tone. "My name is Chris and this is my partner, Shelley. Is this your first turtle watching?"

"Yes." Roger dug his hand in his back pocket and pulled out his wallet. He lowered his voice. "We read about your work and would like to donate something." He handed the man a one-hundred-dollar bill.

The man's face lit up in the dark. "Thank you so much."

He took out his wallet and placed the money inside. "This will help our efforts to prevent turtle poaching." He went on to explain that he had posted people at various points where he expected the turtle to appear. If anyone spotted it, they were to wave both hands and that would be the signal for everyone to congregate at that spot.

"Why do you think she'll come to this part of the beach?" Keith asked.

"Because she was seen here last month. Turtles usually return to the same area for some reason. If you like, you can stay here or you can join one of the other groups, but you must be absolutely quiet. If the turtle senses any activity she'll go back in the water."

"Did you bring a camera?" Shelley asked.

Roger shook his head. "No."

"Good. No pictures, no flashlights." She continued, "Once she begins to lay her eggs, she would be focused on only that, and we can then follow her quietly to see the actual laying."

Chris began to walk, and they followed him. He spoke about his and Shelley's work as conservationists for the threatened species. "Once we find a nesting spot, we place markers and hire local people to patrol the spot in order to keep fishermen from hunting the turtles. They do that despite laws prohibiting hunting."

They stopped near the first group. A man with a foreign accent asked, "Why do they want to keep people from hunting the turtles when the meat is so good?"

"And the shell is beautiful," a woman added. "I saw one at a hotel we stayed at in Trinidad."

Keith had his mouth open. June knew what he was thinking - how could someone ask such a dumb question? Together with two of their classmates, she and Keith had researched the leatherback turtle for a class project, and had learned of its benefits to the ecosystem. Turtles helped preserve marine and beach vegetation in so many ways, as their female guide was now explaining to the group.

June glanced around her. The whole atmosphere appeared surreal. The silvery glow of the beach under the half moon; the dark, velvety sky; silhouetted groups of figures and the distant sound of the waves, even though they were quite near. Chris took a few steps toward the water then flapped his hands excitedly. People further up the beach began walking toward them.

June watched the large turtle emerge from the sea and slowly make her way up the beach. The group inched after her. When she stopped near the edge of the trees, everyone stopped. The air of expectancy was palpable. Then the reptile began moving her flippers, flinging away the sand and burrowing into it, making a pit. June squeezed Keith's hand so hard it almost hurt. They crept closer, watching as she dropped her eggs into the pit. Time passed unnoticed. They counted one hundred and two eggs. Then, as carefully as she had dug the pit, the turtle used her back flippers to pile sand over the eggs until they were all covered.

Whispers came from the crowd, and in silence June and her friends walked back to the car. In the back seat, she snuggled close to Keith, still enthralled by what she'd seen. She never expected she would one day see a member of the endangered species up close and personal. No one spoke for about the first ten minutes, then Keith's sister-in-law broke the silence. "That was a big turtle."

"Probably over 300 pounds," her husband replied.

Keith and June recounted their own feelings in whispers so as not to intrude on their conversation. During a pause, Keith said, "Tomorrow is our last day."

"Don't remind me."

"Spend it with me."

June lifted her head from his shoulder to stare at him. His deep gaze made her heart skip. When the car stopped in front of the guesthouse, he tugged at her hand. "Tomorrow?" he mouthed so the others wouldn't hear.

She nodded and slid out of the back seat.

She ran quietly up the stairs and down the hallway so as not to wake anyone, but as she drew abreast of Miss Stewart's room, the door opened.

June halted. "Miss, you still up?"

Miss Stewart smiled. "Can't sleep until all my girls are in."

"I'm sorry to have kept you up."

She patted her belly. "That's okay. You were not the only one. How did it go?"

June clasped her hands together. "Wonderful," she breathed. "I'll tell you all about it in the morning."

Miss Stewart smiled again. A smile of relief it seemed.

Marva and the others were seated around the pool next morning when the men returned from their fishing trip. Grinning, Mr. Bowen held up the one grouper and the kingfish he'd caught. "Not bad for someone who doesn't do this for a living."

His wife leaned against him. "I'm sure I could have done better."

Marva left them admiring the fishes and ran upstairs to get dressed. While she studied herself in the yellow, flowered dress with the square neckline and wide straps, June came in from the bathroom. "You look very nice, Sister."

Marva smiled her appreciation, hoping Jason would think the same. June had encouraged her to buy the dress when they went shopping, and after she'd tried it on in the store, she thought the color complimented her cinnamon complexion. The gold, heart-shaped pendant he'd given her years ago as a birthday present nestled in the hollow of her neck. She'd applied a little powder and lip gloss and at the last moment borrowed a yellow scarf from Miss Stewart to cover her hair from the wind. She sprayed a little perfume just beneath the pendant and on her wrists and went downstairs.

The sun was a faint glow behind a seamless canopy of gray when she got into Jason's borrowed car. It had rained the night before, and droplets of water still glistened on the crotons and hibiscuses that fringed the building. Marva hoped it wouldn't rain again. But whatever the weather had in mind, she was determined to enjoy the day. She'd thought about

Jason a lot last night and why he'd come to Tobago. Did God have a future planned for them? Maybe He didn't want her to come to Him just yet. After today she would know.

It was around one in the afternoon when June and Keith entered the suite where he and his family were staying, not far from the beach where they'd witnessed the turtle nesting the night before. Keith had informed her that his family was out but should be back soon. The three-bedroom suite was larger than her apartment and tastefully decorated.

Keith led her into the kitchen and opened the fridge. He removed a few plastic containers. "What would you like to eat?"

June peered behind him. "What's in the foil paper?"

"Roti skins."

"That's what I want."

He pulled out the paper. "My mother and Savitri made them yesterday."

June had eaten Mrs. Bishop's roti at Keith's birthday party last year and she knew they were very good.

He took out another dish. "And here's the curry chicken."

June assisted in heating up the food, and minutes later they sat at the little kitchen table enjoying their fare. June eyed his plate, loaded with rice, chicken, stewed peas, half of a roti, macaroni pie and salad. She shook her head. "I don't know where all that food goes."

He winked at her. "I'm a man. I have to eat plenty."

June covered his hand with hers. "No, you love to eat plenty."

He smiled, his eyes crinkling at the corners, as he bit into a piece of chicken. It was good being here with him. She'd brought her swimsuit in case he wanted to go for a swim later, or maybe they would sit around and play dominoes or cards.

Their meal over, they tidied up the kitchen, and June went into the bathroom to brush her teeth. She loved roti, but once she finished eating it, she wanted the spiciness out of her mouth. When she emerged, feeling freshened, Keith was seated in the living-room with two slices of chocolate marble cake on the table in front of him.

June placed her hands on her hips. "Now you're really overdoing it."

He tugged at her hand and pulled her on to his lap. His mouth came down on hers and she returned his kisses eagerly. Apart from a brief peck on her lips when they were on the beach one day, they had not really kissed while on vacation. But this time June sensed an intensity in him that was not there previously. When his hand reached for the zipper on her shorts, she covered it with hers. She tore her lips from his and tried to stand, but he held her firmly.

His eyes burned into hers. "June, I want you so much."

She understood what he meant. Marcus had said those same words to her, and even though she loved Keith, she couldn't bring herself to do what he wanted. Thoughts of her father and what he'd done to her rushed through her mind, and suddenly she wanted to vomit. With an effort, she forced herself up and ran into the bathroom.

When she came back out, he was standing there, a look of puzzlement on his face. "Catty, are you OK?"

Her heart melted at his concern and she touched his face, nodding and forcing back the tears. He brushed them away with his fingers and led her back to the couch. He drew her close. "I'm sorry, Catty. I didn't mean to scare you."

Her voice trembled. "You didn't scare me."

"Then what is it?"

How could she tell him she'd been abused by her father when she was only ten? That there was a time she barely spoke, barely ate. That shortly after her father's death, the mere mention of his name would send her rushing to the bathroom. She felt okay, thought she'd overcome the effects of the trauma, but they still lingered. Would she ever get over it? Had she really wanted Keith to have his way with her? What would Sister say? Miss Stewart? They would be disappointed in her, but most of all God would be too. He'd saved her just in time.

Keith lifted her chin with his finger. "Catty, I love you and I know you love me too. When we're living together it will be different. You'll be more relaxed."

She jerked forward and stared at him. "When we're living together?"

He returned her stare. "I mentioned it before. I want you to come and live with us. I'm going to start working with my dad in August. We won't have to pay rent …"

She held up her hand. "What about what I want? I told you I'm going back to take the CAPE if I get enough passes…"

"You can go back to school if you want to. I won't stop you. I already spoke to my parents —"

She jumped up, feeling the blood rush to her face. "*You* won't stop me. So, this is why you brought me here while your family is away, so you could have sex with me and then I would have to go and live with you? Well, Keith Bishop, you have another thought coming. I —"

The sound of voices in the hallway stopped her and the next moment the door opened and Keith's parents walked in.

Mr. Bishop entered first. "There they are. Well, how are you, my dear? Did you all have a good time?" He eyed the two slices of cake. "Boy, don't tell me you took all the cake from the fridge." Turning to his wife, "This boy will eat you out of house and land, you hear." He went to the fridge, still talking.

June turned to Keith's mother. "Mrs. Bishop, I'd like to go home please."

"Already?"

June looked at her watch. "My sister is expecting me back at a certain time."

"Okay. Steven, June wants to leave."

The man shoved a forkful of cake into his mouth. "Let Keith take her. He can drive."

June glanced at Keith, standing awkwardly near the couch, then back at his father. "Not on these hairpin roads."

The man laughed. "They're all right, once you get used to them. The first time I came to Tobago I rented a car and drove all by myself. You just have to take your time and watch out —"

June tried to close her ears to his chatter as she followed him out the door. She didn't look back at Keith trailing after her.

CHAPTER SIXTEEN

The sun was just a faint glow behind a seamless canopy of gray when Marva got into Jason's borrowed car. She waited while Mr. Brown advised him on the most scenic route to take and then he got in beside her. It had rained the night before, and a few droplets still glistened on the shrubbery.

Jason checked his side mirror before pulling away from the grass. "The fish was really biting this morning."

Marva buckled her seatbelt. "You sound like you had fun."

"I love fishing, but I never went out on a boat before. Man, that was something else." His gaze shifted to her outfit. "You look great, Moe."

She smiled. "You always say that, but thanks."

"And I always mean it."

"Where are we going?"

"I told my aunt we'll pass in to see her since we're going to have lunch near there."

Marva didn't know if that was a good idea, but she didn't want to say anything to spoil the day.

Jason glanced at her again. "You having a good time?"

"Yes. I love Tobago."

"Me, too. I could live here. You been to the Reef?"

"Yes, it's so beautiful. So many fishes, and the coral … The boatman says people are destroying the reef."

Jason nodded. "That's true."

At the Milford Fort, they stopped to admire the canons and walls once used to protect Tobago from invasion. They took pictures of each other near the canons then a New York couple offered to take one of them together.

Marva removed her scarf and shook her hair free. Smiling, she edged closer to him. The man clicked twice then gave the camera back to Jason who returned the favor, using the man's camera. By the time they got back in the car, the sun was more visible, and little patches of white interrupted the boring gray. It was going to be a good day after all.

Jason's aunt, Millicent Burke – "call me Auntie Millie" - reminded Marva of Tantie Beulah, even though she was shorter, younger-looking and didn't carry things stuffed in her bosom. At least, not as far as Marva could see. A widow, Aunt Millie ran a small shop or parlor, as it was called, in the front of her house. She insisted on piling Marva with sweet bread, pone and sugar cakes which she made to sell. Like Tantie Beulah, she was very garrulous and did not hide the fact that she liked Marva.

"But, boy, why you don't marry this pretty young lady? I know she'll make you a good wife. Your mother didn't tell you that?"

Marva glanced at Jason, who seemed not in the least bit put out by his aunt's questions. He leaned over and kissed her on the cheek. "Lemme think about it, okay, Auntie?"

As they got in the car, Marva said, "Your aunt is very nice."

"That's because she likes you. If she doesn't, watch out."

Marva leaned over to place her bag of goodies in the back seat. At the same time, he turned and their lips were inches apart, but he glanced back at his aunt's house then started the car. Marva settled into her seat and buckled her seatbelt. Neither of them spoke until they sighted the sign for Mamie's, the restaurant Aunt Millie had recommended.

The small establishment was an add-on to a bright yellow house at the back. An abundance of greenery surrounded the building. Marva hung back a little as they entered the building, conscious of the eyes of everyone on them. A waitress, her hair in cornrow braids, came up to them. "How you doing, sweetie? Just the two of you?"

Jason nodded. "Yes. My aunt told me you have the best crab and dumplings in Tobago."

She laughed. "Who is your aunt?"

"Miss Millicent, in Bon Accord."

The lady stopped at a square, laminated table. "Oh, Miss Millie? She's my friend." She peered closer at Jason. "How come I never see you before?"

"I live in Trinidad. I came up for the weekend."

Now she turned her attention to Marva. "And this is your wife? She tall and pretty."

Jason pulled out Marva's chair and waited until she'd settled herself before taking his seat. "Thank you. So what you have for us today?"

"Crab, dumplings, a l'il split peas soup. Nothing but the best for Miss Millie's family."

"Sounds good."

The lady took a small pad from her pocket. "What would you like to drink?"

Marva opted for a Coke and Jason a Malta.

The lady disappeared, and Marva raised her eyes to Jason's face. "Why didn't you tell her I'm not your wife?"

He smiled, a dimple deepening on his chin. "Why not? She'll have fun telling everybody Miss Millie's nephew and his wife are here."

"I've been wondering how you happened to be in Tobago this weekend."

"A little bird told me you would be here."

A waitress brought their drinks, and Marva took a sip.

"A little bird?" Then she caught on. "June?"

He grinned, obviously enjoying her surprise.

"She never said a word."

"Smart girl."

She tore her gaze away from his intense look and focused on her hands in her lap. And then it came softly, but as powerful as a wave crashing against the rocks in high tide. "I wanted to see you again, Moe."

Marva struggled for breath. "I … I'm glad you came."

Marva's mind tried to make sense of what had just passed between them. Their words spoke an audible language, but their eyes said something else. They were alone in the room. The chatter and laughter of the patrons came as distant sounds in a sea of fog. The metal chair kept her anchored to the bare, concrete floor, but on the inside, she floated to the handsome young man sitting opposite her. *God, what was happening? This is not what I want.*

It was he who broke the spell. "This is a nice place."

Marva groped her way out of the fog and opened her eyes and mind to her surroundings. It *was* nice – in a rustic way. Bamboo - covered walls, light bulbs shaded with something resembling coconut shells, and candles in coconut lanterns. Calypso music- not too loud- came from a juke box near the bar.

A waitress brought their soup, and Marva bowed her head and said grace. When she looked up, he was gazing at her. "I forgot you always say grace. My mother does too."

She dipped her spoon into the thick, yellow liquid. "You should."

By the time they finished the soup, Marva felt more relaxed and had put her emotional leak behind her. The food came and the aroma of spices went straight to her nostrils. She inhaled deeply. One dish held the blue crabs, their color now disguised by cooking and spices, another, the dumplings. The food seemed enough for four people.

Jason smiled at her. "Go ahead."

Feeling emboldened, she took the dish of dumplings and placed two on his plate then followed with some of the crab.

He smiled. "Now that's how a wife is supposed to behave."

She picked up the banter. "If you tease me, you'll have to serve your-self next time."

The food was delicious, but there was no way a person could eat the dumplings and crab together. Jason showed her how to do it. "You dip a piece of dumpling in the gravy and eat that first. Then you eat the crabs."

Whoever invented such a difficult combination of dishes was either trying to be funny or hadn't expected to be taken seriously. She followed Jason's example, eating only two of the small, round dumplings, before digging into the crab. By the time she finished her meal, Marva under-stood why the dish had become a national favorite. She wouldn't eat it on a regular basis, but on a vacation with plenty time to spare, it was a to-do.

Back in the car, Jason reached for her hand. "What you want to do now?"

She almost said "sleep," but instead she said, "Whatever you want."

He smiled and turned on the engine.

Marva leaned her head against the back of the seat. She awoke to feel Jason shaking her gently.

"You looked so beautiful, I hated to wake you."

Marva's eyes widened. She had no idea where she was. Then she remembered the crab and dumplings and getting into the car. "Where are we?"

Jason looked around. The road stretched before them with bushes on either side and no houses in view. A jitney trundled past. "This is Plymouth. I want you to see something."

"What is it?"

"It's a tombstone."

A tombstone? He'd brought her to a cemetery? Marva rubbed the sleep out of her eyes.

Jason held her hand as they tramped through the beaten-down grass and over mounds of what could have been old graves then stopped at a low, marble stone. Marva peered at the words, some of the letters removed by the passing of time.

Within these walls are deposited the bodies of Mrs. Betty Stivens
and her child. She was the beloved
wife of Alex B Stiven,
to the end of his days will deplore
her death which happened on
the 25th day of Nov. 1783
in the 23rd year of her age.
What was remarkable of her
She was a mother without knowing it,
and a wife without letting her husband
know it except by her kind indulgences to him.

Marva rubbed her eyes again and read the words twice more then she looked at Jason. He shook his head. "Don't ask me. I've no idea what it means. Let's go. This is a lonely place. We'll talk about it in the car. I just wanted you to see it because everyone who comes to Tobago has to see The Mystery Tombstone."

"It's certainly a mystery," Marva said after they drove off. "I can't make out what it means. She was a mother without knowing it. I can understand if she died not knowing she was pregnant … it was 1783 …"

"Yes, but if she didn't know it, how could they know it? It says, 'the bodies of Mrs. Betty and her child.'"

The mystery tombstone provided a lively discussion for them all the way back to Sandy Point. When they got back to the guesthouse, Marva had a lump in her chest. He seemed to feel the same way, for he suggested a walk down to the beach. "It will help to wake me up for the drive back."

He took her hand as they walked. "Enjoy the day, Moe?"

Marva's steps slowed. Her breathing became difficult again. Then he turned and touched her lips with his. Her heart melted, but the kiss was already over. In silence, they walked down the ragged steps to the beach. June and the others were in the water along with other bathers. Marva perched herself on the rock she'd found that first day. He sat near her and she eased herself as close to him as she dared, feeling the hardness of his arm and thigh against hers. He remained statue still. In silence, they gazed at the wide expanse of water. Waves lashed the shore, sea hawks winged their way to their destination, and the sun sank slowly in the horizon.

"Tomorrow we go home."

She didn't take her eyes off the water. "What time is your flight?"

"Eight at night."

"Ours is at two in the afternoon."

"You go to work Monday?"

"No. Tuesday. You?"

"Yeah, I go back on Monday." Pause. "I'm glad you had a good time."

Silence.

"Today was special."

He fixed her with his dark gaze. "I have to be getting back."

A feeling of ennui stole over her. Everything was still the same.

She jumped off the rock and began walking. Near his car, he glanced at her. "I'll call you when I get home."

She watched him get in the car, turn on the engine and buckle his seatbelt, then he turned to her and smiled. "Bye, Moe."

She waved, the lump in her chest growing bigger. A small cloud of dust rose as the car moved away. She watched it until it rounded the bend then she turned to go into the house. She didn't want to admit what she'd hoped for today, but whatever it was, it had not happened. She was still in the wilderness.

In the airport lounge the next day, June hunched over a book of crossword puzzles. Across from her, Marva sat, legs crossed, reading a book. Miss Stewart leaned against her husband, her feet propped up on the chair next to her. The rest of their party were scattered close by. Keith and his family occupied seats on the other side of the aisle. June didn't know if it was by choice or by chance.

The rain drizzled on the rooftop, muting the sounds of conversation and matching the dreariness of her thoughts. She and Keith had not officially broken up, but they'd barely spoken two words to each other since they entered the building. Then he'd gone and sat with his family but didn't seem to be taking part in their conversation. In vain, June tried to push the ache from her heart, but memories of the three years she and Keith had been friends dripped constantly like the raindrops.

From the day she'd first laid eyes on him, she thought him the cutest boy she'd ever seen. And she still did. She loved his boldness too. The way he stepped out of a group of boys and walked with her that first day made her feel special. Then that afternoon he'd waited for her and insisted on carrying her books while he walked her home. They never ran out of things to talk about – whether it was their friends, the latest movie, TV show or his soccer matches, Keith's wit and humor breathed life into every topic.

They were a unit, everyone in school knew that, yet sometimes a boy, or a girl, tried to cut in. Keith or June would pretend to be jealous, observing from the sidelines, then have a good laugh about it afterward. This year their relationship had deepened as they studied for exams, then worked at the chicken place together. How would she go on without him?

Tears stinging her eyes, she rose and went into the bathroom where she let them flow just a little. Someone came into the stall next to hers, and June wiped her eyes and opened the door. While she washed her hands, the lady came out. "June, are you okay?"

Startled, she nodded, still washing her hands.

"Did something happen between you and Keith?"

June reached for paper in the dispenser, but it was empty. "We broke up."

Miss Stewart pulled out a Kleenex from her purse and gave it to her. "Oh, honey, I'm sorry to hear that. Maybe you'll patch it up soon."

June shook her head, keeping her gaze averted. "I don't think so."

Miss Stewart rubbed her soapy hands together. "Why not? These things happen all —"

"He wants us to live together."

The lady's hands remained still under the water. "He what?"

June told her what Keith had said.

Miss Stewart turned off the faucet. "I hope you put him in his place. How dare he disrespect you like that?"

June felt she should defend him. "It's not his fault. His brother and his wife started out living together in his parents' house."

Miss Stewart dried her hands. "Growing up is hard, isn't it? But you're smart. You did the right thing."

Then why does it hurt so much? The tears threatened to spill over again, and she blinked them back. In silence, she and Miss Stewart walked back into the lounge.

CHAPTER SEVENTEEN

Marva slapped her hand on the table, and June jumped up, knocking over her empty juice glass. "What, Sister?"

Marva rose from her chair and advanced closer to June. "What? You've been wearing that nightgown for the three days since we got home, you don't comb your hair, you're not talking, not eating, and I see you watching the phone like a dog waiting for food." Her voice broke. "I want to know what happened between you and Keith."

June's voice shook. "We … we broke up."

Marva's anger drained out of her. "Junie, I … I'm sorry. I didn't mean to snap at you like that."

June placed her glass on the counter and came back to the table.

To Marva's surprise, the news brought her no joy. She always felt Keith seemed too possessive of her sister, but she now realized how important he'd been to her.

She sat back down. "Why did you break up? You looked so happy when you came back from the turtle laying."

June's fingers rolled the edge of the placemat. "He … he wanted me to … to go and live with him."

"What?"

"I told him he shouldn't ask me to do that. He knows I want to go back for my A levels."

"What did he say?"

"Sister, you wouldn't believe this. He said he would let me go to school." June gave a mirthless laugh. "*He* would let me."

Marva felt at a loss for words. Keith wanted June to live with him and his family? Would he have married her eventually? And June had turned him down, put him in his place. Then why wasn't Marva happy?

"Did you try calling him?"

June raised her eyes to Marva's face. "No! Why would I do that? He'd been hinting at that for some time, but I thought he was joking." She returned her gaze to the mat. "I miss him so much, Sister. I lost my best friend. First, Wendy, now Keith."

The dam broke, and she began to sob. Marva pulled her chair closer to June's and drew her against her bosom. "You have me, Junie. You … you'll always have me."

June wrapped her arm around her sister's waist, and Marva allowed her to cry until she was spent. How many times had she cradled June like this when they suffered their father's abuse? How many times had she been there to comfort and reassure her? And how much longer would she be around to do this? Her tears threatened to overflow, and she blinked them back.

Myriad emotions surged through her. She ought to be proud she'd done such a great job raising June, but now … maybe she'd done too good a job.

Gently she shook June's shoulder. "Go and shower. We're going somewhere."

June raised her head and wiped her hand across her eyes. "You're not going to work?"

Marva straightened up. "No. I'm going to call Glen. Go on and shower and put on something nice."

Her baby sister needed her. She could take a day off. They would go to the mall, eat pizza, browse the shops. She couldn't replace Keith or Wendy or any of June's friends but she could at least try to ease the pain.

Seated in the bus on the way to the Gulf City Mall, Marva tried to engage June in conversation. "This is a really nice area of San Fernando."

"Where Keith lives is nicer."

"The sea is not far away too."

"But it's not as nice as Tobago."

At last the bus turned into the entrance to the mall. Even though it was mid-morning, the parking lot seemed almost full. They got out with the other passengers and crossed the busy street.

June's countenance brightened a little when they entered the building. Marva wasn't interested in shopping, but she trailed dutifully behind her from store to store. In one that sold souvenirs, June found a little turtle magnet. She held it up, displaying the first real smile since they returned from Tobago. "This is so pretty. It looks like a hawksbill."

Marva admired the hard shell with scales of golden brown, orange and black. "It will look good on the fridge."

She spotted an oval-shaped tropical fish in bright yellow, blue and black, reminding her of some she'd seen on the reef.

June studied it. "That's nice too."

They paid for their purchases and left the store. By the time they sat in Mario's Pizzeria enjoying their lunch, Marva had made up her mind. "I think you should call Keith."

June coughed on her pizza. "Sister, are you serious?"

Marva wiped her mouth with her napkin. "I know I've been hard on Keith in the past, but he has grown up to be quite a nice boy."

June stared at her open-mouthed.

Marva smiled. "Close your mouth. People are looking at you."

"I can't believe you are my sister. I thought you would be jumping for joy at the news."

Marva recalled the way she'd interrogated Keith the first time she met him. It was at her eighteenth birthday party. He'd seemed petrified, until June came and snatched him away. Those days were long gone. In the years following, Marva had never suspected any reason to mistrust him.

"— I told him I wasn't going for that."

She pushed her thoughts aside. "Not going for what?"

June leaned forward, her eyes wide and accusing. "You weren't listening." She hissed. "He wanted me to do what you told me not to do."

It was Marva's turn to widen her eyes. "You mean —"

June nodded.

"That little good-for-nothing!"

On their way home, Marva closed her eyes pretending to be asleep. What could she do to bring Keith and June back together? From the letters she'd written, she hoped Miss Stewart would take June to live with her when the time came. But with Miss Stewart starting her own family, she might not want the added responsibility of raising a teenager. Keith had provided the perfect solution. He was nice-looking, his parents were well off and they seemed to like June. It could be perfect. All June had to do was ignore his diarrhea-of-the-mouth father. But once June made up her mind on something, there was no talking her out of it. Keith's mother was Indian. Maybe she would be open to arranging a marriage.

Marva took a deep breath and knocked on the large, mahogany door of Keith's parents' home. She'd been there once before last year to meet June after Keith's birthday party. Today she prayed he was not home while she talked with his parents, even though she wasn't sure what she was going to say.

Keith's sister-in-law Savitri opened the door. "Hello."

Marva hesitated. "Hello, I'm Marva, June's sister."

The woman who seemed not much older than Marva smiled, showing nice, even teeth. "I remember you. Come in."

Marva hesitated. "Is … are Keith's parents in?"

"Yes, but Keith is not here."

Marva sent up a quick prayer of thanks as she entered the spacious living-room. The aroma of curry floated out to her nostrils. They were cooking dinner. Maybe she should come back another time. While she hesitated, Keith's mother came in. "Hello, Marva." She extended her hand, and Marva shook it. "How you doing, girl? Take a seat, *nuh*."

Marva sank into the overstuffed chair. "Fine. Fine, thank you, Mrs. Bishop."

The woman took the chair opposite. "You came by yourself? Where's June?"

"Yes. I … I was just passing and saw your house."

"Would you like something to drink? Orange juice, or *mauby*?"

"Mauby, please." Maybe when the woman went to get it she could slip away. But Mrs. Bishop called, "Savitri, bring a glass of mauby for Marva."

Marva sat back, hugging her knees with her hands. She fixed her eyes on a landscape painting on the wall opposite.

The woman caught her gaze. "We bought that in Chaguanas. There's a little store not far from the market. They sell nice things for your house. That is where we buy everything– sheets, bedspreads, everything. Come, let me show you the rest of the house."

Marva rose obediently. The woman seemed much more self-assured in her husband's absence and almost as talkative. On their way to one of the bedrooms, Savitri met them with the frothy, dark-colored drink. Marva thanked her and took a sip. It was good and just what she needed on a hot day like this. She said as much to Mrs. Bishop.

"Yes, I like the way Savitri makes it. She's a good girl."

"Does she work?"

Mrs. Bishop gave her a shocked glance. "No. My son wouldn't let her work. He's old-fashioned like my husband. He believes a woman should stay home and look after her family." Then she added, "I know June is an independent-minded girl. Keith always says that. If they get married … I don't know."

Marva stopped short. "Would you like her to marry Keith?"

The woman placed her hand on her chest. "I love June as if she was my own daughter. She's so pretty and so polite. Just the other day when we were in Tobago, my husband and I were saying —"

She stopped and pointed to a vase on the dresser. "We bought that in Chaguanas too."

Marva looked at the ornate decoration on the vase, which was not at all to her liking. In fact, she disliked most of what she'd seen so far and knew June would too. But she wondered what Mrs. Bishop and her husband had discussed in Tobago. She was sure they would be happy to have June marry their son, though she wouldn't be one to stay at home like Savitri. But Marva was desperate. She had to know that June would be well cared for when she left.

They'd reached the dining-room now and Mrs. Bishop was talking about the chandelier.

"Did you buy that in Chaguanas too?"

"No. We went to Port-of-Spain for this one. Steven wanted something really nice for over the table. He likes to entertain, you know. When his boss and his wife came for dinner and they saw that, the woman told her husband, 'you have to get one like that for me.'" She ended in a burst of laughter.

Marva joined in politely. The chandelier was the only thing worthy of admiration that she'd seen so far.

"Come and see the kitchen."

They entered the large kitchen where Savitri and another woman, maybe the maid, were busy stirring pots. Tiled floors and countertops, pots and pans, sink and stove top all gleamed. Marva could not see a spot anywhere. How many hours of work did it take to keep a large kitchen spotless? She placed her now empty glass on the table, and Savitri immediately picked it up.

Marva turned to Mrs. Bishop. "Thanks for the mauby, Mrs. Bishop. I have to be going."

"You sure you don't want to stay for dinner? Look, we're almost done."

Marva shook her head. "I have to be going. June will be wondering where I am."

"Well, take some of the food with you."

Before she could reply, Mrs. Bishop turned to the other lady. "Kay, put some food in a container for Marva to take home."

Marva almost opened her mouth to refuse, but that would be bad manners. She took the container wrapped in a plastic bag from the lady. How would she explain it to June?

Mrs. Bishop walked her to the door a few minutes later just as Keith came up the driveway, dribbling a basketball. He greeted her politely, but avoided her gaze. Marva walked to the end of the street where she caught a taxi. In the car, she closed her eyes. *Lord, I can't do it. I can't put my sister through that. Show me another way.*

She alighted from the taxi at the corner of Rosewood Lane and began walking toward her house. Her zebra-colored friend came trotting toward her, wagging his tail. He sniffed at the plastic bag, and Marva smiled. "I've something for you, boy."

She removed the container from the bag, opened it and placed it near the edge of the grass. The brindle pounced on it immediately, then he turned back for one second to look at her as if to say, "Thank you."

Marva smiled again and continued on her way.

As Marva was leaving for work a few days later, June emerged from the bedroom wearing a short, slim-fitting skirt, matching jacket and black pumps.

"Where are you going all dressed up?"

June reached for her key on the nail near the door. "To look for a job."

"What happened to the chicken job?"

June stepped in front of her. "I don't work there anymore. I'm going to pick up my last paycheck today, and he better have it ready."

She was obviously in an irritable mood, and Marva didn't want to ask too many questions. She followed her out the door and closed it behind them. As they walked to the bus stop, she asked, "Did you leave because of Keith?"

June paused in her steps. "That's the main reason, but I want something a little less … greasy," she ended with a laugh.

"So, no more free chicken."

"It's not good for us. I'm getting pimples."

Marva glanced at her sister's flawless complexion. "You don't have pimples. You had one and it went away without a trace."

They reached the corner just as the bus approached. There were three other people waiting, and Marva fell silent until they boarded.

After they were seated, she asked, "What kind of job you have in mind?"

June furrowed her brow. "I'm going to try all the insurance companies - Barbados Mutual, Colonial, as many as I can do in one day. I think they hire students during the holidays to file and do other things."

"What if they don't hire you?"

"Then I'll go to the stores."

Marva stifled her sigh and looked out the window.

That afternoon June wore a triumphant grin. "You're looking at the new office assistant at Colonial Life Insurance Company."

Marva could not stop the flood of admiration. "You serious?"

June nodded. "I simply walked up to the receptionist, told her I was looking for a job, she sent me to the personnel manager, and he hired me."

"Just like that?"

June snapped her fingers. "Just like that. The only qualification I have is that I can type forty words a minute."

And beauty. "Is the manager a man or woman?"

"A man."

"How old?"

"He didn't show me his birth certificate. Sister, I know what you're getting at, but this is a reputable company and they hired another temporary girl from Convent. I'll be working in the office with her and two other girls. So, stop worrying."

Marva rose and went into the kitchen. She wished she could take June's advice, but there were too many men like Carlton out there. And June didn't have a rim.

The next day Marva had another reason to worry. The phone rang while she was preparing dinner, and June went to answer it. A few moments later, her raised voice came through to the kitchen. Marva strained to listen. Punctured words and phrases reached her ears. "... must be crazy ... never ... marriage ... don't believe it."

Marva busied herself cutting up the chicken when June stormed into the kitchen.

"Sister, I can't believe you did that. How could you?"

Marva looked at June's reddened face and quickly turned back to the chicken. "Do what?"

"How could you go and talk to Keith's mother about me and Keith getting married?"

Marva paused with the knife upraised. "What did Keith say?"

"He asked me when the wedding is. He sounded like he was grinning from ear to ear."

Marva smothered a smile. "I didn't say anything about a wedding."

"But did you mention me and Keith getting married?"

June was standing closer to her now, and Marva could feel her bristling with anger. She kept her gaze on the chicken pieces. "I … his mother said how much she and her family love you."

"But Sister, you had no right to even go to those people's house. What made you do that? I told you what Keith said to me, and that we broke up. Why did you have to interfere?"

Marva raised her eyes to June's face. "You looked so sad. I thought —"

"You could bring us back together? If we have to get back together, it will be our business. Not yours!"

She stomped out of the kitchen, and the front door slammed. Marva went back to cutting the chicken, paying little attention to what she was doing, until she felt a burning pain and saw the blood dripping on to the meat. She dropped the knife and held her finger under the water until the bleeding ceased. When June returned sometime later, Marva was seated on the couch eating a cheese sandwich. June went past her without a word, and Marva heard her rustling in the kitchen.

They didn't speak to each other that night and for days following.

CHAPTER EIGHTEEN

Showered and in her nightie, June had just curled up on the bed with a book when the phone rang. Could it be Keith? *Let Sister answer it. She'd be happy to hear his voice.*

Marva called out, "Junie, it's for you."

Yep, it was Keith.

She took the receiver from her sister's hand. "Hello?"

"June, how you doing, girl?"

Her face widened in a smile. "Sandra, is that you?"

"None other. How are you?"

"Great. Where are you calling from?"

"Right here in San Fernando. We're moving back."

June gave a little shout. Sandra was the first friend she'd made at Polytechnic Institute and their friendship had continued until Sandra moved to Port-of-Spain when her father was transferred. And now she was back. God was good.

The following day, they met at Woolworth as pre-arranged. They sat at the counter enjoying soft-serve ice-cream and updated each other on what had been going on in their lives while they'd been apart. Sandra had not liked the school she'd attended as much as she did Polytechnic, but she'd liked the bright lights of Port-of-Spain.

"San Fernando is nothing compared to Port-of-Spain. There's always something going on. Me and Arlene, my sister, used to go out every weekend. And the clothes? I bought this outfit in the mall on Frederick Street. Girl, we must go to Town to shop one of these days."

Sandra's purple and white dress was made of batik fabric and featured a ruffled blouse and elasticized waist. It looked cool and expensive.

"This is very pretty. How much did it cost?"

The price was much lower than June had imagined. It would certainly cost more in the South.

June licked the side of her cone, still eyeing the dress. "Did you meet anybody?"

Sandra made a face. "Yeah, but the boys are like the city – fast." She gave a little laugh. "They are never satisfied with one girl. I dumped one as soon as I realized what he was like."

Then she turned to June. "I guess you and Keith still going strong."

It was more a question than a statement and June took another slurp of her ice-cream before replying. "I'm not sure."

Sandra trained wide, curious eyes on her. "What you mean you're not sure? You used to say, 'there's no one in the world like Keith.'"

June swallowed against the lump in her throat. "That's true. But people grow up, and they grow apart."

Sandra seemed lost in thought for a second. "I'm sorry to hear that. Are you seeing anyone else?"

"Not yet."

Their ice-cream finished, they left the store and wandered on to High Street, window-shopping and chatting and the subject of Keith never came up again.

Two weeks had passed since their return from Tobago, and Marva still had not heard from Jason. She was almost tempted to go to her old hometown Egypt Village to see him, but she didn't want to risk running into Joanna. As she came in from work one evening, the phone rang.

She rushed to pick it up. "Hello?"

"Hello, Moe."

Her heart raced. "I was just thinking about you."

"Good or bad?"

"Bad. You didn't call, and I don't have your number."

"Things have been hectic at work. Two men on sick leave, and orders coming in right and left."

"It was like that by us too, just before we went to Tobago."

"Speaking of Tobago, how was your flight?"

"Late, because of the rain, but thank God it was short. We went up in the cotton candy and came back down."

He chuckled. "Yeah, it's only twenty minutes. Mine was delayed too."

They chatted some more about Tobago and then came a pause. Marva wondered if he was going to ask her out, but when he spoke, she detected a note of worry in his voice.

"Moe, you remember Joanna?"

Marva tensed, but tried to remain flippant. "Your girlfriend?"

He didn't correct her. "She … she told me she might be pregnant."

Marva was sure she stopped breathing.

"Moe?"

Her breath returned. "Yes."

"I don't know what to do."

Suddenly she was in control again. "Marry the girl."

"What?"

"You heard me. Marry Joanna!"

She slammed the receiver down and headed for the bedroom. She hadn't got very far when the phone rang again.

She ran back and snatched it up. "Don't call this house again, Jason Smart!"

Fighting back the tears, Marva flung herself on the bed, grateful June wasn't home. How could he do that to her? Why had he come to Tobago, taken her out and treated her so nicely? The sweet memories of the day they spent together turned to ashes in her mouth. Now she understood why he'd seemed so … careful, so distant when they were alone on the beach that evening. And then that kiss, as brief and gentle as a butterfly's wings. Now she understood.

The opening of the front door made her jump up and rush to the bathroom. She didn't want June to see her crying. She let the water wash away her tears, hoping it could wash away the pain, the disappointment. But what did she expect? She shouldn't be upset with him. He deserved someone who would make him happy. She couldn't make him, or any other man, happy. Only God could be her husband. He'd told her that before. And she was going to meet Him. Soon.

June had just reached the part in her novel where the cops were about to close in on the bad guy, when the phone rang. Sighing, she placed the book face down on the couch and went to answer it.

"Hello?"

"I miss you, Catty."

"Keith?"

"I don't have nobody to run with, nobody to play with, nobody …"

She burst out laughing, all thoughts of the cops and the bad guy forgotten. "You sound pathetic."

"I am. I miss you."

She was still laughing. "I'll come and play with you. Only if you promise to be good."

"I'll be there in half an hour."

He hadn't said where they would go, but it was a bit cloudy, not hot, and she hadn't run in a long time. Maybe they could run around the block, cool off under the mango tree in that empty lot on the street that ran parallel to theirs, and maybe later … She'd never stopped missing him. She didn't know about cars the way her sister did, but she guessed the way she felt was like someone driving on a spare tire, just inching along until they could get the damaged one fixed. Or get a new one.

While her thoughts ran, she changed from her blouse and skirt into her shorts then fumbled in her drawer for a tee shirt.

The door opened and Marva walked in. "Going somewhere?"

She found the white tee shirt with the steelpan logo on it and slipped her arms into it. "I was just going for a run."

June hesitated. This cold war between her and her sister had gone on for too long. Maybe Marva wanted to speak to her about something, but June didn't want to miss out on being with Keith. She dug her feet into her sneakers, tied the laces and hurried out of the apartment without a backward glance. Once outside, she looked both ways. She expected either Keith's brother or father to drop him off, and she didn't want Marva to know she was seeing him again. Not yet.

A slight drizzle was coming down when Mr. Bishop's gleaming white Toyota pulled up beside her. She waved at him and averted her head so he wouldn't get into a long conversation with her. Keith got out of the car and came toward her. June fastened her gaze on his face, barely mindful of the car pulling off.

Keith grinned, his eyes crinkling at the corners the way she loved. "Ready? Let's go before this rain comes down."

They took off at a slow trot, not saying anything to each other, because nothing needed to be said. When they neared the end of Rosewood Lane, he asked, "Right?"

June nodded, and they veered right. The drizzle stopped, and they picked up their speed, passing the little parlor where they usually bought their soft drinks and *amchar*. Then on past a couple businesses, houses, an empty pan yard and a vacant lot with a broken chain link fence. A side street ran at right angles to this lot, and they took it back into Rosewood Lane.

June felt her breath coming in gasps. She could tell from the way Keith ran he was still in excellent shape from playing soccer. She slowed her pace, and he immediately did the same.

"Let's stop over there." He pointed to a small grassy knoll in front of a two-story house set way back from the road. They jogged toward it, but before climbing on to it, June placed her hands on her knees and took big puffs of air, feeling her wind returning. Keith was already half way up the little hill. She followed slowly, then plopped down, not caring that the grass was damp.

Keith pulled her up. "See what happens when you don't come out and play? Get up and stretch. You don't want your muscles to tighten up."

Obediently she stood and did as he instructed. After a few minutes, she sat back down. "I feel better now."

"Don't wait too long before you run again."

"It's no fun without you." The words were out before she even thought about them.

"It's no fun without you either, Catty."

She studied his face, stained with sweat marks running down his cheeks to his neck, glistening with sweat. She wanted to touch him, but it was too soon. His gaze flickered over her face and down to her damp shirt that clung to her breasts.

She was the first to look away. "I have a new job."

"Where?"

She told him, and he gave her a look of admiration. "I'm sure they had no trouble hiring you." He paused. "Do you still plan on going back to school?"

She stared into the distance. "Yes."

It began to drizzle again, and they scrambled to their feet. Her house was an easy walk half a block away.

She glanced at him. "How are you getting home?"

"I'll catch the bus."

When they got to her house, she paused. "I can't invite you in."

He nodded understanding. "I'll call you."

He trotted away, and June watched him for a moment before going inside. She was happy to see him, but why did she get the feeling that things would never be the same between them?

When Marva came home from work the next afternoon, June greeted her with her first smile in weeks. "Miss Stewart went in to the hospital."

Excitement surged through Marva, but was quickly replaced by a stab of fear. Would Miss Stewart be all right? Would the babies live? Would everything go well?

She gave a feeble smile. "I hope she's okay."

In the bedroom, she fell on her knees, but words failed her. All she could manage was, "Please, Lord, let her be all right. And the babies …"

June knelt beside her and took her hand. They didn't speak, but Marva felt the silent cry of their hearts go up to God. Eventually, they rose and glanced at each other, then looked away. She knew June felt as ashamed as she did for the way they'd behaved toward each other. She'd prayed that God would soften June's heart toward her and help her understand she only wanted what was best for her. But Marva couldn't explain why she was so eager for June and Keith to get back together, so how could she expect June to understand?

June broke the silence. "Should we go to the hospital?"

"We won't be able to see her now. Better to wait until she comes home."

"That's too long. What if they keep her for a week?"

That was possible. "Okay, we'll ask Miss Sheila when is a good time to see her."

When the phone rang, Marva's heart raced at the sound of Miss Sheila's voice. "Marva, I need a favor. Are you and June doing anything tonight?"

"No, Miss Sheila, what is it?"

"David wants to surprise my sister by having the nursery set up for when she gets home, but we need a little help …"

Marva's worry evaporated. "We'd love to come. What time?"

"In about half an hour?"

"That's good."

She and June were waiting outside the apartment when Miss Sheila arrived with her daughters. When they got to the house, Miss Lucy told them Mr. Bowen was at the hospital. Marva relaxed and focused on the preparations. The painters had done a wonderful job painting white clouds on the pale blue ceiling, and now it formed the perfect canopy for the Winnie the Pooh borders. Matching curtains, crib sheets and lampshade coordinated the decor.

It was almost eleven when they stopped and viewed their handiwork. Afterward, while they feasted on Miss Lucy's fried fish, homemade bread and orange juice, Marva sent up a silent prayer. *Please, Lord, let everything be all right.* The next morning, her prayer turned to praise and thanksgiving when Miss Sheila called to say that the babies were here, and they and their mother were doing fine.

Only one milestone remained before she could take her departure.

CHAPTER NINETEEN

David stretched and patted the space next to him. Hard. And cold. Pale beige walls. Where was he? A couple and another man sat on a long bench opposite. The hospital! He checked his watch. Four-fifty. Cicely? How long had he been asleep? Recollection came to him and he jumped up. A nurse in starched, white uniform, a little cap on her head stood before him. "Are you Mr. Bowen?"

"Yes." *Lord, her face was so serious.* "Is my wife …?"

"Would you like to come and see your babies?"

"Yes, yes." *Why didn't she smile?* "How is my wife?"

"She's fine."

A rush of air escaped from his lungs, and the tears prickled behind his eyes. What would he have done if anything had happened to her? He pushed the thought away and quickened his steps to match the nurse's. They went into the elevator, then down a quiet hallway and came to stand before a room enclosed with glass. A couple stood a little distance away, arms around each other, peering through the glass.

The nurse pointed to two little babies in bassinets on the other side of the room. "There they are."

The babies' eyes were closed and they lay still under a bright yellow light. David glanced back at the nurse. "Are they okay?"

"They are fine. The boy took a little longer to breathe, but he's all right."

"The boy?" He'd forgotten to ask. "You mean …"

The nurse smiled for the first time. "A boy and a girl. A perfect pair."

The tension of the last hours drained from his body, and he felt like dancing. He plied the nurse with questions as they left the nursery. What time were they born? How much did they weigh? Why didn't she call him sooner? Were they going to see his wife now? Was she in a lot of pain?

The nurse laughed as they stepped out of the elevator. "You have a lot of questions. The first one was born at 4. 15 and the second about seven minutes later. Don't ask me which one came first. I don't remember. And you can ask your wife about the pain."

Four-fifteen. He'd taken Cicely to the hospital around noon the day before. Poor darling. They paused in a corridor outside the maternity ward and the nurse became all serious again. She pushed the door open. "Wait here."

She went in and said something to her colleague at the desk, then beckoned to David to come in. "She's over there in the bed by the wall. You can stay for just two minutes, but you have to be quiet."

The dimly - lit room contained three other beds and the occupants all seemed to be asleep. David tiptoed over to his sleeping wife. Gently, he kissed her cheek. Cicely stirred and opened her eyes. Her gaze rested on his face for a moment, then she closed her eyes once more.

"I'll come back a little later," he whispered. "I love you." He kissed her again, but she was already asleep.

A shadow filled the doorway of Glen's office. Expecting to see a customer, Marva looked up with a smile from the bills she was filing.

Carlton stood there. "Well, well. You're the big boss in charge today. When's Glen coming back?"

She felt the scowl darken her features. She still couldn't help thinking the world would be a better place without Carlton McDonald, but she wouldn't let him see how much he rattled her.

"This afternoon."

She stapled an invoice on to a letter, then picked up another one from the stack on the desk. Until he said what he wanted, he could just stand there.

He eventually seemed to get the message. "I need an alternator for the black Mazda."

"Which black Mazda? We have more than one in the yard, and you have to bring the old part so I can order it. You know the rules."

"All right, Miss Boss Lady. Why you showing so much interest? Something going on between you and the boss?"

Marva squeezed the stapler so hard she thought she would break it. "Take your filthy mind out of here and send me the part. Don't bother to come back."

He backed away, hands raised. "All right, all right. A man can't make a joke around here."

Minutes later, the young apprentice brought the old alternator and all the information written on a piece of paper.

Marva nodded to a table in the corner. "Put it over there."

She sighed as the boy turned away. Her day had started off well, but one stupid incident – person - had spoiled it. The phone rang and she snatched it up. "Hello?"

"What, no Glen's Automotive, Miss Garcia speaking, how may I help you?"

Her mood changed immediately and she laughed, then sobered. She was not going to be pleasant with him. She'd told him not to call.

"I knew it was you. Didn't I tell you not to call?"

"Your house. This is not your house."

"All right, don't call me at work either."

"Moe, don't be like that. This is me, Jay, remember?"

Marva wilted at the plaintive note in his voice. "All right, Jay. So, what do you want?" She almost bit her tongue after she said the words. She hoped he wouldn't ask for a date.

"I just want to know that you're not mad at me."

She exhaled with relief, and a little regret. "I'm not mad at you, Jay. I could never be, but I don't want to see you again."

"What?"

"It's for the best. I have my life, and you have yours. Bye, Jay."

She hung up before he could hear the tears in her voice. She went into the bathroom and allowed herself a brief moment of crying, then splashed cold water over her face and returned to her desk.

~

The click of the phone sounded like a death knell in Jason's ear. Slowly he replaced the receiver. He couldn't believe Marva was really shutting him out of her life. But he deserved it. Maybe he shouldn't have told her about Joanna, who was not pregnant as she'd led him to believe. When he told her he would take care of the baby but wasn't ready to get married, she'd recanted her story. He could no longer trust her, and their relationship had cooled. He'd made a mess of things. Marva was the girl he really cared for. The one he would marry if he only had a penny to his name – if she would have him.

According to the words of the song, he'd been loving her so long, he couldn't stop now. He believed she cared for him too. He'd seen the joy and expectation on her face when he surprised her that night in Tobago. And the day they spent together had been magical. How could she turn her back on him?

A hand clamped down on his shoulder, jerking him out of his reverie. "Ay, boy, she must be really good to have you daydreaming like that."

With a shock, Jason saw by the clock that his lunch break had expired ten minutes ago. He left his chair and followed the man into the stock room. While they worked on the inventory of new tires, Jason told the man a little about his predicament with the two women. Thomas was older and happily married with two children. "Boy, you could never understand women, so don't even try. If she wouldn't talk to you, just give 'er time, let her cool off. Don't worry."

Thomas's advice sounded worthwhile.

Marva got off the bus at the corner of her street and trudged home, an ocean of thoughts roaring through her mind: Carlton's inference, Jason's call, her desire to go and be with the Lord. The tiger dog, who seemed always on the lookout for her, bounded toward her from a nearby house.

Marva patted his head briefly. "I have nothing for you today, boy."

But, faithful friend that he was, he followed her almost to her apartment. She had no classes today and no plans for the evening, except sit in front of the television, or read her Bible. She would choose the latter. June could have the TV – if she was home.

As she opened the door, June jumped up from a chair and came toward her, waving a paper. "Sister, look at this! Look!"

Marva stared at her in surprise. Since the night they decorated the nursery together, June had withdrawn again, although not as much as before. Marva guessed she was still hurting over her break-up with Keith, but a new thought had recently surfaced. Did June secretly resent her for killing their father? However, today she seemed really happy. Marva took the paper from her hand, glanced at it and forgot all her problems. "Wow! You did it! Five distinctions and two credits."

She threw her arm around her sister's neck. June returned her hug, then disengaged herself. "I can't believe I got a distinction in math and biology."

Marva was still smiling. "I'm so proud of you, Junie. Now you're definitely going to St. Thomas Aquinas."

"And I have only two weeks to prepare. Sister, I'm so happy!"

Marva gazed at her eyes, now bright gold with tiny green flecks, her cheeks flushed. What a beautiful girl she was. "Let's go over to Miss Stewart and show her your results."

"That's a great idea. I stopped by the chicken place to pick up my last paycheck and Mr. R gave me a box of chicken. I guess business must be slow." Her laughter pealed out.

Marva joined in as she turned toward the bedroom. She dropped her bag on the floor near the bed and threw her arms in the air. "Thank you, Jesus! What a great God you are! Thank you for helping Junie pass her exams. Now I can come to you in peace."

The final milestone had been reached.

Marva paused before entering the Bowen's home. Did Miss Stewart really like her, or was she just taking pity on an orphan girl? Surely the detective would have voiced his suspicion about her to his wife. But she had no doubt that Miss Stewart genuinely loved June and was proud of her success. Even though Marva smiled and said all the right things, she felt a tinge of envy when Miss Stewart drew June to her bosom and said, "You're headed for big things, my dear."

Afterward, Marva shook off the thoughts and immersed herself in the babies. They didn't know her and couldn't judge her. Their scent, the softness of their bodies, even their crying delighted her. She cradled little Junior in her arms, rocking him and singing softly to him, reluctant to put him down. June, seated next to her with little Chrissie seemed equally absorbed. When Miss Stewart came to nurse Junior, Marva said, "Can you take Chrissie first? I don't want to put him down."

"I don't want to put Chrissie down either," June said, but she willingly handed her over.

Miss Stewart laughed. "I never thought you two would be so fond of babies."

Marva kept her gaze on the baby's pink, little face. "They're so cute. And I love the way they smell."

"Well, take as much time as you like, because when you leave, they're going straight to bed."

As Marva stared at the baby's little dark eyes staring back at her, an ache filled her tummy. How old would her baby be now if it had lived? She thought back. Six years. Was it a boy or girl? She never knew. But she would know soon. When she got to heaven. No one should have her baby dug out of her like that. Even if it was her father's.

Marva and June were walking along the beach in the afternoon. Suddenly, a mist descended, and in the mist, she saw a figure coming toward them. As it drew closer, Marva saw that it was shrouded in white. Gaze riveted on the approaching apparition, she kept moving as if on auto pilot, her footsteps barely touching the sand. The figure drew nearer and now she could recognize the features. *Mama!* Her hair, long and curly like Junie's, was parted down the middle, and fell over the front of her right shoulder; a soft flush bathed her cheeks and her smile was gentle. She seemed young, not like the shriveled-up old lady she'd become just before she died. When she got to about four feet in front of Marva, she stopped and stretched both arms toward her. Without hesitating, Marva quickened her steps —

She awoke from her dream smiling, but her smile turned to a frown. The dream had seemed so real. She'd seen Mama. How beautiful she looked. And she wanted Marva to come to her. Marva eased herself out of the bed so as not to wake June. In the dark she fumbled and found her knapsack. She tiptoed into the kitchen and put on the light. She was certain now what she must do. Mama had confirmed it. She brushed a tear from her cheek and pulled out her notebook. She hadn't written in it in a long time.

She began, Dear June,

Tonight, I dreamed of Mama …

The following day she paid a visit to TL. He was in his usual spot, distributing his flyers with the speed of an engine in overdrive. He seemed to spot her the minute she alighted from the taxi. She ran up to him and took some flyers from his hand.

"What? No tracts today, Miss CL?"

"No, I don't have any. I'll pick up some on Sunday."

Then she hurried down the hill to her corner. She would give out tracts once more before she left. It didn't matter whether June found out. She wouldn't be around much longer to listen to her scolding. It didn't take her long to give out her flyers, and when she went back to get more from TL, he was packing up.

"Yeah, Miss CL, ah leavin' early today. Ah have to go an' help my ol' lady. She's not doin' too well these days."

"I'm sorry to hear that, TL. Is there anything I can do?"

He looked up from placing flyers in his bag. "Jus' pray for her. An' for me too."

Marva placed a hand on his arm. "I will. Have time for a Pepsi?"

He grinned. "I'm really thirsty today."

While they sat in the little snackette, she told him all about the twins, her work, and about June passing her exams.

He gave her a look almost of envy. "You have a really nice life."

Marva was taken aback. *She* had a nice life? If he only knew. "Things are not all that nice. I have to take care of my sister. We have no parents, and I," she looked down at the floor. "I don't have a lot of friends. June is the one with all the friends —"

"Yes, but look at me. I don' have no real job, an' I have to take care of a sick mother and sister. If anything happened to me, I don't know what would become of them."

Marva looked back up at his face, noting the creases in his forehead, the tightness of his lips, the sweat on his cheeks. Life was difficult for him, but he didn't carry her guilt. He'd never killed anybody. He didn't have to lie and pretend to be a good person. No matter how difficult his life, it was far better than hers. She opened her purse and took out the two twenty-dollar bills and held them out to him.

He stared at her. "What is this, Miss CL? I can't take your money."

"I'll never speak to you again if you don't take it. You have to buy medicine and food and other things. Take it."

Slowly he stretched out his hand and took the money. "Thanks, Miss CL. Nex' week I'll start working at a car wash. I'll pay you back."

Marva leaned forward. "TL, I don't want you to pay me back. The money is a gift – for your birthday."

"How you know when my birthday is?"

She chuckled. "I don't, but whenever it is, remember I already gave you your gift."

He laughed. "You're a smart chick, you know that?"

Marva sobered. "Besides, I might not be here. When is your birthday?"

"December. I'm a Christmas boy."

It was her turn to stare. "Really? Mine's Boxing Day. But I won't be here."

"Going back to Tobago? I know, you got a boyfriend in Tobago, eh?"

She shook her head and rose. "Where I'm going is much nicer than Tobago."

CHAPTER TWENTY

June closed the filing cabinet and turned around when a voice behind her said, "Good-morning, gorgeous."

Her eyes widened. John Baptiste, one of her former classmates, stood there, a broad smile on his face. June looked him up and down, taking in his neatly-pressed gray pants, striped shirt and matching tie.

She placed a hand on her hips. "Well, well. Good-morning yourself, handsome. What are you doing here?"

"Someone told me you work here, and I should come keep an eye on you."

She chuckled. "Well, you'll have to have a lot of eyes, because I'm all over the place. When did you start?"

"Right after exams, but I was at the Chaguanas branch. It was either I went there or wait until they had a vacancy for me here."

June turned back to the filing cabinet as her boss Mrs. Gordon entered. She wasn't harsh, like Mr. R, but June didn't want to do anything to displease her. Back to John, she said, "That's my boss. What time you go for lunch?"

He glanced at his watch. "In about twenty minutes."

"Wait for me outside if you don't see me."

Small world. She walked over to Mrs. Gordon to inquire if she needed her for anything else.

"Yes." The woman looked at her watch. "We're having a seminar in the conference room in half an hour. Take a quick lunch now and be back here by five after twelve to help set up the room."

June's jaw dropped, but she quickly replied, "Yes, ma'am."

Taking her purse from the desk in the little cubicle where she sat, she hurried toward the elevator. She had to be back here around the time she was supposed to meet John. What awful luck. He would think she stood him up.

June worried all afternoon what John must be thinking of her. He and Wendy dated before she ditched him for the car salesman. June could never understand what they had in common. He was quiet and studious, she, wild and not the least interested in studying. But June supposed they exemplified the saying, opposites attract. Now Wendy had moved to the States, and John was here all alone. Or, was he? She was curious to find out.

When she left work just after three, he was waiting on the sidewalk in front of the office building.

"I'm so sorry …" she began.

"I'm the one who's sorry," he cut her off. "My boss picked today to send me to deliver some papers to Chaguanas."

She stared at him, then burst out laughing.

"What?"

When she explained how her lunch break turned out, it was his turn to laugh. "I guess it wasn't meant to be."

They strolled along the sidewalk, now becoming jammed with the afternoon traffic. He seemed oblivious to the appreciative glances the girls stole in his direction, and she wondered why she'd never noticed before how attractive he was. The answer popped into her mind. Keith. He eclipsed every boy in school, but today she saw John in a new light. He was a little shorter than Keith, but his shoulders were broader, and his biceps bulged beneath his long-sleeved shirt. He was attractive without being showy; reserved, yet interesting.

Before they parted at the top of High Street, he gave her his extension. "Call me tomorrow if you have time for lunch."

She smiled. "I will."

One week passed before they were able to have lunch together. They met at Jenny's, a crowded lunch counter on High Street, which was just that—a long, L- shaped counter where patrons sat on stools with their backs to the road. As soon as a seat became vacant, someone filled it. Jenny's served the most delicious spaghetti and meat balls June had ever tasted.

Through her casual conversation with John, she gleaned he'd not heard from Wendy, and no more mention was made of her. When they walked home after work, he asked just as casually, "So how are things with you and Keith?"

She thought about her answer before opening her mouth. "We still like each other very much."

He laughed. "That's not what I expected you to say."

He was right. Whenever any boy asked her for a date, she'd always said, "You know Keith Bishop? You'll have to speak to him."

That usually put an end to the matter, but her response now was a subtle way of letting him know he may have a chance. When they got to the place where they usually separated, he turned to her. "Keith is my friend. I don't want to do anything to spoil our friendship. Mind if I speak to him?"

June cocked her head sideways. "About what?"

"I want to take you to the BBB concert."

June squealed, and a man walking in front of them turned and looked at her. "They are the best."

John smiled at her excitement. "I saw them perform once in Port-of-Spain. Hearing them on the radio or seeing them on TV is nothing like watching them on stage."

June cupped her hands. "I can only imagine. I want to go. I love the way they dress."

The BBBs, a singing group comprised of Belinda, the lead singer, and her three brothers, the Bad Boys, had gained a large following among the young people because of their ragamuffin outfits and their scintillating performances. To have them come to San Fernando and not go to see them would be a sacrilege.

"I'll talk to Keith."

She lowered her eyes from John's intense gaze. "Okay."

"See you tomorrow."

June watched him stride in the direction of Coffee Street before crossing over to the Promenade. With every step she took, her excitement over John's invitation gave way to growing apprehension. What if Keith invited her to the concert? This was an event that every boy would take his girlfriend to. How could she tell him she wanted to go to the concert with John?

~

June jumped and replaced the receiver when her sister entered then gave her a broad smile. "Hi, Sis, how was your day? You're home early."

"Yes. We were slow today. What you so happy about?"

Did she look happy? She didn't want Sister to guess what she was up to. "I … I'm excited about starting my new school next week."

"You have everything ready?"

"Yep. I'm picking up my uniforms tomorrow when I finish shopping for my books."

"Good."

As Marva turned toward the bedroom door, June called after her. "What are you doing later, Sister?"

"Nothing, why?"

"Er, nothing. I just hate to see you home night after night."

Marva paused. "You're right. There's a young women's group that meets at church every Thursday. They've been asking me to join. Want to come with me?"

"No. I mean, I don't want to start something I wouldn't be able to keep up with. From next week I'll be very busy."

Marva moved away without a word, and June eyed the phone. Hopefully, Sister would go to that meeting and she would get a chance to call Keith. But after they'd eaten dinner, Marva began gathering up their laundry.

June tried to keep the frustration out of her voice. "You're not going to the meeting?"

Marva shook her head. "You know me. I don't like being around strangers. I'll just do the laundry tonight. I'm running out of clean tops for work."

June went into the living room, sat on the couch, and flipped on the television. What could she do? She would have liked to call Keith to see if he would mention the concert. But she hadn't made up her mind what to say to him. *Hi, Keith, I want to go out with John. No, I still love you, but I think we should see other people. We're too young to limit ourselves to each other. If you want … no, you can't go out with anyone else.* No, she could never say that to him. It was a good thing Marva came home early. She would just go with John. It was not as if she was engaged or married to Keith.

The next day, Friday, she and John were again fortunate to have lunch together at Jenny's.

He sipped on his Pepsi then placed the bottle down. "Well, today is our last day."

"Yeah, I'm going to miss these meatballs."

She felt his gaze on her as she stuck her fork in her mouth.

"Is that all you'll miss?"

She kept her head straight. "And this job. It was way better than the chicken place."

He rose from his stool. "I think we should be getting back."

While they waited to cross the street, she asked, "Did you speak to Keith?"

"No. I tried but I couldn't reach him. He must be real busy." He glanced at her. "So, what are we going to do?"

A car stopped for them to cross, and she waited until they got to the other side. "We're going to the concert. I'm not married to Keith, and he doesn't have to know."

John frowned. "You're not married, but you two were so tight in school, air couldn't get between you. And I'm bigger than air."

Smiling, she checked her watch. Five minutes before she had to be at her desk. She faced John, noting his neat attire, his smooth chocolate complexion, neat sideburns and mustache, firm jaw. Suddenly, she realized how much she'd missed out on for the three years she and Keith had been together. They'd spoken on the phone once since that day they ran together. He'd said he was busy with work and soccer, and she'd accepted that. Well, she would no longer wait around for him to call.

"You're not getting between us, John. Things haven't been the same with us for a while. I don't think he'd mind."

"Are you sure?"

"I'm sure."

As she slid behind her desk, she wondered how come Keith hadn't invited her.

June selected her outfit with care. Short, pleated denim skirt, bright pink tee shirt and short denim jacket. Navy blue knee-high stockings, black canvas shoes, and the black purse Marva had bought her for her birthday made up her ensemble. She completed the look with brightly colored bangles and large hoop earrings. She'd gone to the hairdresser that morning and had her hair washed and curled under with a curling iron. Now it hung down her back like a shimmering, silk curtain. At the front, it fell across the right side of her face over her eyebrow and past her ear.

Sister would be home soon and would wonder where she was going. June would just say she was going to the concert with friends. She and John had arranged to meet at the Naparima Bowl, so Sister would never know who she was going with. She may not see John again once school started. He was going back to do the CAPE too, but they would be attending different schools. She told herself it was just a summer fling, but secretly she wanted to get back at Keith for the way he'd treated her.

As she picked up her purse to leave, the door opened, and Marva walked in. Her gaze swept June from head to toe. "Where are you going dressed like that?"

She seemed amused, but June met her gaze without flinching. "I'm going to the BBB concert."

Marva turned away. "Keith picking you up?"

June inched toward the door. "No, I'm taking a taxi."

"All right, be careful. That place is going to be packed."

"Bye, Sister."

How did Sister know about the concert and that the hall would be crowded? June didn't think she paid attention to things of that sort.

Hurrying to the corner, she ran into Cynthia halfway down the block. She and June often met on their way to and from school, or while running errands. They were not friends, but today they had something in common. The girl was dressed in oversized ragamuffin pants and shirt, scarf tied around her head, dark glasses and enough costume jewelry to cover a Christmas tree. They boarded a taxi together.

By the time they got to the Bowl, a crowd already lined the uphill walkway. John was waiting for her at the bottom of the hill. She and Cynthia went separate ways. John took her hand as they threaded their way through the crowd of young people, all dressed in outfits they would never wear anywhere else. John sported a beige ragamuffin outfit, which he'd probably had tailor-made for him. It was loose-fitting, but not loose enough to disguise his muscular chest and arms. Despite his presence, boys still whistled at her and ogled, which seemed not to offend him in the least. At one point, he bent and whispered in her ear, "I'm proud to be out with the prettiest girl tonight. The way you look, I wouldn't be surprised if the BBBs call you up on stage."

June shot him a look of alarm. "I'm not going up there. Uh uh."

The brightly lit hall pulsed with kids dancing to the music of the orchestra, some smooching, while others stood around waiting for the moment when Belinda and her group would make their appearance. They had a reputation for never appearing before midnight, then they would perform for about two hours at most and leave. People complained, but they continued to flock to their concerts.

Suddenly, the lights dimmed, a spotlight was turned on the stage and the crowd began screaming. June didn't care to hear the announcement. She joined in the screaming. And there they were—three young men and one young woman, all in oversized jackets down to their knees, pants rolled up to their ankles. The boys wore black hats and dark glasses, while Belinda wore a Cher-type wig, her cheeks and lips painted blood red. For the next hour or so, June lost herself in the antics of the group. She was aware of John's arms around her waist while they danced and sang along with the music. Then came the moment she and everyone else had been waiting for - the high point of their performance. One of the brothers shouted into the microphone, "Now, boys and girls, it's nursery rhyme time."

The spotlight was turned off, lights dimmed even lower, music stopped, and the crowd held its collective breath. After this break, the group usually returned in new outfits, climbed the walls, swung from trapeze bars or even dispersed among the crowd. No one knew what to expect when the lights came back on. From one corner of the hall, people began to clap and intone, "Itsy Bitsy Spider standing on a wall, Itsy Bitsy Spider …"

An explosion of music shattered the momentary quiet, and when the spotlight came on, the BBB's had changed into jeans and tee shirts and were break dancing on the floor. Two other boys were with them. June clapped her hand over her mouth. *One of them was Keith.* For a moment, she forgot all about John. Keith was so good, his flexible body twisting in all sorts of contortions, rivaling those of the performers.

Then anger and disappointment welled up in her. How could he do this to her? Why had he not invited her to the concert? Who was he here with? She looked back at John to see his expression, but he was busy enjoying the show, unaware of her discomfort. She felt close to tears and for the rest of the performance, all she could do was long for it to be over.

When they finally left the hall, John asked her, "Did you have a good time?"

She nodded, having recovered her composure. She couldn't let him see how she'd been affected by Keith's appearance. She could never attend another BBB concert after this. All she wanted to do was go home to her nice, warm bed. Then as they neared the exit, she spotted them—Keith and Sandra. He had his arm around her shoulder, and she was sipping a coke. June held her breath and cast a swift glance at John to see if he'd noticed them. He took her hand and tried to steer her in the other direction, but she disengaged herself and headed straight over to them. "Hi, Sandra, hi, Keith."

Maybe in an effort to save the night, John clapped Keith on his shoulder. "Ay, man, that was some real good break dance tonight. I didn't know you with BBB now."

Keith's jaw had dropped at the sight of her and John together, but now he seemed to have gotten over his shock and kept his gaze on John's face. He even managed to grin. "Yeah, man. You know me."

June trained her eyes on Sandra, who was sucking life out of an empty cup. "How you doing, Sandra? Did you enjoy the show?"

Sandra kept her eyes down. "Yeah."

An uncomfortable silence ensued, and June suddenly felt drained. But she wanted to give Keith something to think about. Linking her arm in John's, she said, "Come on, John. Your mother must be waiting for us." Then she turned around and fixed Keith with her stare. "Bye, Keith – and Sandra."

CHAPTER TWENTY-ONE

Days later, June still seethed from the unexpected turn of events at the BBB concert. Her plan had backfired, and Keith would be angry with her for going out with John. But if he hadn't invited her, she would have sat at home while he was out having a good time with Sandra. If his behavior had disappointed her before, it now repulsed her. She wanted nothing more to do with him. And as for her two-timing friend, Sandra, she could have him.

June was surprised when he called. Her "Hello," was met with, "So you have a new boyfriend?"

She was floored, but only for a second. "And you have a new girlfriend?"

"Not really. But she's willing."

June felt like she'd been slapped. "What? Keith Bishop, what are you saying?"

He sighed. "Listen, Catty, you're a big girl. You know what I'm talking about. Most girls are not like you, they're moving with the times. But I respect you and love you. I'll never love anybody the way I love you." He paused. "What if we forget everything and start over?"

June couldn't believe her ears. Was he serious? After telling her he'd found a willing partner in her former best friend, he expected her to come running back to him?

But it was tempting, so tempting. She still missed him so much. But love—and respect—wouldn't be enough to sustain their relationship. He wanted a girl who was willing. John's words rang in her ears. "Air couldn't get between both of you. And I am bigger than air."

Sandra was bigger than air too.

"Thanks, Keith, but no thanks. I'll always love you, but I think it's time for us to go our separate ways."

He sighed again. "I thought you would say that. By the way, how did you do in the exams?"

"Five distinctions and two credits. What about you?"

"All distinctions."

Pride surged through her. "I didn't expect anything less. Now you really should go back to school."

"That's what my father said. He even promised to buy me a car."

For him and Sandra to drive in. "So, are you going to go back?"

"I might."

Maybe he'll go to St. Thomas too. It will be like old times.

"Catty, you there?"

"I'm sorry?"

"I said I'm sorry. Can we remain friends?"

"Sure."

His voice held a smile. "Thanks. Take care of yourself, Catty."

"You too."

The line went dead, but June held the receiver to her ear until it began to beep, then she gathered her strength and went into the bathroom.

Marva always paid close attention to Rev. Harris' sermons, but today he seemed to be preaching just to her.

His gaze pierced the congregation. "God does not call everyone to be married. Turn with me in your Bibles to 1 Corinthians Chapter 7. Paul is saying that single women can serve the Lord better than married women can."

Marva's heart skipped a beat. God had told her almost the same thing in Isaiah 54 when He said He was her Husband. He didn't want her to be married to Jason or anyone else. He wanted her for Himself.

The minister went on, "If you are a young lady who is wondering how you can best serve the Lord in your singleness, I have just the answer for you. There's an order of nuns called the Carmelite Sisters at the Corpus Christi Home for Girls. Anybody ever heard of it?"

A couple hands went up. Marva's hand flew to her mouth. She quickly removed it when she saw June's sidelong glance.

"Good. These nuns are a fine example of single women living just for the Lord. They teach and minister to young girls who have been abandoned, orphaned or are delinquents. They also do fine work in the community among the sick and so on. If anyone wants to know more about the Carmelite Sisters, come and see me in my office."

Rev. Harris continued preaching on the gift of singleness, but Marva was no longer listening. Her mind went back to that day, four years ago, when she passed near the Convent and saw a nun going into one of the buildings. Her mother, who was Catholic, had told her a convent was a place where Catholic nuns lived. Something had stirred within her that day as she viewed the peaceful surroundings and a nun walking gracefully, her gown swishing around her ankles.

Marva had long forgotten about the place and, besides, she was no longer a Catholic. But this Carmelite order was non-denominational. She could become one of them. Rev. Harris' words left her confused. She'd already begun to make plans to meet with God. What did He want her to do? What did Mama want her to do?

A gentle shake from June made her look up. People were standing to sing the closing hymn. Marva sighed and reached for the hymn book. If only she had someone to talk to. But what would she say to them? Mama was already calling to her.

Marva opened the hanging wardrobe and groped in the back near the floor. Her hand felt the smooth, plastic bag and pulled it out. She undid the ribbon that tied the top. A white dress was plainly visible among the assortment of clothes she and June no longer wore. She'd been planning to drop them off at the homeless shelter. She pulled out the white dress she'd worn following her baptism. She'd never used it since. It had a high neck with a collar, long sleeves and a belted waist. The skirt was slightly flared. It was perfect.

She retied the bag and stood it in a corner. She would drop it off in the morning on her way to work. She gathered up her and June's laundry and took it and the dress out to the little shed in the back. By the time June came home from her piano lessons, Marva had finished preparing dinner and was folding the clean laundry. The white dress had already been carefully folded and placed in her drawer.

That weekend Marva paid a visit to Tantie Beulah. She was pleased to see the repairs that had been done to the house. It sported a new roof, concrete steps and wooden flooring on the verandah. Tantie Beulah took her through the house and showed her other little improvements she'd made. The broken louvers had been changed, a new gas stove replaced the old one and she'd even put down new linoleum in the kitchen.

"I love it, Tantie Beulah."

Her aunt smiled proudly. "Yes, child, I know you would like it. God bless you, child. You're a good niece. How the little one doing?"

"Good, Tantie. I told you she passed her exams and going to another school?"

Tantie Beulah wiped her face with her towel. "No. More school again? I remember she always like to read."

Marva smiled. "Yes, she wants to go to university, you know."

"Oh, that is good." Tantie Beulah shook her head. "If only your poor father didn't get killed. He woulda been so proud of both of you. But God doesn't sleep, child. He doesn't sleep."

Marva's blood ran cold. Her aunt still held out hope of her brother's killer being found. How would she react if she ever found out it was Marva?

"I have to go, Tantie Beulah. I told Junie I wouldn't be long."

"All right, child. Here, take some of this sweet bread for you an' the little one. And let me give you a bottle of mauby too."

Minutes later she left the house, her aunt's words ringing in her ears. Tantie Beulah would never find out who killed her brother because the killer would soon be gone.

The following weekend, she forced herself to say another good-bye. It was more painful than she expected. Miss Stewart opened the door on her second knock and beamed her welcome. Marva was always happy to see her, but today she hugged her teacher tighter and longer than usual. If Miss Stewart was surprised at her greeting, she didn't show it.

She looked Marva up and down. "Come in, my dear. You look lovely. I don't think I've ever seen you in yellow before."

Marva smiled. "I wore this dress in Tobago, just once."

Miss Stewart smiled back. "Now that you mention it, I think I remember. It fits you well." Marva pushed aside the memory of the day she'd worn that dress on her date with Jason.

"Are the babies sleeping?"

"No, actually, Marilyn and I were just going to bathe them before I nurse them and put them to bed."

She saw no sign of Mr. Bowen as she followed Miss Stewart into the nursery. Maybe he was working today. But Marva had let go of her fear of him. After next week, he would not be able to do anything to her.

They found Marilyn changing little Chrissie's diaper, while Junior lay in the crib. Eyes wide open, he seemed to be focusing on the picture of Winnie the Pooh in the wall border. Marva lifted him out and held him against her chest. He gave a little smile as if in recognition, before turning his head back to Winnie.

She kissed his cheek. "You prefer Winnie to me?"

Marilyn laughed. "He's always looking at that picture."

Chuckling, Miss Stewart took Chrissie from Marilyn's hands. "Maybe he thinks Winnie looks like his mother. Fat and round."

Marva smiled. "No, Miss. You are getting back to your normal size."

Miss Stewart glanced down at her stomach which still showed a little bulge. "Thank you, dear. It can't happen fast enough for me." She glanced at Marva while she sponged the baby's body. "I can't wait to see you girls grown up and married with babies of your own."

Marva didn't answer, and Miss Stewart continued, "How is Jason?"

"He has a girlfriend." The words slipped out before she could think.

"Really? You two seemed so happy that day in Tobago."

Marva remained silent, gazing down at Junior. Miss Stewart continued, "He better make up his mind before someone else snaps you up from under his nose."

How wrong she was. Nobody was snapping her up. Except God. He was her Husband. Now and always. Aloud she said, "I'm not thinking about marriage."

After the babies were fed and put to bed, Marva wandered into the kitchen to say good-bye to Miss Lucy. On her way back through the living-room, she stopped to admire the family photos hanging on the wall. She touched each one on the frame so as not to smudge the glass. How precious they were to her! She would see them again someday.

The sound of the door opening made her turn. "Hi, Marva."

She was glad to be able to say good-bye to him too. "Good-afternoon, Mr. Bowen."

He smiled, showing his even white teeth. "How are you doing?"

"Fine, sir."

"And June, she okay?"

"Yes, sir."

As she walked away, Marva was surprised to find that her thoughts toward the detective were friendly. He was a good husband to her teacher and a good father to his children. That was all Marva cared about.

How could she leave without saying good-bye to her best friend? Despite her words to Miss Stewart and what she'd said to Jason a while back, Marva went to visit him that evening. A short distance away from Miss Stewart's house, she pulled out the white cap Mr. Stewart had given her for a Christmas present, and a pair of sunglasses. When she boarded the taxi for Egypt Village, she was sure no one would recognize her.

Everything seemed the same – the bumpy roads fringed by untrimmed grasses where garbage had been carelessly dumped, plots of cocoa, coffee and citrus trees, and a few well-kept houses standing out among the dilapidated ones like lilies among overgrown bushes.

Despite the unappealing scenery, Marva felt a sudden twinge of nostalgia. When the low-lying, concrete building with the fading sign came into view, her heartbeat quickened. Egypt Village Government School. The place where she'd avenged her anger on her unfortunate fellow students. It was also the place where she'd made two life-long friends – Miss Stewart and Jason.

Marva handed some money to the driver. "Stop here, please."

He pulled off to the side of the road. She thanked him and got out. It was a quiet Saturday afternoon and there were no houses in the immediate vicinity. Sunlight filtered through the thick foliage of forest and fruit trees. With heavy steps, she turned onto what used to be a track, but was now a paved narrow road. Mr. Rampersad had begun to make changes. Marva hesitated. Should she go further? Would she be trespassing? Curiosity, and a desire to see the place where her troubles had begun urged her on.

A few yards brought her to the house. Doors and windows were closed, and there was no vehicle, but at the front of the house, loads of sand, gravel and bags of cement had been deposited. Apparently, the new owner planned to do some remodeling before moving in. She continued along the track, which ended abruptly near the shed where they used to store their crops. The track sloped downward to the river. Marva's heart pounded. Why had she come back to Egypt? Why did she want to relive that fateful night? To justify what she'd done and what she was going to do? Or, was she, as the Bible said, like a dog returning to her vomit?

After checking the grass for ants or anything else, she eased herself down on it and drew her knees up to her chin. She stared at the brown water where she'd rolled her father's body. She'd convinced herself that what she'd done was the best thing for her and June, but now she wasn't so sure. She would do anything to see him coming toward her, tall and lank, his bushy eyebrows hanging over his eyes like a fringe, his expression angry or happy, depending on how much he'd had to drink.

She could throw herself in that water right now and be done with it, but she didn't like the river. It was narrow, for one thing, and dirty. The sea was what she craved. Huge, wide, menacing or embracing, depending on how you looked at it, the sea had called to her even while she was in Tobago.

As if in answer to her thoughts, the bushes scrunched under heavy boots, and Marva jumped. Seconds later, he called her name. "Marva, what on earth …"

She laid her hand over her heart to still its wild beating, then took a deep breath. His dog barked loudly, and he quieted him and tied him to a tree. "Good, boy. Sit!"

By the time he had the dog under control, Marva was composed and she turned to him with a smile. "Jay, I was just coming to look for you."

He lowered himself beside her. "I don't believe you."

He smelt of the woods, that wild, earthy scent that stirred memories of the time they danced right here on the cocoa leaves. She kept her gaze on the river. "It's true though."

"You said you didn't want to see me again."

Now she turned to look at him. "You know I didn't mean that. You're my best friend."

"Only your best friend?"

She picked up a pebble and flung it into the water, watching it eddy into spiraling waves, before returning to its normal flow.

"Moe?"

Still gazing at the water, she said, "That's how my life used to be, Jay. You see how long it takes the water to settle after the pebble hit it?"

She repeated her action and watched with mild fascination. Pebbles flung into the waters of her soul, disturbing its stillness, its peace. But now God had stilled the waters. There were no more pebbles, no more —

He shook her arm gently. "Moe, what are you talking about?"

She rested her hand on her knee. "Jay, you remember the rumors you used to hear about me and ... and my father —"

"Moe. I never believed any of it. You know I used to fight for you —"

"They were true."

"Moe —" The word sounded like a groan.

She stared into the water. "For five years, Jay. Five years, my father abused me. After a while, I think I came to accept it. I thought that was how my life would always be, especially after Mama died. But... then he began doing it to June, too. Seeing her in pain was too much for me to bear." She paused, exhaled deeply. "Jay, I ... I am the person who killed my father."

Jason sprang up as if he'd been stung. Marva looked up at him, furrowing her brows at his reaction. *Will he hate me now? The police suspected him in the beginning, and I said nothing.*

His next words put her fears to rest. "Moe, you could never do a thing like that. Not you."

"Jay, sit down, let me tell you everything."

"I don't want to hear. It can't be true."

She swatted a mosquito on her neck. "I wish it wasn't, but it is true. Now you see why I ... I can't be a girlfriend or a wife to you, or anybody else. I have to take care of what's inside me first."

She stood and began walking along the river bank. He trailed after her. "I didn't plan to kill him, Jay, although the thought was in my mind for a long time. That night when he slapped June, something burst inside of me. I ran in the kitchen, grabbed the pestle and hit him on the back of his head. He fell. I didn't know he would die."

Jason stood stock still, beads of sweat glistened on his forehead. He walked a few feet away from her, wiped the sweat with the back of his hand, looked at Marva, then into the distance. What did he think of her? She hadn't planned to confide in him but knew she could trust him with her secret. And by this time next week she would be gone. When he heard about her death, he would be able to tell people why she did it.

～

Shock and embarrassment jostled for center stage in Jason's mind, and he wasn't sure which one would win. The rumors were true after all. The thing whispered about in rum shops and snackettes was true. The thing that had made him want to snap Sun Sun's neck the first time he heard him say it was really true. No wonder she was always fighting, lashing out at the demon only she knew about. Calm, beautiful. How had she borne it all these years? Something stirred within him.

He bounded over to where she stood and took her hands. "Marry me, Moe."

Her head jerked up to look at him. "What? What did you say?"

"Marry me. Let me take you away from all this. I love you, Moe, I think I've always loved you ..."

"What about Joanna?"

"There's nothing between us. She's not pregnant. Wait, listen to me." He raised his hand as she was about to speak. "I have a little money saved up. I could take you away before the police ever find you. I have an uncle in Grenada. We could leave tomorrow —"

She took his hand then let it drop. "Jay, I ... think I love you, too, but —"

"But what?"

"I have to face up to what I did. I can't go around pretending I'm a good person. I got myself in this mess. I have to deal with it."

"So you're going to confess?"

"I didn't say that."

"Then what are you going to do?"

She took his hand then dropped it. "I have to go, Jay. Don't hate me, okay?"

He stood rooted to the spot, watching her, tall and erect as she walked away from him. He wanted to run after her, force her to say 'yes', but he knew how determined she was. And so, he let her walk away, out of the bushes and out of his life.

CHAPTER TWENTY - TWO

June rolled on to her back still holding the book she was reading. She frowned as her sister passed by carrying a bucket. "Sis, what are you doing?"

Marva glanced at her. "I'm going to wash the windows."

"On Sunday evening? You've been cleaning since we got back from church."

Marva paused. "I know, but I won't have the time this week. I'm going down to the center tomorrow and Tuesday, and Wednesday night is Bible study."

"That's still no reason to do all that cleaning today. And I'm too tired to help."

Marva smiled. "You have every right to be tired."

Was Sister making fun of her? All June had done was wash the dishes after lunch and tidy the kitchen. June watched her go out the door. Who cleans windows on a Sunday? What had gotten into Marva? Uneasiness overcame her. There was nothing in her sister's demeanor to indicate anything was amiss, but her actions were bizarre.

June placed the book down and went outside. "I'll clean the inside while you do the outside."

Marva paused with the rag in her hand. "You don't have to do that."

June turned away. "I want to."

Together they washed the four windows of their apartment. While Marva wiped down the front door, June ironed her school uniforms, muttering to herself, "This is the strangest day."

Her uneasiness had not left her by the time she finished ironing, so she went for a run. When she returned, Marva was seated at the table studying.

"Glad you're feeling better, Sister."

Marva looked up from her book then back down quickly. "What makes you think I wasn't feeling well?"

June frowned. "How many years have I known you? I can tell when something's wrong."

Marva kept her gaze on her book. "You worry too much."

After they retired to bed, Marva lay awake thinking. June was too sharp for her age. Marva would have to be extra careful over the next few days. As she'd said to June, she planned on going to the center Monday and Tuesday after work. On Wednesday morning she would mail her letters – she still had a last one to write to Tantie Beulah.

She'd made all the arrangements. In her letters to Miss Stewart, she'd asked her to adopt June. She'd even gone to the bank and made June her beneficiary so that all her money would go to her. After work on Wednesday she would go and say her good-bye to TL, then come home, eat, shower and go to Bible study. Thursday evening would be her last day with June. She would cook something special – maybe oven- barbecued chicken, macaroni pie, boiled ripe plantains and cole slaw. June would love that. Then on Friday she would put her white dress and her Bible in her bag. And oh, she would be sure to wear the necklace with the heart pendant that Jason had given her.

After work she would take a taxi to the lower end of High Street and walk to the beach. She'd chosen Friday because few people would be on the beach that day. They would be doing their grocery shopping for the week-end. If anyone was there, she would sit and read her Bible until they left. She would make certain she was alone before putting on her white dress and going into the sea. She couldn't bear for anything to foil her plans. This would not be like when she drank alcohol and pills. This time she would succeed. She was a good swimmer, but even good swimmers get tired.

Try as she might, June could not shake the feeling that all was not well with her sister. Her thoughts haunted her all day in school, and she had difficulty concentrating on some of her classes. When she got home that evening, she paced until she heard the door open. When her sister entered, June thought she would burst with relief. "Thank goodness, you're home."

Marva furrowed her brow. "Something wrong?"

June forced a smile. "Not now that you're home." June followed her into the bedroom. "How was work today? What did you do?"

Marva shrugged. "The usual, oil change, adjust brakes and helped Glen in the office."

June had a sudden thought. "Sister, are you in love?"

Marva turned her full gaze on her, then burst out laughing. "Now where did you get that idea?"

"I don't know. It's just that you've been acting strange lately."

Marva removed her bandana and shook her hair out. It had grown back past the nape of her neck. "What about you? Tell me about your love life."

June sat on the bed next to her. "I have a new boyfriend, I think."

Marva paused in the act of removing her sneakers and socks. "Really? Somebody I know?"

June nodded. "You met him a couple times. He was here that time with Wendy."

Marva stared into the mirror opposite. "Oh, the dark, good-looking boy who came to study?"

"That's the one. John. We worked together at that insurance place during the holidays."

Marva seemed genuinely interested. "You all get along well together?"

"Yes, he seems more mature than Keith, but he's not as funny."

Marva laid her hand on June's arm. "Don't compare him with Keith. Every person is different. Try to appreciate him for who he is." Then as if talking to herself, "You never know how things will turn out."

"That's true. John is so nice. I feel happy when I'm with him, but I still miss Keith, even though he treated me so badly."

Marva stared at June's profile. "In what way?"

June met her gaze. "You remember the night of the BBB concert?

Well, I wondered how come he didn't invite me to go with him? Only to see him with Sandra after the show."

"Your good friend Sandra? The one who moved away?"

June nodded. "My good friend Sandra. She and her family came back. I guess it was a mistake to tell her that things weren't so nice between Keith and me. She must have called him, and they got together."

"Never mind, Junie. God has the right person for you. If John is the one, God will show you. After a while you'll get over Keith, watch and see."

June stared at the floor. "I hope so."

The ringing of the phone made her look up. She ran into the living-room to answer it. John's voice came over the line. "June, you doing anything tomorrow evening?"

"No, why?"

"I have a soccer match. Want to come?"

"What time?"

"Around five."

"I'll be there."

Marva came out of the bedroom just as she hung up the phone. "I see that big smile on your face."

June's face grew warm. "John just invited me to his soccer match tomorrow."

"I told you everything will work out. Just trust God, Junie. If you ever remember anything I told you, remember that."

On Wednesday afternoon, Marva alighted from a taxi at the hospital corner and walked down the incline to meet TL. Her mind brimmed with anticipation of this last meeting. She'd bought him a shirt, a blouse for his mother and one for Carol. She passed the newspaper stand, and the woman who sold *amchar*, and walked a little further. TL was nowhere in sight. Marva frowned. She was standing on the same spot he usually stood. Maybe he'd gone to use a bathroom somewhere. Soon he would appear, smiling his colorful smile and dazzling her with his light-ning-fast movements. But when fifteen minutes passed and she still didn't see him, she concluded he might be working at the car wash. Or maybe he'd finished early and gone home. She started down the hill, then turned around. Maybe the *amchar* lady would know if he'd been there earlier.

The woman looked up and smiled at Marva when she approached. "How you doing, girl? I didn't see you in a while."

Marva smiled back. "I'm okay. Did you see TL today?"

The smile vanished from the woman's face. "You didn't hear the news? They killed him last week. He was going home. They robbed him and killed him —"

The sun disappeared. Marva's knees went wobbly, her sight dimmed, and her bag dropped from her hand. Vaguely, she felt the woman slip the bag handle around her fingers, heard her saying something, Marva didn't know what. *Oh God, no, not TL. My friend. The breadwinner of his family. What would they do without him? I didn't get to say good-bye.*

She moved on wooden legs, slowly at first, then faster and faster, the woman's words ringing in her ears. *They killed him. They robbed him and killed him.* Her friend was dead, cut off just like that, like a candle in the wind. Marva couldn't wait. She couldn't bear any more sadness, any more pain. Forget the white dress. She would do it now. This world held nothing for her anymore. The sea was right around the corner. Faster and faster she ran, her feet slapping the pavement with urgency, her bag beat-ing against her side. Racing heart, racing thoughts, racing feet. The bus terminal came in sight, the fish market stood opposite. The sea was right behind it across the road.

A vehicle came speeding toward her. Could she make it in time? Brakes screeched. Marva flew into the air. Clouds, rooftops, treetops spun before her eyes. Then a moment of serenity, a final rendering of conscious thought – *Lord, I'm going to die.* As if in slow motion, she felt herself twirling down like a leaf in the wind. People, places and scenes present and past flashed before her eyes before she slammed into the asphalt and knew no more.

~

June and John turned into Rosewood Lane following his soccer game. June listened to his enthusiastic recount of his exploits on the field. As center forward, he was almost unstoppable, rarely allowing the other side to get the ball. He'd scored one of the two winning goals. She'd enjoyed watching him play, but now she was anxious to get home. She had some homework to complete for school tomorrow.

A small crowd gathered near her house a short distance away. Maybe their landlady was having another one of her Avon parties. As June drew nearer, she realized her apartment was still in darkness. Maybe Sister was still at Bible study, or had stopped at the grocery to pick up something.

She halted and turned to John. "Why is everyone looking at me like that?"

John shrugged. "Maybe they never saw you with a boy before?"

"Yeah, right."

"You want me to come to the door with you?"

She nodded. "Yes."

They reached the small group that included her landlady.

June greeted her with a polite smile. "Good-night, Mrs. Maraj. How you doin'?"

The lady stepped forward, brushing her hand across her eyes. She looked like she'd been crying.

"What's wrong, Mrs. Maraj?"

The woman turned to another neighbor, whom June recognized as Mrs. Teesdale from two houses down. "You tell her."

The woman stepped forward. "Child, your sister …"

At the mention of her sister, June's heart almost stopped beating. "What happened to her?"

Mrs. Teesdale continued, "She … she was involved in an accident. The police was just here."

June felt herself sway. Strong arms came around her, holding her up. Everyone seemed to be talking at once. *They didn't know if Marva was still alive. The accident was serious. She ran in front of the car.* Somebody offered to drive June to the hospital. Vaguely, she heard John ask if she wanted him to accompany her. She must have said yes, for she found herself seated in the back seat with him. He put his arms around her and drew her close.

The drive was the longest June could remember. She tried to pray but couldn't think of a thing to say. Terror like she'd never known before covered her like an icy blanket, and she shivered. She couldn't cry or scream to save her life. Someone said the accident had occurred near the wharf. What was Sister doing down there? She was supposed to have gone to Bible study. Was she giving out tracts again? And what had made her run across the street like that?

As they pulled into the hospital parking lot, Miss Sheila was just getting into her Toyota. June jumped out of the car and ran to her. "Miss Sheila, did you hear, do you know …?"

Miss Sheila got out of her car and closed the door. "Yes, I know. I was just coming to call you. She's still in emergency —"

"She's alive?"

The woman's face seemed strained. "Yes, but she's unconscious. The doctors are with her now —"

June ran back to the man who had driven her. "Thank you. She's alive. I'm going in now." Turning to John, "Can you come?"

He nodded.

Miss Sheila escorted them to the emergency room and gained permission from the nurse on duty. "You and her sister can go in. The young man must wait here."

June couldn't hold back the cry when she entered the small room. Her sister was stretched out on the bed, swathed in bandages and hooked up to machines. Marva's eyes were closed, her swollen face a palette of colors, her body still. But what scared June the most was Marva's head. It seemed to have doubled in size, and the bandage was blood-stained. Dr. Griffith, Miss Sheila's husband, moved from the head of the bed and put his arm around June's shoulder. "I'm sorry about all this, June. We're doing the best we can, but it will be touch and go for the next twelve hours."

June's lips trembled. "What do you mean?"

"She has a lot of fractures and possibly some bleeding in her brain. The neurosurgeon will be here any minute. We have to operate right away."

"Oh my God."

Two strong-looking men in green uniform began wheeling the stretcher away. June ran to the head of the stretcher. "Sister, I love you. Sister, don't leave me. Please, Sister —"

Miss Sheila put her arms around her and held her until she stopped crying. When they emerged from the room, June was surprised to see John still there sitting on a bench. She'd forgotten all about him.

He came to her side, his face showing concern. "How's she?"

June dabbed at her eyes. "They took her to surgery."

Miss Sheila said, "June, Cicely said she'll be here any minute, but I can take you and your friend home if you like."

June shook her head. "I prefer to wait until she comes out of surgery."

Miss Stewart hurried in at that very moment. June ran to her and began crying afresh. The lady put her arms around her, offered words of comfort, but June was too numb to make sense of anything. What if her sister didn't make it through the surgery? Lord, this couldn't be happening. This was far more serious than the time when Marva swallowed pills and alcohol.

The icy blanket tightened itself around her, and she groped her way to the bench, shivering. Why was she so cold? Miss Stewart was saying something. June wrapped her arms around herself. A dark fog was closing in on her. She tried to reach out to someone, something. Voices came from far away. Sounds, footsteps. She felt herself falling. And then, blessed oblivion.

Sunlight streamed in through the long, awning windows. Someone coughed, and June looked in that direction. A young woman spat into a plastic container a nurse held under her mouth. Another nurse wheeled a cart and stopped near her bed. June threw off the cover and tried to sit up, but something tugged at her wrist. A tube taped to her hand led to a bag hanging on a pole. Memories of the previous day washed over her, and she whimpered. She was in the hospital. She looked down at her rumpled uniform and grimaced. She badly needed a shower and a change of clothing, but she had to find out about her sister's condition first. Was she alive? Was she awake?

"Good-morning." The nurse removed the needle from June's wrist.

"Good-morning," June replied. "Where's the bathroom?"

"You can't get up yet. I'll bring you a bedpan."

"A what? I want to go to the bathroom."

The woman looked up from her task. "Did you hear what I said? You can't —"

Another voice intervened. "June, honey, you're awake."

Relief washed over her. "Miss Sheila, thank God you're here."

The other nurse paused with the bag in her hand. "You know her?"

"Yes, she's my friend." Turning to June, "Do you feel well enough to go home?"

Home? The word had a bitter-sweet ring. Home without her sister was no home at all, but she nodded. "As soon as I come from the bathroom."

"Good." Miss Sheila put her arm around her shoulder. "I'll help you and then we'll come back and hear what the nurse says."

June stepped off the bed carefully. She wasn't dizzy but she kept her hold on Miss Sheila's hand. On the way to the bathroom, Miss Sheila said, "Cicely wants you to stay with her until Marva is out of the hospital. If the doctor says it's okay, I'll take you home to freshen up, get clothes for Marva, and then you can come back and see her. How does that sound?"

June turned to her, eyes brimming. "I don't know what I would do without you and Miss Stewart. Thank you so much."

Miss Sheila patted her hand. "That's what we're here for, my dear."

CHAPTER TWENTY -THREE

When June got out of Miss Sheila's car, Mrs. Maraj and Ms. Maureen, another tenant ran down the steps to meet her. June didn't feel like talking, but she told them what little she knew of her sister's status.

The women's gaze showed sympathy. "Just trust God," Mrs. Maraj said.

June nodded and went into the apartment. Alone at last, the numbness overcame her once more. Empty. The emptiness of the apartment echoed the hollowness she felt inside. In the bedroom, she touched her mother's photo hanging behind the bed. *Mama, I lost you, am I going to lose my sister too? Did you see what happened to her, Mama?*

She wandered through the small apartment, remembering. So much had happened since that fateful night. Two frightened girls fleeing to Tantie Beulah's house; the discovery of her father's body on the beach; Marva finding a job; June's first day at school; moving into their new apartment; meeting Keith; Sister's eighteenth birthday party. These walls bore witness to so many memories. Would Sister ever return to make new memories?

The phone rang. Fearing it was the hospital, June stared at the instrument then moved toward it like a zombie.

"June?"

She felt the flicker of a smile. "John, I'm so glad you called."

"How are you feeling? I was so worried about you last night."

June's face grew warm at the memory of her fainting spell.

"I feel better. They kept me overnight. I never fainted before."

She heard the tenderness in his voice. "It was too much for you. You would have fallen if I hadn't caught you."

Her face grew warmer still. "Oh, thank you."

"You're welcome. Any news about your sister?"

June repeated what she'd said to the landlady.

"I'm so sorry." Pause. "Do you need anything?"

My sister. She dabbed her hand across her eyes. "No, but thanks for asking. I don't think I can make it to school today."

"It's all over the news. I don't think the teachers will expect you to come. Did you call them?"

"I don't feel up to it. I think I'll ask Miss Stewart to do it for me. I'll be staying with her for a while."

"That's good. I didn't like you being alone."

"Thanks, John. I'll call you sometime, okay?"

"Okay." Pause. "June, take care of yourself."

"I will, John. Thank you."

She held the receiver to her ear after he hung up. She still had a friend.

Showered and changed, June stared at the phone, then with a deep sigh, she picked it up and dialed Tantie Beulah's number. June had to hold the receiver away from her ears because of her aunt's screams. "Oh, God, that poor child. They kill her father and now they want to kill her too. Oh, God. I goin' to make some fish broth and carry for her right now —"

June had to smile. "She's unconscious, Tantie. She can't eat."

"Oh, God. Unconscious? That's not good, but I'll go for visiting hour today, you hear, child? You keep good, eh? And pray, pray for your sister … Oh God."

She dialed Glen's Automotive next. The man who said he was Glen sounded sympathetic. He even told her she could come and pick up Marva's paycheck whenever she wanted. She thanked him and hung up. She was about to turn away when she remembered one other person. He didn't scream, but his groan pierced June's heart.

"Oh no! That person was Marva? My Moe? I saw it on the news. Oh, my God. I'll go up there this afternoon."

Her sister was going to have a lot of visitors, but she couldn't see any of them. Unless God worked a miracle. In the midst of gathering up her belongings, the phone rang again. This time it was Miss Sheila reminding her to bring clothes for her sister. June had forgotten all about that.

She pulled open Marva's drawer, the first time she'd done so. Everything was neatly folded. Tops in one heap, skirts in another, nightgowns in another. June lifted the heap of nightgowns. Below them was a white dress. June frowned. That was her sister's baptism dress. Hadn't they put both their dresses in a bag in the back of the wardrobe? They'd said they didn't know when they would wear them again. When did Sister put hers in the drawer? Maybe she was going to wear it on Communion Sunday? June shrugged. She had to hurry. She pulled out a smaller drawer and removed some underwear then placed everything in the small suitcase Marva had used when they went to Tobago.

She scratched her head. What else? Toiletries. Marva's deodorant was almost out, she would have to buy one, so was the toothpaste. Might as well buy everything. And some more nightgowns too. A horn tooted just as she finished zipping the suitcase. She grabbed it and her bag and went through the door.

Seated in the car, June reached for her seatbelt. "Did you hear anything?"

Miss Sheila gave her a quick glance. "No, dear, but from what Fred told me, she's still the same."

June tried to keep the tears away, but her eyes stung.

The lady went on, "He and Dr. Chen, the orthopedic, want to speak to you. I'll come up with you in case you need me to explain anything."

June stared straight ahead. "Thanks, Miss Sheila."

June was grateful for her company, but she still felt so alone. All her life her sister had been by her side. Now she was gone, and June had to manage all these things by herself. What was she to do? A sob escaped her lips, and Miss Sheila patted her shoulder. "This must be so difficult for you, but it will pass. Just trust God, my dear. It will pass."

~

Although June had prepared herself mentally for this visit, her sister's lifeless appearance sent fear and shock racing through her veins. Marva's right leg was in a heavy cast up to her waist and her left arm was also casted. Her eyes were closed, and her head, still swollen, swathed in a blood-stained bandage. A tube led from under the bandage to a machine. She had another tube in her mouth, and one taped to her nose.

June went to her head and said softly, "Sister, I'm here. I love you." Between all the tubes, tapes and bandages, there was little of her face exposed, but June kissed Marva's swollen cheek, straightened and looked in vain for some sign of awareness. She brushed away the tears. Would her sister ever open her eyes again? Walk? Talk? Live?

A dull ache spread in her tummy. Part of it was from hunger, but grief, sadness and fear had taken up residence and she couldn't expel them.

She sank down in the only available chair. "What are all these lines for?"

Miss Sheila straightened up from placing Marva's clothes in her little bedside cupboard. "The one in her head is to reduce the swelling, the one in her mouth is a trach tube, to help her breathe." June's gaze followed the tube to where it was attached to a machine.

"That's the ventilator," Miss Sheila said.

"And this one?" June pointed to a tube leading from Marva's nose.

"That's a feeding tube."

While June's mind registered all this, Dr. Griffith and a Chinese doctor walked in. Miss Sheila turned to her husband with a smile. "You're here. We were just about to come to your office."

"Never mind. We wanted to see the patient anyway." Dr. Griffith patted June on the arm. "How are you doing?"

June could only shake her head.

The other doctor extended his hand. "I'm Dr. Chen, the orthopedic surgeon."

June took his hand. "I'm June. Nice to meet you, doctor."

The two doctors turned their attention to Marva. Dr. Chen took out an instrument and looked into her eyes, then listened to her heartbeat.

He turned to June. "Your sister has had some serious injuries, fractures and so on, as you can see from all the casting we did, but we are not too concerned about that…"

"What do you mean, doctor?"

He consulted his chart. "Her left shoulder is dislocated, and she has a humeral fracture, her pelvic bone is broken, her tibia …"

June held up her hand. She didn't want to hear about the fractures. "What are you concerned about, doctor?"

Dr. Chen looked at Dr. Griffith then back at June. "Her brain."

June's heart almost stopped beating. "Her brain?"

Dr. Griffith stepped forward. "I wish Dr. Flechner was here to explain all this to you, but he had to go to Port-of-Spain. He's the only neurosurgeon in the country, you know."

June was becoming impatient. "Can you tell me how soon she will recover?"

The doctors exchanged glances again before Dr. Chen spoke. "Your sister is young. These fractures will heal in time, although she'll be in some pain, but Dr. Flechner found a subdural hematoma - that is when blood collects between the skull and the brain - and he had to drain it. This is why we have the tube here." He pointed to the one Miss Sheila had already told her about. "She's now in a coma. We have to wait and see how quickly she snaps out of it. The quicker she comes out, the better her chances will be. But again, she has youth in her favor."

Moments passed before June spoke, but she didn't ask the question she was too afraid to ask. "So you can't tell how long she'll remain like this?"

Dr. Griffith shook his head. "Only God can."

June stared at her sister's immobile figure. She had youth in her favor, but was youth enough?

Despite Miss Sheila's urging, June refused to leave her sister's bedside. Eventually, Miss Sheila offered to bring her something to eat. "What do you want?"

June thought for a moment. "A Chinese soup, please."

Miss Sheila raised her eyebrows. "Only that?"

"Yes."

A nurse came in and unhooked a bag that June had not seen before from the foot of the bed.

"What is that?"

The nurse didn't look at June. "It's her foley, for her urine."

June stared at the brownish liquid in the bag. Why was it that color, she wanted to ask, but the woman had already walked away.

June rested her elbows on her knees and propped her chin on the back of her fists, gazing at her sister's face. Nurses came and went. Miss Sheila returned with the soup, some noodles and fortune cookies. June's stomach growled and she opened the container immediately. It was wonton soup. "Thanks, Miss Sheila."

"You're welcome. Make sure you drink all of it. I'm going home now. I have to work this evening. Are you sure you don't want to go home?"

June swallowed a spoonful of the soup. It was probably delicious, but right now it could have been dish water. "No, Miss. Could you please let Miss Stewart know?"

"I will. See you later then."

While June was eating, a nurse came to the bed. "Did you bring clothes for your sister?"

"Yes, they're in there." She nodded toward the cupboard.

"Okay, when you're finished eating, step outside so we can clean her up and change her."

"Can I stay, please? My sister is a very private person. She would want me to be here."

The woman gave her a strange look. "I'll have to ask the head nurse."

Minutes later, she returned with another nurse. "You can stay but sit over there. We need some space." She pointed to the corner near the foot of the bed.

June obeyed.

She watched while the nurses removed the bloodied clothing and bandages, not too gently, sponged her in all the exposed places, then dressed her in a clean nightgown. As soon as they left, June returned to the head of the bed. "See? You look so much nicer now, fresh and clean, the way you like to look. Are you ready for visitors? I know Tantie Beulah is coming, Miss Stewart, and guess who else? Jason. I called him this morning." She paused. "You know one thing, Sister? I wish you could look at me the way you look when you're vexed. I'll pay money to hear you say, 'What you did that for?'"

The tears stung her eyes, and she pressed her fingers to them. She would remind her sister of some happy times. She'd read somewhere that comatose patients could hear and were sometimes aware of what was going around them. She took hold of her sister's limp fingers and talked about the good times. The little she could remember before their father's abuse. While their mother was still alive. How she used to take them to church. How she would pray the rosary and read the Bible with June sitting on her lap, Marva on the floor, head leaning against her mother's knee. About bathing in the river, making necklaces out of yellow poui flowers, playing with the cloth dolls Mama made them.

Then she jumped to their life in San Fernando. "Do you remember the first time we went to the movies? How scared we were?" June's eyelids and tongue grew heavy. Still holding her sister's hand, she leaned her head back in the chair.

She awoke to the sound of voices and someone shaking her gently. Dimly, she recognized Miss Stewart's and Miss Sheila's faces. June stretched and closed her eyes again.

"Poor thing, she's really out of it."

"I'm taking her home. She has to get some sleep."

June opened her eyes and glanced at her sister. Memories washed over her and she moaned.

Miss Stewart put an arm around her shoulder. "Honey, I'm so sorry about all this."

June noted her reddened eyes and tear-stained cheeks. How long had she been standing there? June cast her gaze back to Marva. Eyes still closed. Motionless. No sign of life.

A nurse came in and drew Miss Sheila aside. While they whispered, Miss Stewart stroked June's hair. "I'm taking you home, honey. You can't do anything for your sister by staying here."

Tears stung her eyes. "I want to be here when … when she wakes up."

Miss Sheila approached. "June, the nurse said there's a lot of people outside the ward waiting to see Marva, but they're not allowing anyone in. Would you like to come and speak to them?"

June looked from one to the other of the women. Their smiles were encouraging. June pushed herself out of the chair. With a last look at the figure in the bed, she followed them out the door.

The nurse was right, there were a lot of people. She spotted John at the back near the wall. He smiled and waved at her, and she waved back. Tantie Beulah was the first to detach herself from the crowd. Crying, she pulled June to her bosom. "Why they wouldn't let me see the child? I come from so far. Look, you remember Ma Lopez, and this is her son, Winston. He brought us. Oh God, how she feelin'? Why they wouldn't let me go in to see my niece?"

It took some help from Miss Sheila to convince Tantie Beulah that she would be able to see Marva when her condition improved. As June turned away from her aunt, Keith and his parents walked up. June's heart lurched, but she continued greeting the friends, neighbors, her sister's co-workers and people she didn't know. What would she say to Keith and his family? She hadn't expected them all to come.

One tearful lady shook her hand and said that Marva had prayed with her and given her tracts on the street. "Your sister is such a sweet person. Now I'm serving the Lord because of her." The woman patted her eyes. "I'm praying for her."

June's eyes filled. "Thank you, thank you."

Someone tapped her on her shoulder. "Catty?"

She gave him a watery smile. "Keith."

He wrapped his arms around her like no one else was around. "I'm so sorry about what happened."

Was he doing that for John's benefit?

"Thank you," she said and disengaged herself.

His mother hugged her. "How is your sister?"

"Still unconscious."

"You know who hit her?" Keith's father asked. Without waiting for June to reply, he continued, "You should press charges. If you want to find a good lawyer, let me know."

June murmured something, all the while conscious of John's eyes on her. She couldn't read his expression, but she worried about what he, Miss Stewart and Miss Sheila might be thinking. To hide her confusion, she turned to them. "Miss Stewart, Miss Sheila you remember Keith's parents?"

Finally, the crowd dispersed, all except John, and June turned to Miss Stewart. "I want to go back and tell Sister good-bye before I leave. John, can you wait?"

He nodded, and June hurried back to the bed. "Well, Sister, you should have seen the amount of visitors you had. You're a very popular lady." She spluttered. "I have to go now, but I'll be back tomorrow."

She kissed her sister's cheek then hurried back to the hallway. Her mind felt like a glob of spaghetti as she, John and Miss Stewart walked toward the elevator.

A little pleasure seeped into her when the elevator door opened, and Jason and a man with a stingy brim hat stepped out. The greetings over, June gave him the unpleasant news that Marva was not allowed visitors.

He slumped against the wall "I had no idea she was hurt so bad."

Miss Stewart touched his arm. "It's all right, Jason. We're praying for her, and you must pray too."

June's heart ached for him.

His friend squeezed his shoulder. "Take it easy, man. She'll be all right."

Jason bent his head, and two teardrops fell to the floor. Her stomach knotted. She touched his arm. "Jason, we have to be going. I'll call you."

He nodded but didn't look up. "Okay. Bye, Miss Stewart."

Out in the parking lot, they found Mr. Bowen waiting near his car. He opened the back door and June sank into the seat next to John. He squeezed her hand, and she exhaled. This had been the longest day of her life.

CHAPTER TWENTY-FOUR

Despite her exhaustion, June tossed and turned. A dog barked somewhere in the distance, a car drove by slowly, and Miss Stewart padded around in the nursery next door. June was grateful to the Bowens for allowing her to stay at their house until Marva was released from the hospital. She couldn't stay in the apartment without her sister but sleeping in a strange house took some getting used to. Especially in her frazzled state of mind.

The driver of the vehicle that hit Marva had testified that she bolted across the road without looking. Eyewitnesses' statements agreed. What had made her do that? Mr. Bowen told her the driver had turned himself in and was assisting the police with their investigations. So far, he'd not been charged with anything, although he could be. Mr. Bowen had not gone into details, but June took it to mean that if her sister died, the driver may be charged with something.

June stuffed her fist in her mouth to stifle her cries.

When she awoke the next morning, her head ached, and her eyes felt like they had gravel in them. Mr. Bowen offered her a ride to the apartment so she could get fresh clothes. She accepted but declined Miss Stewart's offer of breakfast. The thought of food made her stomach churn.

Cicely tiptoed out of the nursery where the twins lay sleeping, then looked in on June, also sleeping. It was Sunday night and Miss Lucy was off. Cicely went into the kitchen and sat at the table near her husband who had a few envelopes, his checkbook and a pen in front of him. They usually opened their mail and wrote checks on Saturday nights. But everything had been pushed back because of Marva's accident. Five days had passed, and she was still in a coma. Fred had said the sooner she snapped out of it, the better her chances of recovery.

Cicely sighed, and David stroked her arm. "I'll give you a massage before you go to bed."

"I need more than a massage."

He winked. "That too."

Cicely gave him a playful swat. Only a man's brain could conjure up sex out of any situation.

He handed her two envelopes. "These are for you."

The envelopes were addressed in an unfamiliar handwriting. Frowning, she slit the first one open and removed the notebook paper. Her frown deepened as she unfolded it and read, "Dear Miss Stewart." Marva? Why had she written her? Cicely read a few lines and an exclamation burst from her lips. She jumped up from her seat as if she'd been stung.

David also rose. "Honey, what's the matter?"

Cicely put her hand to her mouth. Walking away, she continued reading, "… please take June. You are good. June loves you. I love you too. I didn't mean to kill my father. Will God forgive me? I love God so much. I am going to Him Miss. When I go please take June to live with you. I am a bad person. I feel like I have a bag of grapefruit on my back and I can't put it down. I don't deserve to live. June will be a fine woman one day. I know that. She is very bright. Daddy did bad things to us but I didn't mean to kill him. I feel so bad. Good-bye, Miss Stewart."

Trembling, she turned to her husband. "Open the other one, please."

David quizzed her with his glance, but he obeyed. His reaction was less dramatic than hers, but she could see the tight purse of his lips and the twitching of his jaw.

Eventually, he dropped back into his seat and held his head in his hands. "Oh, my God. Oh, my God."

Cicely took the paper and read it. The contents were similar, but a little more. She added that she respected Mr. Bowen and she knew he suspected her from the start, but he was a good man, and God would bless him. She wrote, "I know you all will be good parents to June. Daddy was a bad father. I can't stay here anymore. I can't fight anymore. He used to drink and he did bad things to me and June. I didn't mind that he hated me but why June? She was so little and so cute. God loves me, that's why I want to go to Him. You know I had an abortion Miss. Because of Daddy. I can't love anybody else, but I'll tell you a secret. It was so painful when I had the abortion but the pain of what he did to June hurt me even more. But I didn't mean to kill him. I hit him with the mortar pestle and he fell. By the time you read this I will be in heaven. I dreamed Mama the other night. Good-bye Miss."

Cicely went and stood behind David's chair, slipped her arms around his neck and laid her head on his shoulder. Moments passed before either of them spoke. Marva had attempted suicide. Again. And this time she'd been determined to succeed. Memories flooded Cicely's mind like rain water in a gutter. Marva was right. David had suspected her of killing her father. He wanted to arrest her, but Cicely had stopped him, with her unreasonable fear and her arrogance. She'd accused him of being callous and insensitive. And, jeopardizing his career, he'd dropped the case. Because of her, Marva lay unconscious in a hospital bed tonight. A sob tore from Cicely's throat. What could she say to him?

She ran to the screen door separating the kitchen from the back porch and pushed it open. A half- moon glided against the velvet of the sky, heedless of the turmoil in the wilderness below, and disappeared behind a cloud. But the large fan-shaped leaves of the dwarf coconut tree bowed mockingly to her in the soft, night breeze. Even the two orange trees, the banana and the baby mango tree David had planted stood like silent sentinels, watching, questioning. *What are you going to do? Is this why you came out of Egypt?*

She felt his arms go around her waist and his head against the side of her neck. "I blame myself."

She spun out of his arms. "No! Never! If it weren't for me, none of this would have happened. I stopped you when you wanted —"

She broke off as soft footsteps sounded in the hallway. June paused. "I'm sorry. I didn't know you were in here. I came to get a glass of water."

Cicely moved quickly and gathered up the letters. "That's okay, honey. We were just paying some bills."

June didn't appear to notice anything. She looked from one to the other with a tired smile. "I had a nice dream about Sister. I dreamed she was walking."

Cicely smiled back. "That's wonderful, honey."

June poured water from the fridge into her glass and padded back to her room. After she left, David voiced Cicely's thoughts. "Not a word."

She nodded and slipped her arm in his.

Lying in bed, Cicely and David talked long into the night about this new turn of events. She couldn't stop blaming herself. Finally, David said, "Look at it this way. *You* didn't stop me from arresting Marva. I didn't take her in because after you told me what had happened to you, I felt like I would be interrogating you instead of her. That shouldn't have stopped me, but it did."

Cicely inched closer to him. "Oh, Dave …"

"On the other hand, if you hadn't objected, and I had arrested her and she'd got life in prison, would you have blamed yourself?"

He was right, as always, and she told him so.

He touched her lips with his. "So, no more blaming yourself. In situations like these it's hard to know what's the best thing to do. We're all guilty. Not just you and me, but society, the law, the government, all guilty. But it's no use crying over spilled milk. We have to learn from our mistakes."

Moments of silence passed before Cicely asked, "What do we do now?"

"We wait until she comes through."

Cicely turned her gaze on him in the darkness. "You mean, she'll still have to go to trial?"

He sighed. "She made a confession, and from what she wrote, it seems she wants closure. The bag of grapefruit, remember? The only way for her to get rid of it is to face up to what she did. Otherwise she'll do something worse the next time."

Cicely shuddered. Her heart went out to the two girls, one lying motionless in the hospital bed, and the other, asleep, dreaming her sister was walking.

"How would we explain to June why her sister is going to trial?"

David slapped his forehead. "You should be a detective. I forgot she doesn't know Marva confessed." He paused. "We'll cross that bridge when we come to it."

Cicely flung an arm across her husband's chest. "Hold me, honey. I'm so frightened."

He drew her to him and his lips sought hers. They clung to each other, whispering, seeking and finding the strength and release that only their love could bring.

When June entered the ICU on Monday morning, she noticed the curtains drawn around her sister's bed. Some unusual activity seemed to be taking place. The curtain was being pushed in and out, and she could hear voices. *God, no!* June sped across the room and came up against a burly nurse, who glared at her. "You can't come in." One shouted to the other, "Call the doctor!"

The nurse pushed past June. "Wait outside!"

But June was not prepared to obey. She inched nearer the bed where two nurses pinned Marva's arms down, while another re-attached her tubes. June could only assume she had pulled them out. But her eyes were still closed, and she made some twitching movements. What did it mean? At least she was alive, but was she out of the coma? Dr. Griffith hurried in just then. He apparently did not notice her. He examined the patient then straightened and addressed the nurses. "Keep on monitoring her breathing, turn her every half an hour —"

At last he spotted June. "Her heart rate seems a little better, but she's still unresponsive."

"What happened just now, Dr. Fred?" June and Marva sometimes called him by his first name.

"She became agitated and started pulling out her tubes."

"Is that a good sign?"

He nodded. "Sometimes it is. We're going to put some medication in the drips to prevent that from happening again and we'll start some Physical Therapy. I've got to run. Take care."

"Physical Therapy?"

"Yes, we don't want her to have any contractures. We want her to be as good as new."

His words stirred hope in her heart, and she smiled. "Thanks, Dr. Fred."

Her mind strayed to a man she sometimes met at the bus stop. He was probably in his late fifties, of average height and build, and always carried a long-handled macramé bag. His head had collapsed into his neck and twisted to his right shoulder. His left hip protruded, so that when he walked, his eyes looked one way while his body seemed to move in the opposite direction. No, her sister would never be like him or any other deformed person.

After the nurses left, June moved her chair to the other side of the bed that Marva faced. She leaned over and kissed her sister's cheek. "Well, it looks like you'll soon be as good as new. That's what Dr. Fred said. No, he didn't exactly say that, but that's what I wanted him to say."

June left at lunch time with Marva's soiled laundry. At the apartment, she put the clothes in the washing machine, then went inside and threw herself on the bed. She would give anything to be back here with her sister. It felt so lonely, so sad, as if the very walls groaned for Marva's presence.

June got off the bed and on to her knees. She hadn't prayed since her sister's accident. Didn't they say that God answers prayer? And Marva was a firm believer in prayer. June prayed, for her sister's quick and complete recovery. "No contractures, Lord. Please, bring my sister back as good as new. Help the doctors and nurses to do the best for her, Lord." She paused. "And help me, Lord. I don't know how much more of this I can take."

When she was leaving, Mrs. Maraj met her with a small pile of mail bound with a rubber band. June thanked her but sighed inwardly. Another responsibility she had to take care of.

She returned to the hospital with fresh laundry, Marva's cassette player and two of her tapes. She'd read somewhere that comatose patients might respond to music. Marva now faced the opposite side, and June moved her chair once more. She switched on the player and slipped in the cassette with one of her sister's favorite hymns, *One Day At A Time*. The nurse came and smiled her approval. "I love that song."

June smiled back.

That day, Marva was allowed her first visitors – Reverend Harris and his wife. June had never spoken to the minister except when he greeted attendees after the church service, but she was happy to see him. He and his wife hugged her, but their faces were grave. His wife said, "We waited a few days until we thought it was okay to come and see her." Then she read a Psalm and her husband prayed.

When June left the hospital that night, a little glimmer of hope nestled in her heart. After she'd reported to Miss Stewart what had taken place, she said, "I'm going to take a shower and come back and play with my babies. I haven't done that in a while."

She let the spray soak into her body before soaping, all the while humming to the tune of *Everything's Gonna Be All Right*. Cool and refreshed, she went into the nursery. Later that night, she eyed the stack of mail on the dresser. She would attend to it in the morning before going to the hospital. Through Miss Stewart, she'd received approval from the principal to return to school the following week. Lying in bed, she thought of how her life had changed drastically in a few days. No more dates, no piano lessons, no running around the block. She sighed and again sent up a prayer for her sister's recovery.

The next morning after she'd eaten breakfast, she said to Miss Stewart, "I'm going to pay a few bills before I go to the hospital. Do you want me to get you anything?"

"No thanks, dear. Miss Lucy and I have to do some shopping today as well and then we'll stop by to see Marva."

"Okay, Miss. I hope Sister opens her eyes today."

June turned away and went into her room. Moments later, she tore into the kitchen, almost breathless, letter in hand.

"Look, Miss, oh my God, I can't believe it … Miss, read this …" She thrust the letter at Miss Stewart who sat holding Chrissie on her lap.

Miss Stewart's hand flew to her mouth. "You got one too?"

Miss Lucy came in carrying Junior in her arms. "Looks like he wants something."

"No, I nursed him a little while ago. Hold him a bit for me." Miss Stewart beckoned to June to follow her.

June stumbled into the living-room after Miss Stewart. What did she mean, you got one too? Had Sister written her that she was going to kill herself? The tears streamed down her face while she waited for Miss Stewart to put Chrissy in her crib, then she followed her, not into the bedroom as she expected, but to the study. Miss Stewart knocked on the door.

Mr. Bowen's voice called, "Come in."

His wife held up the letter. "Honey, sorry to interrupt. She wrote to June as well."

The man laid down his pen and took the letter from his wife's hand.

June stepped forward. "Wait! You all knew about this?"

Miss Stewart seemed near tears. "We can explain."

June's voice trembled. "I can't believe you all knew about this and said nothing to me."

Mr. Bowen rose from his chair, came around the desk and touched her on her shoulder. "We got a letter from your sister just a couple days ago – after the accident. It was as much a shock to us as it is to you. I'm so sorry."

June stared into the man's dark eyes. He seemed sincere. She looked down at the carpet. "I'm sorry I spoke to you that way."

"I understand. I can't begin to imagine what you must be going through."

Suddenly the floodgates burst. She found herself sobbing against his chest, his strong, comforting arms around her. She was vaguely aware of another arm around her and a voice whispering soothing words.

Eventually, she disengaged herself and looked from the wife to the husband. She gave a shaky laugh. "I didn't mean to soak your nice shirt, Mr. Bowen."

He smiled and took his seat. "It will go to the laundry sooner than I'd planned."

June groped for a chair. "I don't understand what would make Sister do something like that."

Miss Stewart sat near June. "From what she wrote to us, she felt that taking her life was the only way to escape going to jail and embarrassing you. She told us all about the abuse and everything. Your sister has been dealing with a lot of depression and guilt for a long time. Do you want to see the letters?"

She shook her head. Letters? How many did she write? Then it hit her. *They know Sister killed Daddy!* The thing they'd struggled so hard to conceal was now out in the open. And her sister was still alive! Worse, the person her sister was most afraid of now knew of her crime. June glanced at the closed door. She wanted to run. But where could she go? She and Marva had run—from Egypt Village to Tantie Beulah to San Fernando—straight into the arms of the man who could throw them both into prison.

June fidgeted. Her bladder burned. She jumped up from her chair. "Excuse me."

In the bathroom she rested her head in her hands. *Sister, what did you do? Oh God, what did you do? It's better you had died.*

June dragged herself back into the study. The husband and wife looked up as she entered.

"You okay?" Miss Stewart asked.

She nodded then shook her head. "I'll never be okay again."

Mr. Bowen glanced at her. "This may make you feel better. Your sister didn't try to kill herself."

June's head jerked up. "What do you mean?"

He read from the letter. "'June, last night I dreamed of Mama. She had on a pretty, white dress her hair was shining and curled over one shoulder and she smiled and held out her hand to me. She didn't speak to me but I knew she was calling me to come to her. June, I'm going to put on my white baptism dress and go to meet her and she will take me to Jesus…'"

He raised his eyes from the letter. "She wasn't wearing a white dress, was she?"

"It was an accident, honey," Miss Stewart looked at June. "Something must have made her run across the road like that."

June gripped the arms of her chair. "I saw the dress. I wondered why it was in her drawer."

Moments passed before she asked the question that nagged at her mind and heart. "What happens now?"

Mr. Bowen came to sit on the edge of his desk nearest her. "We'll cross that bridge when we come to it, but I want you to know, I'll do everything in my power to protect both of you."

June looked at him, and the tears flowed afresh.

CHAPTER TWENTY-FIVE

It was just after nine, but the morning air felt heavy with moisture. Sweat broke out on June's forehead. Dark rain clouds hung like monstrous fingers in the sky as she trudged through the hospital gates, blinking back the tears. She'd been so anxious for her sister to awake from her coma, but now she dreaded it. What would be their fate, if, or when that happened? Would Sister be able to stand up to the rigors of a court trial? Would Mr. Bowen be able to protect them, as he'd said? Would there be a lot of ugly publicity? She could just picture the headlines: James Garcia's Murderer Discovered: Daughter Confesses To Murdering Her Father.

June entered the ICU and nodded to the nurse at the desk. One of the beds was empty. Had the occupant died, or had she been moved to another ward? June was too despondent to ask. When she neared her sister's bed, she saw a young woman in a white coat bending over her. As she drew nearer, she saw the woman raise her sister's casted arm. "Good-morning."

The woman looked up and smiled. "Good-morning. I'm Pat, the Physical Therapist."

June forced a smile. "I'm June, her sister. Dr. Fred told me you would be coming." She rested her bag with Marva's clean laundry on the nightstand. "He said you would help to prevent contractures?"

Pat nodded. "If we don't do this, her joints will become tight and it will be more difficult for her to move them when she wakes up."

"I see."

June momentarily forgot her fears as she watched while the woman worked on her sister's limbs. She bent the elbow, wrist, and fingers of the uncasted arm then moved to her foot, knee and hip. "I like that. May I help?"

Pat showed her how to raise Marva's arm while supporting her elbow. "That's it. Be gentle and watch out for her tubes. You can do her fingers, if you want to, when I'm not here."

Through it all, Marva made no response.

After the therapist left, June returned to brooding about the turn of events. Her initial reaction to Marva's letter had been anger. Why did she want to kill herself and leave June all alone? It was nothing but selfishness. But after talking with the Bowens, guilt, fear and shame had overcome her. She, who had always been occupied with a host of friends and activities, now understood what Marva's life must have been like. Just work, church and home. And for the first time, loneliness enveloped her. Sure, she had Miss Stewart, but this was an impenetrable loneliness, a kind of pathos that no human companionship could satisfy.

She needed God.

June had not yet reached that level of intimacy with God that her sister seemed to have, and now she yearned for it. She wrapped her arms across her bosom and bowed her head. *God, I need you as I've never needed you before. I'm so afraid, Lord, of what could happen to me and my sister. Have mercy on us, Lord. Forgive us for killing our father. I know my sister didn't mean to, Lord. Please, forgive us.* She stopped and fumbled in her mind for a scripture verse she'd heard Marva say. *All things work for God … what was it?*

"June?"

Startled, she looked up. Reverend Harris, his wife, and another lady June didn't know stood there.

She got up. "Good-morning, Reverend. I didn't hear you come in."

He smiled. "That's okay. How's your sister doing?"

June glanced toward the bed. "No better, I think."

"Never mind," the man said. "God is still in control. We are making some morning visits, and the nurse said it was okay for us to come and pray with her."

June nodded. The minister's appearance seemed like an answer from God. They held hands and the three visitors prayed for Marva's recovery. Reverend Harris ended with, "And Lord, please give her sister strength to go through this time of testing. Help her to realize that all things work together for good to them that love the Lord —"

June's eyes flew open. Yes, that was the verse. God had heard her. He would answer. Thank you, Jesus!

That night she shyly recounted to Miss Stewart what had happened during the minister's visit. She said, "I want to learn that verse, Miss. May I borrow your Bible?"

Miss Stewart smiled. "Sure, there's one on the coffee table in the living-room."

With her help, June found the verse, then she wrote it on a piece of paper and tucked it inside her purse. She never wanted to forget it. As she crossed the living-room to return to the kitchen, the phone rang. When she got there, Miss Stewart was saying, "Yes, she's right here. Please hold."

She took the phone from Miss Stewart's hand. When the voice on the other end said, "This is Nurse Cooper from San Fernando General Hospital," June's heart almost stopped beating. She groped for a chair and sat.

"Your sister opened her eyes a short while ago," the nurse continued, "and the doctor said you may come and see her for a few minutes."

June shrieked and jumped up from the chair. "Sister opened her eyes. They want us to come and see her."

She threw her arms around Miss Stewart's neck. "Can you take me?"

Her teacher's eyes shone. "Of course, I'll take you. That is great news."

June ran along the corridor ahead of Miss Stewart when they got to the hospital, then stopped short at the nurse's desk. She expected to be ushered in to her sister's bed, but instead the woman looked at her. "May I help you?"

June had never seen this nurse before. Before she could reply, Miss Stewart came up behind her. "We received a call that Marva was awake and we could come and see her."

The nurse consulted a book in front of her then looked back at Miss Stewart. "Are you Sheila's sister? Yes? How are the twins doing? Sheila showed us some pictures —"

June brushed past the desk and made her way to her sister's bed. In the dim light, Marva appeared to be in the same condition in which she'd last seen her. Eyes closed, she lay on her side, supported by pillows, all tubes in place. But wait! The brain tube, as June called it, had been removed, and Marva's head didn't seem as large as before. That was a good sign. June bent and kissed her sister's cheek.

"I was going to tell you she was sleeping."

June straightened and looked at the nurse in her starched white uniform. "I couldn't wait."

Miss Stewart stepped forward and took Marva's hand. "Marva?"

The girl's eyes fluttered.

Miss Stewart turned to the nurse. "Do you think she heard me?"

"It's possible." She squeezed Marva's unbandaged arm. "Marva, can you hear me?"

Her eyes opened but she didn't turn her head.

June brought her face level with her sister's. "Sister, it's me, June."

Marva's gaze rested on hers, but there was no sign of awareness. Then she closed her eyes.

"I think we should leave her to rest," the nurse said. "She may be like this for a while."

June turned to the nurse. "How long?"

The nurse shook her head. "Every patient is different. It's hard to tell."

June was near tears. It was unrealistic for her to expect her sister to wake up and start talking right away as they do in the movies, but she'd hoped for a miracle.

On the way home, Miss Stewart broke the silence. "You are quiet. What are you thinking, dear?"

June stared out the window. How do you express the anger, the helplessness and hopelessness you feel? How do you tell someone like Miss Stewart that you are angry with God?

Miss Stewart continued, "I know this is difficult for you. It is for me too because I love you girls like you were my daughters. I want you to talk to me. Don't keep it bottled up inside. Your sister wouldn't be where she is now if she'd been able to talk to someone."

June was glad for the darkness in the car so she could give free rein to her fears and her tears. Miss Stewart passed her a napkin, and she blew her nose loudly.

"I'm angry, Miss. So angry."

Miss Stewart glanced at her. "Are you angry with me?"

June shook her head. "I'm angry with God." There, she had said it. "How could He let this happen to my sister? She's such a good, sweet person. Always trying her best to please Him. You remember when she gave out tracts on the street? Because she wanted to please God. And then she met a man named TL. Do you know she bought clothes for him and his sister, invited them to church, and they gave their lives to Christ? And they are not the only ones. What more could she have done? And all the trouble she went through with Daddy. She used to bathe me and comfort me when … when Daddy did bad things to me. Why does God hate her so? Maybe —"

Miss Stewart raised her hand. "Never! Never for one minute must you think God hates your sister. He cannot hate his child. He loves her."

June's eyes widened. "Love? He almost killed her. What kind of love is that?"

Miss Stewart entered the carport and turned off the engine. She took hold of June's hand. "My dear, you have every right to be angry, and to ask the questions you're asking. When bad things happen to good people, it never makes sense. It didn't make sense that Job should suffer the way he did. Have you read the story of Job?"

June kept her gaze down. They'd read it in Sunday school, and she knew it well. Job was a good man who served God, but he lost all his children and all his riches in one day. How unfair was that! "Yes, I read it."

"And he wasn't the only one. Jesus died a cruel death on the cross even though He was sinless. There are many more stories of people in the Bible who suffered for their faith. Child, look at me." Obediently June raised her eyes to Miss Stewart's. "The more we love God and try to serve

Him, the more the devil attacks us, because he wants us to blame God and eventually hate Him. The devil attacked Job to try to prove to God that Job would turn away from Him, but Job never did. You know what he said?"

June shook her head, her eyes riveted on Miss Stewart's face.

"He said, 'Though he slay me, yet will I hope in him.' And that's what we must say when the devil comes against us. We must keep on hoping in God."

June's tired mind couldn't make sense of all that the lady said, but June trusted her. Her shoulders relaxed. She disengaged her hand from Miss Stewart's and unbuckled her seatbelt.

Those were the first words that came to June's mind when she awoke the next morning. *Hope in God.* She looked at the clock. Seven-fifteen. Time to get ready for school. She'd been away for two weeks. She could do nothing for her sister by sitting in that chair staring at her all day long. It was time to trust God and continue with her life, difficult as it was. She got up and went into the bathroom.

Miss Stewart and her husband were at the table having breakfast when she entered the kitchen, dressed in her school uniform.

Miss Stewart smiled at her. "Do you feel up to it?"

June managed a smile. "I think so."

Mr. Bowen looked up from his coffee. "That's a wise decision. You'll feel much better once you're active again. I can give you a ride on my way to work."

June turned to him. "Thank you."

Dressed in a dark-colored vest over long-sleeved blue shirt with matching tie, dark gray pants and gray shoes, hair neatly brushed back from his forehead, Mr. Bowen looked every inch the detective. He sometimes carried a gun in a holster, but he wasn't wearing it this morning. Marva had always been afraid of him, but June thought him a nice man, the perfect mate for Miss Stewart. Under different circumstances, June would have been thrilled to be in his company.

Miss Stewart set a plate of bread, sausage, and eggs in front of her. June suddenly realized she was hungry.

Minutes later, she joined Mr. Bowen in his car.

He reached for his seatbelt. "You have a lot of catching up to do."

She shrugged. "I know."

No more was said until they arrived at the school. June looked out the window at the two-storey building with the sign that read St. Thomas Aquinas. She'd barely been there two weeks. "Now I feel nervous."

He squeezed her hand. "You'll be fine. Just think back to the first and last day at your old school. Just as you fitted in there, you'll do it here."

He really was nice. Suddenly she wished she could kiss him the way other girls kissed their dads when they dropped them off. She'd never kissed her dad. She reached for the door handle.

"Would you like me to pick you up this evening?"

June shot him a quick glance. "If it's not too much trouble."

"No trouble at all."

June thanked him and got out of the car. On the sidewalk, she waved to him and watched as he drove away.

"June, you are back."

She turned to see a tall, brown-skinned girl with a shining, permed bob approaching. June remembered her from her sociology class. She smiled. "Hello, Carlene. Yes, I'm back."

Carlene fell into step beside her. "Is your sister out of the hospital?"

June stifled a sigh. She would hear that question a lot today. "No, but she opened her eyes for the first time yesterday."

Carlene's gaze showed sympathy. "I'm glad. My family and I have been praying for her, and for you too."

June glanced up at the girl who was almost as tall as Marva. "Really? Thank you so much."

The tears welled up. People they didn't even know were praying for them. Surely God would answer.

~

That afternoon when Mr. Bowen came to pick her up, June was apologetic. "I'm sorry I forgot to tell you I wanted to go straight to the hospital from school. But I need to go to the apartment first and get clean clothes for Sister. I can take the bus from there."

He shifted the gear lever. "No problem. I'll take you to the apartment."

June's eyes watered. "You're too kind. I didn't expect all of this."

He was silent while they waited at an intersection. The light changed, and he drove off slowly. "June, I know you and your sister probably looked at me as some type of ogre while I was investigating your father's murder —"

She opened her mouth to speak, but he raised his hand. "I could have arrested your sister very early in the investigations because everything pointed to her, but I didn't. You know why? I didn't have enough concrete evidence, but also, I saw two young girls who had suffered so much. I couldn't add to your suffering. Now I see I was wrong."

June stared at his profile. "What do you mean, you were wrong?"

Mr. Bowen glanced in his rearview mirror before pulling into a little clearing. He left the engine running. "When I took over the position as head of the Point Fortin district, I had big dreams of becoming a top - notch detective. I'd been denied the recognition I thought I deserved in Port-of-Spain, so when your father's murder landed in my lap, I thought here was my chance to prove myself. But it was more than I could handle. I was wrong in thinking that just because I hadn't arrested your sister, she would no longer suffer."

June bit her lip. "I never realized how much she was suffering." She paused. "But why did our case affect you so much?"

He passed his hand over his balding head. "I'd never come across anything like it before. It made me uncomfortable, and in the end, I felt I'd failed as a detective. Not just me, but the whole system."

June frowned at the windscreen. What Mr. Bowen said made little sense to her. She knew nothing about the law or how it operates. Does it help or hurt people? Can you hide behind it the way a child hides behind the bedroom door when playing hide-and-seek? Should you trust it or fear it? Is it like that dark object in your room at nights? You know it's there so you lie still wondering when it's going to pounce.

Maybe if she knew more she could help her sister. "Why do you say the system failed?"

He jerked his head toward her as if just remembering her presence. "Because Trinidad has no law against child abuse. My wife and I both feel that if such a law was in place, the likelihood of your father—and others like him—harming their children would be greatly reduced."

June raised an eyebrow. No law against child abuse? Something that kills a child's self-esteem, renders her almost mute, unable to make friends or achieve the psychological and emotional milestones like other children? Something that drove her sister almost to the point of madness until she felt her only way out was suicide? All because of the lack of a stupid law?

Anger rose within her, and she strained against the seatbelt. The police could only operate within the parameters of the justice system. She knew that much. Without those parameters, sick men like her father were given license to abuse children to their heart's content and not be held accountable.

Mr. Bowen said something to her as he pulled away from the edge of the road, but June's mind was focused on what role she could play in this hapless situation. *I'm going to help put an end to this suffering. No other little girl should have to suffer the way my sister and I did. Thank God, I now have the money.*

CHAPTER TWENTY-SIX

On Saturday morning, June twisted her hair into one long braid, coiled it around at the nape of her neck and secured it with two hairpins. She viewed herself in the mirror. "I'm doing something about this today."

She would go by the apartment, air it out and dust a little before going to the library. Next, a visit to the hairdresser and then the hospital.

About half an hour later, Mrs. Maraj met her at the door to her apartment with a small bundle of mail, and June filled her in on the latest news about Marva.

The woman smiled. "I'm so glad. You know Ms. Teesdale, Ms. Fisher and, I think, Mr. Hamilton over on Riverdale Drive have been meeting once a week to pray for her."

June felt herself becoming teary. "Really? I must go and thank them."

"Yes, do that."

June unlocked the door to the ringing of the phone. She rushed to pick it up.

"Well, finally," a male voice said.

"John! What do you mean, finally?"

"I've been calling. You don't go to your house anymore?"

She sat on the chair near the phone. "Only now and then, to get clothes and things."

"How's your sister doing?"

June smiled even though he couldn't see her. "She opened her eyes the other day, and they removed the tube from her brain, but she still has the ones in her mouth and her nose."

"That's good news. And how are you doing?"

"Better, I think."

Pause. "I miss you."

Her breath caught in her throat. "I miss you too."

And she meant it. She'd been so engrossed in her sister's condition she'd forgotten what it was like to have fun.

"Would you like to go to a movie this evening?"

"I would love it. I have a few things to do today, but later I'll be ready."

"Okay. Where will I meet you?"

"At the Bowens'." She gave him the address and hung up. It would be great to be with John tonight. His quiet, solid presence was exactly what she needed. If Keith had tried to get in touch with her, she had no way of knowing.

And she didn't care.

When June got to the ICU that afternoon, the nurse met her with the news that Marva had kept her eyes open for almost three minutes that morning, but still didn't seem to recognize anything. June went to her sister's bedside and called her name but got no response. June's gaze rested on the cassette player. It seemed the nurses never bothered to put it back on when it stopped. Miss Stewart had given her some cassettes she thought Marva would like. June slipped one in and turned on the player. On an impulse, she took a pen from her bag and wrote on Marva's cast, *I love you, Sister.* She drew a heart next to it and below she wrote, *9/28/86. Eyes open 3 mins.*

She looked up as someone cleared his throat. "Jason!"

He came and put his arm around her, but his eyes were on Marva's still form on the bed. "How you doing, June?"

June smiled at him. "Better." She told him what the nurse had said.

He brushed at the corner of his eye. "That's good. I still can't believe this happened."

June fixed her gaze on her sister's face. Jason wouldn't want her to see him crying. Then something strange happened. He bent and kissed

Marva's cheek and whispered something in her ear. Her eyes opened, and she turned her head in his direction. June's jaw dropped. Her sister seemed aware of his presence. What she'd hoped and prayed for seemed to be happening. Her sister was waking up from that deathless sleep she'd been in for over three weeks. And all because of a kiss. No, not just a kiss. Prayers had played a part too, June was sure of it. You bad girl, you, she wanted to say. You wouldn't open your eyes for me, but you did it for him.

Jason held Marva's hand and spoke words of comfort. They crept to June's ears like vines in a latticework of thoughts.

"---you're coming out of this, Moe. You're strong. Remember how you used to fight those bad kids in Egypt? Now is the time for you to fight, Moe. I'll help you. God will help you. We'll fight this together. Yes, we'll fight it. Be strong, Moe. Now is not the time to give up. I love you, sweetheart ---"

June couldn't take it anymore. She rushed out of the ward, past the nurse, and into a nearby bathroom. She splashed water on to her face and made frantic attempts to blot the tears that gushed forth like a bleeding artery.

When she returned to the ward, Jason was seated on the chair, Marva's hand still in his. Her eyes were closed again, but a ghost of a smile hovered around her lips.

The nurse came in and adjusted the IV. "This is a miracle. I think she has finally come out of the coma, but the doctor has to confirm it."

June tried to dismiss the little demon of jealousy that had sneaked in. Jason had been able to awake her sister to consciousness when she couldn't. But she pushed the thought aside. It was God who did it. Nothing is impossible for Him. He'd only used Jason to do His work.

Jason stretched out his hand to her. "May I borrow your pen?"

June handed it to him. Below June's words he wrote, *I love you, Moe. Jason*

They walked out of the hospital a few minutes later, discussing what had taken place. Jason stopped. "You know, June, I don't know where those words came from, but it was like God was speaking through me.

Marva talked to me about God before. She said she had His light in her, or something like that, and she wanted to live for Him." He gave her a shy smile. "I'm going to start going to church, like she told me to."

June stared at him. Why didn't her sister marry this man? "I'm glad, Jason. Sister will be so happy."

He nodded. "I came a few times before, but they never let me in. I'm glad I was able to see her today."

A feeling of lightness came over her. "It's a pity. Sister would be walking by now."

They laughed as they headed for the elevator.

June's buoyancy remained until she returned to Miss Stewart's house and knocked on her bedroom door. Getting no answer, she went out onto the back porch where she met her and her husband sitting on the swing, each holding a baby.

Miss Stewart's eyes widened. "June! What did you do?"

What had she done? Recollection returned. So much had happened since she left the hairdresser that morning, she'd forgotten that Marva's improvement was not the only reason for the lightness she felt.

She fingered the curls at the nape of her neck. "I wanted to surprise you."

Miss Stewart stared. "You sure have. Turn around let me see."

"It looks good." This came from Mr. Bowen.

"Yes, it does," Miss Stewart added. "I know your hair was probably too hot for you sometimes, but I loved it."

"Maybe I'll let it grow again, but not as long as it was."

Miss Stewart rocked Junior gently. "So, how's Marva?"

June plopped down on the chair opposite. "I have to sit to tell you this."

When she finished relating all that had taken place that morning, the couple's faces were alight with joy.

"That's marvelous news," Miss Stewart said. "I'm going to go over there before Miss Lucy leaves." She turned to her husband. "Honey, do you mind?"

He shook his head. "Not at all. As long as I have Miss Lucy to help, I'll be all right."

Back to the hospital June and Miss Stewart went, but Marva refused to stage a repeat performance. However, June noted a subtle difference in her expression. It didn't seem as blank as it had over the previous weeks. She now looked like a person within that shell.

On the way home, June asked, "Miss Stewart, do you mind if I go out this evening?"

The woman took her eyes off the road for a second. "Not at all. You've been cooped up for so long. Where are you going?"

"You remember John? You gave him a ride from the hospital that first day."

Miss Stewart smiled. "Oh, yes. How could I forget?"

"He invited me to the movies this evening. He should come to meet me around seven-thirty."

"Sure, that's fine. How are you getting back?"

"I believe either his mom or dad will take us and pick us up afterward."

The lady nodded. "Sounds good. He seems like a nice young man."

After a silence came the expected question. "So, is everything over between you and Keith?"

June looked down at her hands. "I think so."

Miss Stewart patted her arm. "Don't worry. God's in charge. Ask Him to direct you."

June dressed for her date in the jeans Marva had bought her. She topped it off with a light pink top and the denim jacket she'd worn to the BBB concert. Gold earrings, a Christmas gift from Marva, black medium-heeled sandals and a small black purse completed her outfit.

John gave her an appreciative glance when she got into his mother's car. He eyed her new short hairstyle. "It looks nice on you. Anything would look nice on you." He paused. "You remember how in school they used to call you 'the girl with the hair'?"

June chuckled. "That was my handle."

His mom smiled at her in the rearview mirror. "I like it too, June."

June smiled shyly. "Thanks, Mrs. Baptiste."

In the theater, he placed his arm around her shoulder and it felt so good to lean against him. When the movie was over, they walked out hand in hand. In the foyer, a small group crowded around the ice-cream stand.

He paused. "Feel like ice-cream?"

She nodded. She hadn't had any in a long time. They strolled over to the group, and June stopped short. But too late. Keith and Sandra turned at the same time and their eyes met. Sandra hastily averted her gaze, but Keith stared at them, then down to their linked hands. Then he smiled. "Ay, John, June how you all doing?"

John's tone was cool. "Great. And you?"

"Never better. We beat Crest Camp 10 - 8 the other day."

"Yeah, I heard. And we beat Presentation 5 - 1 yesterday. I scored 2."

While the boys discussed soccer, June sidled up to Sandra. The girl appeared startled when she saw June next to her, but June had no intention of being mean.

"How you doing, Sandra?"

Her eyes widened and she studied June's face for a moment as if deciding how she should answer. "I'm okay. I heard about your sister. I'm so sorry."

"Thanks. She's doing much better. She seems to be coming out of the coma."

"Oh, that's good. I'll ask Mummy to take me to see her tomorrow."

"That will be nice, Sandra. I might see you there." She turned as John tapped her on her shoulder. "What flavor do you want?"

She smiled up at him. "Chocolate."

He leaned over and whispered in her ear. "I'm having vanilla."

June caught Keith and Sandra's gaze on them. "A private joke," she said.

She and John waited until the others had got their ice-cream, then the four strolled out of the theater together. Outside the entrance, Keith turned to John. "May I speak to June for a second?"

John raised an eyebrow, then shrugged. "Sure."

June glanced at John, who gave a slight nod. After a little hesitation, she joined Keith who had moved out of earshot.

He eyed her hair and smiled. "I always wondered how you would look with short hair. I love it." He paused. "Are you happy?"

June shook her head. "No, but only because of my sister. She means the world to me."

Keith stared at the ground. When he looked up, his expression was pained, which for him was unusual. "I wish things had been different."

She returned his gaze. "Me too. Bye, Keith." She returned to John and linked her hand in his. "Can we wait here for your mom?"

He looked at her with understanding. They said their good-byes to Keith and Sandra and watched as they walked away. June noted he did not hold Sandra's hand. After they'd been swallowed up in the crowd leaving the theater, John turned to her. "You okay?"

She smiled. "I'm fine. Thanks for being so patient with me."

He squeezed her hand. "I know what you and Keith had was special. It doesn't happen to everyone."

Something in his tone made her glance at him. "Have you … have you ever been in love?"

"No, but I think I'm getting there."

They stared at each other, then as if choreographed, they turned, and she was in his arms. A whistle interrupted the kiss and the magic of the moment. They separated, and June gave a shaky laugh. "That was something else."

He smiled down at her. "There's more where that came from."

As June got into bed that night, she reflected on the evening. A chapter of her life had closed. A new one, full of possibilities, was just beginning.

CHAPTER TWENTY-SEVEN

"Behold, I will create new heavens and a new earth. The former things will not be remembered, nor will they come to mind - Isaiah 65: 17.

I see things all around me and I don't know their names. Poles, wires that run from me to machines on tables. One machine has a screen with lines on it that go up and down. They say I'm in the hospital. Why? How did I get here and why can't I walk like everybody else? My bed has rails on either side so I can't get out. The people in the other beds don't walk either. And one of them groans, especially at night. And who is this girl sitting on the chair near my bed reading a book? People are always coming and leaving, but this girl looks like she is staying here.

She has short, curly hair falling forward over one side of her face and she is wearing a blue, pleated skirt, white shirt with a solid blue tie. Now she is looking at me. She has pretty, hazel eyes. And her smile! It's like the sun just came into the room. She has nice teeth and nice skin. She is beautiful!

"Sister, you are awake!"

She gets up from the chair and comes and kisses me on my cheek. Who is she? Is my name Sister? Other people call me Marva. But I don't mind this girl calling me Sister.

"The doctor says you're doing so much better. He says soon they will take all this ugly cast off ..."

My thigh begins to itch. I raise my good arm, and the front of my neck hurts a little. I can't get my hand to go where I want it so I can scratch. Maybe this nice girl can help me scratch? I look at her and try to form the words, but that tube in my throat won't let me speak. I try to pull it out.

The girl holds my hand. "No, don't take it out. That's to help you breathe. Dr. Fred says they'll take it out tomorrow."

My back itches too, but I can't reach it, and this girl is not helping. Tears prickle my eyes.

The girl pats my arm. "What's wrong, Sister? Are you in pain?"

I move my head from side to side. That I can do.

"Do you want me to call the nurse?"

I nod. The girl goes and returns with the nurse. I know her. She is Elise.

She touches my foot. "What's the matter, Miss Popular?"

Miss Popular? Is that my name too? I wave my hand in the air then bring it down to my leg.

"I turned you about fifteen minutes ago. You're still itching?"

I nod.

Elise moves to the head of the bed. "All right. You're making me work. But I like you. You're one of my best patients. Are you happy your sister is here?"

I look at the girl and smile, but her face puckers as if she wants to cry. She's my sister? I'm happy to have such a pretty sister. Elise leaves and returns with a small basin. Yes, a nice back rub is what I need. The water is warm, and it feels good. Afterward, she dries my back and my arm and applies medicine in some places. The medicine burns a little, but I'm used to it now. She leaves me propped on one side so I face the pretty girl. I wish I knew her name.

She looks out the window. When she turns back, I see that her eyes are red and her lips tremble. She sits close to my bed. "Sister, you don't remember me? I'm your little sister June."

Little sister? She doesn't look little. She has a nice height and a nice figure. How old is she? There are so many things I don't know. Tears run down the girl's face and I wish I could wipe them away. I hadn't meant to hurt her.

She smiles and cries at the same time. Then she takes my hand. "I'll help you remember. Your name is Marva Garcia and we live in San Fernando."

I am getting sleepy, although I wish the girl would keep talking.

~

June's head was pounding by the time she got home that night. As soon as Miss Stewart met her at the door, she blurted out, "Sister doesn't know who I am. She can't use her hand, her arm goes all over the place, and she can't speak. I was so happy when she opened her eyes. I can't bear this."

Miss Stewart's eyes widened. "How do you know she doesn't know you? I mean, with the tube in her mouth —"

"The nurse told me when they call her name she just stares at them, but she's not deaf. And when I told her who I am, she looked at me as if she'd never seen me before."

June burst into tears and fled to her room where she stayed for the rest of the night.

Two days later, Marva came down with pneumonia. Dr. Fred said it was not uncommon when patients were immobile as she was. That scared June, but for her the most devastating thing was that her sister really seemed to have lost her memory. June and Miss Stewart increased their prayers. A week later, when June entered the ICU, Nurse Elise—she knew them all by name now—greeted her at the door. "She's not here."

June's heartbeat quickened, then slowed when she noticed the nurse's smile. "They moved her to orthopedic."

June smiled back. "Oh, where's that?"

Elise gave her directions to the ward, and June hurried away. But when she got there, she saw that was not the only surprise. Marva's heavy cast and all her tubes, except the catheter, had been removed.

This time Marva gave her a hesitant smile of recognition. She mouthed, "Hello," which came out like a faint, scratchy sound.

June paused near the bed. "Hello, Sister. How are you feeling?"

Marva's arm snaked its way down to her leg. "Hurts."

June raised the cover and gasped. Beneath her nightgown, her sister's body seemed to have shrunk to half its size. She was as thin as a blade of grass. Her leg, once strong and shapely, now looked like a dried-up bone covered with hair. With trembling hand, June examined her arm next. Also dark and shriveled, but not as hairy as her leg. June covered her up and burst into tears. Then aware that Marva was watching her, she turned toward the window and gave way to wracking sobs.

Someone put her arm around her shoulder. "June?"

Hastily she dabbed at her face and turned around. Miss Sheila stood there, Dr. Fred a few steps behind her.

Miss Sheila drew her close. "I know this is a shock, dear. This must be so hard on you."

Dr. Fred examined Marva, listening to her heartbeat, peering into her eyes and her ears. Finally, he straightened and smiled at her. "How do you feel, my dear?"

Marva croaked her reply. "Pain."

"Okay, the nurse will give you something for the pain and then we're going to have you sitting up and moving, okay? We don't want you getting pneumonia again."

Marva kept her gaze on his face, and June wondered how much she understood.

He beckoned to June and Miss Sheila and they followed him out of the ward. June glanced back at Marva and waved but even though her gaze followed them, she didn't wave back.

Out in the hallway, June faced Dr. Fred. She had a million questions she wanted to ask but didn't know how to phrase them and wasn't sure if she wanted to hear the answers.

The doctor placed a hand on her shoulder. "First, let me say that I admire your courage and your love for your sister."

The tears welled up again.

The doctor dropped his hand. "In the days and months ahead, I want you to draw on that courage, and draw on God. Your sister's making remarkable recovery. To be honest, we didn't expect her to be where she is right now."

June stared at him. "You mean, you didn't expect her to live?"

"No, not that. We try not to make that assumption, but we certainly didn't expect her to progress this quickly."

A little hope stirred within her. "So, when will she be able to get up?"

The doctor shook his head. "I can't say. We're going to start sitting her up in a wheelchair today. She's going to get the best therapy care possible. You saw the physical therapist the other day. Occupational therapy, speech therapy will all be here getting her out of bed, retraining her to walk and talk —"

"What about her memory?"

"That too. Speech therapy will work on that, but usually memory is a spontaneous thing. Over a period of time, we'll see how much of it returns."

"How much of it? She may not regain full memory?"

Dr. Fred scratched his head. "I can't say, June. That's not my specialty. Nothing is cut and dried where memory is concerned. All I can tell you is, keep on doing what you're doing. Talk to her, bring pictures, anything that may help to jog her memory."

Miss Sheila hugged her again. "And try not to worry. When Marva gets better, she wants you to be there for her."

June fought to hold back the tears but lost.

June dropped her fork and rose from her chair as an insistent knocking sounded at the door. Mr. Bowen seated opposite her got up, motioning to her to sit. She looked over at Miss Stewart who continued calmly eating. "It's okay, hon. It's probably one of the neighbors."

But the voice that followed Mr. Bowen into the living-room was one that June recognized very well. She rose from her seat. "Tantie Beulah?"

"I don't like disturbing you an' your family like this, sir. I apologize."

June met them half-way to the kitchen. "Tantie Beulah, what are you doing here?"

Tantie Beulah spread her arms wide and June went into them. "Child, oh, child. Your Tantie got some bad news."

Miss Stewart came up behind them. "Hello, Tantie Beulah."

Her aunt let go of June and embraced Miss Stewart. "Good-night, my dear. You look nice as always. I was just telling your husband how sorry I am for disturbing you at this hour."

June smiled at Tantie Beulah's attempt to speak properly but wondered what the bad news could be.

"No problem," Miss Stewart said. "Come and have a seat. We were just finishing dinner. Would you like something to eat?"

Tantie Beulah followed her into the kitchen. "No, thanks, Mrs. Bowen. My stomach is full."

June pulled out a chair for her aunt. "Tantie Beulah, how did you get here?"

"My neighbor's son. He does take me everywhere I have to go. He's waiting in the car for me. I just show him your teacher's invitation card from the wedding, and he say he could find the house. How your sister feeling?"

"She's doing better, Tantie Beulah." No point alarming her aunt.

"Praise God. I pray for her day and night, you know. For both of you."

Mr. Bowen cleared his throat. "Ms. Beulah, it's nice seeing you again. Will you excuse me please? I'm going to check on the babies."

Tantie Beulah's eyes grew round. "You have babies already?"

Miss Stewart smiled. "We have twins."

Her eyes grew rounder. "Twins! What a blessing from the Almighty. An' I come with all this bad news."

June hovered near her aunt's chair. "What bad news, Tantie Beulah?"

The woman opened her purse. "Oh Lord, child, I don't know what to make of this letter. But I ain't show it to nobody, because I don't know what to make of it." She pulled out a piece of paper and handed it to June.

She recognized it immediately as the same notebook paper Marva had written her suicide letter on. Her heart sank as she took the paper from her aunt's hand. She groped for a chair and read, "Dear Tantie Beulah, I want to thank you for all you did for me and Junie. You are the only aunt we know and you are so good to us. Tantie, I don't know how to tell you this, but when June and I were little Daddy did bad things to us. I am too ashamed to say what he did, but I got pregnant for him when I was fourteen and he and Mama did an abortion on me. I was so ashamed. Miss Stewart found me bleeding in the bathroom and she took me home. But I never told her or anybody else what Daddy did to us and please Tantie Beulah don't tell anybody because I don't want June to be embarrassed. She is doing so well in school I don't want anything to hurt her.

Tantie Beulah I have something else to tell you. One night Daddy came home drunk and started cursing because his dinner wasn't ready. Then he threw some money on the table and told me to go to the shop to buy bread. I knew ---" June paused and swallowed against the lump in her throat. "--- I knew he wanted to do bad things with Junie so I refused to go. Junie started to cry and he hit her. Tantie Beulah I ran in the kitchen and picked up the mortar pestle and I hit him on the back of his head and he fell. I killed my father, Tantie Beulah. All this time I have been hiding and pretending that I'm all right, but I can't hide anymore. Mama is calling me. I'm going to meet her and God soon. I asked Him to forgive me. By the time you get this letter I will be with Him. I can hardly wait.

Bye Tantie Beulah

Your loving niece, Marva."

A deathly silence fell on the kitchen. June looked at her aunt who was wiping away her tears with a handkerchief. Miss Stewart's eyes were full. She reached across the table and touched Tantie Beulah's hand. "I'm sorry, Miss Beulah. We received letters similar to yours, although she told you more than she told us because we knew some of it before."

Tantie Beulah paused with the handkerchief before her eye. "You knew about this before?"

Miss Stewart sighed and rose from her seat. "Let's go in the living-room where we can be more comfortable. June, I'm sure your aunt would like some juice or a cup of tea?"

"Lord, I don't know if I could drink anything. But maybe some tea. Thank you so much."

"Okay. June, will you make it for her? I'll go check on my husband with the babies."

June avoided her aunt's eyes while she put the kettle on. "You want Milo, or tea, Tantie Beulah? I remember you like Milo."

Tantie Beulah stared straight ahead as if in a daze. "Yes, Milo will be good."

While June busied herself, Tantie Beulah said, "So you all was going through all this nastiness and you all never come and tell your aunt nothing? You keep it to yourself and your sister kill she father and you all still didn' say nothing?"

June poured the hot water over the Milo. "Tantie, we were so ashamed. We couldn't tell anybody."

"But I'm your blood …"

"We didn't know if anybody would believe us."

Miss Stewart pushed open the kitchen door, holding a baby in one hand. Tantie Beulah got up and took the child from her hand. "What a beautiful baby. Is this a boy or girl?"

Miss Stewart smiled. "That's Chrissy, the girl."

Tantie Beulah handed the baby back to her mother. "She'll be pretty just like you."

"Thank you," Miss Stewart said. "Miss Beulah, do you mind if my husband joins us? He knows about the other letters."

Tantie Beulah shrugged. "I don't mind. This thing was a secret for too long. The Bible say that whatever happens in the dark will always come to light."

Miss Stewart stood aside for Tantie Beulah to precede her. "That's true."

Her aunt took the chair nearest the coffee table and rested her teacup on it. Mr. Bowen came out carrying Junior. "This little fella wanted to be in the action too."

Tantie Beulah limped over and kissed the child's cheek. "He looks just like his father."

Mr. Bowen moved to the sofa where his wife sat. "I take it that means he's good looking."

"Yes, he is," Tantie Beulah said. "The Lord blessed you with two beautiful children."

Miss Stewart turned to her. "So, Miss Beulah, what do you think about the letter?"

Tantie Beulah placed the cup on the saucer. "My dear lady, I don't know what to think. I was just telling the little one, what's your name again, child? June? I was telling June they had a right to come and tell me something."

"We couldn't go anywhere without Daddy knowing where we were going."

Tantie Beulah nodded slowly. "That's true. But when you and your sister came, you told me your father sent you to spend time with me. You all didn' say he was dead."

June studied Miss Stewart's wedding picture opposite. Her aunt always had trouble remembering June's name, but she remembered that day. June did too. She was so nervous and wanted to say so many things to Marva, but back then she could barely express her thoughts. And the trauma of what happened the night before only made it worse. She took her gaze off the picture to see everyone's eyes on her.

June played with her fingers. "We were scared."

Miss Stewart came to her rescue. "I'm sure you were, dear. I would be scared if I was in your place."

Mr. Bowen glanced at his wife, then at Tantie Beulah. "Miss Beulah, do you think your brother could have done what your niece said in the letter?"

Tantie Beulah looked down at her hands. "I don't know, sir. That is a very serious thing." She paused. "But we have another brother. His wife told me once that somebody accused him of … of the same thing."

June jerked her head at Tantie Beulah. The woman's gaze flitted from the floor to the walls then to the faces of those in the room. Then she fanned herself with her hand.

Mr. Bowen spoke again. "Miss Beulah, will you be willing to testify about this in court?"

Tantie Beulah turned wide eyes on him. "Testify? In court? Why, sir?"

Mr. Bowen adjusted the baby on his lap. "Because your niece may have to go to trial when she gets better."

Tantie Beulah stood. "Go to trial? But that is wickedness, man. After all she went through? No, sir, I don't mean no disrespect, but I don't know. This is too much for me." She threw her hands up in the air. "Lord, what is this? Help us, Lord. I don't know what to do."

June jumped up from her chair and touched her aunt's arm. "Tantie Beulah, calm down. Everything will be all right."

Tantie Beulah looked at her. "Calm down? Your sister killed her father, then she tried to kill herself and you expect me to calm down?" She snatched up her purse from the table. "Sir, Miss Lady, sorry to disrespect your house this time of night. I will be going now. Good-night."

June's eyes filled. "Tantie Beulah …"

Her aunt marched toward the door without looking back, and Mr. Bowen got up and opened it for her. "Goodnight, Miss Beulah."

"Good-night, sir."

June threw herself on the sofa near Miss Stewart and wept on her shoulder. Was there no end to this ugly mess?

CHAPTER TWENTY-EIGHT

I look at the pictures the lady shows me. "Bird. Baby. Book. Grass." She holds up a picture of a lamp. I look at her. "Tired."

The woman shakes her head. "I am tired."

"I am tired."

She smiles. "You did very well, Marva. Tomorrow we'll do some more, okay?"

"Okay." Yawn.

I look past her and smile. The nice girl, June, is back and she has two young men with her. While June talks with the speech therapist, one of the men comes and kisses me on my cheek. "Moe, you're sitting up."

He is nice-looking.

"Marva."

When he smiles, his white teeth light up his face. "You are Marva, but I call you Moe."

The therapist leaves, and June comes and kisses me. "How are you feeling today, Sister?" She looks at the other young man. "You remember my friend, John? And Jason?" She points to the man who kissed me.

"No."

The younger man says, "How are you feeling, Miss Garcia?"

"Miss Garcia?"

June brushes my hair from my forehead with her hand. "Your name is Marva Garcia. I told you, remember?"

"Marva Garcia." I smile. It's a nice name. Then I feel the tears roll down my cheeks. The man Jason pulls out a handkerchief and blots my face. "Don't cry, Moe. It will come back."

I want to nod, but something is holding my head back on the wheelchair. The therapist says it's to keep my head straight. And I have a sponge block between my legs, a belt across my waist and straps on my ankles to keep me from falling out of the chair.

I look at June. "Tired."

June turns away. "Okay, I'll get the nurse."

The nice man holds my hand and talks to me. I don't understand everything he says, but I hear "memory," "getting better" and "walking again."

"Want walk."

"That's what she keeps saying all the time." Nurse Hazel comes with June. "Are you ready to walk?"

I close my eyes and open them again.

"You want to sleep." Hazel turns to June. "She's been up since lunch time. She's staying up longer every day. I think she can go back to bed now."

"We can help you," Jason says.

The nurse tells the men what to do, and they unhook all the things and lift me and put me in the bed. It feels so good to lie down. I close my eyes, wanting sleep, but names and faces are going around in my head. People who came to see me. A tall lady who talked a lot and said she was Tantie Beulah; another lady in a white uniform – Miss Sheila; a man with a white collar who came and prayed with me and told me about God. He asked me if I knew God and I said yes. I could never forget Him. He saved my life. And four men who came and said I worked with them. One said his name was Krishna.

June kisses my cheek again and says she is leaving. They all kiss me. Such nice people. I want to get to know them better.

June sat on the front porch watching the mosquitoes swarm around the streetlamp in front of the Bowens' house. Thoughts buzzed through her mind just like those mosquitoes. Fortunately, she was able to shut them off when she was in school. But the minute she got home, they returned with a vengeance. How long would Marva remain in this amnesic condition? How long would it be before she could speak in sentences? When would she be able to sit unsupported? Stand? Walk?

The orthopedic said he was pleased with her X-rays. Her fractures had healed properly and she would be able to bear weight once her reflexes improved. Which depended on her brain functioning right. And this was what troubled June the most. While strong muscles were important, if the brain could not send them the proper signals, they were useless. They would atrophy.

June had brought home a pile of books from the library and read all she could on amnesia. What she read gelled with what Dr. Fred had told her. Marva appeared to have retrograde amnesia. Her brain was able to form new memories – she now knew June and other people she saw regularly – but could recall nothing about the accident or what happened before that. And the frightening thing was she could stay that way. It wasn't fair to have twenty-one years of one's life hidden in some wilderness never to be retrieved. But which was better, that Marva stay in that wilderness, or grope her way out and face trial for murder? Either one seemed gloomy.

No, she had to switch off the thoughts. John was coming to see her. June wasn't in the mood to go out, and he'd said he understood. He just wanted to see her. What a contrast he was to Keith. As different as a gentle rain to a hurricane.

In a few moments, a car stopped in front of the gate and he got out. June ran down the steps to meet him. She wore a denim capris and a blue tee shirt, which matched his blue jeans, white polo and denim jacket. He kissed her cheek. "How are you doing?"

She shrugged and gave him a half-smile. Whenever people asked her that question, she always felt like crying.

He gave her a keen look. "I worry about you."

She glanced up at him. "Really?"

He nodded. "I wish I could help in some way."

She linked her hand in his. "You are helping." And she meant it. There was something strong, yet calming about him that made her feel good when she was with him. Yet, what did he get in return? "It's not fair to you though."

"What do you mean?"

She took a step forward, aware that the neighbor opposite was sitting on her verandah watching them. "Let's walk a little."

Holding hands, they strolled a short distance, the silence broken only by their soft footfalls.

"You should have someone who is more fun to be with. Not someone who is crying all the time."

He stopped and faced her. "June, you are all I want. Ever since we were in Polytechnic, I had my eyes on you. But nobody could come between you and Keith, so I went along with Wendy and her crazy ways."

June chuckled, her mood lifting. "I had no idea. Have you heard from Wendy?"

"Yes, she called me and said the baby is due in a month or so, but meanwhile she's taking evening classes."

"Good for her. I hope everything goes well."

They reached a little concrete bench near an abandoned lot and they stopped. Light from a nearby streetlamp spilled through a Poinciana tree, it's leaves casting feathery shadows on to the roadway. John pulled off his jacket and spread it on the bench for her to sit.

June sat. "Thank you. Did you practice today?"

"You know I never miss a practice. I think I'm getting better every day."

She smiled up at him. "You're going to be a great soccer player one day."

"That's what I want to be." He took her hand. "June, I want to tell you something. Coach Brenner said that if I keep on playing the way I am now, he would recommend me for the national team."

June cocked her head. "To play for Trinidad and Tobago?"

John looked straight ahead. "A little more than that."

She raised her eyebrows. "More?"

"He would recommend me to the Aston Villa recruiters."

June frowned. Aston Villa? The English soccer team? They were considered the *crème de la crème* of soccer teams, a force to be reckoned with in the World Cup.

She stared at him in admiration. "Oh, John, I'm so happy for you. You're going to be a big soccer star."

He smiled. "It may never happen, but Mr. Brenner has a lot of influence."

June agreed. Since the principal of St. Benedict's had imported him from Germany to coach the school's team they'd never lost a match, and the team had been nicknamed "The Formidable Brenner Boys."

He gazed at her. "If that does happen, will you go with me?"

June's eyes widened. "You mean, to England?"

He gave her a slow nod.

June stood and circled the bench, feeling his gaze on her. This was not what she expected. How could she commit to what he asked, appealing though it was?

She sat back down. "John, I'm pleased, flattered, honored, everything. But, I don't know what to say. At least, not now."

He took her hand in his. "I understand. Just promise you'll think about it. Okay?"

"Okay." And to her embarrassment, the tears welled up again.

Cicely and David ran up the steps, chatting excitedly about their tennis game. As she opened the front door, David patted her on the rump. "I promise I'll let you beat me next time. Today it was too hard to resist."

She turned and gave him a playful shove. "I'll beat you fair and square, as soon as I get back in shape."

They headed for the nursery, but the babies were not in their cribs. They found them out on the back porch, in the arms of June and Marilyn.

"There you are." Cicely flashed a smile around. "How are my little angels?"

June gave a thumbs-up sign.

Marilyn said, "Junior took all of his bottle, but Chrissy only drank half."

Cicely turned toward the door. "Let me go shower and I'll come back and take them."

David put his arm around her shoulder. "Good idea."

Moments later, in the bedroom, Cicely slipped into a housedress. "June doesn't look too good today."

David put down the hair brush and studied himself in the mirror. "My hair seems further back every time I look at it."

"Then don't look at it. You didn't hear a thing I said."

He turned away from the mirror. "June doesn't look too good today."

Cicely slipped her arms around his waist. "I'm worried about her, honey. You know what she said to me yesterday?"

He placed his arms around hers. "No, what?"

"She said she wished her sister had died."

"She doesn't mean it."

Cicely loosened her arms, but he held them in place. "I told her that."

"What did she say?"

"She said death would've been better than her sister living the way she is now."

This time he sighed and moved toward the bed. "I can't begin to imagine what she must be going through."

David opened the nightstand drawer. He took out his checkbook, wrote a check and handed it to Cicely. "Here's something that may help. Take her out to lunch, buy her something."

Cicely gave a little squeal and kissed him on his lips. "Have I told you lately that I love you?"

"No. And you haven't showed me either."

She turned away. He lunged at her, but she dodged him neatly and darted toward the door. "I'll write you an IOU," she threw over her shoulder.

I want to remember so much. June and a nice lady are with me. I look at the lady. "Mother?"

The lady smiles and shakes her head. "No, I'm Miss Stewart. I used to teach you in Egypt Village. Don't you remember me, Marva?"

She is a pretty lady, a little shorter than June and she is wearing a pretty flowered dress and blue sandals. I shake my head. "No."

Tears form in her big, brown eyes. I don't like making people cry. She gives me a hug. "That's okay, honey. You'll remember, one of these days."

June opens a brown envelope, then she puts down one of the bed rails. She sits on the edge of my bed and shows me a picture of a beautiful lady. "This is our mother."

June looks just like her. They have the same plump cheeks, and light-colored eyes. I can't see how long her hair is, but it's parted in the middle and looks silky. I stare at it for a long time then I bend and kiss it. "Want … see her."

The tears are running down June's cheeks. She gets up from the bed, crying even more. Miss Stewart takes June's place and puts her arm around my shoulder. "Honey, your mother died a long time ago. Do you know what that means?"

I nod. It means when people close their eyes and they put them in a grave. I look at the picture of my mother again. "More pictures?"

Miss Stewart gets up and June shows me a picture of two girls. One is a slightly chubby little girl wearing a frilly dress, a hat with a broad rim and she has one braid hanging down the front of her blouse. The other girl in the picture is thin and tall and she is wearing a straight dress with short sleeves. She has thick, curly hair falling around her face and really thick eyebrows reaching almost to her temples. I look at June. She points to the tall girl. "That's you."

I look from her to Miss Stewart. Is that really me? I study the picture again. I was tall. I guess I am still tall, and June was always pretty. She said our mother took us to a studio one day after church and they took that picture of us.

I put my finger on the little girl. "You?"

June smiles, dabbing at her eyes. "That's me."

I smile too. "Very pretty."

"Thank you."

I want to see what I look like now, but I don't know how to say it. "See me."

"That's you," she says again.

I wave my arm and touch my face.

Miss Stewart frowns. "You want to know if that's you?" She smiles and looks in her purse. "I think I know what she wants."

She holds a mirror in front of my face. I look in it and back at the picture. Yes, I can see the same thick eyebrows, the straight nose, a thin light-brown face. I have a scar over my left eye and a bruise on my cheek.

"Not pretty."

June puts her arm around my shoulder. "Yes, you are. You'll always be pretty."

I remember something. "Father?"

This time Miss Stewart is the one who answers. "We don't have one of your father."

"Why?"

June looks down at the bed. "I ... we lost it."

I begin to shake. "Father. See father. See mother." I put my hand on the other bed rail and shake it. I want to get up. Miss Stewart jumps off the bed and raises the rail. I shake and scream even more. Two nurses rush in. I feel a stick in my arm.

June fled from the ward. By the time Miss Stewart found her, she'd dried her tears and held her head up. "I don't know how much more of this I can take."

For once Miss Stewart didn't seem to have any answers.

Marva had acted like a crazy woman. If she continued to carry on like that, they might transfer her to the mental ward.

In the car on the way home, June said, "This is all my fault."

"What do you mean?"

She sniffled. "I was too hard on my sister. I should have left her to live her life the way she wanted to. But instead I criticized her. Wear this, wear that, don't do this, don't do that. Stop giving out tracts. I wanted her to be like me. She would never be like me. We're two different people. Sister was like a young Mother Teresa out there. I'm amazed at the amount of people who come to visit her, all saying how she helped them in one way or another." She paused. "I didn't really appreciate her for who she was. All I did was make her unhappy."

Miss Stewart patted her arm. "I don't think you made her unhappy. Marva was unhappy because of the terrible burden she was carrying. She knew how to help others, but … either she didn't know how, or didn't want to unburden her guilt on God. Maybe she just chose to carry it. Whatever it was, God knows, and this memory loss may just be His way of giving her the peace she couldn't find otherwise."

June stared at the lady's profile. "I never thought of that. You may be right."

CHAPTER TWENTY-NINE

Despite Miss Stewart's words, June dreaded another visit to her sister. But she forced herself to return to the hospital two days later. She regretted her decision the moment she entered the ward. Marva was sleeping on her back, hands tied to the bed rails.

June went to the nurse. "Natalie, why are my sister's hands tied?"

The nurse looked up from the chart. "June, you know we wouldn't restrain her for no reason."

June bit her lip. "I'm sorry. What did she do?"

Natalie smiled. "She wants to feed herself and her hands are not steady yet. She gets food all over herself. This morning she threw a fit when Donna was trying to feed her and she refused to eat."

June's heart sank. "She hasn't eaten all day?"

"She took some of her liquids and her thickened water."

"Do you have anything I can give her?"

Natalie looked at the clock. "Dinner will come in an hour, but I have some Jell-O. Maybe you can try that."

June nodded.

Natalie stood. "Go ahead. I'll bring it."

June returned to her sister's bedside. The bruises seemed to be clearing up and her complexion evening out. June raised the blanket and looked at her sister's legs. The left one was still hairy and scaly and much thinner than the right. The nurse had suggested massaging them with cocoa butter. She would bring it when next she came. She replaced the blanket when Natalie came in with two small containers of Jell-O. She placed them on the nightstand and untied Marva's restraints. Marva moaned softly and opened her eyes.

"Someone's here to see you, Sleepy Head," Natalie said.

Marva's gaze roamed and rested on June's face. She smiled. "June."

June stepped closer to help Natalie sit her up. "Hello, Sister. How are you feeling?"

She nodded. "Good."

Natalie arranged the pillows behind her back. "Feel like eating something?"

Marva nodded again.

"Yes? June is going to give you some Jell-O. Be a good girl, okay?" She turned to June. "Sit close to the bed, but don't put down the rail." She handed June the containers.

"Okay. Thanks, Natalie." June sent up a silent prayer that Marva wouldn't become agitated.

Either God answered, or Marva was really hungry. She ate both containers of the Jell-O and seemed to be looking around for more.

Relieved, June chuckled. "That's all I have, but dinner will be coming soon."

"Want dinner."

June chuckled again. "I'm going to get a washcloth to clean you up, then I'll comb your hair."

Marva smiled. "Pretty."

Did Marva mean June was pretty, or she wanted to look pretty? She wasn't sure, but after she'd washed her sister's face, Marva wriggled her arm toward her. June bent and wrapped her arms around her, and Marva kissed her cheek. June was a little taken aback. Was her memory returning, or did her subconscious mind establish a connection between them? June kissed her sister back and whispered, "I love you."

Later, she combed her hair, staying away from the spot where her brain tube had been inserted. Fine hairs had begun to grow back around the site, and it was just a matter of time before it would be completely covered. But quite a while before she could have a shampoo.

June stood back and viewed her handiwork. "Now you look pretty."

"Look pretty."

June reached into her bag. "I'm going to show you some pictures, but no screaming, okay?"

Marva's eyes lit up. "Okay."

June spent the next few moments showing her pictures of the Bowens, the twins and some of her friends. Marva showed interest in all of them, asking "Who?" and repeating their names after June. As she left the hospital that evening, June whispered, "Thank you, Lord. I think I can do this."

June wondered if it was her changed attitude or God's answer to the prayers that were being sent up for her sister, but gradually Marva's condition improved. She moved from sitting unsupported in her wheelchair to sitting at the edge of the bed then to standing with a walker and taking a few steps with support. But her speech made the greatest improvement. The first day June heard her say a complete sentence, she almost cried. Marva had asked, "Why you call me Sister?"

"You don't like me calling you Sister?"

Marva had looked down at her hands. "No. I just wondered, that's all."

June said, "Because Mama told me to."

She'd watched for her reaction, but none came. In fact, since that day when she'd become agitated over the picture of their mother, Marva had never mentioned her parents again. But June feared that one day she might.

It was already November and she hoped Marva could be home for Christmas and for her birthday on Boxing Day. But Miss Sheila had explained it would not be convenient, since Marva still depended on the bedpan. Until she could go to the bathroom, it was better for her to remain in the hospital.

Meanwhile, June had some important decisions to make. Mrs. Maraj had given her until the end of the year to decide if she wanted to keep the apartment. She was only charging her half-month's rent while they were not occupying it. She'd told her, "I want to help. Your sister is the best tenant I ever had. She was never late with her rent, she kept the place clean and she didn't bother anybody. Just let me know by the end of the year what you want to do."

She'd thanked Mrs. Maraj and promised she would let her know as soon as possible. But it was now the second week of November, and she was still undecided. How long could she keep on living with the Bowens? She had no desire to stay in the apartment by herself, and when Marva left the hospital, who knew if she could be left alone while June was at school? She sighed as she boarded the bus for home.

On a night when a glorious full moon bathed the town in an iridescent glow and lit up trees, bushes and houses like ornaments on a Christmas tree, June and the Bowens took a walk. The twins were bundled up in their hats and booties made by Grandma Rose, and tucked in their brand new stroller, a gift from their Aunt Phyllis. As the moon appeared to float through the clouds, June remembered something she'd heard in church. Something about the eyes of the Lord going to and fro throughout the earth. Was that giant moon the size of God's eye? She stifled a giggle.

June and the Bowens were not the only ones taking advantage of the spectacular night. It seemed like all of Collins Avenue was outside, and they had to pause often so their neighbors could admire the twins.

Eventually, they reached the end of the street and turned around.

Mr. Bowen looked down at his sleeping son. "I bet Junior will sleep through the night tonight."

It was a standing joke that while Chrissy loved her beauty sleep, Junior was the one who usually kept his parents awake.

"He only got up once last night," Miss Stewart replied.

Back in the house, June remained on the porch while the couple settled the babies in their cribs. She admired the way Mr. Bowen involved himself in the care of his children. Marilyn, the nanny, told her once, "I don't know why Miss Stewart hired me. She and her husband do almost everything for the babies. The most I do is wash their clothes and take care of them when their parents are not here."

If I ever have a husband, I would want him to be like that.

Miss Stewart's voice cut into her thoughts. She had a tray with something covered on it. "Do you mind if we join you? We're having a night snack."

"Not at all."

Miss Stewart rested the tray on the little rattan table and seated herself on the love seat opposite June. She uncovered the tray. "David's mother sent us some banana bread, sweet bread and ginger beer."

June salivated with the memory of Mom Rose's goodies. "Where's Mr. Bowen?"

He appeared with a bottle of ginger beer and glasses on another tray. June was not a lover of ginger-beer. "Do you mind if I get a soda or something else from the fridge?"

Miss Stewart reached for a glass. "Sure, there's Coke and orange juice."

June bit into a slice of banana bread. "Mmm, this is delicious." She could really get comfortable living with the Bowens. But she couldn't stay there forever.

Miss Stewart seemed to read her thoughts. "Have you decided what you're going to do about the apartment?"

June glanced at her. "I … Ms. Maraj gave me until the end of the year."

"How much are you paying?" Mr. Bowen asked.

"Three hundred. She's only charging me half the rent."

Miss Stewart set her glass down. "That's very kind of her, but there's no point paying for something if you won't be using it."

June paused with her Coke near her mouth. "What do you mean?"

"Well, look at it this way. We don't know when your sister will be out of the hospital, and meanwhile, you have expenses for school and all that, and there's no salary coming in. It may be a while before Marva can work again. You have the money from your father's estate, but it can go like that," Miss Stewart snapped her fingers, "if you're not careful."

Those thoughts had crossed June's mind, but she'd brushed them away like the pesky mosquitoes. Her sister was the one who made all the important decisions, and June preferred it that way. But now the responsibility was thrust upon her. And she was not ready.

Mr. Bowen poured ginger beer into his glass. "Do you remember the letters your sister wrote?"

June gave a mirthless laugh. "I'll never forget them."

"In every letter she said you should come and live with us."

"And she asked us to adopt you," Miss Stewart continued.

June stared from one to the other open-mouthed.

Mr. Bowen took a sip of his drink. "We know how rough these past months have been for you, and even without the letters, Cicely and I think we ought to help. We don't want you to feel you have to bear all this alone. You can stay in your apartment if you want to, but we think it would be much safer when your sister comes out for her to be here where she has people to help her."

"Her main complaint in the letters is she had no one to speak to." Miss Stewart gazed into her glass. "I guess with me being married, she thought she might be imposing if she asked for help. We don't want either of you to feel that way anymore."

June found her voice. "You mean you want to adopt both of us?"

Miss Stewart laughed. "The courts won't allow us to adopt someone over eighteen, but we can adopt your sister unofficially, if she wants us to."

June dabbed frantically at her eyes. What a fool she was! Miss Stewart's gaze was sympathetic. "Don't cry. We know it's too much for you to think about now. You'll have to ask God to guide you, but the only reason we mention it now is because you'll soon be eighteen."

June stared at the woman's face. Her birthday was only seven months away. A lot could happen in that time. Maybe her sister would have her memory back by then, but right now June felt so helpless, so burdened. Maybe this was how Marva felt. June needed parents right now. If only she could say yes.

The more she thought about the Bowens' offer, the more excited she became. But she hadn't yet given them an answer. She wanted to ask her sister's opinion but was afraid of what her reaction might be. Sometimes at nights she cried, just thinking how wonderful it would be to introduce the Bowens to her friends as "My mom" or "My dad." The words felt strange in her mouth. Should she call them "Mummy" and "Daddy" as some of the kids at school did? No, she wasn't a toddler. Mom and Dad sounded better for someone her age.

She told John about the proposed adoption, and he sounded pleased. "That's the best thing for you and your sister. I wondered how you were going to make out when she came out of the hospital."

Thinking of John always infused her with a warm, comfortable feeling. Not at all the heady, silly excitement she felt with Keith, but something much more mature, something that went well with her short hairstyle and more somber clothing. Her life, which had appeared to take on a downward spiral after her break-up with Keith, now seemed to be on the upswing. Her sister had begun to walk independently with a walker, she was speaking better, and June still hoped she would be home for Christmas.

With a little sigh, June turned her attention to her Christmas shopping list.

I look up from my Bible as Mary, my friend from the bed across from mine, limps over. She stands with hands on her hips and looks at me. She is always smiling, but today she looks sad.

"What's the matter, Mary? You don't feel good?"

She nods and then a tear runs down her cheek. "I'm going home today."

I close my Bible. "You are? Then why are you so sad?"

She brushes away the tear. "Because I'm leaving you here."

I stretch my arms out to her. They don't shake and twist anymore. She bends and we hug. I feel the tears running down my face, but I'm happy for her. "I'll miss you."

She nods. "I'll miss you too, but you should be going home soon. You're doing so much better."

I smile, remembering the night I fell off my bed trying to go to the bathroom. Mary had rushed over and helped me up. "Why didn't you call me? Are you hurt?"

"No," I'd said, even though my leg did hurt. The nurse had come, and I didn't want her scolding me. Some of the nurses are nice, but that one, Linda, is not one of them. She is rough.

I look at Mary. "I don't fall anymore."

"That's true. My husband isn't coming until this evening." She pulls the chair closer to my bed. "What are you reading?"

Mary is three years older than I. She is married and has one child. Mary has some illness that caused her to break her leg bone when she fell down the step at her home. She told me she doesn't have much education and she can't read very well. She'd said, "I didn't finish elementary school. But you look like you went to college."

Her words made me anxious, but I tried to laugh it off. "You know I can't remember anything. Are you teasing me?"

She didn't laugh. "I don't know what I would do if I lost my memory."

I'd tried to change the subject by asking about her husband and her little daughter, but I want to get my memory back so much. When the ward is quiet at night, I ask God to help me remember my family, my friends and my life before the accident. June doesn't answer all my questions. I feel she is keeping things from me.

And I am keeping something from her. I haven't told her about all the sketching I've been doing. It started one day when I realized my hand didn't shake anymore and I was able to write. I tried drawing a picture of a flower from one of my coloring books. When the nurse came to check my vitals, I showed it to her. She took it and showed it to the other nurses and they all complimented me. From that day, drawing and reading my Bible became a great way for me to pass the time. I didn't feel bored anymore. I became bolder, drawing and sketching everything that came to my mind.

Mary touches my arm. "Are you going to stare or are you going to read for me?"

I turn to her with a smile. "I've something for you."

She looks puzzled, and I point to the top drawer of my little cupboard. "Can you get my sketch pad?"

She gets it and gives it to me. I turn the page to a drawing of her. When I give it to her, she covers her mouth with her hand, then she flings her arm around my neck. "Thank you, thank you, Marva. It's beautiful. Nurse Natalie," she limps as fast as she can to the nurse who is sticking a thermometer in a patient's mouth. "Look, Marva did it!"

The nurse exclaims and together they ooh and aah over it, then Mary goes around showing it to everybody. Now they'll all want one. I'll have to work very hard to finish the one I've started of June and the family.

June paused at the sight of a short Indian woman standing near her sister's bed. Who was she? The woman turned when Marva waved to June. She said a polite good-afternoon to the woman before bending to kiss her sister's cheek.

"This is my sister June," Marva said to the visitor.

The woman looked her over. "Your sister told me a lot about you. I sell amchar by the hospital. Your sister used to come there."

A bit of uneasiness crept into June's stomach. This was someone who knew her sister before the accident. How much did she know and how much had she told Marva?

The woman continued, "I was telling her that her friend TL was killed. I told her when she came looking for him and she got so ... so worked up she took off running down the street."

June's heartbeat quickened. "When was this?"

"The day she got in the accident." Tears rolled down the woman's face. "I ... I am so sorry. If I'd known it would affect her so, I wouldn't have said anything." She laid her hand on June's arm. "Please forgive me. Your sister almost died because of me."

June's breathing became shallow, but she tried to reassure the woman. "Don't ... don't blame yourself. She would have found out somehow." June glanced at Marva, and for once she was glad for her lost memory.

Marva frowned. "He was my friend? Why did they kill him?"

June touched her sister's arm. "Don't worry about it now, Sister. He's gone, and we can't bring him back."

Marva stared ahead of her. "I lost a friend."

The visitor turned to June. "Your sister prayed with me many times, and I know God answered her prayer. I want to give her something. I know you have a lot of expenses and I want to give you this." She pulled out a few bills and held them out to June. "It's only two hundred dollars, but please take it."

Other people had brought things for her sister—toiletries, books, pens, pencils, crayons. Those who knew she was only on semi-solids had brought Jell-O and soups as the nurse advised, but no one had given money. June looked at her sister. "Do you want it?"

Marva shrugged, her mind obviously still on what her visitor had said. June took the money from the woman's hand. "Thank you. God bless you."

CHAPTER THIRTY

June slid a photograph into the clear pocket of the album. Then she took a piece of yellow paper, trimmed the edges with a pinking scissors to give them a serrated edge and wrote, *Marva Garcia, maid-of-honor at the wedding of Miss Stewart and Mr. Bowen, Jan. 31, 1985.*

Footsteps sounded in the hallway and stopped behind her chair.

"That looks good," Miss Stewart said.

June stared at the paper. "You think so?"

Miss Stewart came around and took a chair. "Want help?"

June pushed some of the paper scattered on the kitchen table toward her. "Yes, thanks. I have to finish this tonight, so Sister doesn't come and see me working on it. I want it to be a surprise."

Miss Stewart began cutting the edges of the paper. "Are you hoping this will help her memory?"

June propped her chin with clasped hands. "To be honest, Miss, I don't know what to hope for. Part of me wants her memory to come back, but —"

She broke off as another set of footsteps came into the kitchen. She looked up and smiled at Mr. Bowen, clad in tee shirt and pajamas. "I'm working on some therapy."

He peered at the photo. "So I see. Nice shot."

"I wish I had more pictures though."

Miss Stewart turned to her husband. "Junior asleep?"

Mr. Bowen pulled out a chair. "Finally, but he fought it like crazy." He fingered one of the photos. "It doesn't have to be all photos. Anything that might have had significance for her may help."

June creased her brow. "I'll have to look through some stuff." She paused. "Do you think I should put a picture of Daddy?"

Miss Stewart looked up, eyebrows raised. "That may trigger something, maybe more bad than good."

Mr. Bowen leaned his elbows on the table. "Look, with your sister coming home tomorrow, we have to decide how we'll approach this whole thing. I think the best way is to answer her questions as honestly as possible. I can get a copy of your father's photo from the files, but if you think it will upset her, then it might be best to leave it out."

Miss Stewart laid her hand on her husband's forearm. "I agree. God will reveal to her what he wants her to know in his way and in his time."

June waved her hand over the table. "So this is not a good idea?"

"There's nothing wrong with it," Miss Stewart said. "She loves looking at pictures and she's been asking about her past life. This will show her we're trying to help her."

June bit her lip. "I don't have a lot, but I have a picture of us when we were little, that she already saw, I have two of Mama, pictures of her at the wedding, those we took in Tobago and one of her and Jason. If we leave Daddy out, she's bound to say something."

The husband and wife exchanged glances. "All right, I'll call Point Fortin and ask them to make me a copy."

June managed a smile. "Thanks. I pray God this helps, but as I was saying to Miss Stewart, I don't know if I want her memory to return or not."

Mr. Bowen squeezed her shoulder. "Just trust God. That's all we can do."

Someone stands by my bed. I look up from my sketching to see a small, Spanish-looking man with stooped shoulders, twisting his cap between his fingers. I glance at the clock. It's just after ten. I'm surprised they allow a stranger to visit me at this time of day. As I'm thinking this, Elise, the head nurse, hurries up to me. "Marva, I'm sorry, I had to let this poor man in. He said it's important that he speak to you. He came a few times before when you were sleeping, and we didn't want to wake you."

I adjust my head on my pillow to get a better look at the man. He brushes a hand across his eyes, and I smile, hoping to reassure him. Elise lingers, and I give her a slight nod for her to stay.

The man looks away, then back at me, but doesn't quite meet my gaze. "Miss, I'm sorry to bother you, but my wife say if I don't come and see you, she wouldn't talk to me again."

"Why?"

He moves his cap from one hand to another. "Miss, my name is Sonny Odin. I …I'm the driver of the van that hit you."

My heart almost stops. My hand flies to my chest, and I'm glad the nurse is here. Tears are running down the man's face now, and even though I'm not looking at them, I know the other patients are staring.

He looks down at the floor. "All these years, Miss, thirty years, I never hit nobody, not even an animal. I'm a Christian. I don't like to hurt nobody. I don't know what happened to me that day."

I open my arms. "Give me a hug."

He wipes his eyes with the back of his hands and stares at me as if he thinks I'm crazy.

I shake my arms, as if impatient. "Hug me, or I'll never forgive you."

From the corner of my eyes, I see Elise open her mouth as if to say something. Mr. Odin takes a step forward, stops, then bends over and wraps his thin arms around me. "I'm so sorry, so sorry."

He straightens and pulls a not-too-clean handkerchief from his pocket and dabs at his eyes. "How you feel now?"

I reach for the washcloth on my bed to blot my tears. "I feel better. I'm going home today."

This is the man who almost killed me. I'm not sure what my feelings are, but I know I feel sorry for him.

I touch his arm. "It was my fault. They say I ran across in front of you."

"But I should have seen you." He stuffs the handkerchief in his pocket and pulls out his wallet. "The police didn't charge me, but I blame myself." He removes something from his wallet. "Look, Miss, this can't pay for your suffering, but it's just a little something to help you."

He hands me two pieces of paper. One is a check for two thousand dollars.

I hold it out to him. "I can't take your money."

"Miss, you don't understand. I know it's not enough, but my wife say if I don't give you this check, she will leave me. And she'll know when you cash it."

I picture this small man with a big, fat wife bossing him around and I want to laugh, but that will be rude. Elise clears her throat and I glance at her. She gestures wildly behind the man's back. He points to the paper in my hand. "Miss, that is my address and my phone number. My bank is Royal Bank. If you have any trouble, just call me."

Despite my protests, Mr. Odin holds on to his cap and refuses to take back his check. Growing tired, I hug him again and thank him.

After he leaves, Elise draws near my bed. "I can't believe you didn't want to take the money. You and your sister don't work. You're going to need medication for a long time. You did the right thing."

After she leaves, I realize she's right. I'd asked June once how she paid for my walker and other things. She'd said we sold our parents' property, but I don't know how much money we have. With a sigh, I close my eyes and fold my arms. Mr. Odin's visit has worn me out.

My next visitor is Dr. Fred. I'm expecting him. He is a nice man, medium height and build, but his stomach shows just a little under his white coat. He has light-brown skin, wavy hair balding in the middle and a neat mustache. He is Miss Sheila's husband and they both say they knew me before the accident. I stretch my arms out to him. He knows I love to hug and he hugs me back.

"How is our star patient?"

He always calls me that.

"Ready to go home."

He smiles. "Good. Sheila, Cicely and June will be here in a few minutes. I just wanted to tell you how proud the whole team is of you. Dr.

Flechner"—that's my brain surgeon. I wish I could meet him to thank him— "asked me to give you his best regards and says he hopes to be able to meet you one of these days. He wants you to stay on your seizure medicine, for a while. He thinks it will help your moods and hopefully, your memory in the long run."

I try to look happy, even though the mention of my memory always bothers me. Plus, I hate swallowing pills.

He seems to read my thoughts. "I know it's no fun taking pills all the time, but this will help you, trust me. We'll also give you your pain pills to take when you need them, and the nurse will give you your appointments to see me and for therapy. Excited?"

I smile. "Very."

"Good." He gives my shoulder a gentle squeeze. "Oh, here they are now."

I think I am grinning from ear to ear. June, Miss Stewart, Miss Sheila and a man I've never seen before enter the ward. Is he my father? No, my father is dead. Lots of kisses and hugs. June introduces the man as Mr. Bowen, Miss Stewart's husband. If he is her husband, why does June call her Miss Stewart? So many things I don't know.

I open my arms to him. "Glad to meet you."

He wraps me in a nice, warm hug. "I've known you for a long time, Marva. You look great. How do you feel?"

I suddenly feel shy. "Thank you. I feel good."

While I'm talking to him, June and the women put my things into suitcases. I was careful to hide my sketchpad under my clothes. I have a lot of things that people brought me: books, socks, bedroom slippers, toiletries, Jell-O, candy. One woman even brought me a rosary. There is some movement near the door. I look up. Bella, Hazel, Elise and other nurses in a variety of uniforms are coming toward my bed with a bunch of balloons. The other patients begin to cheer. Two who can walk get off their bed and come toward me. People are kissing me and hugging me, and I feel tears streaming down my face. When I look up, some of the nurses are crying too.

Everyone is talking at once. Bella, the oldest nurse, cradles my face against her soft, fat bosom. "We love you, sweetie. Take care of yourself, okay? And don't come back."

"She has to come back for therapy."

"Oh, I forgot."

"Merry Christmas, Marva."

"Happy Birthday. Her birthday is Boxing Day."

"June, look after your sister, you hear me?"

They thrust cards and packages into my hand. I never expected any-thing like this.

"I love you all," I say through my tears.

Finally, a man comes with a wheelchair. A nurse steps forward to help me, but I raise my hand. "I can do it."

Carefully, I get off the bed and into the chair. I wheel myself from bed to bed, hugging, saying good-bye to the five other patients. Everyone calls me the huggy girl. Two of them are casted and bandaged so heavily they can't nod or hug me back, but they smile with their eyes. My heart aches, remembering that at one time I was just like them. When my good-byes are complete, June wheels me through the door. I turn and wave for a last time.

"That was quite a send-off," Mr. Bowen says when we are settled in the car. June and I are in the back seat, Miss Stewart in the front. Miss Sheila has gone back to work.

June turns her beautiful eyes, now slightly red, on me. "You are so popular."

I guess I am, but what next? What does my future hold?

I look out the window at buildings, cars and people walking by. It seems like another world. The sun is so bright I have to close my eyes at times.

Mr. Bowen slows the car at a street corner, and I read the sign. Rose-wood Lane. June had told me we would be making a stop by the house where we used to live. We drive down to a yellow house and I see a lot of people standing in front. Balloons and streamers hang from the windows, and across the front door is a sign that says, "Welcome home, Marva."

Mr. Bowen turns off the engine and people flock to the car. I recognize Mrs. Maraj and others who came to see me when I was in the hospital. I open my car door and extend my arms and hug as many people as I can. A funny-looking brown and black dog barks at me and wags his tail in a friendly way.

Somebody says, "Here's your friend," and makes way for the dog. He tries to jump into the car, but a man pulls him back by his collar.

June opens the door on her side. "I'm going to pick up some clothes, Sister."

She runs down the steps and into the house, leaving me to receive the greetings and answer questions from my neighbors. I begin to feel tired. June comes back just in time with a bag.

Miss Stewart turns around and smiles at me. "Think we can go now?"

"Yes. I'm tired."

We wave good-bye, and Mr. Bowen pulls away from the curb. I lean back and close my eyes. When I open them again, we are in front of a nice, big house. It's painted beige and has brown trim around the windows and doors. I see a little flower garden on one side of the driveway and a lawn on the other. Then I notice the steps, about six of them to go into the house, and I become anxious. I don't know how to climb steps, and these nice people don't know that. I have to be brave. Mr. Bowen takes the car right up to the steps and I am happy for that. Maybe I can make it.

June turns to me. "We're home, Sister."

I open my door, but before I can put one foot out, she and Miss Stewart are there helping me out of the car.

June seems to sense my nervousness. "We'll help you, Sister."

"That's right," Miss Stewart says. "Just take it nice and slow."

This is one thing physical therapy hadn't taught me. Well, I will learn now. Pat had always taught me to put my weak leg first and land on my strong one, so, with June and Miss Stewart each holding my hand, I put my left foot on the first treader, then my right. I wish I could use my walker, but that's impossible on the stairs. I take another step, still holding on for dear life to June and Miss Stewart. When I get to the third, I feel the sweat forming on my forehead and my legs are shaking.

I hear a voice behind me. "Would you like me to carry you?"

Ashamed, I nod. Miss Stewart and her husband exchange places, and the next thing I know, I'm on the verandah. June and Miss Stewart run up the stairs, bringing my bags and my walker. I am so happy to see it. Mr. Bowen opens it for me, and I hold on to it gratefully. I want to hug him again, but I dare not let go of the walker, so I smile. "Thank you so much. I thought I could do it."

June stands beside me. She looks like she was crying again. I hate seeing her cry so much. I haven't known her a long time, but I love her already. She puts one arm around me as if to comfort me. I say to her, "Don't cry. They didn't have steps at the hospital, but I'll learn how to use them. Watch and see."

She nods and squeezes me tighter as if afraid to speak.

Miss Stewart opens the front door. "Let's get you inside so you can sit."

June keeps her arm around me as I enter the living-room. Polished floor, with a rug in the middle, large plush furniture, pretty lace curtains and plants are a welcome sight to my tired eyes. June steers me toward a high wing-backed armchair and I sink down in it gratefully.

"Hello, Marva."

I turn to see two dark-skinned women who look like mother and daughter. I stretch out my arms and the older one comes to me first and hugs me. Then the younger one follows suit.

"Sister, this is Miss Lucy and her daughter Marilyn."

I smile at them. "Nice to meet you."

Miss Lucy hangs her head and runs from the room. Did I make her cry?

Marilyn turns to Miss Stewart. "Lunch is ready. Do you want to eat in here, or in the kitchen?"

Miss Stewart looks at her husband. "What do you say, honey? This is a special occasion."

"Sure, we'll have it in here. I have to be back at work in the next half hour though."

June stands. "I'll help."

Miss Stewart also stands. "No, I'll help. You stay here and chat with your sister."

I don't know if her husband is going to help too, but he follows his wife into the kitchen.

June beams at me. "I'm so glad you're home. How does it feel?"

I smile back. "It feels strange. No nurses, nobody groaning when you're trying to sleep, and that smell. I don't know what they mop the floor with, but I hated it."

June chuckles. "And what about the food?"

I shake my head. "Once I started eating regular food it wasn't too bad. Although some days it had no taste."

I cock my ears at a sound. The babies! I'd forgotten about them. June gets up at the same time. "Somebody is awake."

She disappears into the corridor and returns with a baby. I hold out my hands and she places the baby in them. "This is Junior. He always wakes first."

Junior looks at me with bright, dark eyes like his father's, then he smiles and a dimple appears on one cheek. I kiss it. "Hi, Junior."

He waves a plump little fist and gurgles at me. I raise him to my shoulder.

"He likes you to hold him like that," June says.

Miss Marilyn comes with a platter and places it on the table. Smells like chicken. "I'll check on Chrissy," she says.

The other ladies and Mr. Bowen follow with more dishes. Miss Marilyn returns with the other baby. June takes Junior from me and I reach for Chrissy. She is a doll. Large brown eyes like her mother, hair curling around her face, and lips that curve into a smile as soon as she sees me. I'm going to sketch her the first chance I get. I nuzzle her cheeks and her fat little neck. She has that nice baby smell. Ooh, I just love these babies.

Miss Marilyn stands before me. "I'm going to take her so you all can eat. Everything is on the table."

I hug her to me before giving her up. "Where's the bathroom?"

June gets up. "I'll take you, Sister."

She gives the baby to Miss Lucy who has just entered and she takes me along the corridor. We pass one room with a closed door. June says that's Mr. Bowen's study, then another room which she says is the master bedroom. The door is open, showing a large canopy bed, covered with a beautiful blue bedspread, and blue and white curtains at the large window. Opposite is the nursery and next to it is the bathroom. I go in. It's decorated in pink and lavender and has plush pink rugs on the floor and matching shower curtain and towels. Such a lovely change from the hospital. I like the nurses, but I'm never going back there. Except to outpatient.

CHAPTER THIRTY-ONE

The days go by in one sweet adventure after another. We are preparing the house for Christmas. Schools are closed for the holidays, and June spends a lot of time with me, which gives me less chance to sketch, but I don't mind. She doesn't cry as much as before, and I hug her every chance I get. I want to show her that I'll never give her cause to cry again. I haven't told her about my drawings yet. I'm planning a surprise for her and the family.

I never get tired of watching the babies. They seem to know each other. Chrissy likes to play with her rattle and toss it out of the playpen. I get a lot of exercise picking it up and giving it back to her. Junior is not interested in toys. He just likes to wriggle around and try to turn over. Whenever June and Miss Stewart are out of the house, I sit with them on the back porch and I sketch. I am running out of pencils, the soft kind that I like. One afternoon I give Miss Marilyn some money to get me some. I tell her to not let anyone see her giving them to me. She gives me a strange look but agrees.

Now I see how much I missed while I was in the hospital. It feels like I was in a long, long sleep and I'm now awake. But not quite. I still don't know this girl I see in the mirror every morning when I brush my teeth. Who is Marva Garcia? And who are these people God has placed me with? I like them, and they seem to like me, but I don't really know them.

One day I watched some *bachac* ants, the ones with the big heads, moving in a line like little soldiers, each one carrying a piece of grass, and I thought, they know who they are and where they are going, but who am I? Where am I going? When I said this to June, she looked sad, so I don't say it anymore.

To change my thoughts, I feast my eyes on the back yard, smell the air, ripe and sweet with oranges, coconut and other scents I cannot recognize. I hear the sound of birds and watch them fly, so swift and graceful. Two small birds with dark, green wings and yellow on their bellies chase each other, then light on the telephone pole. I love to watch the green leaves and grass, the lilac bells climbing over the fence. Even yellow leaves hold my attention. I want to touch them, rub them over my skin, feel their textures. Then I go back to sketching. Maybe it will help bring my memory back, but I do it because I enjoy it.

People visit me – Rev. Harris, his wife and some church members, people from where we used to live, Tantie Beulah and others. I am happy to see them, but I long to go out of the house. In the two weeks since I've been out of the hospital, I went back once for therapy and once to see Dr. Fred. He says my kidneys, which were damaged as a result of the accident, are doing better. Pat is also happy with my progress. She says I'll soon be using a cane. I tell her about the steps and she makes me go up and down a wooden box. It's not steps, but it will help. When I'm leaving, she gives me some home exercises.

June's boyfriend comes and he helps us decorate the Christmas tree. Everyone is laughing and talking, the babies are in their playpen, waving their little sausage arms, kicking up their legs and making cute baby sounds. Junior likes to put his big toe in his mouth.

I walk around the tree with my walker, hanging bulbs and candy canes. I thank God I'm alive. Suddenly I hear a pattering on the roof. It's raining! I hobble as fast as I can to the back porch. The rain sparkles like a giant shower of silver threads with the outside light shining through them. I go to the edge of the porch and put my hand out, then my face, then my tongue.

June comes up to me. "Sister, what are you doing?"

"I love the rain." I take her hand and hold it out. "See? Doesn't that feel good?"

She gives me a strange look. "Everything must seem so different to you."

"You don't know how good it feels to be alive."

At last it's Christmas Eve. Miss Lucy and her daughter have gone home, and we sit in the living-room admiring the Christmas tree and the decorations and sipping egg nog. Below the tree is an assortment of boxes wrapped in shiny gift paper and tied with pretty bows. The television shows women in beautiful frilly skirts and blouses with flowers in their hair, singing and dancing. The songs are in Spanish and they call them *parang*.

I'm holding Junior on my lap. June sits on the rug at my feet, her head resting against my legs. Junior tugs at her hair.

"Ouch!" She holds her head, and he squeals.

Across from us, Chrissy, seated on her father, also squeals and drops her rattle.

"Did we do this in Egypt Village?" I ask.

June turns her head. "Do what?"

"Sit around the tree and drink egg nog and watch TV."

"I don't think we ever had a tree. And we didn't have a TV."

No tree? It's such a beautiful thing. I can't understand why everyone wouldn't have one. And no TV either? "We couldn't afford it?"

June shrugs. "I don't know."

That's another thing I don't understand. She never wants to talk about our childhood and Egypt Village.

Junior takes another tug at her hair and she sidles away. "Come here, you." She lifts him off my lap.

I turn to Miss Stewart. "Did you always do this?"

She smiles. "Yes, we did."

I look at Mr. Bowen.

He nods. "We did, too. And you know what else we did?"

Everyone looks at him. "We sang Christmas carols and told the story of the Savior's birth."

"I didn't know that," his wife says.

He gazes at her. "Remember I came from a Christian home. When we lived in New York, we went to church on Christmas Eve night."

"Was it snowing?" June asks.

"Sometimes, but we kids loved it. We would all bundle up in our coats, hats and gloves and sing carols while Dad drove us to church. When we came here, it took us a while before we found a church, so Mom made egg nog and we sat around and did the Christmas thing."

"The Christmas thing?" June asks.

"Yeah. We sat around the crèche and told the Christmas story."

That touches me. We don't have a crèche, but maybe we can do the Christmas thing too.

Feeling shy, I ask, "Can we do that now?"

"Why not?" Miss Stewart gets up and turns off the TV. "Where do we start?"

June bounces Junior on her leg. "Let's start with 'Once upon a time.'"

Mr. Bowen picks up Chrissy's rattle. "Okay, here's how we did it. One person says a few lines of the Christmas story, then we sing a verse of a carol. Then the next person picks up the story from where the last person left off, we sing another verse and so on."

"Sounds great," Miss Stewart says. "I'll go first. Once upon a time there was a man named Joseph, and he had a wife named Mary who was pregnant."

June puts her hand up. "Joseph and Mary journeyed to Bethlehem in order to be taxed, in keeping with a decree from the emperor Cesar Augustus."

"You forgot the song," I say.

June slaps her forehead. "I'm sorry." She clears her throat. "Silent night …"

We all join in the singing. When we finish the first verse, she repeats the lines she'd said, then everyone looks at me. I smile as I continue the story. "While they were there, Mary realized that it was time for the baby to be born."

We sing another verse then Mr. Bowen continues, "Joseph tries to find a room in an inn so Mary could give birth, but he found none."

We continue like this until Mr. Bowen ends with the angels telling the shepherds, "Glory to God in the highest and on earth peace and goodwill toward men."

I look down at Junior now asleep on June's lap. I think of the Baby Jesus who came into this world as small and innocent as this baby even though He was God Himself. What a beautiful story!

June interrupts my thoughts. "Sister, I'm impressed that you remember the Christmas story so well."

I turn to her. "Some things I'll always remember, but the things I want to remember, I don't."

It's Christmas Day, and I'm excited to be going to church at last. I look at myself in the mirror. June has helped me choose a plain blue suit. It's a kind of a smooth, dull fabric. The top is fitted at the waist then flares out over the hips. The skirt is straight and falls below my knees. It hides the scar on my leg, but anyone can see that my left leg is still thinner than the right, and even under my stockings it still looks scaly. I've lost so much weight, the dress just hangs on me. I take off the outfit and look for something else. I find a green and white dress, but that is also too big. I sit on the bed, the dress on my lap, my hand propping my chin.

June comes in from the bathroom where she was putting on her makeup. "Sister, I thought you were dressed already."

"Everything is too big."

She raises an eyebrow then goes to the closet. She finds a pink dress with a lace top, and an accordion-pleated skirt with a belt of the same fabric. It's a bit roomy, but it fits better than the others and it falls almost to my ankles, hiding my skinny leg. I settle for that one. I let part of my hair fall forward and to the side to cover the scar over my left eyebrow. June borrows a silk scarf from Miss Stewart, and I use it to tie my hair back. It curls at my neck. I apply a little bit of makeup and rouge to my cheeks so my complexion doesn't look so pale.

June looks very pretty in her red dress with black irregular circles on the bodice and near the hem.

I still have difficulty with the steps, but I hold on to the railing while Mr. Bowen supports me. At church, lots of people greet me with hugs and kisses and tell me I look wonderful. After the announcements, Rev. Harris goes to the podium. "What a wonderful Christmas present God has given us. Our dear sister Marva is back."

The entire congregation gives me a standing ovation and I smile and wave. I feel so much love.

Back at the house, we open our presents. I'd asked June to purchase gifts for the family and herself, but I'm anxious to give them my gifts. June has bought a pair of black pumps as her gift from me.

I am pleased with the scarf from Mr. Bowen, a blouse and perfume from Miss Stewart, a purse and a new dress from June. I hug and kiss them all, then I hold my new dress in front of me. It's green and sleeveless with a black overall pattern and a cowl collar. It looks like it will fit me better than my old clothes.

June smiles at me. "It's for your birthday."

Miss Stewart hands me another box. "And here's something else for your birthday – to go with that dress."

I open the box. It's a pair of black medium-heeled sandals. I hug and kiss everyone again, then I hurry to the bedroom. I raise the mattress and remove my sketch pad.

They give me curious glances as I re-enter the room with the pad. Carefully, I remove the first page and hand it to Miss Stewart. It's a sketch of her and Mr. Bowen. She looks at it, gasps, then stares at me open-mouthed. Her husband edges close to take a look. He also stares. "You did this?"

I nod, smiling.

June comes around, peers at the sketch. "Sister?"

She and Miss Stewart are both teary-eyed. They hug me, ask questions, study the sketches, dab at their eyes.

June fixes her gaze on the one of her. "Sister, when did you learn to draw? I've never seen you draw. How did this happen? Is this what happens when someone loses their memory?"

Mr. Bowen looks over her shoulder. "It could be that her right brain is making up for what the left brain lost. But don't take my word for it. I'm not a brain surgeon." He smiles and kisses my cheek. "I'm proud of you, Marva." Turning to his wife, "I think we should frame these."

Miss Stewart sifts through the sketches. There are four in all: the one of her and Mr. Bowen, one each of Chrissy and Junior, the backyard and June.

Her eyes are still glued to the sketches. "Maybe I should get you some paints and an easel, so you can paint like a real artist."

I chuckle. "Not yet. I'm comfortable with pencils for now."

June hugs me again, then kisses me. "I thought my surprise would be the best, but you beat me." She takes a box from under the tree. "From me to you, Sister."

Eagerly, I tear the wrapping. It's a photo album. We hug again, then I open the cover. The first picture is one she'd shown me in the hospital, one of me and her when we were little. Below it she has written: *Marva, eight years old, June, four. Taken after church one Sunday.* Even though I'd seen it before, it still grabs me. It's a link to my past.

I am vaguely aware of movements and sounds around me - the crunching of paper, voices, footsteps on the polished floor as they clear the room. I turn another page.

In the afternoon we have lots of visitors. Tantie Beulah brings a bag of bread and cakes, preserved plums and other sweets. I see the resemblance between her and the picture of my father in the album June gave me. I want to ask her about my father, but now is not the time. Tantie Beulah is almost as tall as I am, and when I hug her, she cries. "God is such a good God. Look at you. Nobody thought you would be here today."

June brings her a glass of sorrel and asks about her neighbors. I know June is only trying to get her off the subject of my accident. While they are speaking, there's a knock at the door. Mr. Bowen goes to open it. A young man follows him inside. It's Jason. I remember him from when he came to see me in the hospital. I stretch out my arms and he hugs me and kisses my cheek. He greets everyone else, and Miss Stewart offers him some refreshments, but he pats his flat stomach. "Just ginger beer, thank you. I've been eating all day. Everywhere I went, people gave me things to eat."

Mr. Bowen laughed. "I'll get the ginger-beer."

Tantie Beulah gets up from her chair. "Well, I have to be going. Take care of yourselves."

June walks her to the door, and Miss Stewart leaves the room.

Jason sits next to me on the couch. "How are you?"

"I'm good. And you?"

He smiles. "Great. You look wonderful."

I think he looks wonderful too. He's wearing a beige polo shirt, blue jeans and brown shoes. His hair is neatly brushed, and his sideburns and mustache are well groomed. I think he is handsome. And he smells nice too. I wish I knew him better.

Mr. Bowen brings him the ginger-beer and when he takes it, I see that his nails are clean and neatly trimmed. I like that.

"Would you like to sit on the porch?" I ask.

"Sure." He holds out his hand to me to help me up and I let him, even though I don't need help. I catch the concern on his face as I place my hands on my walker. The sun is going down and a cool breeze blows and stirs the fern leaves in the hanging baskets. When we are seated, Jason says, "You are handling that walker well."

"My therapist says I should soon be using a cane."

He glances at me. "You're such a strong person, Moe."

I remember him calling me that when I was in the hospital. Moe. I love the sound.

"Why do you call me Moe?"

He looks down at his drink. "I … I've always called you that."

"How long is always?"

"Since you were little."

I have an idea. "Wait here. I'll be right back."

I go to the bedroom and get the album. I bring it and open it on my lap. "June gave me this for Christmas. I guess she hopes it will help bring back my memory. What do you think?"

He stares at me for a while. "I don't know, Moe. Some things are best not remembered."

I feel myself frowning. What does he mean by that? Doesn't he want me to remember? Together we look at the pictures. When we come to the ones we took in Tobago, he pauses and looks at me. "That was a nice time we had."

I stare at the one of us standing near something like a canon surrounded by bougainvillea. His arm is around me and I'm leaning slightly against him. I'm wearing a yellow dress. "What place is this?"

"This is Milford. I took you to meet my aunt that day. We spent the day together."

I turn my gaze on him. "Really? Are you my boyfriend?"

He gives me a quick glance. "I'm your friend. Your good friend."

We look at the rest of the pictures and I don't ask any more questions until we come to the one of my father. All June has written is, "Daddy."

I can see he is my father. We have the same thick eyebrows, his hair is almost straight, his nose long and pointed and his eyes appear deep brown like mine.

"Did you know my father?"

Jason nods and turns the page. In this pocket is a birthday card and it's signed "Krishna."

"My mother too?"

"A little bit."

"What do you know about them?"

Jason looks at his watch. "Not much. They sort of … kept to themselves. Your father owned a big estate near the river. Your mother came from Venezuela." He stands. "Look, Moe, I have to go. I'll come back tomorrow for your birthday, okay?"

We hug and he kisses my cheek. "Let's go back inside and I'll say good-bye to the family."

He holds the album while I walk into the living-room. He says his good-byes and hugs June. Then she walks him out to his car.

Jason drove away from the Bowens' house then stopped at the corner of Collins Avenue and Green Acres Drive. He pulled into a narrow, paved alley between two houses and laid his head on the steering wheel. Seeing Marva had drained him. It took all his effort not to burst into tears. To see the girl who had been so strong in Egypt, not caring about her shabby clothes—or maybe she did care but just never showed it—standing up to her tormentors, holding her head high despite the rumors about her family, now reduced to a stranger.

For that's who she was. She didn't know herself, and he didn't know her. The true Marva, the one he loved, had been left on the roadway when she had the accident. June said she couldn't remember anything that happened before that day, nothing about her family or her childhood, and they wanted to keep it that way.

He recalled her startling confession when he met her near the river in Egypt Village. She was the person who had killed her father. How would that affect her if anyone found out? And she was now staying with the detective, the man who could throw her into prison at any time. June was right. It would be better if Marva never remembered who she really was. But from the questions she'd asked him today, he could tell she wanted to.

Tomorrow was her birthday. The family had invited him to her party. He would be there, but after that he would never see her again. He couldn't bear it. He would just have to settle for Joanna.

CHAPTER THIRTY-TWO

The house is crowded. Miss Stewart's father and Mr. Bowen's mother are here. They kiss me and say I look wonderful. And she says, "Call me Mom Rose." Dr. Fred and his family are here too. I'm happy to see him and Miss Sheila. Dr. Fred says I look well. I tell him I've been practicing going up and down the back step, which is shorter, and my knees don't hurt as much as they used to. He smiles and says, "That's good, but don't overdo."

I promise him I won't and then I hug him. Everybody has brought me a present, including money. When is Jason coming? I'm anxious to give him my gift. I'd stayed up late after June went to bed and I'd only managed to sketch his face and neck.

Then I see him at the door. He is wearing a white knitted shirt with some kind of crisscross design and blue jeans. The white shirt shows off his deep bronze complexion and his broad shoulders. He is handsome. I think I'm in love. He bends to kiss my cheek, but I turn my face just in time and the kiss lands on my lips. He straightens, smiles and hands me a little packet.

"Thank you." I tear the wrapping. It's a bottle of White Diamonds perfume. I stand and hug him. "Look, everybody." I hold it up.

I'm waiting for the right moment to give him my gift. Sometime later, Miss Lucy brings in my birthday cake, alight with twenty-two candles. Miss Stewart raises her hand and announces that Jason and I will cut the cake. I fold my walker, and Jason takes my hand and leads me to the table. Mr. Bowen puts on a record. *Endless Love*. A fitting song. I take the knife from Miss Stewart's hand and follow Jason's action as he pushes it gently into the cake. I understand we have to take our time until the song ends. Jason kisses my cheek twice during the song and everyone cheers. I like this.

Later, everyone dances, even Mr. Stewart and Mom Rose. I whisper to Jason that I want to dance. I stand, and he puts one hand around my waist, holds my other hand and we waltz around the room. I'm surprised at how easy it is. I feel I don't need my walker anymore. When the dance ends, everyone claps. I don't remember other birthdays, but I think this one is the best yet.

After the dance, I tell Jason I want to get some fresh air. I really want to get him alone. I tell him I'll meet him on the back porch. When I give him the sketch, he frowns then looks at me. "What? Did you do this?"

I nod, watching his reaction. "Like it?"

He studies it then looks up at me. "When did you learn to draw?"

"While I was in the hospital."

There's a cool, gentle breeze and the sky is just growing dark. A half-moon peeps out from behind a cloud. I sit next to him on the porch swing and tell him how I began drawing. For a while we don't speak then he says, "I love it. I can't believe you did it."

I feel suddenly shy. "Thanks. I'm glad you like it." I wish he would kiss me, but he looks out at the back yard.

I edge closer to him. "I want to get rid of this walker so I can move around better."

"You will. Just take your time."

I continue as if he hadn't spoken. "And I want to remember things. Will you help me?"

"What do you want to remember?"

"What my life was like before the accident. Nobody is telling me."

"Maybe there's nothing —"

Someone interrupts. June has brought Mr. Stewart and Mom Rose to say good-bye. I hug them and thank them for coming and for their lovely gifts.

After they leave, Jason looks at his watch. "Moe, I have to be going. Egypt Village is a long way from here."

"When will I see you again?"

He pauses. "I'll call you, okay? I have your number."

I stand and touch his face. He hesitates, then brushes my lips with his.

I am seated with the family in the kitchen having breakfast. June turns to me. "Looks like you enjoyed your party yesterday."

I take a sip of my tea before placing my cup down. "I did. I think I'm in love."

I'm aware of everyone's eyes on me. "I didn't say anything to him, but I'm sure he knows."

"Are you talking about Jason?" Miss Stewart asks.

I smile at her. "Yes. He's so handsome and so gentle and so nice. I wanted to ask him —"

"Ask him what?" I can hear the tension in June's voice.

"If we ever had sex."

Orange juice squirts across the table, and June jumps up from her chair. So does Mr. Bowen. Only Miss Stewart is still seated. I look at her. "Did I say something wrong?"

June is hastily mopping the spill. Mr. Bowen has left the room.

Miss Stewart pats my hand. "Er, honey, it's a good thing you didn't ask him."

"Why not? I want to know about my life. I want to know who I am."

And for the first time since I left the hospital, I feel like crying.

David settled into bed beside his wife. "I never thought I would hear that word from her mouth."

Cicely stared into the darkness. "We have to do something, but what? She can't stay in this state of euphoria forever. One day she's going to wake up and realize the world is not all hugs and kisses. If her memory does return and she finds out she killed her father and wanted to kill herself …" She turned to her husband. "I'm really worried, honey. What should we do?"

David yawned. "There's a formula I've seen you use before. And I think it works."

Cicely threw off the cover. "Right." In a flash she was off the bed and on her knees. David followed, and together they prayed. They thanked God for sparing Marva's life, for the progress she'd made so far and for her complete recovery. Then they asked that God would give them all wisdom.

Cicely rose from her knees. "I feel better already."

David didn't reply, but he felt reassured.

I stare at Mr. Bowen. I'm liking him more every day. The way he handles the babies, steals a kiss from his wife when he thinks no one is looking, and the way he helps me up and down the steps. I think June and I have come into a nice family, but when he says that he and Miss Stewart want to adopt us, I'm really surprised. Then I smile. "We're too old."

Miss Stewart laughs. "That's a good answer. We can adopt June officially by signing papers, but we can't do that for you because you're over eighteen."

"That's right." I tap the table gently. "And I'll be getting married anyway. As soon as I'm strong enough."

June, sitting next to me, sighs and lowers her head. No one says anything for a few minutes. I cut my chicken and continue eating in silence.

Mr. Bowen lays down his fork and looks at me. "Is it okay then for us to adopt June?"

"Oh, yes. I think you and Miss Stewart are wonderful. June, do you want them to adopt you?"

She turns those gorgeous hazel eyes on me, which now look a little teary. "Yes. I hoped you would agree."

I slap the table harder this time. "I agree. When are you going to do it?"

Mr. Bowen looks at his wife. "I can have all the papers sent to my office. It will be a quick procedure since June already lives with us."

I hug June. "I'm happy for you."

She pulls away. "What do you mean you're happy for me? You talk as if I was a stranger or something. I'm your sister —"

She jumps up and runs from the kitchen. Miss Stewart gives me a look I don't understand then goes after June. I glance helplessly at Mr. Bowen. Once again, I may have said the wrong thing.

Cicely knocked on the bedroom door and turned the handle when June called, "Come in."

She found June sitting on the bed, wiping her eyes. She sat next to her and drew her into her arms. "You have to be strong, my dear. I know this is hard for you. Your sister says the first thing that comes to her head. I wish it was different, but we have to learn to deal with it until she gets better."

June disengaged herself. "That's the thing. What if she never gets better? What if she remains this smiley-smiley, huggy- huggy Pollyanna the rest of her life? I can't handle it, Miss. My sister was so strong and brave. She never took any nonsense from anybody, now all she wants to do is hug and smile. Miss Lucy said she found her on the porch blowing kisses to the men working on the electric pole the other day. And what's this nonsense about getting married?"

Cicely sighed. She wished she had answers. After she and David prayed last night she'd felt better, but the harsh morning light seemed to have burned away any hope her prayers had brought. What could she say to this young girl, her soon-to-be-daughter? Mothers were supposed to always know best. Should she advise June to tell Marva what she wanted to know about her past in the hope that it would jolt her back to reality? Would that bring on the depression, anxiety and suicidal thoughts that plagued her before the accident?

They jumped as the door opened, and Marva stood there. She was not smiling. She looked from June to Miss Stewart. "I'm sorry if I always say the wrong thing to hurt you, June, or to embarrass you, Miss Stewart. I will be very careful about what I say from now on."

June jumped up and rushed to her side. This time she was the one hugging. "Sister, you don't hurt me, and I'm sure you don't embarrass Miss Stewart. We love you. We just … want you to be the way you were before the accident."

Marva pulled away and sat on the bed. "How was I before the accident? I want to know. Don't hide anything from me, please."

Cicely felt a load lifting. This was what she and David had prayed for last night. The answer hadn't come in the way she'd hoped, but she believed it was God's answer.

She placed an arm around Marva's waist, feeling her slight form. Although she'd gained some weight, she was still far from the robust girl she'd been. "Would you like to go for a ride?"

Marva nodded, dabbing at her eyes. Heart breaking, Cicely sent up a quick prayer. "Okay, I'll be right back."

She found David in his study. She threw her arms around his neck. "Honey, I don't think we can keep it from her any longer."

Concern showed in his eyes. "What did she say?"

"She's begging us to tell her who she was. We've got to tell her."

"All right." He turned and drew her on to his lap. "What do you plan to do?"

Cicely laid her head against his shoulder, drinking in his warmth, his strength. "I think we should take her for a ride and explain as we go along."

He seemed to consider the idea. "Okay. Where will we go?"

"To Egypt Village."

I am so anxious to hear what they have to tell me I need very little help going down the steps. But Mr. Bowen still holds my hand and steadies me when I get to the last treader. I think this is a really nice family and I don't expect them to lie to me. It's a warm, sunny day with only white clouds in the blue sky and a gentle breeze takes the edge off the heat.

We get into the car and drive all the way down Collins Avenue without speaking. By now I'm familiar with the route we take to the hospital. But when we get to the corner of Green Acres Drive and Cipero Street near the gas station, we make a right. I have never seen, or I don't remember, this part of the town. We go around a roundabout and keep to the right. I can still see the houses in Green Acres.

Eventually we pass the houses and there are just bushes on either side. Then some large buildings, which look like factories or business offices appear on both sides of the road.

I turn to June who is staring out the window. "What road is this?"

I have to repeat the question before she answers. "South Trunk Road."

She goes back to looking out the window. Shortly after, I catch my breath. The ocean comes into view. I know I've seen it before, but where? I stare at the miles and miles of water held back from the road by a low wall. Opposite the sea on a hill is a large hotel surrounded by fruit and palm trees. Behind us to the right, I see some huge silver tanks and a tall tower with smoke rising from it.

"What are those tanks back there?" I address my question to no one in particular.

Miss Stewart turns her head. "Where?"

I point to the back.

"Oh, that's the Pointe-a-Pierre oil refinery. My father used to work there."

I stare at the ocean through June's window. There is a large red and black boat far out in the distance.

"What ship is that, Mr. Bowen?"

He glances at the ocean. "It's either a cruise ship or a coast guard vessel." He looks at the road then back at the water. "From the colors, I'll say coast guard."

We pass the ocean and come to a hilly area with wide, spreading trees. At the entrance is a sign that says, Shore Of Peace. A road winds through the trees and disappears up the hill.

"What place is this?"

Miss Stewart replies, "That's a cremation site where Hindus burn their dead."

The road we are on goes down a deep bend then up again and I catch another glimpse of the ocean. Small fishing boats are anchored near the shore. Only one is going out to sea. As my mind takes in all of this, I feel so happy to be alive. I must have known all these places before and now God has given me a chance to see them again.

After this, I don't see anything of interest. Only houses, bushes, a few people here and there. My thoughts turn again to what my life must have been like, but I'll wait until they are ready to tell me. I must have dozed off, because when I open my eyes, we are in a place that looks like a storm hit it. Small houses lean to the side; some of the steps have separated from the houses. They don't seem inhabited. The car is rocking. I look out the window and see heaps of asphalt along the way.

Mr. Bowen says with a chuckle, "We're in the hills and gullies, folks."

June says, "The Pitch Lake."

I say nothing because my stomach is churning. Cars are weaving on the side and in front of us, and I'm afraid I'm going to vomit. My head begins to spin. I close my eyes, hoping the feeling will go away, but it grows more intense. I feel things going on in my head, like lights exploding. Images and colors dance before my eyes. I see him, my father. He's on the floor. I see my mother. She's crying, limping, June is crying. I see a river. Things are crashing in my head. I put my hands to my ears. Someone is screaming, yelling. Hands are holding me. I fight to free myself.

"Stop!"

Suddenly the sounds and images cease. I feel faint. I put my forehead in my hands. I am moaning and crying and can't stop. Eventually, I recognize other sounds and someone touching me, holding me. I hear June's voice. "It's all right, Sister, it's all right."

I hear another voice. It's Miss Stewart. "Poor baby. I hope she'll be all right."

A male voice. "Maybe we should take her to the hospital. It's not far from here."

I open my eyes. I know where we are. We are in Point Fortin. The Republic Bank is right around the corner, and the Warden's office is opposite. We are still in the car, parked in a little side street. Three pairs of eyes look at me with concern. June is crying again.

I smile at her. "My memory is back."

I hear a collective gasp. June leans forward to stare at my face. "Sister, are you sure?"

I nod, smiling. "I remember everything." I tell them about the bank and other places where my father used to send me to conduct his business. Then I say, "Egypt Village is not far from here. That's where we lived and went to school. And Miss Stewart, you taught me in school."

Her face remains blank. "Yes, I did."

No one smiles or says anything. I turn to June. "What's the matter? Aren't you happy for me?"

She looks from Miss Stewart to Mr. Bowen then back to me. "Do you remember everything that happened before the accident?"

Some of my happiness goes away. Tears spring to my eyes. I tell them about TL being killed and how I ran, intending to drown myself in the sea. I hadn't planned to throw myself in front of the car. I just didn't see it coming.

Mr. Bowen turns on the engine. "I think we should take her to see Fred when we get back."

June asks, "Do you want to go to Egypt Village?"

I shake my head. "I'm tired. I don't mind seeing Dr. Fred although I feel okay now. I'm so glad to be alive and for all you all have done for me." I dab my eyes. "I'll never want to kill myself again. Life is too precious."

"Do you remember our house in Egypt Village?"

"A little. I know it was small. And I saw my father's face, and my mother."

"Is that all?" June's voice is strained.

I frown. "I saw the river too. Is that near our house?"

She looks out the window. "Yes."

Except for a few casual comments about the villages we pass through, the remainder of the drive home passes in near silence. Questions flood my mind like rain in a gutter, but I don't know where to begin. What is my future going to be like from here on? How much do the Bowens know about me? Will Mr. Bowen throw me in jail when he finds out?

Miss Stewart links my arm in hers to support me as we get out of the car. "How do you feel now?"

I stop and glance around me. "I feel like I've just come from a far, far place."

CHAPTER THIRTY-THREE

June lay on the bed staring up at the ceiling, mulling over the dramatic change that had come over her sister yesterday. Her memory was back! Was that something to be happy about, or did it mean trouble? June had gone over in her mind countless times what this could mean for them. Should they all keep Marva's crime a secret? Would she want them to? And if they didn't, would she be thrown in jail for the rest of her life? Why hadn't Marva remained in her blissful, huggy-huggy state?

She wasn't aware that Marva was looking at her until she spoke, "What are you thinking, Junie?"

June jerked her head toward her sister then looked back at the ceiling. She sighed. "Too much to talk about."

Marva touched her arm. "Look at me, Junie." When June obeyed, she continued, "Don't be afraid, because I am not. God blocked my memory for a reason and He brought it back for a reason. We just have to trust Him."

June frowned. Did Marva have any idea what she faced? "Sister, I'm afraid. I can't pretend. Do you remember anything about Daddy?"

Marva turned her head away. "Now I see why you didn't want to tell me. I'm so sorry, Junie, so sorry." She turned back, her eyes moist. "I wish all of that was just a bad dream instead of a bad memory. I didn't think. That was always my problem. That is what caused me to hit Daddy that blow."

June's tears were close. "I don't think you should blame yourself for what you did. We went through a lot with him and … and that night you were only trying to protect me."

"I would do anything to protect you, but now I know to be more careful." Marva gave a shaky laugh. "God had to knock me flat on my back for me to learn some sense. I wanted to die. Well, I died that day in the accident. As God says in the Bible, 'Behold I make all things new. I'm a new me."

June took a moment to digest this. "So what do you plan to do now?"

"I have to tell the Bowens what … what I did."

"They already know."

Marva gasped. "They do?"

June's eyes watered. "You confessed in those letters you wrote to Miss Stewart, and to Tantie Beulah."

Marva sat up in the bed. "I'd forgotten about that. And I was worrying about how to tell them, and what they will think of me."

"They know everything and they still want to adopt us."

"Mr. Bowen knows too?

June nodded.

"They must be the nicest people on earth."

Moments passed before June asked. "I know you're not strong enough yet, but do you think you'll go back to working as a mechanic?"

Marva shook her head. "I want to be a nun. If God allows it."

"A nun? That is so sudden."

"Not really. You have something to do with it."

June's eyebrows rose. "Me?"

Marva smiled. "It was the day I got into that fight with Marcus. I happened to pass near the Convent on Harris Promenade and I saw a nun going into one of the buildings, then I heard singing. And I remembered Mama telling me about nuns a long time ago. Then, not too long before I had the accident, Rev. Harris preached a sermon about singleness and how God may be calling some of us to serve Him. He mentioned the Corpus Christi Home for girls where Anglican nuns serve alongside others. The idea came to me then, but I'd already decided that … that suicide was the only way out."

June was silent. So many things she didn't know about her sister. "So you don't want to marry Jason again?"

Marva chuckled. "That girl is gone too." She paused. "But if I had to marry anybody, it would be him."

Silence. "Sister, I had no idea you were suffering so much. Why didn't you tell me?"

"I couldn't, Junie. I didn't want to bother you while you were so busy with exams and everything else. And Miss Stewart was just starting her new life."

"Well, from now on I want you to bother me, and I will bother you. No more secrets, okay?" She paused. "And I have a secret too." She cast her sister a shy glance. "I want to be an attorney."

Marva stared at her sister. "An attorney? I thought you wanted to be a librarian."

"Nah, too boring. I want to work with abused girls and women. It's time to help put an end to this suffering."

Marva whistled softly. "A nun and an attorney! We'll be the best."

They slapped their palms in a high five just as someone knocked on the door. June jumped up and opened it.

Miss Stewart stood there. "Hi, girls. I came to see if you were awake."

June threw her arms around Miss Stewart's neck. "Good-morning, Mom. We've been awake for some time and we have so much to tell you."

Miss Stewart laughed. "Mom? That's music to my ears."

June winked at Marva then looked back at the lady. "Er, Mom, can I borrow the car?"

Mom stared then laughed. "Ask your father."

After breakfast, all four of us sit on the back porch and talk for a long time. I thank them for being so kind and understanding and tell them I want to know my fate as soon as possible. "I don't want to go back to worrying about what will happen to me. If I have to go to jail, then I go to jail."

Mr. Bowen looks at me. "You're a very brave young lady. I don't think you'll go to jail. After all you've been through, I think the court will be sympathetic."

Miss Stewart turns to me. "I know you want to get this over and done with, but I'll advise you to give yourself time to heal – physically and emotionally. Maybe a month or so should be okay." She pauses and looks from me to June. "And meanwhile, there's something I would like you both to do."

I smile. "I'll do anything you ask, Mom."

"Me, too," June echoes beside me.

Dad touches his wife's arm. "Honey, I have to get to work." He looks at me. "I agree with my wife, Marva. Give yourself time. Meanwhile, I'll speak to Superintendent Graves. I know he'll keep whatever I tell him confidential." He kisses his wife then gets up from his chair. "See you guys later."

After he leaves, June turns to Mom. "What is it you want us to do, Mom? Clean our room?"

Mom plays with the handle of her spoon then looks straight at me. "I want you to go for counseling. Both of you."

I open my mouth, close it then glance at June who is staring at Mom wide-eyed.

June breaks the silence. "What did you say?"

Mom sighs. "Girls, I know this is the last thing you want to do, but trust me." She rises and beckons to us to follow her.

We trail behind her like two four-year-olds about to be punished. I don't know about June, but memories are blowing through my mind like the wind. Memories of the first time Mom came to invite us to church. I'd protested, saying I had no church clothes. She'd solved that problem by taking me and June shopping. Then when June reported my drinking to her, she came over and emptied all my liquor. When June ran away from home, Mom sent Mr. Bowen to find her and bring her back. What a pair of troublemakers we were! But we couldn't sidestep her then, and we certainly wouldn't do it this time.

We reach her bedroom. She sits on the bed and pats the spot on either side of her.

She looks at me first. "I know you must be wondering why I want you both to go to counseling."

I nod, not daring to speak.

Then at June. "And you?"

June stares in the dresser mirror in front of her. "I know that people go for counseling when … something bad happened to them."

Mom's hand covers mine. "That's a good way to put it. Both of you have had bad things happen to you. And so did I."

I jerk my hand away. My eyes meet June's in the mirror. What is Mom talking about?

She looks at each of us in turn. "I knew I would tell you this one day, but I didn't know when, or how to do it. I think now is the right time."

A cloud passes over the sun, dimming the shaft of light across the bed. A shiver runs up my spine, and I rub my hands up and down my arms. When Mom finishes her tale, the room is silent, and the cloud has lifted. But my mind is heavy. To think that this precious woman suffered the same fate as June and I. And yet, she had come out victorious. Not only that, she took care of her father who abused her, and remained a daughter to him to this day.

"How did you get the courage to go for counseling?" June asks.

"I didn't. The last thing I wanted to do was tell some stranger that I'd been sexually abused by my father. I only went for the premarital counseling that Rev. Harris arranges for all couples before the wedding, but somehow the counselor made me open up and pour out all the pain I'd been holding on to for so long. And with Dave beside me, it was much easier."

I take Mom's hand. "Will you go with us?"

"I certainly will, although she may not let me stay with you."

June leans against her. "We want you there with us."

David parked his car and strode into the San Fernando CID building. So many thoughts churned through his mind. He faced one of the greatest fears of all police officers – having to turn in a relative or someone they knew.

The officer at the front desk greeted him cheerfully, "Ay, Bowen, long time no see."

David shook the man's hand. "Yeah, it's been a while."

"How are things on your side?"

David leaned forward and said in a conspiratorial whisper, "Shocking. When I accepted this job, I thought it would be boring, but it's not."

The man leaned forward on his elbows. "I hear they caught the big man in that bribery scandal the other day."

David straightened. "And we have our eyes on a few others. This thing will be huge. But listen, I don't want to keep the boss waiting."

"Go ahead. He's expecting you."

David walked down the familiar hallway past a row of offices, a few with their doors open. He waved to the occupants then went up the short flight of stairs and knocked on the door on his right.

"Come in."

David entered. A tall graying man in impeccable khaki uniform, looking exactly as David had seen him four years ago, came around his desk and embraced him in a big hug. Superintendent Graves was the only man David knew who reminded him of his father. They had the same erect posture and dignified persona befitting a man of high rank.

Graves released him, then stood back and studied him. "Well, I must say, marriage really does agree with you."

David smiled. "What can I say? I chose the best."

The man gave a hearty laugh. "And so did I. Have a seat, Bowen."

Graves returned to his chair behind the desk. As David took his seat, his mind flashed back to that day four years ago when he sat in this same office and told the man opposite that he was resigning from the police service. Superintendent Graves had fixed him with his steely gaze. "I refuse to accept it."

The man's words cut into his thoughts. "So what brings you by? You sounded very mysterious on the phone."

"Ah, yes, sir, that's because we're on the brink of solving a big mystery."

The man intertwined his fingers. "Ah ha. Go on."

David picked up a picture of his boss and his wife. "You were quite a looker in your days, sir."

The man smiled. "Bowen, you've seen that picture a dozen times before."

David placed the picture down. "Remember that case I was working on in Point?"

The man sobered. "How could I forget? The one that almost drove you crazy?"

"You're right." David picked up a small, weighted globe. "Boy, this thing is heavy."

"That's what you said the first six times you saw it." Graves leaned forward. "Don't touch anything else on my desk, you hear me?"

David met the man's gaze. "I now know who the killer is."

His superior untwined his fingers and leaned back in his chair. David knew the man was waiting for him to continue, but he didn't know how. He wished with all his might he could run out of this office, this building and never say what he had come to say. He was about to reach for a pen but felt the man's gaze on him. David thrust his hands between his legs.

"Has the killer threatened you?"

David looked around. "May I close the door, sir?"

The man waved his hand.

David closed the door and returned to his seat. When he did speak, his voice croaked like an old lady's. "It's his daughter."

"Whose daughter?"

"Garcia's."

David kept his eyes down but heard the gasp that emanated from the man. And for the rest of his life, this moment would remain ingrained in his memory.

The day he shed tears in his boss's office.

He hadn't felt them coming. A feeling of catharsis from the strain he and Cicely had been under these past months washed over him.

When David finally composed himself, his superior stared at the wall opposite, his steepled fingertips touching his chin as if in prayer. "Are we talking about the beautiful young lady who was your wife's chief bridesmaid?"

"Yes, sir." *Damn that croak!*

"Didn't she get in a bad accident?"

David nodded.

"How's she doing?"

David shook his head. "She's using a walker."

During the ponderous silence, David wondered if he should leave. Eventually, the man spoke, "How do you know she did it?"

For answer, David fished in his wallet and handed him the letter Marva had written Cicely. "I suspected her from the beginning but had no concrete evidence."

His boss read the letter silently then, "My God, my God, my God."

He passed it back to David. "You didn't have to tell me this, you know."

"That's true, sir, but Marva wants closure from this. In the letter she said it was guilt that made her want to take her life. Now she says she wants closure. To quote her, 'it's like a bag of grapefruit on her back.'"

Graves shifted in his seat. "I would say she has more than paid for what she did. She should leave it alone. And she does have a younger sister, doesn't she? How is she doing?"

David smiled. "We're adopting her. That's what her sister wanted. She's a very bright young lady, very popular with the opposite sex."

The man nodded. "I remember her from the wedding too. Think of the embarrassment to them both. No, if what Marva says in the letter is true, it sounds like she had probable cause. What did Shakespeare say? '… justice must be tempered with mercy.' I say let's have mercy on this poor girl. The law wasn't there to help her when she needed help, why should it jump on her now when she is down?" He leaned forward. "Bowen, this conversation never happened."

David glanced up. "I appreciate it, sir, but it's not that easy."

"What do you mean?"

"She wants to go to the Corpus Christi Home. To become a nun. They only give priority to court-ordered cases and always have a long waiting list."

Graves drummed his fingers on the desk. "Well, I'll be damned. Then she has to face the court. All right, Bowen. I have friends in high places.

I'll see what I can do. Meanwhile, get her a good attorney."

David stood and extended his hand. "Thank you, sir."

The man shook his hand. "You're welcome. Not a word of this to anyone, except your family, of course."

David nodded and stepped out of the office. Out in the bright mid-day glare, he glanced heavenwards, "Lord, you're in control."

CHAPTER THIRTY-FOUR

Mom, June and I are seated in Rev. Harris's office with him and his wife.

Mrs. Harris breaks the silence. "That's wonderful, my dear. Have you prayed about it?"

I return her gaze. "Yes, ma'am. I believe God does want me to be a nun."

Rev. Harris looks at me. "I know you're a devoted Christian, Marva, and you'll not make this statement lightly. However, I must warn you, being a nun is a very demanding profession. Not a profession, but a calling. The Sisters of Charity have a reputation for being very strict. Do you think you can handle that?"

I raise my chin. "I want to serve God in the best way possible, and if they have to be strict with me, then so be it."

He smiles. "Well, you seem determined. The sisters serve in various capacities. Some of them work with the poor, the aged, some teach …"

"I want to teach, if they will let me."

"They love having young teachers as they have the energy to keep up with the girls," his wife says. "You'll have to be trained, of course."

"My sister is a very good artist," June puts in.

I glance at her then lower my head. I don't consider myself a good artist. I have so much to learn.

Rev. Harris smiles. "Wonderful. Maybe she can teach art. I don't know if any of the nuns do that."

While he is speaking, his wife opens a filing cabinet and removes a large brown envelope. She pulls out some papers and hands them to me. "These will give you more information about the Home. There are some phone numbers that you can call."

While June and I flip through the brochures, Rev. Harris says, "My advice will be, take your time. This is like marriage. Don't rush into anything. Study the brochures, pray and give yourself at least six months before you decide if this is something you really want to do."

I raise my eyebrows. "Six months?"

"Yes, my dear. Your novitiate will be … how should I put it? Rigorous. You need to prepare yourself, physically as well as mentally."

"Sounds like good advice, Reverend," Mom puts in.

June grips my hand. I know she's worried, but I am not. After my life in Egypt Village and the injuries I am still recovering from, my novitiate should be no more difficult than physical therapy.

Someone knocks on the door, and Mrs. Harris gets up to open it. A plump, dark-skinned woman walks in. Rev. Harris stands and shakes her hand. "Good-morning, Andrea. You're just in time."

"Thank you, Rev." She spots Mom, comes over and they hug. "Hi, Cicely, how are you doing? Are these your daughters?"

Mom introduces us, and we shake hands. Andrea seems like a nice lady. Mom told us she is a trained psychologist as well as a minister's wife. She is not a member of our church, and we don't have to tell her anything we don't want to. She and Mom make chit-chat about their families then Mrs. Harris leads us into an adjoining room.

The counseling session is not like anything I'd imagined. I expect Andrea to ask us a lot of strange questions we can't answer, but instead she allows us to speak while she listens. I don't know where to start. June, who usually talks more than I do in front of strangers, seems tongue-tied, so I take the lead. I begin with, "My sister and I were abused by our father."

I look up into Andrea's dark eyes and I can't go on. Eventually, June takes over. When she comes to the part where she says, "For a long time I would vomit whenever someone mentioned his name," Andrea writes something on her notepad.

Head bent, almost whispering, June continues, "When my boyfriend tried to be … intimate with me, I almost vomited. I was so embarrassed."

I jerk my head sideways at her, and Mom puts her arm over June's shoulder. I had no idea she was affected this way. I thought I was the only one who had a problem with men. I didn't vomit. I just couldn't respond to Jason when he kissed me.

Andrea breaks the silence. "Do you think you can ever forgive your father?"

I blurt out. "Forgive?"

She levels her gaze on me. "Yes, forgive. Do you know what a burden we carry around when we don't forgive someone?"

"He's dead," June says flatly.

Andrea lays down her pen. "That makes it easier then. At least you don't have to face him. I'm not trying to sound cold-hearted. But you can ask God to help you heal from the hurt and the unforgiveness you still have in your heart toward your father."

She opens her purse and takes out her Bible. "I'm going to give you a number of passages to study from the Bible. Pray first." She writes as she speaks. "I want each of you to get a little notebook and write your thoughts down as the Holy Spirit speaks to you, then when we meet again, we'll discuss the scriptures and what you wrote. Okay?" She looks up with a smile.

I stare at her, unsmiling.

On the way home, Mom's touch on my shoulder stirs me from my thoughts. "What are you girls thinking?"

June answers first, "Why should we have to forgive daddy? He's the one who hurt us."

My voice sounds faint. "And I turned around and hurt him back. I killed him. That could never be right."

"But you didn't mean to," June says from the back seat. "It was an accident."

"Maybe, but if I hadn't hated him, I would never have done what I did." I feel close to tears. "Even though I'm a Christian, I never thought Jesus could forgive me. Now I know He forgave me a long time ago, and I, too, must forgive."

～

We look up as the door opens and Dad enters the living- room. He is followed by an Indian man, wearing a rumpled suit and carrying a brief-case. He flashes a broad smile. "Good-afternoon, folks."

Dad gestures toward him. "Mr. Clifford Sinanan."

He appears to be in his early fifties, heavy set and balding, with a warm smile and firm handshake. Dad introduces each of us then offers Mr. Sinanan a seat facing me and June.

He looks at me. "I hear you suffered a terrible accident. How do you feel, Marva?"

"Much better, thank you."

"Good. I must say I admire your courage in coming forward with something like this."

"Thank you."

June leans forward. "Mr. Sinanan, do you have any idea how this case might turn out?"

I know she's anxious to get it over with. I am too, but I feel hopeful. I know God is with me.

Mr. Sinanan turns to her. "That's a good question, June. When a case is being tried *in camera*, it can go either way."

June furrows her brow. "*In camera?* What does that mean?"

"It's the British term for a case that is tried in the judge's chambers."

Miss Stewart turns to him. "Does that mean there won't be a jury?"

Mr. Sinanan nods. "That's correct, Mrs. Bowen. And that's why I say the case can go either way. On the one hand we have the privacy of the trial. No one, except those summoned by the court will be allowed to en-ter, and nothing will be in the news. But on the other hand, the outcome of the case is entirely left to the judge's discretion."

Dad clears his throat. "We think this is the best way to protect the privacy of you girls, but as Mr. Sinanan said, it can go either way."

I look at Dad. How kind and sensitive he is. I reach for June's hand. Her head is bowed, but I can feel her anxiety. Mr.Sinanan asks us a lot of questions and takes notes about what happened on the night my father was killed. I'm glad Mom and Dad are there with us because when he is finished, my clothes feel damp with sweat, and June's hand trembles in mine. Mom leaves the room and returns with a tray of cold Pepsi for us. I could kiss her, but all I say is, "Thanks, Mom!"

School reopens and June goes back to her normal routine, but it's less intense than before her CXC exams. She has piano practice twice a week, youth choir practice once, and she and John go out on Saturday nights. I heard her play at church one Sunday and I was really proud. I haven't told her yet, but I've asked Mom and Dad to look into getting a used baby grand piano for her birthday. I'll pay for it from my funds, which have been gathering interest in the bank.

Since the day we met with Mr. Sinanan to discuss my case, June has not spoken about it. Even though the attorney said he may be able to plead self-defense, I sometimes catch her staring into the distance, and I know she's worried. I don't want to speak about it either, but I pray that God will quiet her spirit and help her to not be afraid.

Mom also goes back to work after being away for about half the year. She hugs and kisses me as she and Dad leave the house that first day. "If you get too lonely, pick up the phone and call me around lunchtime, okay?"

I smile. "I won't be lonely. I have lots of company, and lots to do."

That's true. Between helping with Chrissy and Junior, working on my assignments and my sketching, I keep very busy. I have started taking art classes at the center, and that is a special thrill for me. It's amazing what learning the correct technique and having the right tools can do. I now work with charcoal, and it has made a big difference to the quality of my sketches. I want to replace the first sketches I did of the family, but they will not hear of it.

Mom said, "We want to keep them to remind us how far you've come."

And June said, "They're my most precious possessions."

I still depend on my cane, but I love helping around the house. On mornings, I make the bed and tidy our bedroom. I even clean our bathroom. The more I do, the more energy I have. Sometimes I delay my cleaning if Miss Marilyn needs help with the babies. Junior sometimes gets fussy, and she says he could be teething.

Chrissy is more laid back. As long as she has her cloth doll to beat against her crib, or put into her mouth, she is happy. I thank God morning and night for placing me and June into such a nice family. Still, I wonder what my life will be like in a few years. Despite what I said to Rev. Harris about wanting to become a nun, I don't know if it will happen. It all depends on the judge's decision.

That afternoon I hear Dad running up the stairs. I can usually tell from a person's steps what kind of mood he is in. I think he is excited. He goes into his bedroom where Mom is, then someone knocks on my door. I get up and open it. They are both beaming at me.

"Where's June?" Dad asks.

"She hasn't come home yet. What's going on?"

For answer, Dad waves some papers before my face. "June's adoption came through."

I step closer and take the papers from him. It says Order of Adoption and I see David and Cicely Bowen and June's name and I don't bother to read anymore. "Thank you, Jesus. Thank you, Mom. Thank you, Dad. We don't have to go to court?"

Dad grins. "Nah. The judge knows me, most of the people in court know me. It was just a matter of having it entered in the records and signing the papers."

We hug and kiss each other and I think I see Mom dab at her eyes. Mine are watery too. We are a family. Even though I am not formally adopted, it feels wonderful to have parents.

June does a little dance when she hears the news. That night we go out to dinner at Soong's restaurant to celebrate. Miss Lucy and Miss Marilyn stay in and babysit the children. Later, as we prepare for bed, June says, "This adoption doesn't change anything. I've thought of Mom as my mother for a long time."

I get in beside her. "Me too."

I think she is sleeping, but then I hear her say, "Sister?"

"Mmm?"

"You know when you were in the coma, I tried to remember a verse of scripture and couldn't. Then Rev. Harris came and he quoted this verse. *All things work together for good to them that love the Lord.* Since then it has become my favorite Bible verse."

I turn to her. "Why?"

"Because I see everything is really working out for the best."

I ponder over what she said. "It's true. Even my accident was for the best, I think. I learned to love and appreciate life, and God, so much more."

"And you developed a new talent."

From the moment Dad enters the house, I know he has some news. I look at him expectantly, but he doesn't say anything until we have finished dinner. Then as we relax around the kitchen table, Mom holding Chrissy, I with Junior on my lap, he states, "The judge will begin reviewing your case tomorrow, Marva."

My stomach gives a little lurch. "Tomorrow? How long will he take?"

Dad shrugs. "We've no idea. Judge McGregor is a kind of an oddball."

June looks up from her book. "An oddball?"

"I don't know him that well, but from what Mr. Sinanan said, you either love him or you hate him."

June furrows her brow. "Why is that?"

"Well, from what I heard, his methods are somewhat … unorthodox."

Now that's a word I definitely have to look up.

Mom picks up the doll Chrissy has thrown on the floor. "Why do you say that, honey?"

Dad gives her a quick glance. "Well, for one thing, if you meet him on the street, you wouldn't think he was a judge. And when you see him on the bench, you know he's a judge by his robe and his wig, but he has dreadlocks …"

June smiles. "Really? How old is he?"

"Probably in his late forties. From what Mr. Sinanan said, he's the youngest judge in Trinidad. His father is Trinidadian, his mother is English. He was born and raised in England but has been living here long enough to acquire a fake Trinidad accent."

Mom looks at him. "Sounds like you don't like him."

Dad reaches for Chrissy who has been stretching toward him. "It's hard to like a man who calls policemen nincompoops and throws them out of his court. The man looks and behaves crazy. Marva, I don't think you have anything to worry about though. He's sympathetic toward women, especially if they have been abused in anyway. But if you were a man, I would say, pray really hard."

"He's harder on men?" June asks.

"Absolutely. He hates men. He once sentenced a young man to fifteen years in prison for robbing an old lady of her purse. Fifteen years. That's the kind of sentence someone gets for armed robbery."

"What do you mean by reviewing the case, Dad?" I ask.

"He will first go over your file and call witnesses as he sees fit. He can also conduct part of the trial in open court if he feels like it. With him you never know."

I digest everything Dad has said, but I have already decided I will not be afraid, no matter what I hear.

I look at my sister. "What do you think, Junie?"

She considers for a moment. "I hope I get to meet this judge."

Jason arrived at the Bowen's house just after six. Marva met him on the front porch. He bent and kissed her cheek then stepped back and looked her up and down. "You look great, Moe. What happened to the walker?"

She grinned. "I don't need it. I'm going to give it to the old people's home. I only use the cane now. For stability, my therapist said."

Jason feasted his eyes on her. She'd gained a little weight, and her blue denim skirt and matching blouse fitted her just right. Her thick, lustrous hair was tied back with a colorful scarf, and he couldn't see any scars on her face. He could hardly believe this was the same girl whose mangled body had lain in the hospital months ago. He always knew she was a fighter, but her biggest fight was ahead of her.

"Is anyone else home?"

"Mom is here. Dad and June are not home yet. Would you like to come in?"

"Sure." Then he cocked his head. "Mom? Dad?"

"I've so much to tell you. Mom and Dad adopted June. I'm too old to be adopted, but they're still my parents."

"Really? Well, I'm happy for both of you."

"Thanks, Jay. I knew you would be."

Jason stopped short. "You called me Jay."

She smiled. "A lot of surprises. My memory is back."

"It is? Why didn't you call me right away?" He tried to keep the pain out of his voice. Something as significant as that had occurred, and she hadn't thought to call him? She would never love him the way he loved her. To her, he was just a good friend.

She seemed to sense his disappointment, for she hung her head. "I … I was so busy getting used to everything and," she turned to face him, "now I have to go to court."

Jason's mind jerked back to the blue paper in his pocket and the reason for his visit. "That's why I came. Moe, why are you going ahead with this?"

A cloud passed over her face. "It's the only way I can live with myself, Jay. The guilt made me want to kill myself. I have to face the consequences, whatever they might be. But come, let's go inside."

With a sigh, he followed her into the living-room just as Miss Stewart came out carrying her baby girl. Jason kissed Miss Stewart on her cheek then took the baby from her. "Come here, you pretty thing, you. Just like your mommy."

Miss Stewart laughed. "You always were a charmer, Jason."

As they seated themselves, June and Mr. Bowen walked in. After they'd exchanged greetings, Jason pulled out the paper from his pocket and handed it to Mr. Bowen. "I got a summons to testify in Marva's case."

Miss Stewart looked up. "I saw a paper like that with today's mail. June, do you mind getting it for me? It's in the kitchen."

June left and returned with the paper. "It's addressed to me."

She handed it to Mr. Bowen, who scanned it then gave it back to her. "That's your invitation, all right."

Moe looked at her sister. "Are you scared?"

"A little, but I can't wait to let that judge know what I think," June replied.

Mr. Bowen shook his head. "Uh uh, just answer what he asks you as honestly as you can. If you go there with an attitude, you could make things worse for your sister."

How much worse could it get? Marva was facing a murder charge, one she'd pleaded guilty to. It was so wrong. She'd suffered so much. Wasn't there someone who could waive the charge against her? The Attorney General? The Minister of National Security? He addressed this question to Mr. Bowen.

The man sighed. "Believe me, Jason, we've tried every angle. The best thing would've been to keep quiet about the whole nasty business, but Marva didn't want to do that. She says it was what almost drove her crazy, and I think I can understand that. We can only hope and pray that the judge will be lenient."

Jason took Marva's hand. She smiled as if trying to comfort him when she was the one who needed comforting. Later, when he drove away from the house, he sent up a little prayer. "I know you're going to do something good for those girls, Lord."

CHAPTER THIRTY-FIVE

June had only a few seconds to speak to Jason when he emerged from the judge's chambers.

"How did it go?"

Jason's face was tense, but he shrugged. "Not too bad, I guess. The judge didn't ask me anything. But watch out for Alexander."

"Who is Alexander?"

"The prosecutor. He …"

Jason broke off as a policeman approached. "Miss Garcia?"

June followed the burly officer into the wood-paneled room where her dad sat with Mr. Sinanan and a dark-skinned African man, whom she guessed was the prosecutor. He stared at her like a tiger about to sink his teeth into his prey.

June switched her attention to the man seated behind the large mahogany desk. He wore a plain white shirt, black pants, and his sandaled feet peeped out from under the desk. Protruding forehead, light brown eyes under thick eyebrows, and a beak nose gave him the appearance of an eagle. Long sideburns swept down to his mustache, which curled around his mouth to meet an untidy beard. The long dreadlocks her father had mentioned were held together at the back with something, maybe a rubber band. From the way he leaned forward in his chair, he seemed ready to swoop down on her at any moment.

June hoped he would ignore her as he had Jason, but just as the thought came, he called her name. June jumped to her feet. "Yes, sir."

He waved her down. "You don't have to stand. You're not in the army."

Feeling a little silly, June took her seat.

"What do you do for a living?"

"For a living, sir?"

"Do you work?"

June frowned. "I'm a student, Your Honor."

He stroked his beard. "A student? What are you studying?"

"I'm doing my A levels, sir."

He nodded. "And after that?"

"I intend to go to UWI."

"For?"

"To study law."

A smile ruffled the hair on his face. He beckoned to the officer. "Swear her in."

June thought she did well answering the prosecutor's questions, until he asked her to describe what happened on the night of her father's murder. She remembered Marva's words: "Tell them what you know." Her dad had said pretty much the same thing: "They already have your statement, so don't try to hide anything."

She threw him a quick glance before launching into her story. Her father had come home drunk and cursing because his dinner wasn't on the table. Then he gave Marva some money and told her to go to the shop to buy bread. Afraid of being alone with him, June began to cry. Her father slapped her on her face, Marva ran into the kitchen, came back with the pestle and hit him on the back of his head.

"Then what happened?" the prosecutor asked.

"He fell."

"Was he dead?"

Mr. Sinanan sprang up. "Objection, your honor. Miss Garcia is not a doctor."

The judge seemed bored. "Sustained."

Mr. Alexander consulted his notes. "When did you realize your father was dead?"

"Some time after, sir. He didn't get up when my sister called him for his dinner."

"So your sister hit your father on the back of his head, he fell to the floor and neither one of you went to check on him?"

June bit her lip. "No, sir."

The prosecutor took his seat. "No further questions, your honor."

Mr. Sinanan rose. "Judge, I have a question for the witness."

Mr. Mc Gregor nodded.

"Miss Garcia, you said a while ago that when your father gave your sister money to go to the shop you became afraid. Why was that?"

June looked down at the carpeted floor. The attorney had warned her this was coming, but still she wished she didn't have to answer. She put her hand to her chest. She couldn't vomit now. Not now. Dad was standing. "Your Honor —"

Her stomach churned, and she could feel the bile rushing to her throat. She couldn't stop it. She turned and ran from the room.

In the bathroom, June lost her breakfast. Afterwards, she rinsed her mouth as best she could, washed and dried her face. Surprisingly, no one came to get her. What were they saying in there? How long could she stay? Should she run away? No, Dad had brought her, she had to wait for him. Besides, she'd promised her sister she would be brave.

Feeling a bit calmer, she returned to the chambers. Her dad came over and put his arm around her shoulder. "How do you feel?" he whispered.

"Okay."

"The judge said we can adjourn if you don't feel well."

"Until when?"

"Tomorrow."

June shook her head. "I want to get it over with."

Her father stepped away and relayed what she'd said to the judge.

"Proceed, counsel."

"Do you remember the question, Miss Garcia?"

June looked him squarely in the face. "Yes, sir, I remember. I became afraid because whenever Daddy wanted to ... to molest me he would send my sister out of the house."

Mr. Sinanan asked some more questions concerning their relationship with their father, which she answered as best she could. But when he took his seat, Mr. Alexander stood. "Your Honor, I would like the young lady to explain what she means by 'molest'."

June swallowed. *Not that. Why did he have to ask that?* Helplessly, she stared at her father and the other men in the room. Mr. Sinanan got to his feet. "Objection, Your Honor. Surely Mr. Alexander knows what the witness means."

"It can mean anything, counsel. Let the young lady speak." Looking at June he said, "You may remain seated if you wish."

As if that would make a difference. But haltingly, staring at the clock on the wall opposite, hearing her voice as if it came from someone else, June gave her testimony. Silence followed, and this time all she could hear was the pounding of her heart and the loud ticking of the clock. It was a relief when the judge said, "We will adjourn until tomorrow. Be here at 10.00 sharp."

June hopped out of her chair and ran ahead of her father and out to the car. She spoke not a word on the way home and was glad for her father's sympathetic silence.

The next morning, June sat on a bench outside the courtroom while her attorney and Dad consulted with the judge and the prosecutor. She'd had time to recover from her embarrassing experience the day before, and when the bailiff came to escort her in, she was ready. As soon as she sat down, Judge Mc Gregor called her name.

She stood. "Yes, Your Honor."

"You said you want to study law?"

"Yes, Your Honor."

"Well, you can't put on a display as you did yesterday every time something upsets you."

June felt close to tears. "It was not a display, Your Honor."

The judge continued as if she hadn't spoken, "Now, I want you to imagine you're your sister's attorney and you're addressing the jury. Tell them why your client should be found not guilty."

What? June looked around. Her dad, the attorneys and the court reporter all stared at the judge, open-mouthed. The court reporter raised her hand. "Judge McGregor, is this for the record?"

The judge rolled his eyes. "Of course not, Miss Reynolds. Loosen up a bit, will you? Miss Garcia, go ahead."

June pushed herself out of the chair. This was worse than she expected. She wasn't an attorney. Was the judge trying to make fun of her? But when she glanced at him, his face was unsmiling.

June gulped and looked around at the small number of people in the room. Disgust showed on her dad's face, irritation on Mr. Sinanan's, and Mr. Alexander twirled a pen between his fingers. Miss Reynolds' penciled eyebrows were raised in surprise.

Do I have to do this? Maybe I should just say, I can't. But she owed it to Marva to convince an invisible jury—and this intractable judge—that her sister deserved to be acquitted. An image of her sister's face the night of the murder flashed before her eyes. She'd never seen her so frightened before or since. Angry, but never scared. Despite the years of abuse, Marva hadn't planned to kill their father.

An old movie that featured a lawyer who successfully defended a young man accused of murder came to June's mind. The lawyer won the case, not by trying to prove the man's innocence, but by invoking sympathy for the young man. She would do the same.

She cleared her throat. "Ladies and gentlemen of the jury, my client Marva Garcia has already confessed to murdering her father on the night of July 15, 1981. Therefore, I'm not going to waste your valuable time by saying she didn't do it. She did, but it was an accident. You heard the last witness testify that her sister hit her father on the back of his head and he fell. You may be asking yourself why she did it.

"For answer, let me take you to that little house by the river in Egypt Village. A little concrete dwelling set about half a mile from the main roadway, with the nearest neighbor about a mile away. The shop where Marva would have gone that night to buy bread was also about a mile away in the opposite direction. Marva grew up seeing her mother being beaten by her father. He made her perform an abortion on Marva at the tender age of fifteen because she'd become pregnant by him. Marva thinks that may have hastened her mother's death."

Aware that everyone was listening intently, June's confidence grew.

"At the age of fifteen, Marva was forced to become mother to her younger sister, plus take on the responsibility of running the home and helping on the estate. She and her sister lived a life of seclusion and drudgery. On the night she killed her father, Marva wished she knew someone she could call, but her father had kept them so isolated she had no one to turn to.

"Burdened by guilt, she later contemplated suicide. She spent four months in the hospital following an accident. During that time, she suffered amnesia. But the moment her memory returned, Marva decided she must face up to her crime. She is happy that this is out in the open and she doesn't have to carry this burden of guilt anymore. Still, she thinks she has suffered enough. *I* think she has suffered enough, and this is why I ask you to find Marva Garcia not guilty of murder in the second degree."

Once she'd stopped speaking, nervousness washed over her, and her hands shook. In the silence that followed, June took her seat, not daring to look at anyone. Then the applause broke out. The judge pounded with his gavel, and when June looked at him, all the hair on his face was moving. A broad grin parted her lips.

I bow my head as Dad says grace, finishing with, "Thank you, Lord, for all that you're doing in our lives and for this meal you have provided. Amen."

"Amen," we echo.

Mom passes the platter of stewed red snapper to him. "I hear we have an attorney in the family."

He takes it from her hand. "Your daughter was magnificent." He looks at June. "When did you get the idea to be an attorney?"

June spoons rice on to her plate. "Dad, you remember that day when you told me you felt helpless about sister's case because of the restrictions in the law?"

Dad seemed puzzled. "I don't remember but go on."

"You said you felt you'd failed as a policeman, but you later realized that the system had failed us because there was no law against incest."

I look at Dad's bent head and pause with my fork to my mouth. Before my accident, I'd thought he was just out to arrest me, when all the time he was struggling to keep me out of jail.

I put my fork down. "Dad, I owe you an apology."

"Why?"

I struggle to keep the tremor from my voice. "Because … because I thought all you wanted to do was throw me in jail. I was so afraid of you."

Dad pats my hand. "I'm glad you realize that's not the truth. The more I studied your case, the more I saw you were not a hardened criminal. Not only that, you acted to protect your sister more than yourself. Am I right?"

Images of that night fill my mind and I can only nod.

Mom looks at me. "I want to hear everything that went on in court, but first, Dave and I have some more good news."

Her smile warms my heart, and I wait, barely daring to breathe. Dad nods at her and she continues, "We wrote a letter to the Attorney General, copied to the Minister of National Security, asking that they make incest a crime punishable by law."

June gasps and raises her hand heavenward. Mom goes to the drawer where she keeps bills and other papers and fishes out a brown envelope with the coat-of-arms and the words Trinidad and Tobago Government Service printed on it. She passes it to me and I take it with shaking hands. I try to steady my voice as I read, "Dear Mr. Bowen,

We appreciate your concern about the grievous incidence of incest in our community, and the failure of the law to address it. We thank you for bringing this to our attention. We are pleased to let you know that we have forwarded your letter, along with one of ours, to the Prime Minister, and he has given the go ahead to bring this matter before Parliament. We will keep you informed of our progress."

June, who had been reading with me, jumps up from her chair and rushes over to Mom. "Oh, thank you, thank you."

I join her and we hug our wonderful parents in a long embrace.

When we separate, Mom wipes her eyes. "So, let's hear what our attorney said in court."

As Dad tells the story, with June filling in bits and pieces, my heart swells with admiration for my little sister. Although, she's not little anymore. She has grown up and is bright and confident. Today, she just might have kept me from spending a lifetime in prison.

I have mixed feelings as I enter the judge's chambers a week later. He is as weird looking as June described him, but I'm not concerned about his looks. I'm concerned about what decision he has come to. I was not allowed to testify, for which I am grateful. I am anxious to put all of this behind me and move on with my life, wherever that life may be. My family and I prayed together the night before and if anything, it has given me a spirit of calm. Dad sits beside me on one side and Mr. Sinanan on the other.

The judge looks at me and at my cane, but I can read nothing from his expression. The prosecutor and my attorney spend a long time presenting what the judge calls their closing arguments, each trying to influence the judge why I should or should not be found guilty. Mr. Sinanan speaks last and I feel satisfied with what he has said.

After Mr. Sinanan takes his seat, there is a moment of silence. Everyone looks at the judge who is leaning back in his chair, eyes closed. Finally, he opens his eyes and looks straight at me. "Miss Garcia, how do you feel?"

I moisten my lips. "Fine, sir."

"Tell me, how do you think I should rule in your case?"

I blink. "Not guilty, sir."

He smiles. "You already pleaded guilty, Miss Garcia." He looks at the papers in front of him. "Okay, I won't take up much of your time. Have you ever heard of Corpus Christi Home for Girls?"

My heart is pounding so fast I can hardly breathe. I manage to gasp, "Yes ... yes, sir."

"Well, that's where you're going. You're hereby sentenced to three years at the Corpus Christi Home for Girls. During that time, you will be under the jurisdiction of the court. You will appear before me once a year to review your conduct. You are not to leave the country …"

I stop listening. Tears are streaming down my face. Dad thrusts some Kleenex in my hand. I'm aware that the judge has stopped speaking and is leaving the room. The attorneys are shaking my hand and Dad is helping me to my feet. I am free at last. I'm going home. Thank you, Jesus!

~

I go into the kitchen to get a glass of water. Smiling, June looks up from a letter she is reading. A photograph lies on the table. I give it a quick glance as I go to the fridge. "Looks like you got some good news."

June chuckles. "It is good news, in a way. Listen to this."

I pour my water and remain standing near the counter. Holding up the photo, June waves me over. "Sister, see if you recognize this person."

I take it from her hand. It's a picture of a girl holding a baby. "Is this Wendy?"

June nods. "She has the baby. It's a boy."

I pull a chair and sit. "How's she doing?"

June returns her attention to the letter. "She seems to be doing okay. The baby is four months old, and Wendy has started going to school. She says her aunt is trying to get her to stay in Florida. But hear this part. She says, 'June, I made so many stupid mistakes. One was leaving John for Daryl. If you see John, tell him I miss him.'"

June looks at me with a grin. "What do you think of that?"

"Sounds like she missed the bus."

June explodes into laughter.

"Who missed the bus?" We don't hear Mom come up.

Still laughing, June looks at Mom. "My friend." She fills her in on Wendy's story. When she finishes, Mom says, "I feel sorry for her, poor thing."

June sobers. "I do too, but it's a type of justice. Somebody stole what was mine, and I … well, I didn't steal hers. She handed him to me."

Her chair scrapes as she gets up.

"So, does that mean you are serious about John?" Mom asks.

A little smile turns up the corners of her mouth. "John is exactly what I need right now." She pauses. "But the man I marry, he'll rock my world."

With a wink at us, she flounces out of the room.

Mom and I stare at her back as she leaves the kitchen. Mom turns to me. "You think she's still pining over Keith?"

I take a sip of my water. "I doubt it. But you know how it is, you never get over your first love."

Mom stares into the distance. "You're right."

I touch her hand. "Thinking of your first love?"

She looks at me with a smile. "Yes, who has left me to go fishing with his buddies."

We chuckle, then we fall silent. Eventually Mom asks, "So, do you think you can forget your first love when you become a nun?"

Her question startles me. How can I? He'll always be a part of me. The boy who helped me fight my battles, danced with me on the cocoa leaves, took me on the only two dates I've ever had, gave me my first kiss—and asked me to marry him. I can never forget any of that. I finger the gold heart pendant he gave me for my eighteenth birthday.

"I'll never forget my first love. I have too many precious memories of him. And that's what I'll tell him when I see him tonight."

The End

Dear Reader,

It is my pleasure to bring you *In The Wilderness* the second book in the *Egypt* series. I trust that you enjoy it as much as you enjoyed the first book *Coming Out of Egypt.* This second book builds on the suspense of the first and tested my emotions in ways I didn't imagine. Writing about suicide was especially harrowing for me. In my opinion, suicide is never an option. It is always too soon to give up.

If you enjoyed *In the Wilderness,* would you kindly leave a review on Amazon so that other readers can be guided in their reading choices? This simple process takes just a few minutes but is so crucial to an author's success. Please visit my website at http://angelasfreelancewriting.com and sign up for my newsletter where you can get updates on my books and giveaways. Follow me on Facebook at https://facebook.com/AJose6 and on twitter at https://twitter.com/trincity.

Thanks for reading,

Angela

Other books by this author:
Women For All Seasons
Coming Out of Egypt
In the Promised Land

Following are some questions for your reflection and discussion:

1. How does Marva's perception of herself change by the end of this book?
2. June has been subjected to extraordinary pressure in this book. What do you think of the way she rose to the challenges in a) dealing with her sister's accident and b) losing her boyfriend at a time when she needed him most?
3. Experts say that most people contemplating suicide may drop subtle hints. Can you identify any hints that indicated Marva's intention?
4. Does Marva show character weakness by wanting to attempt suicide? Why or why not?
5. Is a Christian's faith enough to insulate her from becoming depressed or suicidal?
6. In what ways could Jason have responded differently to Marva's advances before her memory returned?
7. Both June and David expressed frustration over the limitations of the law to help and protect victims of sexual abuse. Do you think the law is doing enough to help these victims in today's society? What can you do to help effect positive change?
8. David cried in his boss's office when he related the circumstances that led to Marva killing her father. Do you see this as a form of weakness in a police officer? Give reasons for your answer.
9. Forgiveness is one of the themes portrayed in this book. How is this played out in the Bowens' interactions with the sisters?
10. There are many examples of friendship in this book. What are your thoughts on June's friendship with Wendy?